Joseph Rickaby

Notes on St. Paul

Corinthians, Galatians, Romans

Joseph Rickaby

Notes on St. Paul
Corinthians, Galatians, Romans

ISBN/EAN: 9783743383494

Manufactured in Europe, USA, Canada, Australia, Japa

Cover: Foto ©Andreas Hilbeck / pixelio.de

Manufactured and distributed by brebook publishing software (www.brebook.com)

Joseph Rickaby

Notes on St. Paul

NOTES ON ST. PAUL:

CORINTHIANS, GALATIANS, ROMANS.

BY

JOSEPH RICKABY, S.J.

LONDON: BURNS AND OATES, LIMITED.
NEW YORK, CINCINNATI, CHICAGO: BENZIGER BROTHERS.

1898.

PREFACE.

"Listening assiduously to the reading of Blessed Paul's Epistles," says St. John Chrysostom, "I exult with joy; I am delighted with that spiritual trumpet : I am warmed with affection, listening to the voice of a friend, whose person I almost think I see, and hear his words. But I do grieve and am annoyed to think that not all know this man, as they should."

Not for want of commentators certainly does St. Paul remain unknown. I have kept before me steadily St. John Chrysostom and Theodoret. On the Galatians I have been helped by Lightfoot. Nearly throughout I have been aided by the sagacity and borne up by the erudition of Father Cornely (*Commentarius in S. Pauli Epistolas*, Paris, Lethielleux). Still I have not absolutely deferred to any authority, except, I trust, to that of the Holy Catholic Church.

These four Epistles form a group. I have taken them in the order in which I believe they were written, and in which they lead naturally one

to the other. I have printed almost exactly the
text of Challoner's 1752 edition of the Rheims
Testament, reissued by the Art and Book Company,
Leamington. For the history of that text, see *The
Month* for July, 1897, *Our English Catholic Bible*.
I have often endeavoured to improve the translation. Nor have I always adopted the reading
of the Latin Vulgate. With regard to the decree
of the Council of Trent, Session IV., commending "the old Vulgate edition, which has been
approved by long usage of so many centuries in the
Church," it is to be observed that where a reading
has always been matter of controversy among
Catholics, the text of the Vulgate has never been
there approved to the condemnation of other
readings. Thus Melchior Canus, otherwise a strict
interpreter of the Tridentine decree, writes of that
much debated passage, 1 Cor. xv. 51, 52 : " Neither
reading has been rejected by churchmen : rather
they have always given warning that the reading is
doubtful and various, and neither of the two alternatives has been embraced by them as certain and
fully established. We are therefore compelled to
neither reading, because the Doctors of the Church
have asserted neither side for certain and fully
proved " (*Loc. Theol.* ii. 14). See further Father
Hunter's *Outlines of Dogmatic Theology*, vol. i. p. 221,
or my *Oxford Conferences*, 1897, pp. 52, 53.

I am afraid I have not made St. Paul quite easy reading. Popular notes on the Apostle might go the way with popular notes on the great Greek historian Thucydides, whom he greatly resembles in abruptness of style. With the one author as with the other one must face difficulties, and not be afraid of the original Greek. Still one need not be a Greek scholar to profit by these Notes. I have laboured everywhere to elucidate what exactly the Apostle meant to say; and as he was inspired for all time, to bring out that portion of his inspiration which is addressed to our age.

I earnestly recommend the reader, if he has perused my Notes, to open a New Testament in which the Text appears continuously, and let his eye range over it as over a map. Thus only can he appreciate the connection of the several parts: thus only can he rescue the Apostle from the misfortune of being overlaid by the Commentator.

I should be glad if these Notes might find a place by the side of the greater Commentaries, in that humble companionship which Theodoret asks for himself in his Introduction: οὐδὲν τοίνυν ἀπεικὸς οὐδὲ ἡμᾶς οἷον κώνωπάς τινας σὺν ταῖς μελίτταις ἐκείναις τοὺς ἀποστολικοὺς περιβομβῆσαι λειμῶνας. "There is then nothing unseemly even in our going like gnats in company with those bees, buzzing round the apostolic meadows."

FIRST EPISTLE TO THE CORINTHIANS.

INTRODUCTION.

LATE in the autumn of A.D. 52, St. Paul left Athens, little satisfied with his work there, and landed at Cenchreæ, the port of Corinth. At Corinth he found hospitality with Aquila and Priscilla, two Jews, man and wife, who had already embraced Christianity. They were tent-makers by trade ; and as that was St. Paul's trade too, he worked with them. On the Sabbaths he repaired to the Jewish synagogue, and preached there Christ, but encountered violent opposition, which induced him to quit the synagogue and hire a room hard by, where he preached to the Gentiles and to any Jews that were willing to listen. Thus was founded the church of Corinth. The work occupied St. Paul a year and six months. Early in 54 he left the city, and travelled by Asia Minor to Jerusalem. Thence he went to Ephesus, and there he dwelt for three years. Towards the end of his sojourn there, at Easter, A.D. 58, he wrote this first Epistle to the Corinthians, to answer certain difficulties which the Corinthians had submitted .to him, and still more to quell the party feuds that had become rampant in their church.

B

1. Paul, called to be an apostle of Jesus Christ, by the will of God, and Sosthenes, a brother, 2. To the church of God that is at Corinth, to them that are sanctified in Christ Jesus, called to be saints, with all that invoke the name of our Lord Jesus Christ in every place of theirs and ours : 3. Grace to you, and peace, from God our Father, and from the Lord Jesus Christ. 4. I give thanks to my God always for you, for the grace of God that is given you in Christ Jesus; 5. That in all things you are made rich in him, in every word, and in all knowledge; 6. As the testimony of Christ was confirmed in you : 7. So that nothing is wanting to you in any grace, waiting for the manifestation of our Lord Jesus Christ ; 8. Who also will confirm you unto the end without crime, in the day of the coming of our Lord Jesus Christ. 9. God is faithful, by whom you are called unto the fellowship of his Son Jesus Christ our Lord. 10. Now I beseech you, brethren, by the name of our Lord Jesus Christ, that you all speak the same thing, and that there be no schisms among you ; but that you be perfect in the same mind, and in the same judgment. 11. For it hath been signified unto me, my brethren, of you, by those who are of the house of Chloe, that there are contentions among you. 12. Now this I say, that every one of you saith : I indeed am of Paul ; and I am of Apollo ; and I of Cephas ; and I of Christ. 13. Is Christ divided ? was Paul crucified for you ; or were you baptized in the name of Paul ? 14. I give God thanks that I baptized none of you, but Crispus and Caius : 15. Lest any should say that you were baptized in my name. 16. And I baptized also the household of Stephanos : besides, I know not whether I baptized any other. 17. For Christ sent me not to baptize, but to preach the gospel ; not with wisdom of speech, lest the cross of Christ should be made void. 18. For the word of the cross, to them indeed that perish, is foolishness; but to them who are saved, that is, to us, it is the power of God. 19. For it is written : I will destroy the wisdom of the wise, and the prudence of the prudent I will reject. 20. Where is the wise ? where is the scribe ? where is the disputer of this world ? hath not God made foolish the wisdom of this world? 21. For seeing that in the wisdom of God the world by wisdom knew not God, it pleased God by the foolishness of preaching to save them that believe. 22. For now the Jews require signs, and the Greeks seek after wisdom : 23. But we preach Christ crucified, to the Jews a stumbling-block, and to the gentiles foolishness ; 24. But to them that are called, both Jews and

Greeks, Christ the power of God, and the wisdom of God. **25.** For that which appeareth foolish of God is wiser than men ; and that which appeareth weakness of God is stronger than men. **26.** For see your vocation, brethren, that not many are wise according to the flesh, not many mighty, not many noble : **27.** But the foolish things of the world hath God chosen that he may confound the wise ; and the weak things of the world hath God chosen that he may confound the strong ; **28.** And the mean things of the world, and the things that are contemptible, hath God chosen, and things that are not, that he might destroy the things that are : **29.** That no flesh should glory in his sight. **30.** But from him you are in Christ Jesus, who is made to us wisdom from God, and justice, and sanctification, and redemption : **31.** That, as it is written : He that glorieth may glory in the Lord.

1. *Sosthenes.* We know of no other Sosthenes than the one mentioned in Acts xviii. 17, whom we must suppose to have become a Christian. His name is in the Roman Martyrology, 28 November. He seems to have been St. Paul's amanuensis in writing this letter.

2. *Called to be saints.* Literally, *called, saints,* κλητοῖς, ἁγίοις, two distinct general names of all Christians in the New Testament : *called* by Christ, or by His ministers, and having answered the call to the faith ; and *saints,* as having been sanctified in baptism. The *many called* of Matt. xxii. 14 cannot be understood as inclusive of persons who reject the faith. And see *v.* 24 of this chapter.

Of theirs and ours. Understand *their Lord and ours,* and omit the word *of* before *theirs.*

5. *Rich in him, i.e. by him,* as Matt. v. 13, *Wherewith* (literally, *in what) shall it be salted ?*—and also, *in union with him :* cf. Rom. vi. 11.

In every word and in all knowledge. St. Chrysostom explains : "Many have knowledge, but no power of utterance ; but you are not such : you have the faculty at once of thought and of expression,"—even a mira- culous faculty, xii. 8.

6. *i.e.* The *testimony* rendered to Christ by the Apostles who have preached Him to you, has been *confirmed* by the graces which you have received upon believing that testimony. For these graces see chs. xii. and xiv.

8. The antecedent of *who* is *God* in *v.* 4. *Without crime*, so that there be no matter of condemnation against you at the day of judgment. Cf. Col. i. 22, where the same word ἀνεγκλήτους is translated *blameless*.

9. *The fellowship of Christ* is *the adoption of sons* (Galatians iv. 5); *that he might be the first-born amongst many brethren* (Rom. viii. 29); and incidentally also the *chastisement* of sons (Heb. xii. 7—10). In this chastisement, which fell even upon His Only-begotten (1 Pet. iv. 13; 2 Tim. ii. 11, 12), *God is faithful, who will not suffer you to be tempted above that which you are able* (1 Cor. x. 13). The fellowship of Christ means also union with the body of the Church (1 Cor. xii. 11—14; Rom. xii. 4, 5; Eph. v. 29, 30).

10. From this to the end of ch. iv. the Apostle deals with the divisions among the Corinthians, the healing of which was his principal object in writing the Epistle.

Perfect, κατηρτισμένοι, *i.e.* perfectly joined together without *schism*, or rent. The verb is used of the *mending* of nets (Matt. iv. 21).

In the same mind, as to belief, *and the same judgment* as to action; *i.e.* in union of faith and charity.

12. We have here four parties, not divided in faith, but contending with one another within the bounds of the Church. There was first the Pauline party, St. Paul's own converts, or such of them as continued to admire Paul above every other teacher. This pre-eminence was challenged by the party of Apollo, who had come to teach at Corinth after St. Paul had left the city, *watering* what the Apostle had *planted*. For

Apollo see Acts xviii. 24—28. Grieved at the failure of his eloquence at Athens (Acts xvii.), St. Paul had employed at Corinth an exceedingly simple style of address, far removed from the sublimities of Greek philosophy and the intricacies of Hebrew lore. Apollo had done just the reverse of this. Being an Alexandrian, *mighty in the Scriptures*, he had delighted Corinthian ears with the allegorical expositions for which the school of his native city was famous. Thus, without intending it, Apollo had got a party at Corinth, who extolled his subtlety and eloquence above the apostolic plainness of St. Paul, a plainness which the Apostle adopted on principle, as he says in this Epistle (ii. 1—5; iii. 1, 2). Apollo himself gave no countenance to faction, and was ever accounted by St. Paul a loyal fellow-labourer (iii. 6; xvi. 12; Titus iii. 13).

A third party took their stand on the observance of the Jewish law, and arrogated to themselves the honoured name of St. Peter. Cf. Gal. ii. 11—14. There seems to have been yet a fourth party, consisting of a few who had seen Christ in the flesh, and traced their Christianity immediately to His teaching. These affected to despise St. Paul, as not having been one of our Lord's disciples. To them he justifies his position, ix. 1, and still more pointedly, 2 Cor. x. 7. Many commentators however deny the existence of this fourth party, and reduce the parties to three.

13. They were baptized, not *in the name of Paul*, but *in* (literally, *unto*, εἰς) *the name of the Lord Jesus* (Acts viii. 16), taking Him as their head (cf. x. 2), and making *one body* under Him (xii. 13). The phrase *to baptize unto the name* is illustrated by a phrase common in the Roman historians, *e.g.* Tacitus, *Hist.* ii. 14: *provincia Narbonensis in verba Vitellii adacta*—"the province was sworn unto the words of Vitellius," *i.e.* took the oath to him as emperor.

18, 19. There is an antithesis between *wisdom of speech* (*word*) and *the word of the cross*. Eloquence and subtlety of argument may be used to commend the gospel to men : but the acceptance of gospel truth ultimately is not a recognition of argument, but an act of faith in the Crucified. Furthermore it was in the Providence of God that the earliest preaching of Christianity should be done with no display of argument or eloquence, but in plain words confirmed by miracles, that the success to follow might be evidently divine. This does not debar the modern successors of the Apostles, not having the gift of miracles, from availing themselves of philosophy, rhetoric, and erudition ; yet even they should beware of placing their main reliance on such arms. They should remember that *the weapons of our warfare are not carnal*. Rhetoric, science, and philosophy, by themselves, will never bring any *understanding into captivity unto the obedience of Christ* (2 Cor. x. 4, 5 : cf. Luke xviii. 17).

To them that perish, ἀπολλυμένοις, literally, *are perishing*, *i.e.* unbelievers. The next words may be literally translated, *to us who are in the way of salvation*, σωζομένοις.

19. The quotation is from Isaias xxix. 14, according to the Septuagint, or Greek version, except that for *I will hide*, St. Paul says, explaining the phrase, *I will reject*. The prophet speaks of the counsellors of Ezechias : it was not by their worldly wisdom that the invasion of Sennacherib was to be repelled.

20. The Apostle alludes to rather than quotes Isaias xxxiii. 18, the general sense of which passage, according to the Hebrew, is *where is now the tribute-collector ?* The cross has triumphed over human learning, as Israel once triumphed over the Assyrians. By *the wise* understand the Greek philosophers, for *the Greeks seek after wisdom* (*v.* 22). *The scribe* is the doctor of the Jewish law. *The disputer of this world* is the product

of all the learning of the day combined, apart from Christianity.

21. The meaning is that whereas, notwithstanding the wisdom of God shown forth in Scripture to the Jew (Rom. iii. 2), and in the book of nature to the Greek (Rom. i. 20), still the world with all its wisdom knew not God practically so as to glorify Him (Rom. i. 21, 22; iii. 9, 10); therefore God has sent His Divine Son (Heb. i. 1, 2) and His Apostles to preach that *obedience of faith* (Rom. xvi. 26) which the world derides as folly. The text announces the failure of "free thought" to attain to religious truth.

22. *Signs*, as that asked from heaven (Matt. xvi. 1). *Wisdom, i.e.* rational and philosophic proof, not miracles.

23. It was well observed by Dean Bradley in Westminster Abbey on Easter Day, 1891, that the *scandal* and *folly* of the non-Christian mind in our day is not Christ Crucified, but Christ Risen. Our age delights in Passion Plays and the Three Hours: but its predominant devotion to physical science is shocked by the fact of the Resurrection.

24. *Called*, see on *v.* 2.

In *vv.* 22, 23, 24, observe the antithesis involved in the pairs of contrasted terms:

Jews . . . *signs* . . . . *stumbling-block* . . *power.*
Greeks . . . *wisdom* . . . *foolishness* . . . . *wisdom.*

The *signs* are *signs* of *power;* and the *stumbling-block* comes from the seeming breakdown of *power* in *Christ crucified.* So He foretold: *All you shall be scandalised in me* (Matt. xxvi. 31).

It is not Jesus Christ as God the Word, but *Christ crucified*, who is here called *the power of God and the wisdom of God; power*, to overcome the world by what seemed to be His defeat and overthrow; *wisdom*, to teach the world the lesson of renunciation (Gal. vi. 14 with note).

25. The foolishness of God is wiser than the wisdom of men, and the weakness of God stronger than the strength of men. *Foolishness* and *weakness*, appearing in the doctrine and mystery of the cross.

26—28. A large proportion of the early Christians were slaves; and a slave was a nobody, one of the things that in the estimation of the world *are not*. Cf. Gal. vi. 3: *If any man think himself to be something, whereas he is nothing.* Cf. also John vii. 48, 49.

Christianity, unlike philosophy, is for the simple, the illiterate, the slave. It is a democratic principle. But like a wise democracy, it offers attractions to and has attracted the highest intellects, beginning with Paul of Tarsus, the first powerful mind that bowed to receive baptism,

30. *You are in Christ Jesus.* To *be in Christ* is to be a member of His Church (Rom. xvi. 11, 17; *ib.* viii. 1; Gal. i. 22).

Christ is not said to have made us wise, but Himself to be *made unto us wisdom*, to show the abundance of the gift. As the wisdom of Christ is not imputed to us, but is really communicated to us, so also His justice and sanctity are not imputed but really communicated to us, making us inwardly and really just and holy. "Justification is not the mere forgiveness of sins, but is sanctification also and the renewal of the inner man. . . . Receiving the gift of the justice of God, not that wherewith He Himself is just, but that whereby He makes us just, we are renewed in the spirit of our mind, and are not only reputed, but are truly called and are just" (Council of Trent, Sess. 6, c. 7).

31. An abridged quotation of Jer. ix. 23, 24. It was vainglory that had set the Corinthians first despising and then quarrelling with one another.

CHAPTER II.

1. And I, brethren, when I came to you, came not in loftiness of speech or of wisdom; declaring to you the testimony of Christ: **2.** For I judged not myself to know any thing among you, but Jesus Christ, and him crucified. **3.** And I was with you in weakness, and in fear, and in much trembling: **4.** And my speech and my preaching was not in the persuasive words of human wisdom, but in the showing of the Spirit and power; **5.** That your faith might not stand on the wisdom of men, but on the power of God. **6.** Howbeit, we speak wisdom among the perfect; yet not the wisdom of this world, neither of the princes of this world, who are destroyed: **7.** But we speak the wisdom of God in a mystery, which is hidden, which God predestinated before the world, unto our glory; **8.** Which none of the princes of this world knew: for if they had known it, they would never have crucified the Lord of glory. **9.** But, as it is written: The eye hath not seen, nor ear heard, neither hath it entered into the heart of man, what things God hath prepared for them that love him. **10.** But to us God hath revealed them by his Spirit: for the Spirit searcheth all things, even the profound things of God. **11.** For what man knoweth the things of a man, but the spirit of a man that is in him? So the things also that are of God no man knoweth, but the Spirit of God. **12.** Now we have received not the spirit of this world, but the Spirit that is of God; that we may know the things that are given us from God: **13.** Which things also we speak, not in the learned words of human wisdom, but in the doctrine of the Spirit, comparing spiritual things with spiritual. **14.** But the sensual man perceiveth not the things that are of the Spirit of God: for it is foolishness to him, and he cannot understand; because it is spiritually examined. **15.** But the spiritual man judgeth all things: and he himself is judged by no one. **16.** For who hath known the mind of the Lord, that he may instruct him? But we have the mind of Christ.

1. It seems likely that the Apostle came from Athens to Corinth much mortified and abashed; and that his addresses to the Corinthians were delivered in a tone and style unusually subdued and simple, like the speech of a man heavy with recent disappointment and apprehensive of further failure. We must beware therefore

how we take these verses to indicate St. Paul's normal
manner of preaching. By nature and by education, as
his writings show, the Apostle of the Gentiles must
have been a great orator, subject doubtless to those fits
of depression which frequently beset genius. Cf. note
on Gal. iv. 13.

2. The cross is honourable in our eyes; but in the
first century of the Church it required considerable
enthusiasm in a preacher of the gospel, to avow and
set in a strong light the fact that his Master and his
God had recently died the death of a slave.

3. *In weakness.* The phrase ἐν ἀσθενείᾳ may mean *in
lowly estate*, and allude to his working as a tent-maker,
Acts xviii. 3.

In fear and in much trembling. " What sayest thou ?
did Paul actually fear dangers ? Yes, he did fear and
was very much afraid : for he was human, though he
was Paul. This is no charge against Paul, but a
weakness of nature, and a commendation of his resolve,
in that, for all his fear of death and stripes, he did
nothing unseemly through that fear. They who say
that he had no fear of stripes, not only do not elevate
his character, but detract much from his praises. For
if he had no fear, what constancy or what philosophy
was there in his braving dangers ? It is for this that
I admire him, that fearing, aye even trembling as he
did at dangers, he everywhere ran his race victoriously "
(St. John Chrysostom).

If then at Corinth (*a*) the believers were generally
mean and illiterate people (i. 26) ; (*b*) the preacher and
founder of the church there was a man who made a
poor show to human eyes (ii. 3, 4) ; (*c*) the truth
preached and believed in was Christ crucified, to
human intelligence a scandal and a folly (i. 23 ; ii. 2) ;
then Christianity at Corinth was of no human creation ;
it was created by the power and inward motion of the

Holy Ghost, working in the hearts of them that believed. The final conclusion is that the Corinthians had no matter for self-glorification, no matter for despising their neighbour, no matter for contention and strife, in any gift that Christianity had brought to them.

5. *The power of God* shone forth by the miraculous gifts enumerated in ch. xii.

6. *The perfect* here are not the whole multitude of the faithful, but, according to the definition given of the designation, Heb. v. 14, they *who by custom have their senses exercised to the discernment of good and evil. The perfect man* is *the spiritual man* (*v.* 15), the full-grown Christian who is arrived *unto the measure of the age of the fulness of Christ* (Eph. iv. 13). He is marked off from the *children*, who are deceived by *cunning craftiness* (Eph. iv. 14); from the *partaker of milk, unskilful in the word of justice* (Heb. v. 13); which was the condition of the Corinthians themselves (iii. 1, 2). *Wisdom*, the *strong meat* (Heb. v. 14), is the higher teaching of Christian theology, such as we read in Heb. vii. viii. ix; Rom. ix. x. xi.: as distinguished from *the first elements of the words of God* (Heb. v. 12), or the primary truths of the catechism, *e.g.* those mentioned in Heb. vi. 1, 2. But by *wisdom* here we are particularly to understand the doctrine of sanctifying grace, the theme of Eph. i. ii. iii.; 2 Pet. i. 4: set forth, after all, not ignobly in this very epistle under the head of the *more excellent way* of charity, ch. xiii.

The princes of this world are the devils, *the spirits of wickedness, the rulers of the world of this darkness* (Eph. vi. 12: cf. John xii. 31; xiv. 30; Eph. ii. 2; 2 Cor. iv. 4): not however the devils only, but their human instruments, the misled great ones of this earth, such as Caiphas and Pilate; also the whole crowd of professors and poets, philosophers and politicians, men of leading, but not of Christian light: none of these have had any practical insight into the mystery of Christian life.

7. The meaning is : We deliver as a mystery, under-stood only of the few, the wisdom of God in the scheme of our salvation.—The Church has never kept back any of her doctrines from the baptized. At present she publishes them to all the world. They are published, but not understood : they are preached on the house-tops, and still remain a mystery. The unbeliever hears, and as mere notions he understands, the dogmas of faith : but he has no real appreciation of them. To the enunciation of Christian truth, considered as an intelligible proposition, he gives what Cardinal Newman calls a *notional assent*, not a *real assent*. See *Grammar of Assent*, ch. i. § 2.

And even among believers there are differences of appreciation : *the spiritual man* (*v.* 15), *the perfect* man (*v.* 6), understands higher lessons, that would be lost upon the yet *carnal* Christian, the mere *little one in Christ* (iii. 1, 2).

Predestinated before the world, as a father makes provi-sion for his children ere they are capable of enjoying it.

8. That is, if the authors of our Saviour's crucifixion, the devils and the men whom they instigated, had understood how Christ crucified was to take away sin, to overcome death and hell, to open heaven, and to reign glorious on earth, they would have shrunk back from a deed so ill-judged for Satan's purposes, and so sacrilegious for man to dare. Thus Annas, Caiphas, and those about them knew not what they did (Luke xxiii. 34), in that sense in which St. John says : *Whoso-ever sinneth, hath not seen him nor known him* (1 John iii. 6). There is ignorance in every sin, but the ignorance in this case was least excusable in the chief priests, and most excusable in the rude executioners nailing Him to the cross, who were the immediate objects of our

Lord's prayer. St. Peter repeats this assertion of ignorance: *And now, brethren, I know you did it through ignorance, as did also your rulers* (Acts iii. 17): and St. Stephen—*they that inhabited Jerusalem, and the rulers thereof, not knowing him, nor the voices of the prophets* (Acts xiii. 27). Cf. John viii. 19. But when after the triumph of the cross, and the wonders wrought in the name of the Crucified (Acts iv. 10), the Jews as a people remained still incredulous, Divine justice handed the unbelieving city over to Titus the besieger.

9. A free rendering of Isaias lxiv. 4, which should not surprise us, when we remember that the same Holy Spirit, who was the author of the prophecy, was likewise the author of this epistle. An author often explains a previous saying of his own by putting it in another and more striking dress.—*The things which God hath prepared* are *the unsearchable riches of Christ* (Eph. iii. 8), grace on earth and glory in Heaven. The passage, Eph. iii. 3—9, should be compared with *vv*. 7, 8, 9 here.

10, 11. A strong proof of the Divinity of the Holy Ghost.

12. *The spirit of this world* is *the wisdom of the flesh.* Read Rom. viii. 5—18, which also declares what the things are which we know by the Spirit to be given us from God. On *the spirit of this world* see 2 Cor. iv. 4; Eph. ii. 2; 1 John iv. 3—6; v. 19; James iii. 15. It is the special office of the Spirit of God to make us appreciate and be careful of things supernatural : while on the other hand heedlessness of supernatural good, as pastors of souls by bitter experience know, is the commonest and at the same time the most desperate of evils in a Christian congregation. The people do not want their priest : socially he may be welcome, but not in his spiritual capacity. See however Luke x. 16; John xii. 48.

13. *Learned words of human wisdom :* more literally, *words which are taught by human wisdom.*

Comparing spiritual things with spiritual, i.e. taking the measure of spiritual things by spiritual standards, not judging of spiritual things carnally. There is a Greek epitaph : μή με τάφῳ σύγκρινε, " Take not my measure by the modesty of my tomb " : where the same word is used which St. Paul has here, συγκρίνοντες.

14. *The sensual man* here is not necessarily the man given up to sensuality and sin, but the merely *natural* man, the man who rests satisfied with his own human reasonings and the promptings of his nature to goodness, not recognising his need of light and grace from a superhuman source. To such a man the things of God are foolishness, and he cannot understand them, because they need to be examined on spiritual principles, of which he has none.

15. *The spiritual man,* in spiritual things, *is judged of no man,* that is not spiritual.

16. This verse amounts to an argument as follows. —None knoweth the mind of the Lord, to instruct Him (a quotation from the Greek text of Isaias xl. 13). But we, as spiritual men, have the mind of Christ, that is, of the Lord. Therefore none is in a position to instruct us : that is to say, no mere natural-minded man can fathom, judge of, or add to our knowledge of the things of the spirit.—The doctrine requires this caution, that any one who assumed himself to be a spiritual person, and his superiors in their several places and degrees to be carnal-minded men, would show little of that humility, which is the surest indication of *the mind of Christ.*

CHAPTER III.

1. And I, brethren, could not speak to you as to spiritual, but as to carnal. As to little ones in Christ, 2. I gave you milk to drink, not meat : for you were not able as yet : but neither indeed are you now able; for you are yet carnal. 3. For whereas there is among you envying and contention, are you not carnal, and walk according to man ? 4. For while one saith, I indeed am of Paul ; and another, I am of Apollo; are you not men ? What then is Apollo, and what is Paul ? 5. The ministers of him whom you have believed ; and to every one as the Lord hath given. 6. I have planted, Apollo watered ; but God gave the increase. 7. So then neither he that planteth is any thing, nor he that watereth ; but God who giveth the increase. 8. Now he who planteth and he who watereth are one : and every man shall receive his own reward, according to his own labour. 9. For we are God's coadjutors ; you are God's husbandry ; you are God's building. 10. According to the grace of God, that is given to me, as a wise architect, I have laid the foundation, and another buildeth thereon. But let every man take heed how he buildeth thereupon. 11. For no one can lay another foundation but that which is laid, which is Christ Jesus. 12. Now if any man build upon this foundation gold, silver, precious stones, wood, hay, stubble; 13. Every man's work shall be made manifest : for the day of the Lord shall declare it, because it shall be revealed by fire; and the fire shall try every man's work of what sort it is. 14. If any man's work abide, which he hath built thereupon, he shall receive a reward. 15. If any man's work burn, he shall suffer loss : but he himself shall be saved; yet so as by fire. 16. Know you not that you are the temple of God, and that the Spirit of God dwelleth in you? 17. But if any man violate the temple of God, him shall God destroy : for the temple of God is holy, which you are. 18. Let no man deceive himself. If any man among you seem to be wise in this world, let him become a fool, that he may be wise. 19. For the wisdom of this world is foolishness with God : for it is written : I will catch the wise in their own craftiness. 20. And again : The Lord knoweth the thoughts of the wise, that they are vain. 21. Let no man, therefore, glory in men. 22. For all things are yours, whether it be Paul, or Apollo, or Cephas, or the world, or life, or death, or things present, or things to come : for all are yours; 23. And you are Christ's, and Christ is God's.

1. *Carnal.* The *carnal* man here meant is the man who is spiritualised to a certain extent, but only to a

very small extent—a *little one in Christ*, retaining much of the *sensual*, or *natural* man (ii. 14) still about him. If to be *carnal* in this limited sense is a hinderance to the appreciation of the heights of Christian teaching, no wonder if being *carnal* in the fuller sense of being *sold under sin* (Rom. vii. 14) is in many cases a total obstacle to the reception of the truths of faith. Cf. John iii. 20.

2. *Milk, not meat.* Cf. Heb. v. 12—14. The reproach was graver as addressed to the Hebrews, whose local church had existed over thirty years, than it is here as uttered to the Corinthians, Christians as yet of scarce six years standing.

3. *Envying and contention,* ζῆλος καὶ ἔρις. The two are enumerated among *the works of the flesh* in Gal. v. 20, where our version has *contentions, emulations*. The word ζῆλος in Aristotle, *Rhetoric* ii. 11, means *emulation*, as distinguished from *envy* by this, that the *envious* man wishes his neighbour not to have the good, which the *emulous* wishes to share with him. The word is used in a good sense also by St. Paul, 2 Cor. vii. 7, 11; ix. 2; xi. 2.

Walk according to man. To *walk* is the common Hebrew idiom for *to conduct oneself, e.g.* Eph. iv. 17: *walk not as also the gentiles walk.* To *walk according to man* is to conduct oneself according to the dictates of human nature, divorced from the Spirit of God.

4. *Paul, Apollo*, see on i. 12.

Are you not men? The Greek *textus receptus*, but not the best Greek manuscripts, has *Are ye not carnal? Men* here are *flesh and blood* (Matt. xvi. 17, 23; 1 Cor. xv. 50), as opposed to those whom our Saviour calls *gods* (Matt. x. 34, 35). These Corinthians were not mere *flesh and blood*, else there would have been no Christian holiness in them at all: but the process of sanctification, deification (that is, assimilation to God), and divine faith

(John i. 12, 13) in them was as yet very imperfectly accomplished.

5. A better reading is that of all the Greek MSS. and Fathers, *ministers through whom you believed*, δι' ὧν. St. Augustine has both this and the Vulgate reading.

Paul, Cephas, Apollo, are *ministers*, but Christ is much more, *as he hath inherited a more excellent name than they* (Heb. i. 4)—*the author and finisher of faith* (Heb. xii. 2); the Crucified, in whose name men are baptized (i. 13).

6. *I have planted; for in Christ Jesus by the gospel I have begotten you* (iv. 15).

Apollo watered; who, when he was come, helped them much who had believed (Acts xviii. 27).

God gave the increase. There is more meaning in this, if we hold that all manner of increase, germination, or generation, involves a certain special concurrence of the Almighty, as St. John Chrysostom teaches.

" Though men till the earth, and have the help of cattle for the purpose, and pay great attention to the tillage, and though there be fair weather, and all other earthly requisites combined, still, apart from the Master's assent, it is all vain and to no purpose; and nothing will come of those many labours and toils, unless the hand of Heaven joins in the work, and gives it to the crop to fructify and come to maturity (μὴ καὶ τῆς ἄνωθεν χειρὸς συνεφαπτομένης, καὶ τὴν τελεσφόρησιν χαρι- ζομένης τοῖς γινομένοις). Hom. v. *On Genesis.*

8. *Are one*, as having the same ministry and dispensation of the mysteries of God (iv. 1). St. Paul seems anxious here to show his union with Apollo, and to waive any claim of ecclesiastical superiority. He goes on to say however, as a warning against idleness, that oneness of ministry does not mean oneness of merit, but merit varies according to the quantity and quality of the labour done. Of the labour, not of the

c

fruit: at the same time it is the part of a *wise servant* (Matt. xxiv. 45), to lay out his labour with an eye to returns (Luke xviii. 23).

Thus then "there is an individuality, as well as a unity in the work of the ministry. This is, however, not a thing to be noticed by men, but it will be recognised by the great Master" (Shore).

9. *We are God's coadjutors* (συνεργοί). Cf. Mark xvi. 20, *the Lord working withal* (συνεργοῦντος), *and confirming the word.* St. Paul here speaks of apostolic labours, but the text has its application to all works done in and with grace, and consequently meritorious. See the Council of Trent, Sess. 6. c. 16.

Husbandry, building. The metaphor is suddenly changed, and the new metaphor is carried on for the next eight verses. "If you are a building, you must not part asunder" (St. Chrysostom).

10. Dropping the metaphor, we have this meaning: "I have been the first to preach Christ and make Christians at Corinth: others are proceeding with the instruction of the Christians whom I have made. Only let these my successors look to the character of the instruction that they impart."

Of these instructors, whom the Apostle evidently means to censure, we may observe:

(*a*) They were not teaching heresy: for they were *building on the foundation of Christ* (*vv.* 11, 12), and they were in a condition to be *saved* (*v.* 15).

(*b*) Their style of teaching was such as to argue a motive of vainglory and emulous desire to eclipse St. Paul (i. 31; iv. 7; 2 Cor. x. 15; xi. 12—18).

(*c*) The matter of their teaching was faulty, though not heretical,—not improbably in this, that they were Judaisers, over-much insisting on the observances of the Mosaic law (2 Cor. xi. 21, 22).

(*d*) They would then have been of the party that

called themselves *of Cephas.* Apollo was not of them, for at this time he was away with St. Paul at Ephesus (xvi. 12).

11. *That* (foundation) *which is laid, which is Christ Jesus.*

" Upon this then," says St. Chrysostom, " let us build, and hold to it as a foundation, as a branch to a vine, and let nothing come between us and Christ : for if anything does come between, we are immediately lost. So the branch by its continuity with the trunk draws the sap ; and the building stands by being knit together ; whereas, if it opens into clefts, it is lost, not having support for itself. Let us not then merely cling to Christ, but let us knit ourselves fast to Him. If we part from Him, we are lost, as the text says : *They that go far from thee, shall perish* (Ps. lxx. 6). Let us then cleave fast to Him, and cleave fast by deeds : for *he that keepeth my commandments, he it is that abideth in me* (John xiv. 21 ; xv. 10). And by many illustrations He signifies His union with us. Just consider. He is the head, we the body : can any gap come between head and body ? He is the foundation, we the building : He is the vine, we the branches : He is the bridegroom, we the bride : He is the shepherd, we the flock : He is the way, we the wayfarers. Again, we are the temple, He the indweller : He the firstborn, we the brethren : He is the heir, we the co-heirs : He is the life, we the living : He is the resurrection, we the raised : He is the light, we the enlightened. These are all so many significations of union, and exclude anything, even the least separation, from coming between us. For he that stands off ever so little from Christ, in time will stand off far."

12. The *gold* and *silver* will be proved by the *fire*, melted down and purged of dross. The *precious stones* are not gems but marbles, which have some capacity

of standing fire. But the *wood*, *hay*, and *stubble*, will be utterly consumed. In Corinth, as in Ephesus where the Apostle wrote, there might have been seen hovels built of lath and plaster (*wood*), the chinks in the walls stuffed with straw (*hay*), and the roof covered with thatch (*stubble*). These wretched tenements would perish utterly, and no doubt often did perish, in conflagrations from which the temples with their marble pillars and gilt capitals escaped uninjured.

By the materials here mentioned are we to understand doctrines or works? Not exactly either the one or the other: that is to say, not doctrines in the sense of things taught: nor again works in general, not at least primarily; but the primary reference is to works of teaching, to the act of delivering these or those doctrines, to the various ways in which the office of preaching the gospel was discharged either in the Church at Corinth or elsewhere. No doubt from this special kind of work, and its testing by fire, a generalisation may be drawn to all other works of Christian men, so far as those works are *built upon the foundation, which is Christ Jesus.*

The act of teaching heretical doctrine is not *built upon the foundation of Christ* at all; there is therefore no question of heresy in this verse. Heresy would come under the *violation of the temple of God* (*v.* 17). So this verse can by no licit generalisation be extended to mortal sins. It can however and should be extended to all venial sins, committed by a person in the state of grace. Not that a venial sin, precisely as it is sinful, is built upon the foundation of Christ: but the man who commits it, even while he sins, remains founded on Christ, and in His grace. Moreover the venial sin is frequently an imperfect way of doing a good work, as when a priest says his office with distractions, or a person approaches the altar-rail led partly by vanity.

Thus St. Thomas says: "A venial sin is not *against* the law: because in sinning venially one does not do what the law forbids, or omit to do what the law binds one to under precept; but it is *beside* the law, because it does not observe the mode of reason which the law intends" (1a 2æ, q. 88, art. 1, ad. 1).

13. *The day of the Lord. Of the Lord* is not in the Greek: but that *the day* here is *the day of the Lord, i.e.* the day of judgment, is clear from iv. 3, 5.

It shall be revealed. The pronoun may refer either to the *day* or to the *work;* or we may read the phrase impersonally, *there shall be a revealing in fire.*

The fire shall try, τὸ πῦρ αὐτὸ δοκιμάσει, which means, *the fire, without further experiment or testimony, will prove.* I take αὐτὸ to be nominative, not accusative. The *textus receptus* omits αὐτὸ.

The understanding of the whole passage turns on the sense we attach to the word *fire,* metaphorical or not. Is there question of a real, flaming fire, or is no more alleged than that the judgment of God is sharp and keen? On the one hand we observe that throughout the passage the language is metaphorical—*foundation, precious stones, wood, stubble:* why should *fire* alone be taken in the proper sense of the word? The answer is, because we know from other places of the New Testament (2 Pet. iii. 7; 2 Thess. i. 8), that the world is to perish by fire at the day of judgment, as it perished by water at the deluge. St. Paul knowing that, and speaking of the day of judgment, could not have had in his mind any mere metaphorical *fire.* As well say that it is a metaphorical *heat* which is attributed to the sun in the text: *There is no one that can hide himself from his heat* (Ps. xviii. 6).

At the same time we must allow that there is something figurative in the expression: for fire cannot by itself *try,* test, and distinguish, works praiseworthy and blameworthy: a man's *work*, his preaching or other action, cannot literally *burn* (v. 15). We must understand then by *fire* here the judgment of God at the last day, the first act of which will be a consuming flame of real and true fire, which God will direct to the purposes of His justice.

14. St. Thomas (Supplem. q. 74. art. 8) argues that the good, in whom no fault is found, will suffer no pain from the fire that is to devour the world before the day of judgment. If then the wicked perish in that conflagration, and also the just who have upon them the liabilities of unexpiated sin, though not of sin unto death ; it follows that they alone shall remain alive to be *changed* at the last day (xv. 51, 52), and *overclothed* (2 Cor. v. 2), who are so pure as to be ready at once for heaven. *Their work shall abide* the trial of fire : they shall *receive reward*, for to them it may be said : *I find thy works full before my God* (Apoc. iii. 2).

15. The minister who mingles vanity with his motives and unauthorised additions with his words, in preaching the gospel, shall *suffer loss* of reward for that vain and superfluous portion of his work. That portion of his work shall *burn* and be brought to nought so far as reward goes ; and further, he, the doer, shall *burn* for it. The fires that go before the judgment-day, if he happen to be alive at that age of the world, shall have in his suffering of them an expiatory character. He shall find in them his Purgatory on earth : a Purgatory which the prudent and safer builders up of God's word shall escape. Still, inasmuch as he is after all a good Christian, finishing his course in the grace of God, *he himself shall be saved*, and the *just judge will render him the crown of justice* (2 Tim. iv. 7, 8). He shall be saved, *yet so as by fire*. That is to say, the fire that shall consume the world, coming to burn him, shall form an essential preliminary to his attaining his crown. The prudent

and safer builders will not need to pass through that fire. Indeed they must escape it, to be alive at the day of judgment. God's Providence will arrange it so, as St. Thomas says. But the builder up of *wood* and *stubble* must burn along with his works.

St. Paul throughout speaks as though the day of judgment might come in the lifetime of those Corinthians to whom he writes. We must not be surprised if even an inspired writer was left in ignorance of a *day and hour* which *no man knoweth, no not the angels of heaven* (Matt. xxiv. 36). Cf. vi. 14 and note.

The argument of Catholic theology on this passage proceeds as follows. If those venially offending Corinthian teachers required to pass through fire before they could reach their salvation and final reward; then in default of the fire of the last day, of which immediately the Apostle speaks, coming upon them in their lifetime,—and also in default of their furnishing any other satisfaction in their lifetime,—some equivalent of purging fire must overtake after death all such debtors to God's justice.

This is the argument for the doctrine of Purgatory, drawn from this passage. Like other scriptural arguments, it must be taken in support of, and not wholly independent of, the tradition of the Catholic Church and her living, speaking authority. Viewed as involving a reference to Purgatory, St. Paul's note of warning to the Corinthian teachers has a depth and a gravity about it that strikes the heart. Set Purgatory aside, and there remains a faintly appreciated metaphor: *The trumpet gives an uncertain sound* (xiv. 8).

We must observe, however, that the *fire* which is mentioned in this text, is not precisely the fire of Purgatory, but the fire which will burn upon the face of this earth before the day of judgment. From what St. Paul says of that fire we argue the existence of

Purgatory. An argument is also drawn from the same source that there is fire in Purgatory; but this second conclusion is not of faith. It is generally ignored by the Greek Fathers, and not admitted in the Greek Church; nor was it pressed upon the Greeks by the Latins at the Council of Florence as a condition of reunion. That Council was content to define that "the souls of those who have died truly penitent and in the charity of God, before they have satisfied by worthy fruits of penance for their sins of commission and omission, are cleansed by the pains of Purgatory after death;" and this, with the addition made by the Council of Trent (Sess. 25), that "that the souls there detained are aided by the suffrages of the faithful, and especially by the acceptable sacrifice of the Altar," is all that is of faith in this matter. Catholics however generally believe that fire is one of the punishments of Purgatory. Against this purgatorial fire St. Paul here seems to caution the Corinthian doctors, and all others who do good works with a large admixture of imperfection and disorder.

16. The connection is: Be not surprised at the punishment in store for those who would build you up with imperfect teachings, you who are the temple of God. The temple of God spoken of here is the Christian body at Corinth collectively. An argument is hence drawn for the Divinity of the Holy Ghost thus:

You are the temple of God.

He who dwells in God's temple as in his own abode is God.

The Spirit of God dwells in you as in His own. Therefore—

17. Better, according to the best Greek reading: *If any man shall destroy the temple of God, him shall God destroy.* The triple repetition of *If any man, vv.* 14, 15, 17, is to be noticed, pointing as it does to three classes:

(*a*) those who teach perfect truth perfectly, and have an entire reward: (*b*) those who teach truth with imperfection, and have their reward, but with some loss and punishment annexed: (*c*) teachers of heresy and false doctrine; destroyers of the Church, so far as in them lies; themselves to be destroyed by God in turn.

19. *The wisdom of this world* is the wisdom that is void of the grace of the Spirit, and uses only human arguments, even in religious matters. We have here not a condemnation of learning or science simply, but of learning and science thus isolated and misapplied.

The words of Eliphaz, Job's friend (Job v. 13), are here quoted as inspired. Job xxxix. 30 is quoted by our Saviour, Matt. xxiv. 28. He is mentioned by St. James (James v. 11). St. Paul again, Rom. xi. 35, quotes Job xli. 2.

22. This is the final answer to: *I am of Paul, I am of Apollo, I am of Cephas*, i. 12. You are not of them as appendages or adherents, but they are yours. It is an application to Church matters of the grand political maxim, that all government is for the governed.

The climax reads much better, if the second *for* (*enim*) in this verse is omitted: it is not in the Greek.

23. *Christ is God's.* The Arians made much of this, that St. Paul does not say that Christ is God, as though he thereby implied him to be a creature of God. But that word *creature* is all of the Arians' putting in. As St. John Chrysostom says: "We are Christ's in a different way from that in which Christ is God's, or that in which the world is ours. We are Christ's as being His work: Christ is God's as His natural-born Son, not as His work, as neither is the world our work. Thus though the manner of speaking is one, the sense varies."

Possibly *Christ is God's* is added for their sake who said, *I of Christ*, i. 12 (where see note).

1. Let a man so look upon us as the ministers of Christ, and the dispensers of the mysteries of God. 2. Here now it is required among the dispensers, that a man be found faithful. 3. But as to me, it is a thing of the least account to be judged by you, or by human judgment : but neither do I judge myself. 4. For I am not conscious to myself of any thing ; yet in this I am not justified : but he that judgeth me is the Lord. 5. Therefore judge not before the time, until the Lord come, who both will bring to light the hidden things of darkness, and will make manifest the counsels of the hearts ; and then shall every man have praise from God. 6. But these things, brethren, I have in a figure transferred to myself and to Apollo, for your sakes ; that in us you may learn, that one be not puffed up against the other for another, above that which is written. 7. For who distinguisheth thee ? and what hast thou that thou hast not received ? and if thou hast received, why dost thou glory, as if thou hadst not received it ? 8. Now you are satiated, now you are become rich, you reign without us ; and I would to God you did reign, that we also might reign with you. 9. For I think that God hath set forth us apostles the last, as it were men destinated to death : because we are made a spectacle to the world, and to Angels, and to men. 10. We are fools for Christ's sake, but you are wise in Christ : we are weak, but you are strong : you are honourable, but we without honour. 11. Even unto this hour we both hunger, and thirst, and are naked, and are buffeted, and have no fixed abode : 12. And we labour, working with our own hands : we are reviled, and we bless : we are persecuted, and we suffer it : 13. We are ill spoken of, and we entreat : we are made as the refuse of this world, the offscouring of all even till now. 14. I write not these things to shame you ; but I admonish you, as my dearest children : 15. For if you have ten thousand instructors in Christ, yet not many fathers : for in Christ Jesus I have begotten you through the gospel. 16. Wherefore I beseech you, be ye followers of me, as I also am of Christ. 17. For this cause have I sent to you Timothy, who is my dearest son, and faithful in the Lord ; who will put you in mind of my ways, which are in Christ Jesus, as I teach everywhere in every church. 18. Some are so puffed up, as though I would not come to you. 19. But I will come to you shortly, if it please the Lord, and will know, not the speech of them who are puffed up, but the power.

20. For the kingdom of God is not in speech, but in power.
21. What will you? shall I come to you with a rod, or in charity,
and in the spirit of meekness?

1. This verse is a resumption of iii. 4, 5: *What then
is Apollo, and what is Paul?   The ministers of him whom you
have believed.*

The mysteries of God, of which there is question
throughout this argument, are the mysteries of divine
truth, *dispensed* by preaching.   The reference to sacraments is only indirect, inasmuch as the dispenser of
the word of God likewise dispenses the sacraments.

3. This is not pride: for the Apostle not only
declines other men's judgments, but even his own
judgment upon himself.   Rather it is a specimen of
that *scorn* which St. Thomas (II-II. q. 129, art. 3, ad 4),
after Aristotle, assigns as a mark of magnanimity, and
quite consistent with humility.

By man's day, *i.e.* by man while his day lasts, and it
is yet his turn to sit in judgment.   *Man's day* is contrasted with *the day of the Lord* (Isaias ii. 11 ; xiii. 6, 9),
the great judgment-day.   So we read of *the day of Jerusalem*, the hour of Jerusalem's triumph and restoration
of the city (Psalm cxxxvi. 7: cf. St. Luke xxii. 53).
Again it is said: *I have not desired the day of man* (Jerem.
xvii. 16), the fleeting hour of human pre-eminence.

4. *Of anything*, that is, of any shortcoming in my
dispensation of the word of God.   The statement is
particular, but admits of generalisation to all the duties
of a Christian man, upon the performance of which his
finding acceptance with God depends.   Hence it involves
the rejection of the doctrine of *assurance*, that to be just
before God, we must believe with the firm certainty of
faith that we are just in His eyes.   And so it is used
by the Tridentine Fathers (Sess. vi. c. 16) : " Because
we all offend in many things, every man, as he ought to
have mercy and goodness, so also should have severity

and judgment before his eyes, and not judge himself, though he be conscious to himself of nothing; because all the life of men is to be examined not by human judgment, but by that of God, *who will bring to light,* &c., *v.* 5."

St. Paul's argument to the Corinthians is: ' I cannot judge with absolute assurance of my own merits as a Christian teacher, how then can you judge me?' After all, the Apostle must have had fair ground for believing himself faultless (see 1 John iii. 21): only he says his own acquittal of himself is not an authoritative and final acquittal: that is reserved for God alone, authoritatively to acquit or condemn. Accordingly it is by divine authority that he presently proceeds to judge the incestuous Corinthian, v. 3, 4. They to whom he was writing had no such authority to judge *him.*

6. *I have in a figure transferred,* μετεσχημάτισα, *transfiguravi,* literally, *I have transformed.* The word is used 2 Cor. xi. 13, 14, 15; Philip. iii. 21. The Apostle says that he has altered the form of his language from what he might have used with propriety and truth. He refers to iii. 4, 5, 6. Instead of *What then is Apollo, and what is Paul?* he might have set down the names of certain other Corinthian teachers, whom he will not name, but whom he addresses, *vv.* 7, 8.

One puffed up against another for another. They formed parties, called from the names of their several teachers, and contended with one another, each taking credit for the merits of his own teacher, as schoolboys brag of the schools where they are severally brought up.

Above that which is written, Jerem. ix. 23, 24 quoted above, i. 31.

7. This and the next verse is addressed, not to the Corinthians generally, but to certain unnamed teachers among them, ringleaders of faction.

Who distinguisheth thee?—as having any good gift which

others have not. And if thou hast any distinguished excellence, is it not after all a gift? The text refers literally to natural gifts, such as eloquence, learning, and ingenuity, the makings of a popular teacher. But by controversialists, from St. Augustine downwards, it has been alleged to evince the gratuitousness of super-natural graces. The allegation is just, considered as an argument *a minori ad majus*. If the less is not *of ourselves, as of ourselves* (2 Cor. iii. 5), certainly not the greater.

8. *You reign*, ἐβασιλεύσατε, literally, *you have come to be kings*. Ironical of course.

9. *Hath set us forth the last, i.e.* has made us appear the meanest of the mean.

Men appointed to death. Tertullian, *De pudicitia*, c. 14, quotes this text, reading here *bestiarios*. The *bestiarii* were men who fought with wild beasts in the amphi-theatre. Some of them, like the Spanish *matadors*, were armed, and expected to show their prowess, and slay the beast. Others were condemned criminals—ἐπιθαν-άτιοι, St. Paul's word, as being ἐπὶ θανάτῳ, bound for death — thrown unarmed among the beasts to be devoured by them, while the people looked on. This was the treatment of the Christian martyrs in the generation immediately following St. Paul, men who actually became that "food for beasts" to which St. Paul here likens himself and his fellow-apostles.

To angels. As St. Chrysostom says, some perform-ances are a sight and a spectacle to men, but con-temptible to the angels, as the vainglorious displays of the Corinthian doctors; not so the acts of the apostles.

10. *Wise in Christ*, that is, in the Church and under the gospel. "You enjoy security, and are much courted: but that is not permitted by gospel condi-tions. The present is not a time of honour and glory,

such as you enjoy, but of persecution and ill-treatment, such as we suffer. It is impossible for one to be accounted a fool, another wise; one strong, and another weak, under a gospel that does not admit of both the one and the other alternative. If it were possible for some to be one thing and some another, there might be some reason in your position; but now that is not possible: it is not possible for a Christian teacher to pose as a wise man, great and glorious, and out of reach of danger."—So St. John Chrysostom, declaring the mind of St. Paul and of all the Saints.

11. *Have no fixed abode.* Cf. Matt. viii. 20.

12. *Working with our hands* at tent-making, St. Paul's trade, Acts xviii. 3; xx. 34.

13. *We are blasphemed, and we entreat,* βλασφημούμενοι παρακαλοῦμεν, *i.e.* we are *spoken ill of* and still go on *exhorting* men to good.

Refuse, offscouring, περικαθάρματα, περίψημα. This translation may be exact. Or the two words may both mean *scapegoat*, as περικάθαρμα does in Proverbs xxi. 18, and περίψημα in Tobias v. 18. At Athens a *worthless person,* called κάθαρμα, was flung into the sea in time of public calamity, with the words, "Be thou our scape-goat (περίψημα)." The words in the Vulgate are *purgamenta* and *peripsema,* the latter itself the Greek word, the former ambiguous as the Greek. The translation *worthless fellow, scapegoat,* would go well with the idea of *food for beasts* in *v.* 9.

14. *To confound you,* ἐντρέπων, the only instance in the New Testament of the active form of this verb. In the middle it is not uncommon, meaning to *reverence, e.g.* Matt. xxi. 37.

16. *Be ye followers of me* (repeated xi. 1), that is, be modest as I am, suffer as I suffer, and glory in your sufferings, not in your gifts: let there be no more of the contrast set forth in *v.* 10.

17. See xvi. 10, and Acts xix. 21, 22. Timothy was not the bearer of this letter, which was despatched after he had left Ephesus, to reach Corinth before him, he going round by Macedonia.

18. *As if I would not come to you.* Rumour had noised abroad that St. Paul dared not return to the city where he had been outshone by Apollo. His sending of Timothy might seem to confirm this report.

19. *But I will come,* xvi. 5—8, as he did, Acts xx. 2. " As the presence of the lion makes all the beasts crouch down, so the presence of Paul overawed the corrupters of the Church." (St. Chrysostom).

19, 20. *Power,* the power of the Holy Ghost working in men, whether unto miracles, as in Acts iv. 33 ; x. 38 : or unto good works and works of edification, as here.— Here ends the first part of the Epistle, dealing with the subject that is introduced i. 10.

1. It is heard for certain that there is fornication among you, and such fornication as the like is not among the heathens; that some one hath his father's wife. 2. And you are puffed up, and have not rather mourned, that he might be taken away from among you who hath done this deed. 3. I indeed, absent in body, but present in spirit, have already judged, as though I were present, him that hath so done: 4. In the name of our Lord Jesus Christ, you being gathered together, and my spirit, with the power of our Lord Jesus Christ, 5. To deliver such a one to Satan for the destruction of the flesh, that the spirit may be saved in the day of our Lord Jesus Christ. 6. Your glorying is not good. Know you not that a little leaven corrupteth the whole mass? 7. Purge out the old leaven, that you may be a new mass, as you are unleavened. For Christ, our pasch, is sacrificed. 8. Therefore let us feast, not with the old leaven, nor with the leaven of malice and wickedness, but with unleavened bread of sincerity and truth. 9. I wrote to you in an epistle not to keep company with fornicators. 10. I mean not with the fornicators of this world, or with the covetous, or the extortioners, or the servers of idols; otherwise you must have gone out of this world. 11. But now I have written to you not to keep company, if any man that is called a brother be a fornicator, or covetous, or a server of idols, or a railer, or a drunkard, or an extortioner; with such a one not so much as to eat. 12. For what have I to do to judge them that are without: do not you judge them that are within? 13. For them that are without God will judge. Take away the evil one from among yourselves.

1. *Have his father's wife.* It was a case of a man marrying his stepmother, and that while his father was yet alive, 2 Cor. vii. 12. No doubt he had gone through the form of marrying her. Any connection short of that would not have been so abiding a scandal, nor so entirely unprecedented among the Gentiles. The woman was probably a pagan, as the Apostle has no word of reproach for her.

2. *And you are puffed up.* The Apostle's vehement and pointed language finds its full explanation only in

the hypothesis of the Greek Fathers, that the offender was one of those very teachers *wise in Christ*, who had supplanted St. Paul in the estimation of the Corinthians. He reproaches them (here and *v.* 6) for glorying in the man, when they ought to have put him out of the Church.

3. *Absent in body, but present in spirit*, as Eliseus was to Giezi, *Was not my heart present etc.?* (4 Kings v. 26).

Him that hath so done. Him is the object, not of *have judged*, but of *deliver, v.* 5.

4, 5. *You being gathered together, and my spirit, i.e.* you being present bodily, and I spiritually, and both of us fortified *with the power of our Lord*, we are (*v.* 5) *to deliver such a one* (*v.* 4) in the *name of our Lord—to Satan.* The phrase *to deliver to Satan*, taken by itself, might mean no more than to expel the offender from the Church, the world outside the Church being taken to be the kingdom of Satan (Luke xi. 21 ; Eph. vi. 12). But the addition, *for the destruction of the flesh*, which is evidently the body, as distinguished from *the spirit*, or soul, shows that some bodily harm is threatened, to ensue upon ejection from the Church. The idea is to hurt his body, yet so as to save his soul. It would appear that with the apostolic grace of curing diseases, Matt. x. 8, there went also the power of striking with illness, or even with death, as St. Peter struck Ananias and Saphira (Acts v) and St. Paul struck Elymas (Acts xiii. 11). Cf. Apoc. xi. 5. One variety of this power to hurt would be to hand the offender over to Satan, as Job was handed over (Job ii. 6, 7), though for a different reason. The excommunicate thus handed over might actually become a demoniac. Similar language used of Hymenaeus and Alexander, 1 Tim. i. 20.

The Apostle tells them what his judgment is on the case as he hears it. Still it is not apparent that he wished to preclude the authorities at Corinth from trying and passing sentence upon their subject. They were to

D

bring him to trial, and punish him severely, if he was found guilty and contumacious.   From 2 Cor. v. 5, it appears that they did try him, and condemned him, and (*v.* 10.) abated his sentence upon his repentance.

6. *Corrupteth*, ζυμοῖ, more properly, *leaveneth.*   There is an unlikely reading, δολοῖ, *adulterates.*   But the Vulgate version, *corrumpit*, is sufficiently borne out by the consideration that for the rites of the Passover, here referred to, to *leaven* was to *corrupt* and make the bread legally uneatable.

7. This Epistle was written about Easter time, xvi. 8.   The Apostle had before his eyes the carrying out of the law of Exodus xii. 15.   *Seven days shall you eat unleavened bread ; in the first day there shall be no leaven in your houses ; whosoever shall eat anything leavened from the first day until the seventh day, that soul shall perish out of Israel.*   So scrupulously did the Jews observe this ordinance that, as St. Chrysostom says of them, "they go vexing their souls about mouse-holes," to see if any morsels of leavened bread had been carried there.

What is meant by *leaven* in *v.* 6 is evidently the evil company of the incestuous man ; cf. xv. 33.   From evil company the thought of the Apostle passes to evil manners. That is the *old leaven* of *vv.* 7, 8—as Theodoret puts it, " the leaven that was before baptism." These two verses then are parenthetical to the main drift of the chapter, which is resumed in *v.* 8.

Christ our Pasch is sacrificed.   The pronoun *our* is to be emphasized.   Not only the Jews have, or had, their Paschal Lamb : but Christ, our Christian Pasch, that is, Paschal Lamb (cf. Luke xxii. 7), *by one oblation hath perfected for ever them that are sanctified* (Heb. x. 14) ; and therefore the life of the Christian convert should be, not for one week, but for all time, lived aloof from the *old leaven of malice and wickedness*, that was cast out of his house at baptism.

The translation *purge out* is misleading. The word ἐκκαθαίρετε, *purgate*, here has no medical significance: it means *clear out* (of your house). When everything leavened was cleared out, a new paste was made, unleavened. St. Paul says to the Corinthians, *you are*, metaphorically, that *new paste*, you are *unleavened*.

9. *An epistle*, now lost.

11. *A server of idols*, such a Christian as the Samaritans were Israelites, 4 Kings xvii. 28, seq. History shows how pagan worship died hard, even within the fold of the Church. For traces of it at Corinth see viii. 10; x. 20, 21. Cf. 1 John v. 21.

With such a one not so much as to eat. Cf. 2 Thess. iii. 14. It is open to any individual, of himself and for himself, to break off from the company of a fellow-Christian, whom he considers a bad man. But to put that person under a ban, and command and even compel others to keep aloof from him, can only be done by sentence of a competent tribunal. The Church reserves to herself the right of excommunication, and most rarely exercises it to the extent of declaring any one an *excommunicatus vitandus*.

12. *What have I to do to judge them that are without?* Quoting this text St. Thomas writes: "It does not belong to the Church to punish unbelief in those who have never received the faith: but the infidelity of them who have received the faith is amenable to her sentence and punishment," 2a 2æ, q. 12, art. 2. The Council of Trent, sess. xiv. cap. 2, also alleges it, to bring out the difference between the sacraments of Baptism and Penance: "The minister of Baptism need not be a judge, since the Church exercises judgment on none who has not first come into her by the door of Baptism."

13. *Put away the evil one from amongst yourselves*, a phrase of the Mosaic law, Deut. xiii. 5; xvii. 7; xxi. 21.

CHAPTER VI.

1. Dare any of you, having a matter against another, go to law before the unjust, and not before the saints? **2.** Know you not that the saints shall judge this world? and if the world shall be judged by you, are you unworthy to judge the smallest matters? **3.** Know you not that we shall judge angels? how much more things of this world? **4.** If, therefore, you shall have judgments about the things of the world, set them to judge who are the most despised in the church. **5.** I speak to your shame. Is it so, that there is not among you any wise man, that is able to judge between his brethren? **6.** But brother goeth to law with brother, and that before unbelievers? **7.** Already, indeed, there is plainly a fault among you, that you have lawsuits one with another. Why do you not rather take the injury? why do you not rather suffer the fraud? **8.** But you do wrong and defraud, and that to your brethren. **9.** Know you not that the unjust shall not possess the kingdom of God? Be not deceived: neither fornicators, nor idolaters, nor adulterers, **10.** Nor the effeminate, nor sodomites, nor thieves, nor the covetous, nor drunkards, nor railers, nor extortioners, shall possess the kingdom of God. **11.** And such some of you were: but you are washed, but you are sanctified, but you are justified, in the name of our Lord Jesus Christ, and in the Spirit of our God. **12.** All things are lawful to me, but all things are not expedient. All things are lawful to me, but I will not be brought under the power of any. **13.** The meat for the belly, and the belly for the meats: but God shall destroy both it and them: but the body is not for fornication, but for the Lord, and the Lord for the body. **14.** Now God hath both raised up the Lord, and will raise us up also by his power. **15.** Know you not that your bodies are the members of Christ? shall I then, taking the members of Christ, make them the members of a harlot? God forbid. **16.** Or know you not that he who adheres to a harlot is made one body? for they shall be (saith he) two in one flesh. **17.** But he who adheres to the Lord is one spirit. **18.** Fly fornication. Every sin that a man doeth is without the body; but he that committeth fornication sinneth against his own body. **19.** Or know you not that your members are the temple of the Holy Ghost, who is in you, whom you have from God, and you are not your own? **20.** For you are bought with a great price. Glorify and bear God in your body.

1. The *unjust* are the Gentiles, and the *saints* (cf. above, i. 2) are the Christians. Cf. Gal. ii. 5: *We*

are by nature Jews, and not of the Gentiles sinners. The early Christians marked themselves off from the pagan world as severely as the Jews marked themselves off from the Gentiles. Cf. Rom. ii. 17—20. In all the cities of the Roman Empire where there were Jewish communities, they had their own tribunals of civil procedure, and the Rabbis took care that no Jew should go to law with another Jew before a heathen judge. Similar was the discipline of the early Christian Church. To understand it, we may consider what would have been thought in Spain in the tenth century of Christian prosecuting Christian in a court of Moors. Hence the practice arose of bringing suits before bishops, even for temporal matters. See the Life of St. Augustine in the Maurist edition of his works, lib. 4, cap. 5, n. 4.

2. *The saints shall judge the world,* a quotation from Wisdom iii. 8: *They* (the just) *shall judge nations.* Cf. Matt. xix. 28. The judgment shall be, first, by the manifest opposition, which shall appear at the last day, between the innocence of the saints, or their repentance, and the wickedness and impenitence of the reprobate. Thus our Lord says that the queen of the south and the men of Niniveh shall rise in judgment and condemn the generation that rejected Him (Luke xi. 31, 32); and if they, much more the generation who heard and obeyed Him, and all generations since who have heard His voice in the Church. Secondly, the saints shall judge the world as assessors of Christ our Lord at the last judgment. For after the Judge has pronounced sentence of blessing upon them, *Come ye blessed of my Father* (Matt. xxv. 34), they shall come to Him as they are bidden; and surrounded by them, with their assent and approval, He shall utter the final doom of the wicked, *Depart from me, ye cursed* (Matt. xxv. 41). Thus we are not only to be *crucified with* Christ (Rom. vi. 6;

Gal. ii. 20), and *to die with* Him (2 Tim. ii. 11), and to
be buried with Him (Rom. vi. 4), and to *rise with* Him
(Eph. ii. 5, 6; Col. ii. 13; iii. 1), and to *live with*
Him (2 Tim. ii. 12; Rom. vi. 8), and to *be coheirs
with* Him (Rom. viii. 17), and to *be glorified with* Him
(Rom. viii. 17) and to *sit in heavenly places with* Him
(Eph. ii. 6), and to *reign with* Him (2 Tim. ii. 12), but
also with Him to *judge the world*.

3. *Judge angels*, ἀγγέλους, not τοὺς ἀγγέλους, *the angels*.
We shall judge *some* angels, namely, the evil angels,
whom God *hath reserved under darkness in everlasting chains
unto the judgment of the great day* (Jude 6). St. Thomas
(Suppl. q. 89, art. 8, ad 1) says: "This word of the
Apostle is to be understood of the judgment of comparison, because some men shall be found superior to
some angels."

5, 6. *Set them to judge, who are the most despised in the
church.* This is hyperbolical speaking, as St. Chrysostom
says, and as is evident from the next verse, *Is there not
among you any one wise man*, &c.? The Apostle is meeting
a possible objection, that as in the Corinthian church
there were *not many wise according to the flesh*, it was
necessary to go outside to find a competent judge.
What, says the Apostle, is there not even *one wise man*,
or as we should say, "one man of business," among
you? Take him then for your judge: but it would be
better to *set the most despised in the church to judge* than for
brother to go to law with brother before unbelievers.

7. *A fault.* This translation of ἥττημα makes St. Paul
say more than he does say, more indeed than is true.
The word means a *falling off*. It is used in Rom. xi. 12,
where it is translated *diminution*, and is opposed to
fulness, πλήρωμα; also in the Greek of Isaias xxxi. 8,
where we read, *the young men shall be* εἰς ἥττημα, that is,
they shall fall off in numbers. The word does not occur elsewhere in the Bible, nor in classical Greek. Here then

it denotes a *falling off* from perfection, that perfection which is commended to us, Matt. v. 40, but not commanded, except, as St. Augustine and St. Thomas teach, " in readiness of soul, so that a man be prepared to act thus, if need be " (St. Thomas, II-II. q. 72, art. 3).

The Athenians were notorious for their love of litigation, a feature satirised by their comic poet Aristophanes in *The Wasps*. Corinth, also a commercial city and a near neighbour, can hardly have been less litigious. The Apostle's caution against lawsuits was then particularly in point for the persons to whom it is addressed. The recommendation is still often given, even from a worldly point of view, to compromise a matter in dispute before it comes into court.

9, 10. Cf. Ps. xlix. 21 ; Gal. vi. 7—9. These texts are directed against antinomian notions, which were making some way in the Church of Corinth; cf. Rom. vi. 1, 15. They show the perfect accord of St. Paul with what Luther called the *straminea epistola* of St. James.

11. " He clearly shows the equality of the Son and of the Holy Ghost, and brings in the mention of God, that is, of the Father ; for it is by the invocation of the Holy Trinity that the nature of the waters is sanctified, and the forgiveness of sins afforded " (Theodoret).

12. *All things are lawful to me, but all things are not expedient.* These words are repeated, x. 22, 23, where *are not expedient* is paraphrased, *do not edify*. When the Apostle says, *All things are lawful*, he evidently means to except such things as those he has just condemned, *vv.* 9, 10. He insists on the observance of the moral law of the ten commandments, but beyond that, in the region of things indifferent, he says that Christians are free, yet so that they do not turn their liberty into a snare (Gal. v. 13); nor take in immoderate amount that which in itself they may lawfully take, and so by this very immoderation come to be *slaves of sin* (John

viii. 34); nor again give scandal to the weak by doing things which, however right in themselves, still present some apprearance of evil, cf. viii. 13. The Apostle goes on to point out, what was very necessary to point out in a pagan city like Corinth, that fornication was not in the number of things indifferent (Acts xv. 29), or only venially evil. Understand simple fornication, as distinct from the more generally acknowledged sin of adultery. St. Thomas in the thirteenth century found it worth while to prove the sinfulness of simple fornication by elaborate arguments, II-II. q. 154, art. 2 ; *Contra Gentiles*, iii. 122 : which are still of value.

I will not be brought into the power of any. St. Chrysostom explains: " Are you master of your own eating ? Then remain master, and see that you do not become the slave of that passion." The pronoun *any* here is neuter, any of *all things* mentioned above. There is a play on the words ἔξεστι and ἐξουσιασθήσομαι, which might be Englished : " All things are *lawful* to me, but I will not be *brought under the law* of any of them:" understanding *law* as in Rom. vii. 23.

13, 14. The argument is: If you wish to eat, eat : stomach and food are made for one another : and yet one day the Lord shall *destroy*, or literally, καταργήσει (cf. xiii. 8, 10, 11, where the same word is used), *make the occupation gone* of them both. But for fornication, that you must not commit : your body is not made for that, but for the Lord ; and though it be destroyed, the Lord shall raise it up. It shall then perish as a *natural body*, eating and drinking; but it shall rise again as a *spiritual body* (xv. 44), *equal to the angels* (Luke xx. 36).

Will also raise us up—*us* who are dead. Cf. xv. 32 : *The dead shall rise, and we* (living at that time) *shall be changed*. And 1 Thess. iv. 16: *We who are alive*, &c. The Apostle speaks of *us*, now as living till the day of judgment, now as dead before it, not knowing which would be the case.

15. Nowhere does Holy Scripture contain a better medicine against the vice of impurity than is to be had from these verses, 15—20. Nothing could be better adapted to the Greek mind, to which it was first addressed, or to modern minds and modern needs. It is an appeal resting at once on the innermost mystery of Christianity, the union of Christ with His Church, and the noblest thought of the ancient world, such as that of Plato when he speaks of some one θείᾳ φύσει δυσχεραίνων τὸ ἀδικεῖν, "by an endowment of divine nature disdaining wrong " (*Republic*, 366, C). Cf. 2 Pet. i. 4.

Know ye not that your bodies are the members of Christ. This argument loses all its cogency, if no more than a mere metaphor or analogy is seen in it. The union of the faithful with Christ is a mystery, obscure as any other mystery, but a reality and a revealed truth of the first importance. Christ is Head of the whole Church, which is His mystical Body ; and the faithful all and each are members of Christ, not in soul only but also as to their bodies. The Incarnation is an alliance contracted, not with that Soul and that Body only which was united in the unity of one Person with the Eternal Word *made flesh*, but likewise with all mankind, by their entrance into the Church, in which that Word has dwelt amongst us (John i. 14). Thus *we are members of his body, of his flesh and of his bones* (Eph. v. 30; and here xii. 27; also John vi. 55—57). Hence though we die and turn to dust, our resurrection is a consequent necessity : it is impossible for death finally to hold us, as *it was impossible that he should be holden by it* (Acts ii. 24).

16. *Two in one flesh.* Physically, the union of the sexes is the same, whether it be licit or illicit. The text relating to the former is applicable in a physical

sense to the latter, at the same time showing its moral turpitude.

17. " He says: When you are joined to a harlot, you make your members members of a harlot. Again when you are joined to the Lord by the Spirit, you make your members members of Christ. If then you have been joined to the Lord, and again go off to her, the insult redounds upon the very Person of the Lord : for it is His members that you bring to the harlot, and make the members of Christ members of a harlot." (Theodoret).

18. *Sinneth against his own body.* Because, as St. Augustine explains (Serm. 162), other sins are either spiritual, as pride and apostasy, or require for their commission some external goods, or some outside person to deal with; but the fornicator sins about his own body alone, and that of his accomplice which is conjoined with his, and has no other instrument or matter of his sin.

The Apostle points out what manner of body it is that he sins against, if he is a Christian.

19. *Temple of the Holy Ghost.* The Holy Ghost is said to be the *soul* of the Church, of which Christ is the *head*, and the faithful the *members*. There is a special indwelling of the Holy Ghost, and through Him and with Him of the Father and the Son, in the soul and body of every Christian that is in the state of grace.

20. *Great price.* The word *great* is not in the Greek, and is not wanted for the argument, which turns not on the greatness of the price paid, but on the fact that we have been bought, or redeemed, and are not our own to spoil. *And bear* also is not in the Greek, though it is well supported by the use of such words as χριστοφόρος, *Christifer* (Christ-bearing) in early Christian tradition.—Here ends the second part of the Epistle, which commences with chapter v.

Chapter VII.

1. Now concerning the things whereof you wrote to me: It is good for a man not to touch a woman: **2.** But because of fornication, let every man have his own wife, and let every woman have her own husband. **3.** Let the husband render the debt to his wife: and the wife also in like manner to the husband. **4** The wife hath not power over her own body, but the husband: and in like manner the husband hath not power of his own body, but the wife. **5.** Defraud not one another, unless, perhaps, by consent for a time, that you may give yourselves to prayer; and return together again, lest Satan tempt you for your incontinency. **6.** But I speak this by indulgence, not by commandment. **7.** For I would that all men were even as myself. But every one hath his proper gift from God, one after this manner, and another after that. **8.** But I say to the unmarried and to the widows: It is good for them if they so continue, even as I. **9.** But if they do not contain themselves, let them marry: for it is better to marry than to burn. **10.** But to them that are married, not I, but the Lord commandeth that the wife depart not from her husband: **11.** And if she depart, that she remain unmarried, or be reconciled to her husband: and let not the husband put away his wife. **12.** For to the rest I speak, not the Lord. If any brother have a wife that believeth not, and she consent to dwell with him, let him not put her away. **13.** And if any woman have a husband that believeth not, and he consent to dwell with her, let her not put away her husband. **14.** For the unbelieving husband is sanctified by the believing wife; and the unbelieving wife is sanctified by the believing husband: otherwise your children should be unclean; but now they are holy. **15.** But if the unbeliever depart, let him depart: for a brother or sister is not under bondage in such cases; but God hath called us in peace. **16.** For how knowest thou, O wife, whether thou shalt save thy husband; or how knowest thou, O man, whether thou shalt save thy wife? **17.** But as the Lord hath distributed to every one, as God hath called every one, so let him walk: and so I teach in all churches. **18** Is any man called, being circumcised? let him not procure uncircumcision. Is any man called in uncircumcision? let him not be circumcised. **19.** Circumcision is nothing, and uncircumcision is nothing; but the keeping of the commandments of God. **20.** Let every man abide in the same calling in which he was called. **21.** Art thou called, being a bondman? care not for it: but if thou mayest be made free, use it rather. **22.** For he that is called in the Lord, being a bondman, is the freeman of the Lord: likewise he that is called, being free, is the bondman of Christ. **23**. You are bought with a price; be not made the bondslaves of men. **24**. Brethren, let every man, wherein he was called, therein abide with God. **25**. Now concerning virgins I have no commandment of the Lord: but I give counsel, as having obtained mercy of the Lord to be faithful. **26**. I think, therefore, that this is good for the present necessity, that it is good for a man so to be. **27**. Art thou bound to a wife? seek not to be loosed. Art thou loosed from a wife? seek not a wife. **28**. But if thou take a wife, thou hast not sinned; and if a virgin marry, she hath not sinned. Nevertheless, such shall have tribulation of the flesh: but I spare you. **29**. This, therefore, I say, brethren: The time is short: it remaineth, that they also who have wives be as those who have not; **30**. And they who weep, as they who weep not; and they who rejoice, as they who are not rejoicing; and they who buy, as if they were not possessing any thing; **31**. And they who use this world, as if they used it not: for the figure of this world passeth away. **32**. But I would have you to be without solicitude. He that is without a wife is solicitous for the things that belong to the Lord, how he may please God: **33**. But he that is with a wife is solicitous for the things of the world, how he may please his wife: and he is divided. **34**. And the unmarried woman and the virgin thinketh on the things of the Lord, that she may be holy both in body and spirit: but she that is married thinketh on the things of the world, how she may please her husband. **35**. And this I speak for your profit; not to cast a snare upon you, but for that which is decent, and which may give you power to attend upon the Lord without impediment. **36**. But if any man think that he seemeth dishonoured with regard to his virgin, for that she is above the age, and it must so be, let him do what he will: he sinneth not if she marry. **37**. For he that hath determined, being steadfast in his heart, having no necessity, but having power of his own will, and hath judged this in his heart to keep his virgin, doeth well. **38**. Therefore, both he that giveth his virgin in marriage doeth well; and he that giveth her not doeth better. **39**. A woman is bound by the law as long as her husband liveth; but if her husband die, she is at liberty: let her marry to whom she will; only in the Lord. **40**. But more blessed shall she be if she so remain, according to my counsel; and I think that I also have the Spirit of God.

1. *Now concerning the things that you wrote to me of.* From here to the end of ch. xv. the Apostle solves

various questions that the Corinthians had proposed
to him by letter. And first in this chapter, of marriage
and celibacy.

It is good for a man. What the Apostle says is that
virginity is a high state, but all are not suited for it.
By their personal example and by teachings such as
this, as St. Chrysostom says, "the Apostles have filled
the whole world with the plant of virginity."

2. There has been an unnecessary amount of controversy about this very plain text. On the one hand,
it has been taken to be an indiscriminate exhortation
to all men to marry, against *vv.* 1, 7, 8, 34. On the
other hand it has been said to be addressed exclusively
to persons married already. This is not apparent on
the face of the text. It seems to be addressed to both :
to the married, in the sense of *v.* 3, and to the unmarried,
in the sense of *v.* 9.

5. *Give yourselves to prayer*, literally, *take time for it*,
σχολάσητε. There must be question here of some extraordinary time or season of prayer : since even for
married persons the injunction holds, *pray always*, 1 Thess.
v. 17. Such an extraordinary time of prayer would be
the time of Holy Mass, when one is called to celebrate
it, as most priests now do, daily. For them therefore
this text supplies a counsel, which the law of the
Western Church converts into an obligation.

6. *I speak this by indulgence.* It refers to the words
in the previous verse, *return together again.* But how is
this an *indulgence*, not a *command*, if it is a necessary
safeguard against sin ? The answer is that such a safeguard is not absolutely necessary, nor the only safeguard possible, but it is a safeguard suitable to human
weakness, and therefore is called an *indulgence.* Observe,
there is not question here of any indulgence to sin,
even the slightest venial sin. It is not a sin to take
advantage of the married state as a remedy for *incon-*

tinency. St. Augustine (*De peccato originali,* 38), makes the use of matrimony on this motive a venial sin : while St. Chrysostom, on the contrary (*De Virginitate,* c. 19), declares it to be the only use of matrimony in these latter days, which again is an exaggeration. Evidently Doctors differ. But we have our guide. As St. Thomas says (II-II. q. 10, art. 12) : " The greatest authority attaches to the custom of the Church, which is always to be followed in all things; since even the teaching of the Catholic Doctors has its authority from the Church. Hence we must rather stand by the authority of the Church than by the authority of either Augustine or Jerome, or any Doctor whatever." St. Augustine's opinion is obsolete in the Church of the present day : which obsoleteness in a practical matter is sufficient to mark that opinion for an error.

7. *I would that all men were even as myself.* This has been explained to mean, " not that the Apostle wished that every one was unmarried, but that every one had the same grace of continence which he himself was endowed with, that they might without risk of sin remain unmarried." But why should he wish that, unless the state of continence, unmarried, were in itself higher than the married state ? As Archbishop Porter said : " There is no heroism in marrying." At the same time this verse implies that, while virginity is a gift of God, marriage is a gift likewise, and a *good gift, from above, coming down from the Father of lights* (James i. 17).

On the oft-repeated difficulty about *all men* St. Jerome writes : " Be not afraid of all putting in to be virgins : virginity is a hard thing, and rare because it is hard." (*C. Jovin,* i. 36). Or more briefly, as our Lord said it, *All men take not this word* (Matt. xix. 11).

8, 9. These verses join on to *v.* 7 rather than to *v.* 10, which should begin a new paragraph.

To burn. " It is not the annoyance of concupiscence that he calls *burning*, but the enslavement of the soul, and the falling away for the worse. What he says comes to this:—It is better for you that are not yet entered into the state of matrimony, and for you that have entered it and have been set free from it by death, to choose a state of continence. But if you cannot sustain the assault of passion, but are weak in soul for such a struggle, owing to the warmth of your admiration for what is beautiful, there is no law restraining you from marriage." (Theodoret).

10. *Not I, but the Lord.* And *v.* 12, *I speak, not the Lord.* And yet he writes to these same Corinthians: *Do you seek a proof of Christ that speaketh in me?* (2 Cor. xiii. 3). And in this Epistle: *Know the things that I write to you, that they are the commandments of the Lord?* (xiv. 37). The distinction then is between the precepts promulgated by the lips of Christ Himself on earth, and the precepts or counsels published by the Apostles, inspired by the Spirit of Christ. The precept here given is read in the Gospel, Matt. v. 32; xix. 9; Mark x. 2—12.

12. *To the rest.* In *v.* 8 we have *to the unmarried:* in *v.* 10, *to them that are married.* Who then are *the rest?* On consideration it appears that *v.* 10 refers to married persons, in marriages where both parties are Christians. *The rest* then are those Christians whom this letter finds already married to unbaptized persons. Such marriages are invalid by the present discipline of the Church, and have been invalid perhaps for a thousand years, by the ecclesiastical impediment known as "disparity of worship," an impediment, be it observed, that affects marriages between a baptized Christian on the one side, and on the other a person who is not simply a member of an heretical communion, but is actually unbaptized. This impediment did not exist when the Apostle wrote. At the same time he strongly deters

any Christian from marrying a heathen (2 Cor. vi. 14),
as the Jews were forbidden to marry Gentiles (3 Kings
xi. 2). The marriages here spoken of are those contracted when both parties were heathen, one of the
parties having since received baptism.

Let him not put her away. And *v.* 13, *let her not put
away her husband.* A counsel, not a command. But
as times then were, and as they are now, the party that
neglects this counsel must remain single, and can have
no benefit of the privilege contained in *v.* 15.

14. *Your children,* all children born of Christian
parents. The *holiness* here predicated of such children
even before baptism is the same as the *sanctification* that
is said to pass to the *unbelieving husband,* or the *unbelieving
wife,* from the believing partner. But no one has ever
pretended that an unbeliever was fully sanctified and
justified before God by mere cohabitation with a
believer. Therefore the contention of the Pelagians,
and of Calvinists after them, that before any baptism
children are fully justified and acceptable to God by
being born of Christian parents, falls to the ground.
What sort of holiness these children possess is declared
by Tertullian (*Ad uxorem,* ii. 7): "The children of the
faithful are called holy as being candidates for the faith,
and unstained by any filth of idolatry." To be born
of, or to share in, the union of a Christian marriage,
is a kind of anticipated holiness, a prelude to baptism,
an earnest of the full grace of the faith. Cf. the note
on *adoption,* Rom. ix. 4.

15. "If of an unbelieving couple one is converted
to the faith, while the other will in no way cohabit
with the convert, or not without blasphemy of the
Divine name, or without going about to draw the convert into mortal sin ; the convert at discretion may go
off and marry again. And this is the construction that
we put on the Apostle's saying: *If the unbeliever depart,*

let him depart; for a brother or sister is not under bondage in such cases" (Innocent III.). Sanchez, *De Matrimonio*, l. 7, disp. 74, n. 4, says: "This conclusion is most certain, and cannot be departed from without manifest error in faith." That does not mean that it is always prudent to act upon it, especially where the privilege is not recognised by the laws of the State. The conclusion points to unbaptized persons only, not to heretics.

The law of Catholic Europe forbade the convert to continue to live with the unbeliever on any terms short of the conversion of the latter. In case the latter refused to be converted, it was held that the convert might marry again, the reason of the divorce in that case being that the convert should not on occasion of conversion be reduced to the alternative of either an intolerable state of marriage or a life of continence. See Sanchez, *De Matrimonio*, l. 7, d. 74, nn. 9, 10.

In peace; say *unto peace.* This is not inconsistent with Matt. x. 34: *I came not to send peace, but the sword:* for as Theodoret says: "The teaching of salvation does not bring confusion into life, but rather procures that peace which is true and loved of God; yet not before destroying that other harmony, and by creating discord effecting concord."

16. *How knowest thou whether thou shalt save?* better, *how knowest thou but what thou shalt save?* This refers, as St. Chrysostom says, to *vv.* 12, 13, *let him not put her away,* and *let her not put him away:* the possibility and hope of saving the partner is alleged as a reason against separation. The Greek Fathers know no other interpretation than this of τί οἶσθα εἰ σώσεις. It is borne out by Joel ii. 14: τίς οἶδεν εἰ ἐπιστρέψει; and by the lines of Euripides quoted by Plato (*Gorgias,* 492 E):

τίς δ' οἶδεν εἰ τὸ ζῆν μέν ἐστι κατθανεῖν,
τὸ κατθανεῖν δὲ ζῆν;

E

The modern interpretation, favoured by the Rheims version, joins this verse with the preceding, and makes it mean; 'there is great uncertainty and little hope of saving the partner;' which however is not the meaning.

18. *Procure uncircumcision*, 1 Mac. i. 16.

19. *Circumcision is nothing :* therefore St. Paul did not insist on Titus undergoing it (Gal. ii. 3). *Uncircumcision is nothing*, therefore St. Paul, for a grave reason, made no difficulty about circumcising Timothy (Acts xvi. 3). There was *one baptism* (Eph. iv. 5) for circumcision and uncircumcision, for *Jew and Greek*, making all *one in Christ* (Gal. iii. 28). The present verse is one of many out of St. Paul, condemning the antinomianism that St. James ii. 14, seq. denounces. This verse is repeated in substance, Gal. v. 6; vi. 15. The *new creature*, and the *faith that worketh by charity*, is conjoined with *the observation of the commandments of God*.

20. *Calling*, κλῆσις. The word does not mean "occupation," or "condition of life," but "invitation," "summons," and in the New Testament always an invitation or call to Christianity, given and accepted: cf. i. 26. Thus, as the next verse and the verses preceding show, the *calling* of the bondman is to be a Christian bondman, and the *calling* of the married is to live in Christian marriage. Only those conditions cannot cleave to a vocation to Christianity, which are of their own nature, as St. Chrysostom says, "obstacles to piety :" such would be the condition of a heretic or schismatic : St. Paul was indifferent to circumcision, but not to heresy (Gal. i. 8, 9; 1 Tim. i. 19; Titus iii. 10, 11).

21. *But if thou mayest be made free, use it rather.* Better, according to the Greek and the Vulgate Latin, *but if even thou hast it in thy power to become free, rather keep to it*, that is, as St. Chrysostom explains, *rather remain in*

slavery. "This hyperbole," says Theodoret, "he has not set down idly, but as an advice not to fly from slavery under pretence of serving God." It is simply a counsel to the Christian slave not to run away from his master, as Onesimus did, whom St. Paul sent back to Philemon (Philem. 12). Cf. Tit. ii. 10.

To have denounced slavery as an institution, of itself against justice and the privileges of Christianity, would have convulsed society, and brought down on the nascent Christian Church the strong arm of the Roman power. Rome had had bitter experience of servile wars. The rising of slaves against their masters was in Roman eyes the last extreme of anarchy. Still no fear of consequences could have induced the Apostles to countenance a downright injustice. Slavery is not absolutely unjust, when it is understood that what comes under the ownership of another is not the man himself, but all the labour of the man. A slave-owner is strictly a slave-labour owner. Slave-labour was at the root of human society, as the Church found it, and it was only when the Church had succeeded in re-founding and reconstituting society, the work of centuries, that the general emancipation of slaves became possible, and was actually achieved.

22. *Freeman,* ἀπελεύθερος; say *freedman.* The original Rheims version has, *the franchised of the Lord.* The bondman, in his conversion, received his freedom from sin (John viii. 34; Rom. vi. 14; vii. 14; viii. 2), as the freeman, becoming a Christian, is bound over as a *servant of justice* (Rom. vi. 18). See the whole passage, Rom. vi. 12—22, with St. Thomas's explanation, 2a —2æ, q. 183, art. 4.

23. *Ye are bought with a price,* vi. 20. *Be not made slaves of men*: that is, *obey your master. . . not serving to the eye, as pleasing men, but . . . do it from the heart, as to the Lord . . . serve ye the Lord Jesus Christ* (Col. iii. 22—24).

25. *Concerning virgins.* St. Paul speaks here of both sexes. Cf. Matt. xix. 12 ; Apoc. xiv. 4.

No commandment of the Lord, but counsel. Our Lord never forbade marriage, but spoke of virginity permanently chosen *for the kingdom of heaven,* as a gift given to some (Matt. xix. 12). This evangelical counsel of virginity St. Paul here rehearses.

To be faithful, i.e., to be a faithful counsellor, as Theodoret explains: "I am a counsellor worthy of credence, called by the Lord's great mercy, and entrusted with the ministry of preaching."

26. The second clause in the verse is all a development of the pronoun *this* in the first clause. So we may translate: *I think therefore touching this fact, the fact that it is good for a man so to be, that the goodness arises out of the present necessity.*

So to be, that is, to be a *virgin, v.* 25, or unmarried.

The present necessity. Does the word *present* mean *actually present,* as in iii. 22, or *close at hand and imminent* (2 Thess. ii. 2) ? Of itself the word, *instantem,* ἐνεστῶσαν, may mean either the one or the other. And what is the *necessity* spoken of ? Many Catholic commentators take it to mean the *constraint, hardship* and *difficulty* of married life. Such interpretation however seems to make void the prefixed adjective *present* or *imminent.* For the difficulties of married life were not peculiar to the time in which St. Paul wrote, or to the age to which he looked forward as immediately coming on : they are difficulties of all human history, beginning with the Fall and to end only with the day of judgment.

Rather the *necessity,* or *distress* (ἀνάγκην) referred to, is the *great distress* (ἀνάγκη μεγάλη) that *there shall be in the land* (Luke xxi. 23) at the approach of the judgment-day. Consequently the participle ἐνεστῶσαν, *instantem,* is to be translated *imminent,* not *actually present.* Continence from marriage is recommended by reason of the imminent approach of the distress of the last day.

We are not however, with the Protestant commentators, to jump to the conclusion that, since the world has rolled on for eighteen centuries from the date of this Epistle, and is likely, for all that we can see, to continue on its course for eighteen centuries more, we are therefore right in taking the Apostle's allegation for a note of groundless alarm, and in ignoring the counsel of virginity springing from such alarm. Yes, if the Epistle to the Corinthians is a mere human work, marked with errors and prejudices; but certainly not, if it is the inspired and unerring word of God. The truth is, that every Christian is bound to live in daily expectation of the day of judgment, or what comes to the same thing for him, of the day of his death, after which he will have no more time to prepare for the day of judgment. He is bound by the plain command of his Saviour, delivered Matt. xxiv. 36—50. And he is counselled as part of the *watching* there enjoined, if God offer him grace to lead a life of virginity, to accept that offer, and even to make it matter of a vow, being, as every vow should be, *de meliori bono*, " of the better good."

28. *If thou take a wife, thou hast not sinned.* " Spoken, not of those who once for all have renounced the world, but of those who have not yet chosen either the one or the other state, but are yet on the debatable ground between marriage and unweddedness," says Theodoret.

But I spare you, i.e., I will not insist: I have no mind to erect a counsel into a command: do as you will, it is no sin to marry, *v.* 36.

29. *The time is short.* Short is the time allotted to any individual for preparing for the day of judgment, however that event seems to linger and hold back, lengthening out the history of the world. *Surely I come quickly* (Apoc. xxii. 20),—to every individual man.

30. *As though they possessed not :* literally, *as though not taking fast hold* of their purchase.

31. *Use as if they used it not :* literally from the Greek (χρώμενοι, καταχρώμενοι) *use as not using to the full.*

Fashion, or outward show. The same word in the Greek appears in Phil. ii. 7 : *and in habit found as a man.*

33. *And he is divided.* This word, μεμέρισται, in many manuscripts and versions is taken as belonging to the next sentence. The authorities who so take it, also alter the place of the word *unmarried*, so that *woman* comes to mean *wife.* Thus they translate : *There is a difference between a wife and a virgin. She that is unmarried thinketh on the things of the Lord.* In point of antiquity there is little to choose between this reading and the other. In point of doctrine there is no difference. In the Vulgate reading, *is divided* is explained by what our Lord says to Martha : *Thou art careful, and troubled about many things* (Luke x. 41).

34. *And the unmarried woman and the virgin thinketh. Et mulier innupta et virgo cogitat*, as though the Greek were καὶ ἡ γυνὴ ἡ ἄγαμος καὶ ἡ παρθένος μεριμνᾷ. The article, which certainly stands before παρθένος, shows that *the unmarried woman and the virgin* are not the same person. *The unmarried woman* then must be the widow, of whom *vv.* 39, 40. The translation of our present Greek text is given in the previous note.

35. *Not to cast a snare upon you*, that is, not cunningly or violently to put you under a necessity of precept not to marry or give in marriage. Cf. Matt. xix. 10, 11, 12.

36. In this and the next two verses, which regard the conduct of a father, *his virgin* means *his virgin daughter.*

Seemeth dishonoured, ἀσχημονεῖν, ·in opposition to τὸ εὔσχημον, *that which is decent*, of the verse before. The word is used here in the sense in which it is usually found in Greek writers, *e.g.*, Plato, *Republic* 517 D, and

Theaetetus 165 B, where it has the meaning, *to cut a bad figure*, as also Deut. xxv. 3 (LXX.). Cf. note on xiii. 5, where the word recurs.

The meaning of the whole verse is: ' If any man is unable to bear up against the scorn of his neighbours, taunting and teasing him about the "old maid," the undisposable merchandise, that he keeps in his house, and marriage seem on this and other grounds a necessity, for the father's comfort and the girl's happiness, perhaps even her honour,—well, there is no harm in marriage: if she finds a proper partner, *let them marry.*'

Let·them marry, γαμείτωσαν, not *if she marry*, is the best reading.

37. *For he that hath determined, being steadfast.* The correct rendering is, *But he that standeth steadfast.* *Statuit* in the Latin should be *stat*, ἔστηκεν.

The father who *standeth steadfast* is the antithesis of him who fancies himself *dishonoured, v.* 36, and is moved at the thought of the bad figure that he makes in the eyes of his neighbours, not seeming able to dispose of his daughter. The *steadfast* parent does not mind that reproach. Moreover, he is supposed to be *having no necessity*, that is, there is no reason, whether strong inclination in the girl or danger to her virtue, why *it must so be, v.* 36, that he give her in marriage; but he *having power of his own will*, and she of hers, he *hath judged to keep his virgin*, and she to remain a virgin. Such a father *doth well*, and such a daughter. Nay even, he *doth better, v.* 38; and she doth better also, God calling her to a state which is a better good than marriage. Such is the Apostle's plain teaching.

39. *By the law*, omitted in some MSS., while others read, *to her husband.* The law spoken of is the marriage law, laid down, Rom. vii. 2, 3.

The Greek gives, *she is at liberty to marry whom she will.* *Only in the Lord*, that is, let her marry a Christian.

40. *I think that I also.* St. Paul says: ' You will tell me, these are only counsels. True, I give no authoritative command: yet know ye that the Spirit of God counsels you by my mouth, at least no less (ix. 1, 2) than by the mouths of those other your admired teachers' (referred to in the first three chapters). Cf. 2 Cor. xi. 5.

———

Chapter VIII.

1. Now concerning those things that are sacrificed to idols, we know that we all have knowledge. Knowledge puffeth up, but charity edifieth. 2. And if any man think that he knoweth any thing, he hath not yet known as he ought to know. 3. But if any man love God, the same is known by him. 4. But as for the meats that are offered in sacrifice to idols, we know that an idol is nothing in the world, and that there is no God but one. 5. For though there be that are called gods, either in heaven, or on earth, (for there are many gods, and many lords,) 6. Yet to us there is but one God, the Father, of whom are all things, and we unto him; and one Lord Jesus Christ, by whom are all things, and we by him. 7. But knowledge is not in every one: for some until this present, with a conscience of the idol, eat as a thing sacrificed to an idol; and their conscience, being weak, is defiled. 8. But meat doth not commend us to God: for neither, if we eat, shall we have the more; nor, if we eat not, shall we have the less. 9. But take heed, lest perhaps this your liberty become a stumbling-block to the weak. 10. For if a man see him that hath knowledge sit at meat in the idol's temple, shall not his conscience, being weak, be emboldened to eat those things which are sacrificed to idols? 11. And through thy knowledge shall the weak brother perish, for whom Christ died? 12. Now when you sin thus against the brethren, and wound their weak conscience, you sin against Christ. 13. Wherefore, if meat scandalize my brother, I will never eat flesh, lest I should scandalize my brother.

1. *Concerning those things that are sacrificed to idols.* The ancient sacrifices, pagan as well as Jewish, consisted principally in the slaughter of animals, the flesh of which was partaken of by the offerers. Great part

of the meat was not consumed at the place of sacrifice, but was carried off for private consumption, or even found its way to the butchers' shops. These sacrificial meats were called by the Greeks ἱερόθυτα. The Jews and Christians called what had been offered to the pagan gods εἰδωλόθυτα, or "idol offerings," the word used by St. Paul here. The article was found everywhere, in the market and in the rites of private hospitality. Some Christians made no scruple in eating any meat set before them, idol-offered or not : others ate with a bad conscience : some few perhaps endeavoured to discern meat from meat, though that must have involved much scrupulous questioning under no little risk of deception.

We know that——Here St. Paul breaks off into a parenthesis, to the end of *v.* 3. In *v.* 4 he resumes : *we know that*——

We all have knowledge. There seems to be, as Theodoret says, some irony in this statement (for another example of irony see iv. 8), since in *v.* 7 the Apostle says, *there is not knowledge in every one.* The fact is, there is a difference between knowledge and knowledge. We all know many things, if we only choose to think, which things nevertheless many of us do not know for want of resolutely thinking them out. The point of knowledge here referred to is that stated in *v.* 4, *that an idol is nothing, and that there is no God but one.*

Knowledge puffeth up. Knowledge, without charity, bloats out the individual in his own empty conceit ; but *charity edifieth*, or *buildeth up* the good of the Christian community. The Apostle proceeds to show that promiscuous eating, the practice of these men of knowledge, did not promote the good of the community, but gave scandal.

The use of the verb " to build," meaning " to edify,"

seems to have been started by St. Paul. It is perhaps
a Hebraism: cf. Ps. xxvii. 5; Jerem. xxiv. 6; xxxiii. 7.
It falls in well with the metaphor of the temple,
iii. 9—16; Eph. ii. 20—22.

2. The sentiment of this verse is exactly that of
Prov. xxvi. 12: *Hast thou seen a man wise in his own
conceit ? there is more hope of a fool than of him.*

3. *Known by him*, that is, recognised and approved
by Him. Cf. Ps. i. 6; Matt. vii. 23; and Exod. xxxiii. 12:
*I know thee by thy name, and thou hast found favour in my
sight.*

4. *But* (oὖν, *autem*) . . . *we know.* Rather, *well then, as
I was saying, we know.* The conjunction employed carries
us back to *v.* 1, after the parenthesis.

An idol is nothing, nothing but wood or metal, stone
or plaster, no God. This is the theme of Baruch vi.

5. *Gods many and lords many.* This reads like a
proverb current at the time.

6. As in the previous verse there was mention of
lords many, who were all taken to be so many gods, so
in this verse *God* and *Lord* are not mutually exclusive.
The Son is no more excluded from the *one God* than
the Father from the *one Lord.* Cf. Tit. ii. 13. Moreover, as St. Chrysostom observes, if the word *God* were
sufficiently distinctive of the Father, and exclusive of
the Son, the very mention of *the Father* in this verse
would be superfluous.

Of whom, as Creator, are all things in the order of
nature; and *unto whom*, as our Father in the order of
grace, *we* Christians stand supernaturally related as
His children.

By whom, that is, upon whom as an exemplar, as
the Son is the Word or Wisdom of the Father (cf. John
i. 3), *are all things* created; and again *by whom*, as the
Word made Flesh, all mankind and *we* Christians more
particularly (cf. 1 Tim. iv. 10) are redeemed. *By whom,*

literally, *through whom*, δι'οῦ. Touching this preposition, δια, St. Chrysostom observes on i. 9, *God is faithful, by whom* (through whom, δι'οῦ) *you are called* : " Since he continually uses of the Son the expressions *through Him* and *in Him*, to prevent any from taking that fashion of speech to imply any inferiority in the Son, he here (i. 9) applies it to the Father."

7. *With conscience of the idol*, that is, making the idol a matter of conscience, making a scruple of the idol, and of the fact of these meats having been offered to it. So 1 Pet. ii. 19, *for conscience towards God,*—literally, *conscience of God* : which passage seems to have been overlooked by those who insist on taking the other reading, *through being habituated to the idol*, συνηθείᾳ, instead of συνειδήσει.

8. *Meat* (food) *doth not commend us to God*, Rom. xiv. 17.

Have the more, have the less, i.e. have merit or demerit in God's sight.

10. The mere eating of flesh-meat that had been offered to idols was no harm of itself, apart from scandal ; but to *sit at meat in the idol's temple* was taking an immediate part in a religious rite, and that rite an idolatrous sacrifice, and therefore could never be allowed. The Apostle severely inveighs against the practice, x. 14—22.

Emboldened, the Greek word is *edified*, used not without some sarcasm.

There is a difficulty here. The eating of idol-offerings, away from the temple and all idolatrous rites, is of itself no sin. Where then consists the harm of the *weak brother* being *emboldened* to follow on such a course ? And how can he be said (*v.* 11) to *perish* by it ? The answer is found in *v.* 7, and Rom. xiv. 23. He is too weak to divest himself of the idea that, in eating such meats, he is in some measure identifying himself with those who sacrifice to idols. Thus he eats with a bad

conscience; and *all that is not of faith*, *i.e.* is against
conscience, *is sin*, Rom. l.c.

St. Thomas, 2a 2æ, q. 43, artt. 7 and 8 (*Aquinas
Ethicus*, i. pp. 417—419), examining whether good
things are to be abandoned for fear of scandal, lays
down three rules. First, that things necessary to
salvation are not to be abandoned. But clearly the
eating of idol-offerings has no bearing on salvation, *v.* 8.
Secondly, that no notice need be taken of the "scandal
of Pharisees," which proceeds from malice. Thirdly,
that for the "scandal of little ones," which is the scandal
in question here, even things spiritually good are to be
concealed, or deferred, till the scandal can be removed
by an explanation. Much more then mere material
goods, such as a meal on roast pork that was offered
the day before to Jupiter, are to be foregone, *lest I should
scandalize my (weak) brother*, *v.* 13.

11. *Through thy knowledge.* St. Chrysostom reads
through thy eating (βρώσει for γνώσει), cf. Rom. xiv. 15, 20.
He goes on : " He has then four complaints, and those
very serious ;—that it is the case of a brother, and him
a weak one, and one for whom Christ had so much
regard as to die for his sake, and after all he perishes
for a matter of eating."

13. *Meat* here is *flesh-meat*, κρέας. Cf. Rom. xiv. 21.

CHAPTER IX.

1. Am not I free? Am not I an apostle? have not I seen Christ Jesus our Lord? are not you my work in the Lord? 2. And if I be not an apostle to others, but yet to you I am: for you are the seal of my apostleship in the Lord. 3. My defence with them that examine me is this: 4. Have not we power to eat and to drink? 5. Have we not power to lead about a woman a sister, as well as the rest of the apostles, and the brethren of the Lord, and Cephas? 6. Or I only and Barnabas, have we not power to do this? 7. Who serveth as a soldier at any time at his own charges? who planteth a vineyard, and eateth not of the fruit thereof? who feedeth a flock, and eateth not of the milk of the flock? 8. Speak I these things according to man? or doth not the law also say these things? 9. For it is written in the law of Moses: Thou shalt not muzzle the mouth of the ox that treadeth out the corn. Doth God take care for oxen? 10. Or doth he say this indeed for our sakes? For these things were written for our sakes: for he that plougheth should plough in hope; and he that thresheth, in hope to receive fruit. 11. If we have sown unto you spiritual things, is it a great matter if we reap your carnal things? 12. If others be partakers of this power over you, why not we rather? Nevertheless, we have not used this power; but we bear all things, lest we should give any hindrance to the gospel of Christ. 13. Know you not that they who work in the holy place eat the things that are of the holy place? and they who serve the altar partake with the altar? 14. So also the Lord ordained that they who preach the gospel should live of the gospel. 15. But I have used none of these things; neither have I written these things, that they should be so done to me: for it is good for me to die, rather than that any one should make void my glory. 16. For if I preach the gospel, it is no glory to me: for a necessity lieth upon me; for woe is unto me if I preach not the gospel! 17. For if I do this thing willingly, I have a reward; but if against my will, a dispensation is committed to me. 18. What is my reward then? That preaching the gospel, I may deliver the gospel without charge, that I abuse not my power in the gospel. 19. For whereas I was free as to all, I made myself the servant of all, that I might gain more persons. 20. And I became to the Jews as a Jew, that I might gain the Jews. 21. To them that are under the law, as if I were under the law, (whereas myself was not under the law,) that I might gain them that were under the law; to them that were without the law, as if I were

without the law, (whereas I was not without the law of God, but was in the law of Christ,) that I might gain them that were without the law. 22. To the weak I became weak, that I might gain the weak: I became all things to all men, that I might save all. 23. And I do all things for the gospel's sake, that I may be made partaker thereof. 24. Know you not that they who run in the race all run indeed, but one receiveth the prize? So run that you may obtain. 25. And every one that striveth for the mastery refraineth himself from all things: and they indeed that they may receive a corruptible crown; but we an incorruptible one. 26. I therefore so run, not as at an uncertainty; I so fight, not as one beating the air: 27. But I chastise my body, and bring it into subjection; lest, perhaps, when I have preached to others, I myself should become reprobate.

1. *Have I not seen Christ Jesus our Lord?* A necessary qualification for the apostolic office (Acts i. 21). His vision (Acts ix. 9) to which he alludes again in this Epistle, xv. 8, was evidently matter of notoriety in the Church.

2. *The seal,* that is, the proof and confirmation.

4. *To eat and to drink,* at the public expense of the faithful. The argument opening this chapter is to show that the concluding words of the last chapter were no empty boast, but that the Apostle actually did, at great cost to himself, abstain for edification's sake from things otherwise permissible.

5. *A woman a sister.* The Anglican version is, *a sister, a wife,* the word γυναῖκα being susceptible of either translation. *Sister-woman* is the literal translation of ἀδελφὴν γυναῖκα, and the fairest ; as not pre-judging the question, whether at the time St. Paul wrote St. Peter and the rest of the apostles were married men, and were accompanied by their wives in their missionary journies. Of course the words might mean this: they might also mean what Theodoret tells us was an interpretation current in his time—" that as our Lord was followed by faithful women, who supplied the disciples with the sustenance they required, so some of the

apostles were attended by women fervent in faith, who
hung upon their teaching and helped the work of the
gospel." Between this and the previous interpretation
we must choose under the guidance of other portions
of Holy Writ and the authority of Christian tradition.
That St. Peter was married we know from Mark i. 30,
where there is mention of his *wife's mother*. Otherwise there is no mention in Scripture of his wife, nor of
the wife of any other Apostle. St. Peter says (Matt.
xix. 27) : *Behold we have left all things ;* and our Lord in
reply enumerates *wife* among the things left *for my
name's sake*. That *woman* in this passage does not mean
wife is maintained by Clement of Alexandria, *Strom.*
iii. 6; Tertullian, *De monogam*, 8 ; St. Augustine, *De op.
monach*, 4, 5 ; St. Jerome, *In Matt.* xxvii. 55 ; and *Contra
Jovin*, i. 26. Till we come to the Reformers, this
Jovinian seems to have been the only authority for the
rendering *wife*.

The *brethren of the Lord*, enumerated, Matt. xiv. 55,
James and Joseph, and Simon and Jude. The word *brother*
is used in Hebrew in a very loose sense, and no
argument can be built upon that word as to the
relationship in which these persons stood to our Blessed
Lord. The relationship is otherwise determinable from
Scripture. In Matt. xxvii. 56, we read of *Mary the
mother of James and Joseph :* who again is called (John
xix. 25) *his* (our Lord's) *mother's sister, Mary of Cleophas*,
and again, *Mary the mother of James the less and of Joseph*.
Lastly, in the enumeration of the Apostles (Acts i. 13),
James of Alpheus—and Jude the brother of James. Now
Cleophas and Alpheus are two Greek forms of the
same Hebrew name. Cleophas then, or Alpheus, was
married to Mary, sister of the Blessed Virgin, and of
these parents were born Joseph (of whom we know
nothing further: he *may* be the Joseph of Acts i. 23),
James (that is, the Apostle, St. James the less, Bishop

of Jerusalem, Acts xv. 13; xxi. 18), Jude, the Apostle;
and as it seems, also Simon the Apostle. All these
were cousins of our Lord, and three of them members
of the Apostolic College. Yet, as they were not all
Apostles, they (and probably with them their brothers-
in-law, or their sisters' husbands, that is, of the women
who are called *sisters* of Christ, Matt. xiii. 26) are ranked
apart from the Apostles in Acts i. 14. It remains to
observe, what Eusebius (*Hist. Eccles.* iii. 11) tells us on
the authority of Hegesippus, that Cleophas was the
brother of St. Joseph, and consequently that the Mary
who is called (John xix. 25) *sister* of the Blessed Virgin,
was really her sister-in-law. Thus all these "brethren
of the Lord" were related to Him only on the side
of Joseph, his foster-father. See further on Gal. i. 19.

And Cephas. "See his wisdom. He puts the chief
after the rest, putting the stronger of his heads of
argument then when the others have been enumerated.
It was not so wonderful to show the rest acting in this
way, as to show that this was the conduct of the fore-
man, of him who had been entrusted with the keys of
heaven" (St. Chrysostom).

6. This looks as though the dissension between Paul
and Barnabas (Acts xv. 35) had been already made
up. Further evidence of reconciliation is found in
Col. iv. 10; 2 Tim. iv. 11. Cf. St. Thomas 2a 2æ, q. 37,
art. 1 (*Aquinas Ethicus*, i. pp. 404—406).

To do this. The right reading seems to be μὴ
ἐργάζεσθαι, *not to work.* But *to do this* means the same
thing, *to live without working.*

7. "This shows what a priest should be, having a
soldier's courage, and a husbandman's care, and a
shepherd's solicitude; and for all that seeking no
more than bare necessaries" (St. Chrysostom). The
shepherd here only *eateth of the milk*, unlike those
shepherds (Ezech. xxxiv. 3), who *killed that which was*

fat. St. Paul confesses to having *taken from other churches, receiving wages of them* (2 Cor. xi. 8, 9).

9. *Doth God take care for oxen?* God has not of His irrational creatures that principal care which He has of men, but a secondary care (Matt. vi. 30; Jonas iv. 6, 7; Ps. ciii.).

13. *They who serve in the holy place.* The priests and levites in the temple at Jerusalem.

Partake with the altar. On the altar were burnt *the two kidneys, with the fat wherewith the flanks are covered, and the caul of the liver* (Levit. iii. 4); *the shoulder and the breast* were *the priest's due* (Deut. xviii. 3; cf. 1 Kings ii. 12—16).

14. The Apostle does not mention the Christian altar in contrast with the Jewish altar, because he is speaking of the remuneration due, not precisely to the sacerdotal, but to the apostolic office; and the first work of an Apostle is to preach and make converts, and to teach his people the truths of the gospel.

15. *But I have used none of these things.* "What things? These many examples. For whereas I have license offered me on many hands, from the soldier, from the husbandman, from the shepherd, from the Apostles, from the law, from the priests, from the command of Christ, none of these considerations have persuaded me to set aside the law I have made for myself, and to accept of remuneration" (St. Chrysostom).

17. *Willingly* in this verse means *uncommanded;* and *against my will* means simply *under the necessity* (*v.* 16) *of a command imposed upon me. This thing* is preaching the gospel *without charge.* The meaning then is:—'If, as in point of fact is the case, uncommanded, I abstain from making any charge for my preaching, I have a reward for such abstinence as being a work of super-erogation: but if, as is not the case, the abstinence were *against my will*, that is to say, commanded me,

F

then I do not say that I should have no reward, but I should have no further reward than is proper to one who fulfils the dispensation committed to him to be fulfilled under pain of sin and disobedience.'

18. *What then is my reward?* The answer to this question is really given in *v.* 23. St. Paul preached the gospel for the gospel's own sake, not looking for any reward in this life. For *abuse not*, a better rendering would be *use not to the utmost*. The *power* includes the power of taking temporal remuneration for his preaching. St. Paul refrained from using his power to this length, that he might gain souls as the reward of his abstinence (*vv.* 19—22); whereas those men with *know-ledge* (viii. 1, seq.) used the *liberty*, which their knowledge afforded, to the ruin of souls.

19. *Gain more persons*, should be, *gain the greater number*, or *the majority*, τοὺς πλείονας.

21. *Them that are under the law*, a rhetorical variety of expression for the *Jews*, mentioned in the previous verse, those Jews namely who still held out against Christianity.

Instances of St. Paul's compliance with the Mosaic law are Acts xvi. 3; xviii. 18; xxi. 26. But when certain Jewish converts wished to make the observance of that law a necessary point of Christianity, St. Paul resisted stoutly, Acts xv. 2, a resistance which inspires the whole Epistle to the Galatians.

Myself was not under the law. He says elsewhere, *I am dead to the law*, Gal. ii. 19.

22. *To the weak*, the weak Christian brother, who easily takes scandal, viii. 7, 9—12. To these weak brethren St. Paul accommodated himself in such a way, as to abstain from the indifferent action, which they took to be wrong, as though it really were wrong.

That I might save all, rather, that anyhow (πάντως for πάντας) *I might save some*. In *v.* 19 he speaks of gaining

only the *greater number*, and in *v.* 24, x. 5, he intimates
that not all are saved.

24. The Apostle proceeds to sober these over-con-
fident men of *liberty* and *knowledge* (viii. 9, 10), by
showing, first by a reference to a Greek custom, *vv.* 24,
25, then by a typical example from the history of the
Jews (x. 1—12), that their salvation is not yet a certain
and accomplished fact.

One receiveth the prize. " Not as though one only of
them all was going to be saved, but to indicate the
intensity of the earnestness that we ought to display.
For as there, though many enter the course, not many
are crowned, but on one head only the crown is set,
so here faith is not sufficient, nor a mere perfunctory
effort, but unless we run so as to show ourselves not
to be laid hold of at the last, we shall get nothing for
our pains. Even though you think yourself perfect in
knowledge, you have not yet secured the main issue "
(St. Chrysostom).

So run, as that one victor runs, *that you may obtain.*

25. *Refraineth himself from all things*, better, *practises
self-restraint in all things.* The athletes, who were to
contend at the Greek games, spent ten months in
training.

A corruptible crown of bay leaves, olive, pine, or even
parsley.

26. *At an uncertainty.* The sense is given by St.
Chrysostom: " I run as having an eye to the goal. I
do all things for my neighbour's salvation (*vv.* 19—22),
not as you do, entering into temples of idols. What
good comes of your entering such temples and eating
there? For *meat does not commend us to God* (viii. 8). You
then are running anyhow and at random, that is, *at an
uncertainty.*"

Beating the air, wildly and impotently, as though
there were no adversary to contend against.

27. *I chastise*, ὑπωπιάζω. The word is taken from the boxing-ring, a more honoured profession in St. Paul's day than now, and means *I beat the face black and blue*.

Bring into subjection, δουλαγωγῶ, literally, *I lead about as a slave*. In some Greek games, it appears, the conqueror had the right to lead the conquered party round the arena, and exhibit him as though he were a slave. The two verbs then together mean : ' It is my study to quell and gain a thorough mastery over those *lusts of the flesh, that fight against the law of my mind*' (Gal. v. 16, 17; Rom. vii. 23).

Lest when I have preached to others. The word for to *preach*, κηρύττειν, has for its primary meaning, ' to act the herald.' The herald at the games had a prominent part to play : he made all the announcements of the combatants, and finally proclaimed the victor. It also would be the duty of the herald to announce if any, for any defect or foul play, was excluded from the contest and banished the arena. Such a one would be ἀδόκιμος, *rejected*, here translated *castaway*. Keeping up the metaphor then St. Paul says, ' lest having played the herald for others, I myself be declared by sound of herald's voice no fit person to be crowned.'

If Paul was afraid, says St. Chrysostom, how much more may we be! He adds, as if in view of heresies to come, " Think not that, once you have believed, that is enough for your salvation."

1. For I would not have you ignorant, brethren, that our fathers were all under the cloud, and all passed through the sea; 2. And all in Moses were baptized in the cloud and in the sea: 3. And they all eat the same spiritual food; 4. And all drank the same spiritual drink; (and they drank of the spiritual rock that followed them: and the rock was Christ.) 5. But with the most of them God was not well pleased; for they were overthrown in the desert. 6. Now these things were done in a figure of us; that we should not covet evil things, as they also coveted. 7. Neither become ye idolaters, as some of them; as it is written: The people sat down to eat and drink, and rose up to play. 8. Neither let us commit fornication, as some of them committed fornication, and there fell in one day three and twenty thousand. 9. Neither let us tempt Christ, as some of them tempted, and perished by serpents. 10. Neither do you murmur, as some of them murmured, and were destroyed by the destroyer. 11. Now all these things happened to them in figure; and they are written for our correction, upon whom the ends of the world are come. 12. Wherefore, let him that thinketh himself to stand take heed lest he fall. 13. Let no temptation take hold on you but such as is human: and God is faithful, who will not suffer you to be tempted above that which you are able; but will make also with temptation issue that you may be able to bear it. 14. Wherefore, my dearly beloved, flee from the service of idols. 15. I speak as to wise men; judge ye yourselves what I say. 16. The chalice of benediction which we bless, is it not the communion of the blood of Christ? And the bread which we break, is it not the partaking of the body of the Lord? 17. For we, being many, are one bread, one body, all who partake of one bread. 18. Behold Israel according to the flesh: are not they who eat of the sacrifices partakers of the altar? 19. What then? Do I say that what is offered in sacrifice to idols is any thing? or that the idol is any thing? 20. But the things which the heathens sacrifice, they sacrifice to devils, and not to God: and I would not that you should be made partakers with devils. You cannot drink the chalice of the Lord, and the chalice of devils: 21. You cannot be partakers of the table of the Lord, and of the table of devils. 22. Do we provoke the Lord to jealousy? are we stronger than he? All things are lawful for me, but all things are not expedient: 23. All things are lawful for me, but all things do not edify. 24. Let no man seek his own, but that which

is for the welfare of another. **25**. Whatsoever is sold in the shambles eat, asking no question for conscience sake. **26**. The earth is the Lord's, and the fulness thereof. **27**. If any of the infidels invite you, and you be willing to go, eat of any thing that is set before you, asking no question for conscience sake. **28**. But if any man say : This hath been sacrificed to idols, do not eat of it for his sake that told it, and for conscience sake. **29**. Conscience, I say, not thy own, but the other's : for why is my liberty judged by another man's conscience? **30**. If I partake with thanksgiving, why am I evil spoken of for that for which I give thanks? **31**. Therefore whether you eat or drink, or whatsoever else you do, do all things for the glory of God. **32**. Give no offence to the Jews, nor to the gentiles, nor to the church of God : **33**. As I also please all men in all things, not seeking that which is profitable to myself, but to many, that they may be saved.

1. *Our fathers.* The people of God in the Old Law are the spiritual ancestors of all Christians: for *they who are of faith, the same are the children of Abraham,* Gal. iii. 6—9; Rom. ix. 6—8.

Under the cloud. This *pillar of cloud,* before the Israelites had crossed the Red Sea, hung as a screen between them and the Egyptians (Exod. xiv. 19, 20), so that it is written : *He spread out a cloud to cover them,* Psalm civ. 39. Cf. Num. xiv. 14.

2. *All in Moses were baptized,* literally, *took on themselves baptism unto Moses. Baptism,* the thing typified, is here made to stand for the type, the type being the passage of the Red Sea (Exod. xiv.), where the Egyptians were drowned, and the people of God delivered, as our sins are taken away in the waters of baptism, and we are rescued from the power of evil spirits. *Unto Moses* means passing under the leadership of Moses: cf. on i. 13. He entered the Red Sea first, and the people followed him to the opposite shore, and thence through the desert. Moses, the passage of the Red Sea, and the people of Israel under his leadership in the desert, were types respectively of Christ our Saviour, of the

Sacrament of Baptism, and of the Church of God on earth.

3. The same spiritual food, the manna (Exod. xvi.), a type of the Holy Eucharist (John vi. 49, 52).

4. *The same spiritual drink*, the water produced miraculously from the rock (Exod. xvii. 6; Num. xx. 8).

The spiritual rock that followed them.

We have here, *vv.* 3, 4, *spiritual food, spiritual drink*, and *spiritual rock*. The food and drink spoken of are not things metaphorically so called; but a corporal food, manna, and a material substance, water. It is fair to conclude that the rock also is not any being, figuratively called a rock, but an actual geological rock, that in fact which Moses struck. It seems also a fair conclusion, that the word *spiritual* bears the same meaning in all these three applications. In the first two cases it clearly connotes two things:—(1) being a term of miraculous action; (2) being typical of a higher and holier reality to come. And in no other sense is the rock struck by Moses called a *spiritual* rock. For, first, a miracle was wrought upon it, causing it to well forth water; and, secondly, the rock thus struck and welling forth water was a figure of Christ, for, as Theodoret says, "the rock imitated the side of the Lord." Cf. John xix. 34.

The difficulty remains, how such a rock can be said to have *followed* the Israelites. There is a Rabbinical fable, seemingly as old as St. Paul, that the rock, once struck, followed the camp, and daily supplied the people with water; in which case of course the distress, mentioned in Num. xx. 1—13, could not have occurred. Possibly the phrase "companion rock," ἀκολουθοῦσα πέτρα, may have become familiar to Jewish ears from this legend. St. Paul then, without endorsing the legend, would use the familiar phrase, loosely employing the word ἀκολουθούσης, where otherwise he would have written παρατυχούσης : *i.e.* saying *the rock that followed them*, where all he really meant was *the rock that met them on the way*, any rock, to wit, that they came across, and which Moses was directed by God to strike. We have the records of two such strikings (Exod. xvii. ; Num. xx.) ; and there may have been others, not recorded in our Scriptures.

And the rock was Christ. This phrase would be harsh, if it were not clear from the previous words that the rock spoken of was a *spiritual rock*, a rock, that is to say, typical of a high and holy reality to come. This being made clear, there is no more difficulty in the expression than if, pointing to the head on one of our coins, a person were to say, " This is Queen Victoria." When the *spiritual rock* is *spiritually examined* (ii. 14), it is found to be a showing forth of Christ, as type shows forth antitype. The rock then is Christ *in figure*, τυπικῶς, *v.* 11.

The attempt to draw a parallel between this verse and Matt. xxvi. 26 fails altogether, because nowhere in the context of St. Matthew is there mention of *spiritual bread*, or bread having the function of a type ; while here there is mention of a *spiritual rock*, which prepares us to read the ensuing proposition typically. The manna that fell from heaven was a *spiritual food, v.* 3, a type of Christ ; but the bread that our Lord took into His hands at His Last Supper was no type of Him ; but being converted by transubstantiation into His Sacred Body, it became the antitype of the manna (John vi. 31, 59).

5. *With most of them.* St. Paul understates his case : he would not afford ground for any one to argue that of any Christian congregation all but one or two would perish eternally. But of the Hebrews who went out of Egypt, all except two, Caleb and Josue, perished in the desert (Num. xxvi. 64, 65).

6. *These things were done in a figure of us.* " For," as

St. Chrysostom says, "as you eat the Lord's Body, so did they eat manna; and as you drink His Blood, so did they drink water from the rock." He goes on to show that as the gifts given to the Hebrew people were typical, so were their punishments typical; and as we have received far greater gifts, so shall we receive far greater punishments also, if we abuse our gifts.

As they also coveted the fleshpots of Egypt (Num. xi. 4, 5, 18, 33, 34). And the Corinthians were coveting the meats offered to idols, not without danger of idolatry, as hinted in the next verse.

7. *The people, &c.*, Exod. xxxii. 6, at the worship of the golden calf.

8. *Three and twenty thousand.* The record of this transaction in Num. xxv. 1—9 says *twenty-four thousand.* This may be an instance of the same understatement for safety's sake, which led St. Paul's countrymen to inflict thirty-nine strokes where the law allowed only forty (2 Cor. xi. 24; Deut. xxv. 3).

The worship of Aphrodite of the Corinthians involved the same impurities as that of Beelphegor, the idol of Moab. This was the danger of *sitting at meat in the idol's temple*, namely, the temple of Aphrodite.

9. *Neither let us tempt Christ*, by growing weary of the modest religious rites of the infant Christian church at Corinth, and harking back to the gorgeous ceremonial and carnal sacrifices of paganism, as the Israelites (Num. xxi. 4, 5, 6; Psalm cv. 14), spoke against God and Moses, asking why they had been brought out of Egypt to die in the wilderness, without bread, without water, their hearts sick of the light food of the manna.

10. *Some of them murmured.* After the deaths that ensued upon the schism of Core, Dathan, and Abiran, we read that *all the multitude murmured against Moses and Aaron, saying, You have slain the people of God* (Num. xvi. 41). From c. iv. it appears that some of the

Corinthians had been murmuring against and depreciat-
ing St. Paul.

Destroyed by the destroyer, Num. xvi. 49. We read in
Wisdom xviii. 25: *To these* (prayers of Aaron for the
people, Num. xviii. 24) *the destroyer gave way*, which text
St. Paul seems to have had before him here. The other
Scripture references to *the destroyer* are Heb. xi. 28;
Exod. xii. 23; Josue iii. 10.

11. *The ends of the world*, the consummation and
accomplishment (τὰ τέλη, not τὰ πέρατα) of the figures of
previous ages (τῶν αἰώνων). The period from the first
coming of the Messiah to His second coming is *the last
hour* (1 John ii. 18) in this sense, that there is no further
dispensation to be expected. It is *the end of ages* (Heb.
ix. 26), *the fulness of time* (Gal. iv. 4), comprising indeed
old age and decrepitude, prevarication and apostasy,
but before that, and much more than that, middle age
and maturity, and the ripe strength of the faith of
Christ on earth.

12. "This is the practical conclusion of the whole
matter. We are to look back on that strange record of
splendid privilege and terrible fall, and learn from it the
solemn lesson of self-distrust. Led forth by divinely-
appointed leaders, overshadowed by the Divine Presence, supported by divinely-given food and drink, the
vast hosts of Israel had passed from the bondage of
Egypt into the glorious liberty of children of the living
God; yet amid all those who seemed to stand so secure
in their relation to God, but a few fell not. Christians,
called forth from a more deadly bondage into a more
glorious liberty, are in like peril. The murmuring
against their apostolic teachers, the longing to go so far
as they could in indulgence without committing actual
sin, were terribly significant indications in the Corinthian
Church. When we feel ourselves beginning to dislike
those who warn us against sin, and when we find our-

selves measuring with minute casuistry what is the
smallest distance that we can place between ourselves
and some desired object of indulgence without actually
sinning, then *he that thinketh himself to stand, let him take
heed lest he fall*" (Ellicott's *New Testament Commentary for
English Readers*).

13, 14. Verse 14 is a corollary from *v.* 12. It is the
immediately practical conclusion of the whole exhortation, as addressed to the Corinthians. Verse 13 seems
rather to break the thread of the argument. It is really
of the nature of a note, put in perhaps as an afterthought, *lest perhaps one be swallowed up with over-much
sorrow* (2 Cor. ii. 7), or alarm, at a lesson so terribly
enforced. We should read, with nearly all the Greek
MSS. and Fathers: *Temptation hath not taken hold of you
but such as is human.* The sense is: 'You have had no
intolerable trials yet (cf. Heb. xii. 4); and as for the
fear of intolerable trials to come, know that God will
always provide an issue. Your perseverance in good
then is in your own hands.'

To guard against the seeming Pelagianism of this
interpretation, we must add with St. Chrysostom: "So
there are temptations beyond what it is possible to bear.
And what are they? All, so to speak. For the possibility of our bearing them depends on God's intervening
on our behalf, which intervention we draw down upon
ourselves by our good-will. Not only those temptations
that surpass our ability, but even these human temptations, it is impossible easily to withstand without aid
from heaven. For not even with these temptations,
proportionate to our nature, shall we go through by our
own strength, but even here we need God as our ally
to go through with them, and before going through, to
bear them."

16. *The chalice of benediction.* According to Matt.
xxvi. 26, our Saviour blessed the bread before con-

secration. Doubtless He blessed the chalice also, as is the traditionary practice of the Church to this day. Hence this phrase of St. Paul. The chalice is mentioned before the bread, because in the pagan sacrifices, against which St. Paul here puts in opposition the Christian sacrifice, wine was poured out at the beginning.

The communion of the blood of Christ. "What is here in the chalice is that which flowed from the side [of Christ], and of that we partake" (St. Chrysostom).

This passage, by the antithesis that it involves, is an argument of the sacrificial character of the Holy Eucharist. The Apostle sets out table against table, that is, altar against altar, and sacrifice against sacrifice, ἱερόθυτον against εἰδωλόθυτον. See *Council of Trent*, sess. 22, cap. 1.

17. This verse is better translated: *Because it is one bread, we are one body, many as we are: for we are all partakers of that one bread.* But for the fact of transubstantiation, this argument would not hold. But for that fact, it would not be *one bread.* The bread on the altar at Constantinople, so long as it remains bread, is not the bread at Rome, even as the victims slain on the altar of holocausts in the Jewish temple were all so many several oxen and sheep. What Jewish Rabbi ever wrote: 'We are all partakers of one lamb'?

One bread, one body. "What is the bread? The Body of Christ. And what do they become who receive it? The Body of Christ: not many bodies, but one Body" (St. Chrysostom). To the same effect St. Augustine writes (*Conf.* vii. 10): "Nor shalt thou change Me into thee, as thou dost the food of thy flesh: but thou shalt be changed into Me." The real Body of Christ in the Holy Eucharist is the food and consolation of His mystical Body, the Church (Eph. i. 23; v. 20; Col. ii. 19; 1 Cor. vi. 15). It was a saying of the

Fathers: " The body of the baptized man is the flesh of the Crucified."

18. *Israel according to the flesh*, the unconverted Jews of the time, as opposed to *the Israel of God*, Gal. vi. 16.

Partakers of the altar. Better, *with the altar.* Part of the sacrifice was burnt on the altar : the rest was eaten by the offerer, or by the priests (1 Kings ii. 13—16). The unconverted Jews then were partakers, not *with devils*, as the heathens were (*v.* 20), nor yet with God, but simply *with the altar*, a thing now *in Christ made void* (2 Cor. iii. 14).

19. An idol represented no real person (viii. 4), Jupiter, Venus and the rest being mere figments. Nor was the meat offered to an idol thereby altered so as to become pernicious of its own nature any more than any other meat.

20. *They sacrifice to devils.* Cf. Deut. xxxii. 17; Ps. xcv. 5. Not that the Gentiles commonly were conscious of worshipping evil spirits, or that there was a devil locally resident in every idol, or even that to every deity of heathendom there was some devil corresponding; but that heathen worship had grown generally so inane, so superstitious, and so impure, as to be ruinous to the souls of the worshippers, and thereby a grateful service to the enemies of mankind, who found in the legends, rites and emblems of such a religion a powerful instrument of corruption and incentive to sin, and who also seem to have been permitted not unfrequently to mingle their personal action with such rites, causing false signs and wonders, as happens in the unchristian regions of the East even to this day.

21. Cf. 2 Cor. vi. 15. *The chalice of devils.* A libation, as it was called, at a heathen sacrifice was performed with a full goblet, pouring out a little in honour of the god, and drinking the rest.

22. A text for waverers, whether in belief, or, as the Corinthians were, in practice.

Do we provoke, &c.? From Deut. xxxii. 21 : *They have provoked me to jealousy over one who was not God, i.e.* over an idol.

All things are lawful, &c., repeated from vi. 12. Some things, *lawful* in themselves, are neither *expedient* for the doer's own sanctification and salvation, nor *edify* (*v.* 23) the looker on.

24. Cf. Rom. xiv. 14—23 ; xv. 1—3.

25. This concession does not extend to sharing the sacrificial meals in idols' temples, viii. 10, which is the practice condemned in *vv.* 20, 21.

28. *Sacrificed to idols*, εἰδωλόθυτον. Better, *sacrificed to holy beings*, ἱερόθυτον, the reading of our three oldest MSS. The words, so St. Chrysostom apparently understands them, are spoken by a pagan, who would not call his own gods *idols*.

29, 30. The previous verse 28 (like v. 13 above, which see) is parenthetical, and in a modern book would stand as a footnote. Commentators, failing to recognise the parenthesis, have made various unsuccessful efforts to connect *vv.* 29, 30, with *v.* 28. The real connection is with *v.* 27. Then the sense runs : —' Eat, and ask no questions for what other people's conscience, or consciousness, may tell them, as to the meat set before you having been offered to idols. That is not in your consciousness, nor on your conscience either. You are free, and untrammeled by what others may know and think. You eat, and thank God for the good gift : you deserve not to be evilly spoken of for so doing. And thus much of meats about which no question is asked, nor information volunteered. But (to revert to *v.* 28), if any pagan draws your attention to the fact that this or that meat has been offered to his false gods, he may justly be shocked at your continuing to eat it.   Do not eat it then, for his sake, for now his conscience and consciousness come to be also yours. Do not eat it, not as though it had any power of itself to hurt you, but for loathing, now that it is pointedly placed before you as meat once made over to the enemies of God.'

St. Paul here gives the Corinthians an authoritative interpretation of the decree, passed at the Council of Jerusalem a year before, *that you abstain from things sacrificed to idols*, limiting it to things certainly known as such, and, in the absence of certainty, excusing from enquiry, and allowing the benefit of the doubt.

31. Cf. Col. iii. 17.   On the similar verse of Psalm xxxiv. 28, *All day long thy praise*, St. Augustine writes : " Whatever you do, do it well, and you have praised God.   When you sing a hymn, you praise God : but what good is there in your tongue's performance, unless your mind and heart also joins in the praise ?   You have given over the hymn-singing, and go away for a meal : be temperate, and you have praised God.   You retire to rest : do not rise to do evil, and you have praised God.   You are in business : practise no fraud, and you have praised God."

33. The flatterer too makes it his object to *please all men*, but all the while *seeking that which is profitable to self*.

CHAPTER XI.

1. Be ye also followers of me, as I also am of Christ. 2. Now I praise you, brethren, that in all things you are mindful of me, and keep my ordinances as I delivered them to you. 3. But I would have you know, that the head of every man is Christ; and the head of the woman is the man; and the head of Christ is God. 4. Every man praying or prophesying with his head covered disgraceth his head. 5. But every woman praying or prophesying with her head not covered disgraceth her head : for it is all one as if she were shaven. 6. For if a woman be not covered, let her be shorn : but if it be a shame to a woman to be shorn or shaven, let her cover her head. 7. The man, indeed, ought not to cover his head, because he is the image and glory of God ; but the woman is the glory of the man. 8. For the man is not of the woman, but the woman of the man. 9. For the man was not created for the woman, but the woman for the man. 10. Therefore ought the woman to have a power over her head, because of the angels. 11. But yet neither is the man without the woman, nor the woman without the man, in the Lord. 12. For as the woman is of the man, so also is the man by the woman; but all things of God. 13. Judge you yourselves : doth it become a woman to pray to God uncovered ? 14. Doth not even nature itself teach you that a man indeed, if he nourish his hair, it is a shame to him ? 15. But if a woman nourish her hair, it is a glory to her, for her hair is given to her for a covering. 16. But if any man seem to be contentious, we have no such custom, nor hath the church of God. 17. Now this I ordain, not praising you, that you come together not for the better, but for the worse. 18. For first of all, I hear that when you come together in the church there are divisions among you, and in part I believe it. 19. For there must be also heresies ; that they also who are approved may be made manifest among you. 20. When you come together, therefore, into one place, it is not now to eat the Lord's supper. 21. For every one taketh before his own supper to eat : and one indeed is hungry, and another is drunk. 22. What ! have you not houses to eat and to drink in ? or despise ye the church of God, and put them to shame that have not ? What shall I say to you ? Do I praise you ? In this I praise you not. 23. For I have received of the Lord that which also I delivered to you, that the Lord Jesus, the night in which he was betrayed, took bread, 24. And giving thanks, broke, and said : Take ye, and eat; this is my body which shall be delivered for

you : do this for the commemoration of me. **25.** In like manner also the chalice, after he had supped, saying : This chalice is the new testament in my blood : this do ye, as often as you shall drink it for the commemoration of me. **26.** For as often as you shall eat this bread, and drink this chalice, you shall show forth the death of the Lord until he come. **27.** Wherefore whosoever shall eat this bread, or drink the chalice of the Lord unworthily, shall be guilty of the body and blood of the Lord. **28.** But let a man prove himself, and so let him eat of that bread, and drink of the chalice. **29.** For he that eateth and drinketh unworthily, eateth and drinketh judgment to himself, not discerning the body of the Lord. **30.** Therefore are there many infirm and weak among you, and many sleep. **31.** But if we would judge ourselves, we should not be judged. **32.** But whilst we are judged, we are chastised by the Lord, that we may not be damned with this world. **33.** Wherefore, my brethren, when you come together to eat, wait for one another. **34.** If any man be hungry, let him eat at home ; that you come not together unto judgment. And the rest I will set in order, when I come.

1. This ought to have been made the concluding verse of the preceding chapter. It sets the crown on the whole argument of cc. viii. ix. x. against the scandal of idol-meats.

2. So the Corinthians seem to have assured St. Paul in their letter.

3. *Of every man*, that is, of every Christian man. Cf. Eph. v. **23.** Christ is our Head in His Sacred Humanity, and in respect of that Humanity *the head of Christ is God*.

5. *Woman prophesying.* Further on, xiv. 34, he writes : *Let women keep silence in the churches.*

As if she were shaven, Isai. iii. 17, 24.

7. Man is *the image and glory*, or the glorious reflection, *of God*, both in other respects, and (what makes for the present argument) in this, that he is the lord of creation (Gen. i. 26). " Woman," as Theodoret says, " being under the power of man is *the glory of the man*, and as it were, the image of an image."

8, 9. This reasoning of St. Paul from Gen. ii.

G

21—23 is a weighty consideration in favour of taking the account of the formation of the first woman literally as the words sound.

10. *A power*, that is, a cap or veil in token of her being under the power of man, not necessarily of her husband, for the words apply to all women, not to married women only.

A power over her head : the Greek means simply *a power on her head*, ἐπὶ τῆς κεφαλῆς. Similarly in Isaias ix. 6, in the Septuagint version, which St. Paul often used, we read, *the principality was upon his shoulder*, ἐπὶ τοῦ ὤμου. It must be decided from the context whether the emblem of power, borne on head or shoulder (cf. Isaias xxii. 22), signifies power wielded by the bearer over others, as in Isaias, or power wielded by another over the bearer, as here.

Because of the angels. From the way these words are introduced, they cannot contain an entirely new argument for women covering their heads in churches : they can be only the complement of the argument already given. The modesty and submission proper to a woman has been argued to require her head to be covered, especially in the Lord's House. The angels, the *ministering spirits* (Heb. i. 14 : cf. Eph. iii. 10; and above, iv. 9), gathered there, expect such modest covering : be it worn accordingly *because of the angels*.

14. If *he nourish his hair*, *i.e.* wears it long, it *is a shame to him*. In Greece it was customary for boys to have their hair cut for the first time at the age of eighteen. To wear long hair after that age was the recognised mark of a fop.

15. Nature provides for woman a more abundant growth of hair on the head, an indication of the natural propriety of a woman's head being always covered.

16. *Seem to be*, better, *thinks fit to be*, δοκεῖ. "Although then the Corinthians were contentious, now the whole

Christian world has received and observes this law: such is the power of the Crucified" (St. Chrysostom).

17. *Now this I ordain; not praising you.* Literally, according to the best reading, *Now giving this word of command* (concerning women covering their heads), *I praise you not* (for what I am going to mention). *I praise you not* refers back to *v.* 2, and is taken up again in *v.* 22.

You come together for the worse. "All gregarious animals," writes St. Thomas on this passage, "by natural instinct come together for their better bodily good: hence man also, being a gregarious or social animal, ought to act rationally by the assembling of many for some purpose of improvement; as in worldly matters many meet in the unity of one State for the bettering of their worldly condition in the way of security and sufficiency of life. And therefore the faithful ought to come together for the bettering of their spiritual condition: but these Corinthians came together for the worse on account of the faults they committed in their assemblies."

Hence the Apostle hints, *v.* 34, that rather than come together *unto judgment*, they had better have stayed at home.

18, 19. *First of all.* The second heading commences at xii. 1.

In church, ἐν ἐκκλησίᾳ. The word means properly *the meeting of a multitudinous, corporate and legal body, as such.* It is not clear that the name was given to any building till the third century of our era.

Schisms, heresies, better perhaps here, *divisions, parties.* The separation of rich from poor, presently spoken of, did not amount to a *schism*, in the sense which that theological term bears now. The word αἵρεσις, here translated *heresy*, occurs in eight other places of the New Testament (Acts v. 17; xv. 5; xxvi. 5; xxiv. 5, 14; xxviii. 22; Gal. v. 20; 2 Pet. ii. 1). In six at least of

these places it means no more than *sect.* The best
realisation of the modern theological meaning is Titus
iii. 10, *A man that is a heretic* (αἱρετικὸν) *avoid.* St. Paul
does not here simply say *there must be also heresies,* which
would be a general declaration parallel to that of our
Lord, *it must needs be that scandals come* (Matt. xviii. 7) ;
but he says, according to the best readings, *there must be
also heresies* (rather, *sects, parties*) *among you.* Now what
is true in the abstract, is not necessarily true of any
particular church : nor, as a matter of fact, do we know
of any *heresies* springing up in the early church of
Corinth.

A printer's error has here crept into at least some
modern editions of the Rheims version, *reproved* for
approved (*probati*, δόκιμοι).

20. *It is not now to eat the Lord's supper,* more correctly,
there is now no eating the Lord's supper.

The first converts to Christianity, the three thousand
converted on the day of Pentecost, had all things in
common (Acts iii. 41, 44). This community of goods
ceased to be insisted on, as the Church spread. But
there continued what St. Chrysostom calls " an emana-
tion " of it, in the *agapae* or *love-feasts.* These were
meals, to which each guest brought provisions in kind,
according to his means ; and what was thus brought
together was supposed to be shared alike by all. This
was a Greek institution, as old as Homer. The Greek
name for such a meal was ἔρανος, said to be from ἐρῶ, *I
love,* as the Graeco-Christian name was ἀγάπη, which in
Christian language meant *brotherly love.* The Church
then in this, as in so many other instances, adapted to
her own purpose what she found already in existence.

The *agapae* are mentioned only once by name in the
Bible, by St. Jude, *v.* 12, who condemns the abuse of
them. At Corinth, as we learn here from St. Paul, they
were tarnished by a triple abuse. (1) The rich eating

the good things that they had themselves brought, before the poor could get at them, *vv.* 21, 33. (2) Some drinking to excess, *v.* 21. (3) The extreme irreverence of such an ill-conducted meal taking place in close connection with the celebration of the Holy Eucharist, *vv.* 23—29, which was celebrated, St. Chrysostom says, "before" (St. Augustine says, "after") the *agape*, or love-feast; which any way became either a bad thanksgiving after, or a bad preparation before Holy Communion.

We may remark incidentally that to extol the primitive Christians to the depreciation of the faithful in modern times, as was the fashion with the Jansenists, must argue a strange inability or reluctance to conceive the manner in which these primitive Christians at Corinth "went to their duties." Yet these were the parents of the martyrs!

The Lord's supper is the *agape*, or love-feast, preceded or followed by the celebration of the Holy Eucharist. The meats brought to the *agape* ought to have been shared alike by all, as the Holy Communion was partaken of by all alike. The selfish gluttony of the rich subverted the whole institution by destroying the essential idea of equal participation.

21. *Before* any distribution of the provisions brought could be effected, they were consumed severally by the several persons who had brought them.

Is drunk, μεθύει. The word need mean no more than *drinks freely,* as in John ii. 10; Gen. xliii. 34.

22. "Is it not preposterous that within the temple of God, where the Lord is present who has set before us a common table, you should riot, while the needy are hungry, and blush for their poverty?" (Theodoret).

23. *I have received of the Lord.* Evidently St. Paul means that a special instruction had been vouchsafed to him, beyond that which other Christians of his time

had received concerning the Last Supper from the Apostles there present. Elsewhere he says: *For neither did I receive it* (the gospel) *of man, nor did I learn it, but by the revelation of Jesus Christ* (Gal. i. 12). Our Saviour Himself then, appearing after His Ascension to St. Paul, had deigned to instruct him in this and other mysteries. St. Paul was a seer of visions (xv. 8; 2 Cor. xii. 2—4; Acts ix. 12; xxii. 17; xxiii. 11; xxvi. 15).

This is the oldest record of the Last Supper. St. Luke xxii. 19, 20, closely follows St. Paul, whose companion he was. St. Matthew xxvi. 26—28, writes as an eye-witness; and St. Mark xiv. 22—24, records the story as he learnt it of another eye-witness, St. Peter.

24. *Giving thanks*, εὐχαριστήσας, means the same thing as εὐλογήσας, which is translated *blessing*. The two words are used as synonymous in xiv. 16, where εὐλογήσῃς and εὐχαριστίᾳ are translated *bless* and *blessing*. Again they are interchanged in Mark xiv. 22, 23. And St. John vi. 11, has εὐχαριστήσας where the other three evangelists (Matt. xiv. 19; Mark vi. 41; Luke ix. 16) have εὐλόγησε, of our Lord *blessing* the loaves and fishes.

Take ye and eat: this is my body which shall be delivered for you. To represent these words, all that we find in the three oldest manuscripts is, *This is my body that is for you.* The other Greek manuscripts read, *This my body that is broken* (*i.e.* given in food) *for you.* For the Hebrew phrase of *breaking bread* cf. Isaias lviii. 1; Lam. iv. 4; Mark viii. 19; Acts ii. 46; xx. 11. Our present reading, *given*, διδόμενον, is found in Luke xxii. 19; while *take ye and eat* is in Matt. xxvi. 26. The variation then is unimportant.

25. *After he had supped* (also in Luke xxii. 20). We may argue from these words, with St. Mark's *whilst they were eating* (Mark xiv. 22), and St. Matthew's *while they were at supper* (Matt. xxvi. 26), that the institution

of the Holy Eucharist took place when supper was in
the main over, but they had not yet risen from table.
The chalice used in the institution may have been the
fourth cup of wine, that legally terminated the Jewish
paschal supper. ·

The new testament in my blood, i.e. *my blood of the
new testament* (Matt. xxvi. 28). *For when every commandment
of the law had been read by Moses to all the people, he took the
blood of calves and goats, . . . and sprinkled both the book
itself and all the people, saying, This is the blood of the
testament, which God hath enjoined unto you* (Heb. ix. 19;
Exod. xxiv. 8). With this sprinkling of *the blood of oxen
and goats*, it was *impossible that sins should be taken away*
(Heb. x. 4). Nor again could the law take away sin
(Rom. iv. vii.; Gal. iii.). Sins are taken away, not by
the real, living blood of goats and oxen, but by what
that blood was a figure of, the real, living Blood of
Christ, which He gave to His disciples to drink (Matt.
xxvi. 27, 28). In this was the *new testament*, in which
God said: *I will be merciful to their iniquities, and their sins
I will remember no more* (Heb. viii. 8—12; Jer. xxxi. 31
—34).

This do for the commemoration of me. "If any one says
that by the words, *This do for the commemoration of me*,
Christ did not institute His Apostles priests, or did not
ordain that they and other priests should offer His
Body and Blood, let him be anathema " (Council of
Trent, sess. 22, can. 2). This is one of the comparatively few texts, the sense of which has been dogmatically declared by the Church.

26. *You shall eat, you shall show forth :* better, *you eat,
you show forth* (καταγγέλλετε, *you declare*).

The eating and drinking here spoken of, being the
completion of the celebration of the Holy Eucharist, is
put for that celebration itself. Every time the Holy
Eucharist is celebrated, every time Mass is said, the

death of the Lord is shown forth by the separate consecration of the bread into His Body, and the wine into
His Blood, which separate consecration is symbolical
of the actual separation of that same Body and Blood,
which was the actual death of that same Lord on
Calvary.

27. *Or drink.* The reading *and drink* is now generally
discarded. It has disappeared in the Anglican Revised
Version. It used to be maintained for fear of the
inference in favour of Communion under one kind.

Guilty of the body and blood of the Lord : because, his
unworthiness depriving him of the fruit of what he
receives, that Blood, so far as he is concerned, has
been shed in vain, as well in the original sacrifice of
Calvary, as also in the renewed sacrifice of the altar at
which he communicates; and thus, as St. Chrysostom
puts it, like the crucifiers of our Saviour, " he has made
of the proceeding a butchery, and not a sacrifice."
Or again, as Theodoret explains : " As Judas betrayed
Him, and the Jews insulted Him, so do they dishonour
Him who receive His all-holy Body with unclean
hands, and approach it to a guilty mouth."

28. *Let a man prove himself.* " The custom of the
Church declares that such proving is necessary, as that
no one conscious to himself of mortal sin ought to
approach the Holy Eucharist without previous sacramental confession, however contrite he may think
himself " (Council of Trent, sess. 13, ch. 7). Going to
confession, a man *proves himself*, examines his own
conscience, and is in the first instance his own judge.
Cf. 2 Cor. xiii. 5. Let him *prove himself, i.e.* make sure
of the state of his conscience. That this proving of
oneself, where it reveals mortal sin, further implies the
confession of that sin, is not evident from the bare
words of this text, but from the tradition of the Church.

29. In this verse the words *unworthily* and *of the Lord*

are wanting in the three oldest manuscripts. Even so, however, the adverb must be mentally supplied from *v.* 27: and *the body* can be no other than *the body of the Lord*, spoken of *vv.* 24, 27, no other *body* being mentioned anywhere in this chapter. The Church is indeed the mystical *body* of Christ, x. 16; Rom. xii. 5; Eph. i. 23; but after speaking pointedly of the *body* of Christ as it is in the Holy Eucharist, then suddenly to use the term, without any qualification, to mean His mystical *body*, would be a mere equivocation. St. Paul then teaches that the unworthy communicant does not *discern the body of the Lord* in the Holy Eucharist. But how could he discern it, if it were not there?

Not discerning, "that is, not examining, not reflecting on the greatness of what is set before him, not taking account of the vastness of the gift: for if you were accurately to learn who it is that is set before you, and who it is that gives Himself, and to whom, you would need no other inducement" (St. Chrysostom).

Judgment to himself, κρίμα ἑαυτῷ. The same phrase is applied to those who resist lawful civil authority, Rom. xiii. 2.

30. *Therefore.* In any community, congregation, or country, where there are many unworthy communions, the effects will soon be visible,—scandals will occur, and miseries will break out into the light. This is a sin which never sleeps. The Corinthians were visited with temporal punishments, sicknesses and deaths, for the greediness and disorder of their agapae, so close to the reception of Holy Communion.

Many sleep, i.e. are dead. The word occurs ten other times in the New Testament, never of the death of the unrighteous. Hence it may be argued that the irreverence of the Corinthians, who were thus punished, in regard of their reception of the Holy Eucharist, did not go the length of grievous sin. This conclusion is made further probable from *v.* 32, with which compare Heb. xii. 5—11. *We are judged* (*v.* 32) and *chastised* with a temporal chastisement; while the *condemnation of this world* (that will not know Christ, John i. 10, 11) is eternal.

31. *Judge ourselves,* literally, *discern ourselves,* the same word as in *v.* 29. It means here that a man should *prove himself* (*v.* 28), and *discern the body of the Lord* present in the Eucharist, and also his own conscience, how that stands prepared for the reception of it.

33. *Wherefore,* at the *agapae, wait for one another.* This would prevent the abuse mentioned in *v.* 21, and the consequent irreverence to the Holy Eucharist (*vv.* 27, 29), and the judgments that thereon followed (*v.* 30).

34. *Let him eat at home.* "He leads the man out of the church, and sends him home, making such persons (those mentioned, *vv.* 21, 22) ridiculous, as slaves to appetite and wanting in self-control" (St. Chrysostom).

The rest I will set in order when I come. The written inspiration of the Apostle needed to be eked out by a living guidance, also divine.

1. Now concerning spiritual things, my brethren, I would not have you to be ignorant. 2. You know that, when you were heathens, you went to dumb idols, according as you were led. 3. Wherefore I give you to understand, that no man, speaking by the Spirit of God, saith anathema to Jesus; and no man can say, The Lord Jesus, but by the Holy Ghost. 4. Now there are diversities of graces, but the same Spirit. 5. And there are diversities of ministries, but the same Lord. 6. And there are diversities of operations, but the same God, who worketh all in all. 7. But the manifestation of the Spirit is given to every man unto profit. 8. To one indeed, by the Spirit, is given the word of wisdom; and to another the word of knowledge according to the same Spirit; 9. To another faith in the same Spirit; to another the grace of healing in one Spirit; 10. To another the working of miracles; to another prophecy; to another the discernment of spirits; to another divers kinds of tongues; to another interpretation of speeches: 11. But all these things one and the same Spirit worketh, dividing to every one according as he will. 12. For as the body is one, and hath many members, and all the members of the body, whereas they are many, yet are one body; so also is Christ. 13. For in one Spirit were we all baptized into one body, whether Jews or gentiles, whether bond or free; and in one Spirit we have all been made to drink. 14. For the body also is not one member, but many. 15. If the foot should say: Because I am not the hand, I am not of the body; is it therefore not of the body? 16. And if the ear should say: Because I am not the eye, I am not of the body; is it therefore not of the body? 17. If the whole body were the eye, where would be the hearing? if the whole were hearing, where would be the smelling? 18. But now God hath set the members every one of them in the body, as it hath pleased him. 19. And if they all were one member, where would be the body? 20. But now there are many members, indeed, yet one body. 21. And the eye cannot say to the hand: I need not thy help; nor again the head to the feet: I have no need of you. 22. Yea, much more, those that seem to be the more feeble members of the body are more necessary: 23. And such as we think to be the less honourable members of the body, upon these we bestow more abundant honour; and those that are our uncomely parts have more abundant comeliness. 24. But our comely parts have no need: but God hath tempered the body together, giving the more

abundant honour to that which wanted it; **25.** That there might be no schism in the body; but the members might be mutually careful one for another. **26.** And if one member suffer anything, all the members suffer with it; or if one member glory, all the members rejoice with it. **27.** Now you are the body of Christ, and members of member. **28.** And God indeed hath set some in the church, first, apostles; secondly, prophets; thirdly, teachers; after that, miracles; then the graces of healings, helps, governments, kinds of tongues, interpretations of speeches. **29.** Are all apostles? are all prophets? are all teachers? **30.** Are all workers of miracles? have all the grace of healing? do all speak with tongues? do all interpret? **31.** But be zealous for the better gifts: and I yet show to you a more excellent way.

"This passage is very obscure, owing to our ignorance and inexperience of things that happened when St. Paul wrote, but do not happen now. In those days, after baptism, one immediately spoke in strange tongues: many also prophesied; some worked miracles. Coming from their idols to the faith, with no previous accurate knowledge or acquaintance with the books of the Old Testament, they received the Holy Spirit in the instant of their baptism. But they could not see the Spirit, as He is invisible; and therefore the miraculous grace gave them a sensible proof of His operation. Thus at once one there was speaking the language of the Persians, another that of the Romans, another that of the Indians, and so of the rest. This was a sensible proof to those outside the faith that the Spirit was in the person of the speaker. They also raised the dead, chased out devils, and did other wonders. Some had more, and some fewer of these miraculous gifts; and those who had more, extolled themselves over those who had fewer, while the latter felt vexation and envy. The same jealousies occurred also at Rome (Rom. xii. 3—8), but not so much as here" (St. Chrysostom).

1—3. The connection of these three verses is something as follows:—'I would not have you ignorant:

you were ignorant as heathens, senseless followers of
senseless divinities: but Christians ought not to be
ignorant of spiritual things: wherefore I give you this
rule of discernment between good and bad spirits: *No
man speaking in the spirit of God,'* &c.

Dumb idols, Baruch vi. 40; Wisd. xi. 16.

Anathema means in Greek a thing devoted to Heaven;
and in New Testament Greek, a thing devoted to the
anger of Heaven. *Anathema to J.*, or more correctly,
Be J. anathema, means *Let him be accursed*. Any spirit
that prompts to such an utterance, St. Paul says, is an
evil spirit. But if the spirit prompts the man whom it
possesses to cry out, *the Lord Jesus*, or more correctly,
Jesus is Lord, that spirit either is, or at least is ruled by,
the Holy Ghost. It is true that evil spirits occasionally
gave this testimony (Mark i. 24; Acts xvi. 17), but
that was under compulsion of the Spirit of God.

St. Paul's rule for *trying the spirits if they be of God*,
is the same as St. John's (1 John iv. 1—3).

This verse, 3, thus explained, has no bearing upon
the controversy of St. Augustine with Pelagius as to the
necessity of grace. St. Paul is not speaking of the
ordinary workings of grace, but of the extraordinary
manifestations of spirits, good and evil.

4—6. Under the names of *Spirit, Lord,* and *God*, we
have here mentioned the Holy Ghost, the Son, and the
Father. Cf. i. 3; 2 Cor. xiii. 13. *Graces, ministries*, and
operations, are all the same thing, the extraordinary
manifestations of divine indwelling which then followed
upon baptism, all the work of one and the same God.

8. *The word of wisdom* seems to transcend *the
word of knowledge* by involving a deeper penetration of
mysteries. *We speak wisdom among the perfect*, ii. 6. A
catechist must be possessed at least of *knowledge*, but
wisdom is looked for in a theological lecturer. In those
to whom this Epistle was first addressed, these gifts

came, not of study, as they must in us, but of an extraordinary *manifestation of the Spirit*.

9. *Faith.* "Faith, not in doctrines, but to the working of signs and wonders, of which Christ says: *If you have faith as a grain of mustard-seed, you shall say to this mountain*, &c. (Matt. xvii. 19); and this the Apostles asked for, saying: *Increase our faith* (Luke xvii. 5). This faith is the mother of signs" (St. Chrysostom). In those to whom it is given, over and above the divine assurance that all the faithful have of God's power to work miracles, it involves a special assurance from God of His will to work a miracle in this or that case.

It is to be remembered throughout this passage that the Apostle is not speaking of any graces given to the receiver for his own salvation, or making or tending to make him holy and just.

10. *The working of miracles* may be distinct from the *faith* previously mentioned, as when one works miracles without being aware of it, *e.g.* Acts v. 15; xix. 12: cf. Luke vi. 19.

Discernment of spirits. Since there were prophets abroad at that time who deceived men, there was given to some of the faithful a special grace of the Holy Ghost to discern such cases of diabolic operation.

The other graces mentioned in this verse are discussed at length in ch. xiv.

11. This text shows the Holy Spirit as a Divine Person, who *worketh all these things*, which in *v.* 6 *God* is said to work.

12. *So also in Christ*, that is, the mystical Body of Christ, His Church. "The whole Christ," says St. Augustine, "is head and body: the head the only-begotten Son of God, and His body the Church, bridegroom and bride, two in one flesh" (*De unit. eccles.* 4). And St. Chrysostom here: "As head and body are one man, so, says the Apostle, the Church

and Christ are one; wherefore he puts *Christ* instead of *the Church.*" Cf. vi. 15 with note; Eph. i. 23; iv. 12; v. 30; Col. i. 18.

13. Cf. Col. iii. 11; Gal. iii. 27, 28.

In one Spirit we have all been made to drink. The preposition *in* is better away: it is absent in the oldest MSS. The meaning then is: 'We all have had given us to drink, that is, we all have received, one Holy Ghost.' For the metaphor see our Lord's words, John iv. 13, 14; vii. 37, 38; where the Evangelist explains: *Now this he said of the spirit which they should receive who believed in him* (*v.* 39). The metaphor is also in the Old Testament, Isaias xii. 3; Ezech. xlvii. 1, seq.; Zach. xiv. 8. "He seems to me now to speak of that descent of the Holy Ghost, which is after baptism, and before the reception of the [Eucharistic] mysteries" (St. Chrysostom). The reference is to the Sacrament of Confirmation, which in early times, as in the Greek Church still, was given immediately after baptism.

There is a conjectural reading, ἐν πόμα ἐποτίσθημεν (πόμα, *drink*, for πνεῦμα, *Spirit*) which would refer to the Eucharistic chalice. But the tense of the verb points to a rite performed once, not habitually. And the given reading of the oldest MSS. leaves nothing to be desired.

14. St. Paul appeals to that "differentiation," the having a variety of parts with so many several functions, which appears more in the higher animals, and less and less as we sink in the animal scale.

15, 16. The foot compares itself with the hand; and not the foot, but the ear, with the eye: we envy rather those with whom we have more points in common.

22. *More necessary.* The Greek has the positive degree, ἀναγκαῖα, *necessary.* The members spoken of are not the internal organs, as brain, heart, liver, but the

outer parts. An instance of a *feeble*, or delicate, but *necessary* member, would be the eye.

23, 24. *Honour* of raiment and *comeliness* of clothing, which our most *uncomely parts* nowhere go deprived of: while our most *comely part*, the face, goes most of all exposed. The uncomely parts of the Church are criminals, lepers, lunatics, and such unhappy persons, the objects of charitable care.

26. "When anywhere the finger of any of us receives a blow, the whole commonwealth of the body, attuned to one accord with the soul that rules it, feels the infliction; and for the distress of the particular member the whole body sympathises and feels pain together; and thus we say that the man has a pain in his finger; and the same with any other portion of the human frame, there is pain for the distress of any part and pleasure at its recovery. Very much like this is the social tone of the best constituted city. Whatever good or evil befalls one of the citizens, the city will say that that is her good or her evil, and will all rejoice or grieve together, necessarily so in the city that has good laws " (Plato, *Republic*, 462, a passage to which St. Paul can hardly have been a stranger). Obviously, this comparison must not be pressed too closely, where the body politic, civil or religious, has grown very large.

27. *Members of member*, μέλη ἐκ μέλους, is explained to mean 'members dependent one on another.' But much better is the reading of nearly all the Greek MSS., μέλη ἐκ μέρους, 'members severally.' We find ἐκ μέρους in xiii. 9, 10, translated *in part*. The Apostle then says to the faithful: 'Collectively, you are the body of Christ; and taken severally, or distributively, you are His various members.' These several memberships are set forth in the next verse.

28. The classes here mentioned are not the hierarchical grades of the Church, which still exist, but

classes marked out by the possession of various extraordinary gifts, which have for the most part ceased in
the Church, though we still find instances of them in
the lives of the saints and of great missionaries.

Apostles. The word is used here in a wide sense
(as in Acts xiv. 13; Rom. xvi. 7; 2 Cor. viii. 23; Phil.
ii. 25; 2 Pet. iii. 2; Apoc. ii. 2) to denote one who
broke new ground in the conversion of the heathen, and
for that purpose was endowed with a profusion of
miraculous gifts, as was St. Francis Xavier in later
times.

Prophets. " There were many more prophets at that
time than there had been in the Old Law. The gift
was poured out abundantly, and every local church had
numbers prophesying" (St. Chrysostom). Cf. Acts ii. 18;
xi. 27, 28; xv. 32.

Doctors, who had the infused *word of knowledge* (*v.* 8
with note).

Helps, persons with an extraordinary power of helping the sick and poor.

Governments, extraordinary powers of church administration.

Chapter XIII.

1. If I speak with the tongues of men and of angels, and have not charity, I am become as sounding brass, or a tinkling cymbal. **2.** And if I should have prophecy, and should know all mysteries, and all knowledge; and if I should have all faith, so that I could remove mountains, and have not charity, I am nothing. **3.** And if I should distribute all my goods to feed the poor, and if I should deliver my body to be burned, and have not charity, it profiteth me nothing. **4.** Charity is patient, is kind; charity envieth not, dealeth not perversely, is not puffed up, **5.** Is not ambitious, seeketh not her own, is not provoked to anger, thinketh no evil; **6.** Rejoiceth not in iniquity, but rejoiceth with the truth: **7.** Beareth all things, believeth all things, hopeth all things, endureth all things. **8.** Charity never faileth; whether prophecies shall be made void, or tongues shall cease, or knowledge shall be destroyed. **9.** For we know in part, and we prophesy in part. **10.** But when that which is perfect shall come, that which is in part shall be done away. **11.** When I was a child, I spoke as a child, I understood as a child, I thought as a child; but when I became a man, I put away the things of a child. **12.** We see now through a glass in an obscure manner; but then face to face. Now I know in part; but then I shall know even as I am known. **13.** And now there remain faith, hope, and charity, these three; but the greatest of these is charity.

1. *Charity.* Throughout this chapter the Apostle speaks of the *charity of God* which *is poured forth in our hearts by the Holy Ghost who is given to us* (Rom. v. 5). That is, he speaks of the theological virtue of charity, which is either identical with, or inseparably attached to, the gift of sanctifying grace, by the possession of which we are said to be in 'the state of grace.' Being in this state of grace, or *having charity*, is the sole and indispensable condition for admission to the vision of God in heaven. If a man *have not charity*, that is, be out of the state of grace, no work that he does is meritorious of heaven. A *sounding brass* trumpet or a *tinkling cymbal* may be of occasional use to others, but it is a poor thing of itself; such is the man out of grace

and without charity, though he have the miraculous gift of speaking *divers kinds of tongues* (xii. 10; Acts ii. 4) *of men*, or even could catch and repeat the mysterious locutions in which the *angels* communicate with one another, and hymn the praises of their Creator.

The burden of this chapter is declared by St. Chrysostom: " Thanks be to God, that while He gives extraordinary gifts, He knows how to save by common gifts: for the gifts without which it is impossible to be a Christian, are more useful than those which are attainable by few." The extraordinary graces of the Corinthians (chs. xii. xiv.) are rarely ever witnessed now: but *there remain faith, hope, and charity* (*v.* 13); and of these, charity and sanctifying grace is a better gift of God to man than all the miraculous favours that we read of in the history of the early Church and in the lives of the Saints.

2. *Knowledge*, the miraculous gift, called *the word of knowledge*, xii. 8.

Faith, not the theological virtue, but the extraordinary gift of miracle-working faith, mentioned xii. 9.

3. *Distribute all my goods to feed the poor*, ψωμίσω πάντα τὰ ὑπάρχοντά μου. The verb here means 'to break up food into little pieces to put into other peoples' mouths.' The Apostle says that if I should continue this process till all my goods were spent upon it, it would profit me nothing for heaven, unless I were in the state of grace. Philanthropy without charity does not merit the vision of God.

To be burned. By the change of a letter, καυχήσωμαι for κανθήσωμαι, the three oldest MSS. yield the sense, *to make a vaunt of it.* The text then means: ' If I spend all my substance in philanthropy, or give over my body to death or slavery, in a spirit of bravado and for human glory, and not out of charity, or the grace of God, indwelling in me and impelling me, it profits me nothing for heaven.' Indeed such is the meaning, whichever of the two readings we prefer. In favour of καυχήσωμαι we may observe that that is exactly what the Corinthians were doing with their extraordinary graces: they were making them matter of vain display, and vaunting themselves one above another. A converse confusion of the same two letters, χ and θ, in Ps. cxxxi. 16, has given us χήραν (*viduam*, widow) for θήραν (*venationem*, hunting). We may further observe that καυθήσωμαι (future subjunctive) is a non-existent tense in Greek. Many accordingly edit καυθήσομαι. But the reading ω makes another argument for καυχήσωμαι.

4—7. In these verses the Apostle describes charity, not simply as indwelling, in the form of sanctifying grace, but as operative, by the aid of actual grace. A man of course may be in the state of grace, and commit many venial sins of impatience, unkindness, selfishness, &c.: he may be in charity, and fail to produce the fruits thereof: still these are the fruits of charity. Cf. Luke xiii. 6—9 for the danger of a tree long failing to bear fruit.

Dealeth not perversely, οὐ περπερεύεται. The word was a difficulty even to the Greek Fathers. St. Chrysostom explains it: "Is not forward (οὐ προπετεύεται); charity makes a person discreet and grave and staid; forwardness being a defect that appears in base and guilty lovers." Theodoret says: "The meaning is, that charity meddles not with what does not concern her, does not grope after the measures of the substance of God, nor examine the matter of His dispensations: charity endures to do nothing rash." Cicero, writing to Atticus (i. 14), says: ἐνεπερπερευσάμην *novo auditori Pompeio*, which clearly means, "I made a fine display of myself before my new hearer, Pompey." Hence the Anglican Authorized Version here has *charity vaunteth not itself*.

The conjecture however seems to amount to a certainty, that in the Vulgate originally the translation of οὐ περπερεύεται was *non est ambitiosa*, *is not ambitious* (or better, *is not ostentatious*), which now appears in *v.* 5: while *non agit perperam* was meant, plausibly enough, to translate οὐκ ἀσχημονεῖ in the same *v.* 5. For οὐκ ἀσχημονεῖ the Vulgate now gives *non est ambitiosa*, which is confessedly no rendering of the Greek at all. The mistake arose from some ingenious person remarking the etymological correspondence of *perperam* and περπερεύεται, and thereupon interchanging *non agit perperam* and *non est ambitiosa*.

The phrase οὐκ ἀσχημονεῖ, misrendered *is not ambitious*, is otherwise explained as follows: "Charity excuses herself from no mean or lowly service, as though such service were unseemly (ἀσχημον), on behalf of brethren" (Theodoret).

St. Chrysostom in like manner takes the word to mean, not *to misbehave*, but *to make a bad figure*, the meaning it bears in Plato, who uses it four times, as also in Euripides, *Hecuba*, 407. So St. Chrysostom explains: "Charity, while suffering extremities for the beloved, does not count the position a sorry one. The Apostle does not say, 'Charity maketh a bad figure, to be sure, but she beareth the shame manfully?' he implies that she has not even a perception of the shame. So our Lord Jesus Christ was spat upon and beaten, and not only did not consider that He made a bad figure, but exulted and called the situation His glory." Cf. Heb. xii. 2: *And despised the shame.*

If St. John Chrysostom and Theodoret knew their own language, both the original Vulgate, *non agit perperam*, and the Anglican, *doth not behave itself unseemly*, are mistranslations of οὐκ ἀσχημονεῖ, and we might translate perhaps, *charity weareth not a rueful countenance*, or *charity doth not pout or sulk*, when called upon to act.

Seeketh not her own, x. 24; Phil. ii. 4. These paral-
lelisms render improbable the reading of the Vatican
MS., *seeketh not what is not her own*, which moreover
represents not charity but justice.

Thinketh no evil, literally, *imputeth not the evil* that she
suffers, *does not score it down* to the doer's account.

Rejoiceth with the truth, *i.e.* with righteousness, as in
Eph. iv. 15, the Apostle speaks of *doing the truth in
charity*.

Beareth all things, whatever is put upon her. The
verb στέγει is used of ice *bearing*. It appears in ix. 12,
we bear all things: also 1 Thess. iii. 1, 5. The three
following verbs are rhetorical amplifications of this.
"Charity," says St. Chrysostom, "not only *hopeth*, but
believeth from excess of love, despairs not of the loved
one, and if he turn out not according to hope, but
grows still more insupportable, charity *endureth* that
also." This feature of charity is never shown more
seasonably than by a priest in the confessional dealing
with his penitents.

8. *Charity never falleth away*, not that a man may not
fall from charity, Apoc. ii. 4, but that charity is never
superseded, as the miraculous gifts here mentioned are
superseded, by the development of the Church on earth,
and finally in heaven.

Whether prophecies shall be made void. The Greek εἴτε
δὲ προφητεῖαι, *but whether prophecies*, shows that we should
punctuate, *but whether there be prophecies* (or rather,
prophetic powers), *they shall be made void* (*i.e.* come to an
end); *or tongues, they shall cease; or knowledge, it shall be
destroyed*. The reference is clear to the gifts of prophecy,
tongues, and knowledge, things of common experience
at Corinth, which, so far as our common experience
goes, have entirely ceased, but not so charity.

9—12. The Apostle shows that man on earth has
small cause to boast of any gift of knowledge or

prophecy bestowed on him. It is little compared with what there is to know, and with what shall be known one day in the vision of God.

Through a glass, δι' ἐσόπτρου, *by means of a* (metallic) *mirror.* The best mirrors were made at Corinth.

In an obscure manner, literally, *in an enigma.* Our knowledge of God is so limited, that for one thing we know, two others we are left to conjecture; and many puzzles, perplexities, or *riddles*, wait upon faith. The Apostle seems to have had in view what the Lord says of Moses: *I will speak to him face to face; and openly, and not by enigmas and figures doth he see the Lord* (Num. xii. 8): wherein it is insinuated (cf. *v*. 6 l.c.) that the prophetic knowledge, of which the Corinthians boasted, was only *by enigmas and figures.*

Face to face. Cf. 1 John iii. 2. " We shall see God face to face, because we shall have an immediate vision of Him, as of a man whom we see face to face. By this vision we are most of all made like to God, and are partakers in His happiness, for this is His happiness, that He understands Himself. They therefore *eat and drink at the table* of God (Luke xxii. 9), who enjoy the same happiness wherewith God is happy, seeing Him in the way in which He sees Himself" (St. Thomas, *Contra gent.* iii. 51).

I shall know even as I am known. " I shall see Him more accurately for being brought into close intimacy with Him. *I am known* is put for *I am become intimate.* Thus God said to Moses, *I know thee above all* (Ex. xxxiii. 17); and the Apostle, *The Lord knoweth who are His* (2 Tim. ii. 19), that is, He takes more care of them " (Theodoret). The verse means simply: ' I shall be intimate with God, and He with me.'

13. *And now*, marking the logical conclusion, or summing up, *there remain*, as the permanent endowments of the Church on earth, when the extraordinary graces

of her infancy are almost lost in the calm strength
of her mature age,—*there remain* on earth *faith, hope,
charity.*

CHAPTER XIV.

1. Follow after charity; be zealous for spiritual gifts; but
rather that you may prophesy. 2. For he that speaketh in a
tongue, speaketh not to men, but to God: for no man heareth.
But by the Spirit he speaketh mysteries. 3. But he that prophesieth speaketh to men unto edification, and exhortation, and
comfort. 4. He that speaketh in a tongue edifieth himself; but he
that prophesieth, edifieth the church. 5. And I would have you all
to speak with tongues, but rather to prophesy: for greater is he
that prophesieth than he that speaketh with tongues; unless,
perhaps, he interpret, that the church may receive edification.
6. But now, brethren, if I come to you, speaking with tongues,
what shall I profit you, unless I speak to you either in revelation,
or in knowledge, or in prophecy, or in doctrine? 7. Even things
without life that give sound, whether pipe or harp, except they give
a distinction of sounds, how shall it be known what is piped or
harped? 8. For if the trumpet give an uncertain sound, who shall
prepare himself to battle? 9. So likewise you, unless you utter by
the tongue plain speech, how shall it be known what is spoken?
For you shall be speaking into the air. 10. There are, for example,
so many kinds of tongues in this world, and none is without a voice.
11. If then I know not the power of the voice, I shall be to him to
whom I speak a barbarian, and he that speaketh a barbarian to me.
12. So you also, forasmuch as you are zealous of spirits, seek to
abound unto the edifying of the church. 13. And, therefore, let
him that speaketh a tongue pray that he may interpret. 14. For if
I pray in a tongue, my spirit prayeth, but my understanding is
without fruit. 15. What is it then? I will pray in the spirit;
I will pray also in the understanding: I will sing with the spirit;
I will sing also with the understanding. 16. Else if thou shalt
bless in the spirit, how shall he that holdeth the place of the
unlearned say Amen to thy blessing? because he knoweth not what
thou sayest. 17. For thou indeed givest thanks well, but the other
is not edified. 18. I thank my God I speak with all your tongues.
19. But in the church I had rather speak five words with my
understanding, that I may instruct others also, than ten thousand

words in a tongue. **20.** Brethren, do not become children in sense;
but in malice be children, and in sense be perfect. **21.** In the law
it is written: For in other tongues and other lips I will speak to
this people; and neither so will they hear me, saith the Lord.
22. Wherefore tongues are for a sign, not to believers, but to
unbelievers; but prophecies, not to unbelievers, but to believers.
23. If, therefore, the whole church come together into one place,
and all speak with tongues, and there come in unlearned persons or
unbelievers, will not they say that you are mad? **24.** But if all
prophesy, and there come in one that believeth not, or one unlearned, he is convinced of all, he is judged of all. **25.** The secrets
of his heart are made manifest; and so, falling down on his face,
he will adore God, affirming that God is among you indeed.
26. How is it then, brethren? when you come together, every one
of you hath a psalm, hath a doctrine, hath a revelation, hath a tongue,
hath an interpretation. Let all things be done unto edification.
27. If any speak in a tongue, let it be by two, or at the most by
three, and in course; and let one interpret. **28.** But if there be no
interpreter, let him hold his peace in the church, and speak to
himself, and to God. **29.** And let the prophets speak, two or three;
and let the rest judge. **30.** But if any thing be revealed to another
sitting, let the first hold his peace. **31.** For you may all prophesy
one by one, that all may learn, and all may be exhorted. **32.** And
the spirits of the prophets are subject to the prophets. **33.** For he
is not the God of dissension, but of peace; as also I teach in all
the churches of the saints. **34.** Let women keep silence in the
churches: for it is not permitted to them to speak, but to be
subject, as also the law saith. **35.** But if they would learn anything, let them ask their husbands at home: for it is a shame for a
woman to speak in the church. **36.** Or did the word of God come
out from you? or came it only unto you? **37.** If any man seem to
be a prophet, or spiritual, let him know the things that I write to
you, that they are the commands of the Lord. **38.** But if any man
know not, he shall not be known. **39.** Wherefore, brethren, be
zealous to prophesy, and forbid not to speak with tongues. **40.** But
let all things be done decently and according to order.

1. *Spiritual gifts*, the miraculous gifts mentioned
xii. 8—10. The advent of these gifts was announced
by St. Peter on the day of Pentecost, quoting the
prophecy of Joel, then to have its fulfilment (Acts
ii. 16—18).

Prophesy. They who had the gift of prophecy in the early Church were sometimes foretellers of future events (Acts xi. 27, 28; xxi. 10, 11); but their principal function was to be ' forth-tellers,' exhorting and praying extempore, not as regularly ordained ministers, *fulfilling their ministry* (2 Tim. iv. 5; Acts xiii. 2), but under an extraordinary divine inspiration.

2. *He that speaketh in a tongue,* that is, in a strange language, which neither he himself understood, nor those about him. Such was the gift of tongues, the use of which was not for preaching, but for praying (*v.* 14), to *confess to the Lord, because he is good* (Ps. cxvii. 1). Such prayers and praises the multitude heard the Apostles putting up, *speaking in divers tongues the wonderful works of God.* The first sermon was preached after this (Acts ii. 14, seq.), probably in the Hebrew tongue, and understood only by those who knew that language. We cannot however deny, nor yet can we prove it by any text of Scripture, that the Apostles had the gift, which was given to St. Francis Xavier and St. Vincent Ferrer, of preaching the faith to peoples whose languages they had never learnt.

Speaketh not unto men, but unto God. Clearly therefore this gift of *speaking in a tongue* was not used for preaching.

No man heareth, i.e. *understandeth,* as in Gen. xi. 7; xlii. 23.

Mysteries, as well in the matter, the *wonderful works of God* (Acts ii. 11), as also here still more in the form, the language spoken being an unknown tongue to speaker and hearers.

4. *Edifieth himself,* inasmuch as he surrenders to a divine impulse to utter words which he does not understand, except in so far as he knows them to contain the praises of God; like a nun, ignorant of Latin, devoutly chanting the Breviary.

Interpret (xii. 30). The miraculous power of inter-
preting the utterances of one who had the gift of
tongues, was itself a distinct gift. The two gifts might
or might not be conjoined in the same person.

6. One must receive *revelation* before one can speak
in prophecy; and one must be filled with *knowledge* before
one can instruct *in doctrine.*

7, 8. In listening to a language that we do not
know, we cannot catch the words, where one word ends
and another begins. The speaker is to us as a musical
instrument, that makes not music, but *an uncertain sound*,
without *distinction,*—mere noise.

9. *Plain,* not merely absolutely, the language itself
being correct and fraught with meaning, but relatively,
it being understood by the company present. Thus
the language of Socrates is not *plain speech* in the streets
of London.

10. *There are, for example, so many,* any number you
like to make it, as sixty or a hundred. *For example*
(εἰ τύχοι) occurs again in xv. 37, *as, for example, of wheat.*

Kinds of tongues, different languages.

None is without voice, better, *without tongue.* No tongue
is tongueless, *i.e.* no language is meaningless. The
word translated *voice* in this and the next verse had
better have been translated *tongue,* or *language,* being the
same word that appears in *kinds of tongues.*

For γένη φωνῶν, *kinds of tongues,* which is in all the
MSS., it has been proposed to read γένη φωνῶντα,
speaking races. Then what follows would be translated,
and no race is without speech.

11. *The power of the voice,* the meaning of the language.

A barbarian, βάρβαρος, a maker of inarticulate sounds
(*bar-bar,* like our *bow-wow*). Any language that we do
not know, is to us made up of inarticulate sounds, or
gibberish.

12. *Zealous of spirits,* the *spiritual gifts* of *v.* 1.

13. *Let him pray that he may interpret.* To *pray* here means what it means in the next verse, to *pray in a tongue.* The Apostle then says: ' He who has the gift of tongues, let him use it by all means, with the intention that the prayers he puts up in a strange language may be interpreted, either by himself, if he have the further gift of interpretation (*v.* 5), or by another (*v.* 27).'

14. *My spirit, i.e.* the divine impulse in me, *prayeth;* but the human faculties of my mind have no hold on the meaning of my prayer.

15. *With the spirit,* under the divine impulse above mentioned.

With the understanding, finding out from some one who can interpret to me the meaning of the words I use.

The verse is simply an exhortation to use the gift of tongues intelligently, with some knowledge of the meaning of the ecstatic prayer or hymn.

16. *Bless* (εὐλογῇς), *blessing* (εὐχαριστίᾳ), see note on xi. 24.

Not *the unlearned,* but *the unofficial person, the layman* (ἰδιώτου). The person who had the gift of praying in a strange tongue, might or might not be one of the ministering body, bishop, priest, or deacon (1 Tim. iii. 1, 12; v. 17): but for the time he put up his prayer he acted as an extraordinary minister of the Church; and any one who had not the gift was fain for the time being to *hold the place of the layman,* and say the Amens.

18. *I speak with all your tongues.* There is a double mistranslation here. The English has wandered wide of the Latin Vulgate, which has *lingua,—tongue,* not *tongues.* The original Rheims version renders the Latin literally: *I speak with the tongue of you all.* But the Latin has departed from the Greek by disregard of the word μᾶλλον, *more.* It should be rendered, *I speak with a tongue more than you all.*

20. Cf. Matt. xviii. 3; 1 Pet. ii. 2, 3.

In sense, i.e. in wits. The Corinthians were to have more wits than a child, but not more malice. Whereas, continues the Apostle (*v.* 23), any stranger coming in, and hearing their childish display of their gifts of tongues, would say they had lost their wits.

Perfect, τέλειοι. The word means *grown up men.*

21. *In the law*, Isaias xxviii. 11, 12. The Psalms are quoted as *the law* in John x. 34; xv. 25; xii. 34, the last being also a reference to Isaias and Ezechiel.

The *other tongues and other lips* were those of their Assyrian conquerors, whose barbarous and unknown languages the Jews were to be constrained to listen to in punishment for having mocked at the utterances of the prophets and complained of their obscurity.

22. *Wherefore*, as the hearing of strange tongues was a sign of old to the unbelieving Jews, so it is now *a sign*, primarily, *not to believers, but to unbelievers*, calling their attention to the Christian community, exciting their curiosity, and bringing them to listen to instruction, all which process is exemplified, Acts ii. 6—41.

Prophecies (see note on *v.* 1) were a sign, primarily, *to believers:* they were mainly for the edification and consolation of the faithful: which however did not prevent their being a sign, secondarily, also to unbelievers, as we gather from *vv.* 24, 25.

23. *Unlearned persons*, ἰδιῶται, the same word as in *v.* 16. It is a relative term, and varies in meaning, according to the various antitheses into which it enters. Here it means *strangers*, whether Christians from elsewhere, or catechumens, who had not had experience of the gift of tongues, or *unbelievers.*

Will they not say that you are mad? Thus the gift of tongues, unless borne out by prophecy, moves the persons for whose benefit it was principally intended, rather to derision than to faith. All that the Apostles would have got by it would have been a name for being *full of new wine,* had not Peter *lifted up his voice and spoke* (Acts ii. 13, 14).

24. *He is convinced,* i.e. *convicted and proved guilty, of all,* i.e. by all whom he hears preaching and prophesying: *he is judged,* i.e. sentenced. The words of inspired exhortation and prayer do for him that which the Jews could never do for our Lord (John viii. 46), they *convince* him *of sin,* and move him to seek for baptism (Acts ii. 28).

25. *The secrets of his heart are made manifest,* not to the assembly, but the man's own conscience is roused, and speaks to him of secrets of the past that had been glossed over: which same is to this day, except in scrupulous persons, the fruit of a good sermon.

26. *How is it* to be done?

Hath a psalm, the power of breaking out into an original, spiritual canticle, as our Lady uttered the *Magnificat,* and Zachary the *Benedictus.* This power has not been mentioned before.

Hath a doctrine, the word of knowledge, xii. 8.

Hath a revelation, prophecy, xii. 2, and above, *v.* 1.

29. *Let the rest judge;* let them who have the gift of *discerning of spirits* (xii. 10) exercise their gift.

32. The *spirits,* that is, the spiritual gifts, notably the gift of prophecy. The spirit, or gift of prophecy, is a sort of habit which one can use when he will, and withhold at pleasure. No excuse therefore for disobedience to these regulations.

33. *Dissension,* rather, *disorder,* ἀκαταστασίας. The gifts, with which the Corinthians were endowed, were of God: but their disorderly way of using them was not of God.

A better reading places a full stop at *peace.* The verb *I teach* is absent from the best manuscripts.

34. The better reading is: *As in all the churches of the saints, let women keep silence in your churches.* The Apostle

here restricts women still further than he had done in
xi. 5. The restriction is so absolute and so general as
to exclude women, not only from the public exercise in
church of extraordinary gifts, such as prophecy and
tongues, but also from ordinary ecclesiastical functions.
But it is saying too much to contend that the Apostle
had in view our modern female choirs.

As the law saith, Gen. iii. 16.

36. He justifies the induction of *v.* 34 (al. 33) from
the practice of other churches to that of Corinth,
reminding the Corinthians that Corinth is neither the
mother-church of Christendom, nor the only church:
therefore she ought not to be singular, but conform to
the practice of the other churches. Thessalonica had
had the start of Corinth, 1 Thess. i. 7, 8.

38. The meaning is: If any man will not recognise
these written commands of the Lord, the Lord will not
recognise him, nor admit him to familiarity. Cf. xiii. 12.
The Greek MSS. vary between ἀγνοείσθω, *let him be
unknown, i.e.* unrecognised of God: and ἀγνοείτω, *let him
remain not knowing, i.e.* be left to himself and his own
wilful ignorance.

It would be a mistake to suppose that gifts as
miraculous as those referred to in this chapter have
altogether disappeared from the Church. The lives of
the Saints in all ages are evidence to the contrary.
And there are names, and faces too, familiar amongst
us, of men and women who have built churches and
schools, founded congregations, influenced for good
and commanded all about them, with such paucity of
human resources as to argue the presence and over-
shadowing of Him, who is still *wonderful in his holy place*
(Ps. lxvii. 36).

CHAPTER XV.

1. Now I make known unto you, brethren, the gospel which I preached to you, which also you have received, and wherein you stand; 2. By which also you are saved, if you hold fast after what manner I preached to you, unless you have believed in vain: 3. For I delivered to you first of all that which I also received, how that Christ died for our sins, according to the Scriptures: 4. And that he was buried, and that he rose again the third day, according to the Scriptures; 5. And that he was seen by Cephas, and after that by the eleven. 6. Then he was seen by more than five hundred brethren at once; of whom many remain until this present, and some are fallen asleep. 7. After that he was seen by James, then by all the apostles: 8. And last of all, he was seen also by me, as by one born out of due time. 9. For I am the least of the apostles, who am not worthy to be called an apostle, because I persecuted the church of God. 10. But by the grace of God I am what I am: and his grace in me hath not been void; but I have laboured more abundantly than all they: yet not I, but the grace of God with me. 11. For whether I or they, so we preach, and so you have believed. 12. Now, if Christ be preached that he arose again from the dead, how do some among you say that there is no resurrection of the dead? 13. But if there be no resurrection of the dead, then Christ is not risen again: 14. And if Christ be not risen again, then is our preaching vain, and your faith is also vain: 15. Yea, and we are found false witnesses of God: because we have given testimony against God that he hath raised up Christ; whom he hath not raised up, if the dead rise not again. 16. For if the dead rise not again, neither is Christ risen again: 17. And if Christ be not risen again, your faith is vain, for you are yet in your sins. 18. Therefore they also, who have slept in Christ, have perished. 19. If in this life only we have hope in Christ, we are of all men the most miserable. 20. But now Christ is risen from the dead, the first-fruits of them that sleep. 21. For by a man came death, and by a man the resurrection of the dead. 22. And as in Adam all die, so also in Christ all shall be made alive. 23. But every one in his own order: the first-fruits Christ; then they that are of Christ, who have believed in his coming. 24. Afterwards the end, when he shall have delivered up the kingdom to God and the Father; when he shall have abolished all principality, and authority, and power. 25. For he must reign, until he hath put all enemies under his feet. 26. And the enemy death shall be

destroyed last: For he hath put all things under his feet. And whereas he saith, **27.** All things are put under him, undoubtedly he is excepted who put all things under him. **28.** And when all things shall be subdued unto him, then the Son also himself shall be subject to him who subjected all things to him, that God may be all in all. **29.** Otherwise what shall they do who are baptized for the dead, if the dead rise not again at all? why are they then baptized for them? **30.** Why also are we in danger every hour? **31.** I die daily, by your glory, brethren, which I have in Christ Jesus our Lord. **32.** If (according to man) I fought with beasts at Ephesus, what doth it profit me if the dead rise not again? let us eat and drink; for to-morrow we shall die. **33.** Be not deceived: evil communications corrupt good manners. **34.** Awake, ye just, and sin not; for some have not the knowledge of God: I speak it to your shame. **35.** But some man will say: How do the dead rise again? or with what manner of body shall they come? **36.** Senseless man, that which thou sowest is not quickened, except it die first. **37.** And that which thou sowest, thou sowest not the body that shall be, but bare grain, as of wheat, or of some of the rest. **38.** But God giveth it a body as he will, and to every seed its proper body. **39.** All flesh is not the same flesh: but some is that of men, another of beasts, another of birds, another of fishes. **40.** And there are bodies celestial, and bodies terrestrial: but the glory of the celestial is one, and that of the terrestrial another. **41.** There is one glory of the sun, another glory of the moon, and another glory of the stars; for star differeth from star in glory. **42.** So also is the resurrection of the dead; it is sown in corruption, it shall rise in incorruption: **43.** It is sown in dishonour, it shall rise in glory: it is sown in weakness, it shall rise in power: **44.** It is sown an animal body, it shall rise a spiritual body. If there be an animal body, there is also a spiritual body, as it is written: **45.** The first man Adam was made a living soul, the last Adam a quickening spirit. **46.** But not first that which is spiritual, but that which is animal; afterwards that which is spiritual. **47.** The first man was of the earth, earthly; the second man from heaven, heavenly. **48.** Such as is the earthly, such also are the earthly; and such as is the heavenly, such also are they that are heavenly. **49.** Therefore as we have borne the image of the earthly, let us bear also the image of the heavenly. **50.** Now this I say, brethren, that flesh and blood cannot possess the kingdom of God; neither shall corruption possess incorruption. **51.** Behold, I tell you a mystery: We shall all indeed rise again, but we shall not all be changed, **52.** In a moment, in the twinkling

I

of an eye, at the last trumpet; for the trumpet shall sound; and the dead shall rise again incorruptible, and we shall be changed. **53.** For this corruptible must put on incorruption, and this mortal must put on immortality. **54.** And when this mortal hath put on immortality, then shall come to pass the saying that is written: Death is swallowed up in victory. **55.** O death, where is thy victory? O death, where is thy sting? **56.** Now the sting of death is sin; and the power of sin is the law. **57.** But thanks be to God, who hath given us the victory through our Lord Jesus Christ. **58.** Therefore, my beloved brethren, be ye steadfast and unmoveable, always abounding in the work of the Lord, knowing that your labour is not in vain in the Lord.

1. *I make known*, γνωρίζω. The word means to make one recognise what before he had under his senses, or in his mind, without grasping the import of it. The doctrine of the resurrection, given in this chapter, is by way of explanation and interpretation. The Corinthians had not to learn it now for the first time; but their ideas needed correcting, and their memories refreshing.

As we gather from *v.* 12, some of the Corinthians went the length of denying that there was any resurrection from the dead—at least for us. The resurrection of our Saviour seems to have been admitted by them all, living, as they did, twenty-five years after the event. From that admission St. Paul proceeds to argue our resurrection. The Corinthians might naturally share in that incredulity, which had led their neighbours, the Athenians, to scout the idea of any resurrection, even that of our Saviour (Acts xvii. 31, 32). The immortality of the soul was a favourite tenet of the Greek philosophers, especially of Plato and his school. But those same philosophers had a particular antipathy, theoretical of course, to the body. The resurrection of the body, if preached to Plato, would have struck his ears as the announcement of a dire calamity. No wonder then that there were at Corinth unsent and unlicensed teachers who gave out, as

St. Chrysostom tells us, that "the resurrection was the purification of the soul." Of this sort were Hymenæus and Philetus, "saying that the resurrection is past already" (2 Tim. ii. 16, 17), and consequently that it is not a resurrection from the dead. For Jewish prejudice against the resurrection see Luke xx. 27; Acts xxiii. 7, 8.

2. *After what manner I preached unto you.* In the Greek, and in the Latin, these words do not depend on *if you hold fast*, which comes after them, but on the main verb, *I make known*. The original might be rendered thus: *I press upon your recognition the gospel which I preached to you,* . . . (reminding you) *in what terms I preached to you, if you hold it fast* (*i.e.* hoping you hold it fast, as indeed you do), *unless your acceptance of the faith was a mere freak of the hour.*

Believed in vain, that is, 'unless your acceptance of the faith was a mere freak of the hour.' An instance of such *believing in vain* are *they upon the rock, who receive the word with joy, believe for a while, and in time of temptation fall away* (Luke viii. 13).

You have believed, ἐπιστεύσατε. This aorist, which appears again in *v.* 11, called by grammarians the *inceptive aorist*, would be better rendered, *you accepted the faith*. So in Rom. xiii. 11, *now nearer than when we* (first) *believed*, ἢ ὅτε ἐπιστεύσαμεν. It refers to the past act of receiving the faith, not to present abiding faith and settled conviction, which is expressed by the perfect tense, as in 2 Tim. i. 12, *I know whom I have believed*, ᾧ πεπίστευκα.

3. *Which I also received.* For St. Paul's instruction in divine truth see on xi. 23; also Gal. i. 11—19.

According to the scriptures, Ps. xxi.; Isaias liii.: cf. Acts viii. 32—35.

4. *According to the scriptures.* See the references made in Matt. xii. 40; Acts ii. 25—28; xiii. 33—37.

5. *Seen by Cephas* (Luke xxiv. 34). We have no details of this apparition.

By the eleven. All the best MSS. read *by the twelve*, the more difficult, and no doubt, the more correct reading. The reference is to the apparitions recounted, Luke xxiv. 36—43; John xx. 19—29, where at first only ten Apostles were present, St. Thomas being away. Yet we read in Luke xxiv. 33, *They found the eleven gathered together.* Clearly *eleven* and *twelve* are both official numbers of the same assembly of persons from two various points of view. St. Thomas is called by St. John, l.c. *v.* 24, *one of the twelve.*

6. *More than five hundred brethren at once;* probably the apparition recounted in Matt. xxviii. 16—20. The evangelist speaks only of *the eleven disciples* (the Apostles) being there: but in the next verse, where he says *some doubted*, he seems to recognise the presence of other witnesses; for after even the doubts of Thomas were removed (John xx. 28, 29), it is not likely that any further doubt was harboured in the apostolic college. Thus this statement of St. Paul removes what would otherwise have been a difficulty in St. Matthew's narrative.

7. *Seen by James.* When St. Paul wrote, there was only one well-known apostolic bearer of this name, *James the brother of the Lord* (Gal. i. 19: cf. above, note on ix. 5), or *James the Less* (Mark xv. 40), bishop of Jerusalem (Acts xv.), and author of the Canonical Epistle. It was some fourteen years before St. Paul wrote, that Herod *killed James the brother of John* (James the Greater, the Apostle of Spain) *with the sword* (Acts xii. 2). We have no other record of this apparition.

Then by all the apostles. Not the apparition, eight days after the resurrection, when Thomas was present (John xx. 26), but the apparition which ended in the

Ascension (Luke xxiv. 50; Acts i. 9). On Ascension Day the Risen Saviour was seen by the full college of twelve Apostles, including St. Mathias, who, a few days later, was chosen, as St. Peter says, *a witness with us of his resurrection* (Acts i. 22).

That the reference here is not to John xx. 26, is proved by the following considerations. From that verse of the evangelist, compared with the previous verse 19, it appears that *fear of the Jews* kept the Apostles from stirring far abroad that week, and therefore from journeying all the way to Galilee and back to Jerusalem. Therefore the apparition of Matt. xxviii. 16, 17, took place after those eight days: that is, at a later date than the apparition referred to in John xx. 26. But the Apostles can have had no further doubt after that apparition, John xx. 26. Therefore the *some* who *doubted* in Galilee (Matt. xxviii. 17), were other than the eleven Apostles there present. That warrants our identification of the apparition in Matt. xxviii. 17 with the apparition to the five hundred, mentioned by St. Paul, *v.* 6. But St. Paul is evidently relating the apparitions, as many of them as he mentions, in chronological order. The conclusion is manifest.

8. *He was seen by me*, Acts ix. 17, 27; xxvi. 15, 16. St. Paul on this occasion must have seen, not a mere vision of the imagination, such as has often been vouchsafed to other saints, but the real Body of Christ in its proper appearance: else he could not have been, as he here ranks himself, and as it was the especial function of Apostles to be (Acts i. 8, 22; iv. 33), *a witness of the resurrection*.

One born out of due time. The word used, ἔκτρωμα, means a child such as Macduff describes himself: " from my mother's womb untimely ripped." Observe the article, τῷ ἐκτρώματι, *the child born by the caesarean operation*, and therefore born last of all, *youngest and least* (ἐλάχιστος) of the apostolic brotherhood (*v.* 9). Paul was called when the apostolic college was complete, and the Holy Spirit had been sent from heaven. He had none of that formation in the school of Christ on earth, which the other Apostles, even St. Mathias (Acts i. 21, 22), had benefited by.

9. Eph. iii. 8; 1 Tim. i. 12—16.

10. *More abundantly than all they*, whether singly or collectively, the Apostle does not express. For his labours, Rom. xv. 16—20; 2 Cor. xi. 23—28.

The grace of God with me. Better, *the grace of God that is with me.* *Not* here, as in Matt. ix. 13, means, according to Hebrew usage, *not so much.* The grace here spoken of is the grace given for the external work of the apostolate (Eph. iii. 8; Gal. i. 15, 16; Rom. xv. 15, 16), not that given for the receiver's own sanctification: though an argument may be drawn from the one to the other.

13—16. Evidently, if Christ is not risen again, other dead men have no chance of rising again. But this proposition does not logically involve the other, that if other dead rise not, neither is Christ risen. To establish the connection here asserted between Christ's resurrection and that of His saints,—to show that the two resurrections must stand or fall together,—we must observe that the two are bound together at least in the order of possibility. If Christ is risen again in a human body, it is possible for a human body to rise from the dead. Again, if life from the grave for any man is intrinsically impossible and absurd, as those Greeks thought, then neither is *the man Christ Jesus* (1 Tim. ii. 5) risen from the dead. But further than this, the two resurrections reciprocally involve one another in the order of actuality, as appears by the previous doctrine of the head and the members, vi. 15; xii. 27. If the Head is risen, the members must rise after Him, or the mystical Body, which is Christ and His Church, would remain eternally incomplete; and conversely, if the members are never to rise, neither is the Head risen. It may be remarked that this particular argument avails only for the resurrection of the just. Elsewhere (Acts xxiv. 15) St. Paul asserts, *there shall be a resurrection of the just and unjust.*

14—17. If Jesus is not risen, He is not the true Messiah, the taker away of sin, who was to rise again *according to the scriptures* (*v.* 4 with note), as He declared that He would rise again (John ii. 18—22; Matt. xii. 38—40),—not the Son of God, Rom. i. 4.

But more than this. There is argued an objective connection between Christ's resurrection and our justification. To see the connection, we must observe that the Apostle has in mind the present order of Providence, in which holiness and the life of grace for man mean membership with a living Christ (vi. 13—15; xii. 27). But such membership could not be, if Christ had died and not risen again. There would have been then no human holiness, and consequently no remission of sin, since none is justified who is not made holy.

18. *Have perished*, that is, are lost eternally, being *yet in their sins;* since the Jesus in whom they trusted for their expiation, is no true Messiah, if He be not risen from the dead.

19. *We are of all men most miserable*, considering what our eternal lot will be, if we have not *an advocate with the Father*, and if *Jesus Christ the just* is not *the propitiation for our sins* (1 John ii. 1, 2). Most miserable, if we have lost Moses, and have not found the Christ. From the context it would appear that this was all that St. Paul meant to say. He was not thinking of the aids to happiness that Christianity has provided for human society, substantial aids, even apart from the fulfilment of the promises of Christ in the world to come. If,

however, those eternal promises were vain, that temporal happiness would be all based on a delusion, no better than the fancies of children, of which Aristotle writes: " No one would choose to live with a child's mind all his life long, going all lengths of delight over what gives pleasure to children " (*Ethics*, X. iii. 12). Such fond happiness would really be a great misery. You cannot cut Christianity in two, keep the first half only, and call it good. It is no good for earth, if it is no good for heaven.

20. *But now*, as things are. Cf. *And now*, xiii. 13. For *first-fruits* see Leviticus xxiii. 10—21; and for the harvest of the just to rise up out of the earth, *vv.* 42—44 of this chapter.

21. *By a man came death.* Death comes by nature to man as to other animals; but by a supernatural privilege mankind would have been exempt from death but for Adam's sin.

22. The meaning of this verse is, that as no man dies except in consequence of the sin of the first Adam, so no man shall be made alive in the resurrection to glory except through the merits of Christ, the second Adam. For a similar combination of *all* and *all* see Rom. v. 18: *As by the offence of one unto all men to condemnation; so also by the justice of one unto all men to justification of life.*

23. *Who have believed.* These words are absent in all the Greek MSS. except two, not of the best. Two early editions of the Vulgate have them not, nor St. Augustine, nor St. Jerome. Omitting them, we have the text, *then they that are of Christ, in his coming:* to say, that is Christ's saints shall arise at His second coming.

24. *Afterwards the end*, the end of the world, giving place to *a new heaven and a new earth* (Apoc. xxi. 1).

God and the Father is simply *God the Father* (Rom. xv. 6; 2 Cor. i. 3).

He shall have delivered up the kingdom. " The Scripture recognises two kingdoms of God, the one by appropriation, the other by creation. He is King of all, Greeks and Jews, demons and adversaries, on the title of creation. He is King of the faithful, and of the voluntarily obedient and submissive, on the title of appropriation " (St. Chrysostom). It is of the second of these kingdoms that there is question here. As Creator, Jesus Christ is Lord of all for eternity, with the Father and the Holy Ghost. As Redeemer, His kingdom is the Church. This kingdom He will deliver up to His Father, when the warfare of the Church Militant is over, and all enemies are overthrown ; when no more Church government is needed, nor care of Pastor, nor intercession of Priest, nor teaching with authority unto the obedience of faith (Matt. xvi. 19 ; xxviii. 19, 20 ; John x. 11 ; xxi. 17 ; Heb. vii. 25, 26 ; Rom. xvi. 26). Then will be verified the full meaning of His words to His Father : *I have glorified thee on earth ; I have finished the work which thou gavest me to do* (John xvii. 4). Then will He present to His Father His Bride (Apoc. xix. 7), *a glorious church, not having spot or wrinkle, or any such thing* (Eph. v. 27). These must have been some of the *secret words*, which St. Paul heard when he was *caught up into paradise.* (2 Cor. xii. 4).

For *delivered up*, it would suit the Greek as well, and render the meaning truer to our ears, if we read *handed over*, as a victorious general is said to *hand over* to his Sovereign a kingdom which he has won and pacified. Or yet more correctly, taking the Sinaitic and Alexandrine reading, ὅταν παραδιδῷ, *when he hands over. Because thou hast redeemed us to God in thy blood, and hast made us to our God a kingdom* (Apoc. v. 9, 10).

Principality and power and virtue. The two following verses, 25, 26, show clearly that these powers here mentioned are evil, hostile powers, whether of demons, or of men leagued together against Christianity.

25. *For he must reign until*, &c., Ps. cix. 1. *Until* may denote cessation, or it may not; as in Isaias xlvi. 4, according to the Septuagint, we read, *Till you grow old, I am* (God). It depends on the context. The important words in the context here are *reign* and *kingdom*. The reign of Christ will continue or cease according to the nature of the kingdom that He is said to reign over. St. Gregory Nazianzen (Orat. xxx. 4) proceeds as St. John Chrysostom, above quoted, to distinguish what needs distinction here. " He is said to reign in one respect as Almighty, King over willing and unwilling alike: in another respect, as effecting subjection, and placing under His kingly rule us, who are willing to have Him for our King. Of His kingdom, understood in the former way, there shall be no end. But what of the second sort of kingdom? It shall end by His taking us into thorough possession, when we are saved. This shall be the end of it, for why go on effecting subjection, where subjection is perfect and complete ? "

The sum is this. Christ's kingdom as God is eternal as that of His Father, with whom and the Holy Ghost He is one God. The kingdom of *the Man Christ Jesus* (1 Tim. ii. 5) over the Church Militant, as such, ceases when the Church ceases to be militant. The fact is obvious, and St. Paul asserts it here.

Of the kingdom of Christ in the Church Triumphant, St. Paul says nothing. Of such a kingdom, with every member wrapped in the vision of God seen face to face, we have simply no conception. Only St. John tells us that *the Lamb is the lamp thereof* (Apoc. xxi. 23). And the Church, in the Nicene Creed, after the mention of the Last Judgment, rehearses the prophecy: *And of his kingdom there shall be no end* (Luke i. 32 ; Daniel vii. 14), giving us thereby to understand that, in some mysterious manner, the kingdom of the Word Incarnate will continue even after the Judgment day; as He will still be *a priest for ever* (Heb. vii. 21), although " He will then no longer make intercession for us, after He has handed over the kingdom to God the Father " (St. Augustine, *De Trin.* i. 11).

26. *Death destroyed last*, by the general resurrection. The quotation is from Ps. viii. Cf. Heb. ii. 6, 7, 8. Literally the Psalm deals with the beauty of heaven and earth, and the position of man as lord thereof; but in a more exalted sense it points to the Messiah, the chief of the human race.

28. *The Son also himself shall be subject.* There are different sorts of subjection according to the condition of the person made subject. The enemies of Christ, the principalities and powers of evil, wicked reprobates and devils (*vv.* 24, 25) shall be subjected by force. The friends of our Saviour, His elect, saints and angels, shall be subject in adoring love. Christ Himself as God shall be subject to His Father, not by any subjection of inferiority as less to greater, but as true God of true God, owning His Father for the source of the Divinity which He has of Him by way of generation. Christ as Man shall be truly subject to the Father, according as He said, *the Father is greater than I* (John xiv. 28). For though the Humanity of Christ is of divine dignity and sanctity, and calls for the same adoration that is given to God; yet it has not this dignity, sanctity, and title to adoration, of itself, but by reason of the Divinity to which it is united, whereas the Divinity is of itself adorable. In this way Christ as Man is, and ever since the Incarnation has been, subject to and less than the Father, less than Himself as God, and less than the Holy Ghost. Why then does St. Paul say that at the end of the world He *shall*

be subject? No doubt, because when He stands finally with the whole multitude of His elect, with all the members of His Mystical Body complete, the subjection which, as Man and Chief of mankind, He will then exhibit to God, will be of greater amplitude, fulness, and extension. He will be subject to His Father then in us, and—as Man—with us, and we with Him.

That God may be all in all. This takes up the saying of Isaias (ii. 11, 17): *The Lord alone shall be exalted in that day.* The majesty of God shall stand out above all humanity, and all flesh shall be subject, willingly or unwillingly. God is in the living members of the Church on earth, according to the text, *I in them, and thou in me* (John xvii. 23): but He is not yet *all in all.* Imperfection is still in them, and even sin (1 John i. 8); and *the wages of sin, death* (Rom. vi. 23) still awaits them: but in that day sin shall be cast out, and death shall be undone.

29. *They that are baptized for the dead.* Of the many interpretations of these words the least unsatisfactory is the literal, to wit, that when a catechumen died without baptism, a friend had the rite of baptism performed upon himself on behalf of the departed, by way of testifying that the latter had had at least the faith and the baptism of desire, and might therefore be laid to rest in hope of a glorious resurrection. Without either praising or blaming this custom, the Apostle cites it as an instance of faith in the resurrection. The custom was carried on and became an abuse in the hands of heretics, as St. Chrysostom tells us of the Marcionites: "When one of their catechumens is dead, they hide the living man under the bed of the dead one: then they approach the corpse, and converse with it, and ask if it wishes to receive baptism: thereupon, when it answers nothing, the man hidden underneath answers for it, that he would like to be baptized; and so they baptize him

instead of the departed." Punctuate, *If the dead rise not again, why then are they baptized for them?*

30. That is, 'Why do we Apostles lead a life exposed to so many risks (2 Cor. xi. 26), except it be *concerning the hope and resurrection of the dead* (Acts xxiii. 6)? If this be the only life, we ought to take more care of it.'

31. *I die daily,—pressed out of measure above my strength, so as to be weary even of life* (2 Cor. i. 8).

I protest by your glory, νὴ τὴν ὑμετέραν δόξαν, that is, by the glory I have in you, who are *my joy and my crown* (Phil. iv. 1). The Greek possessive pronoun, as used here, represents an objective genitive. Cf. *your mercy*, Rom. xi. 31, with note.

32. Punctuate, *If according to man I fought with beasts at Ephesus, what doth it profit me? If the dead rise not again, let us eat and drink*, &c.

According to man, that is, on mere human motives, as vanity, obstinacy, and the like: as he says (Gal. i. 11), *the gospel preached by me is not according to man, i.e.* does not rest on grounds of mere human credibility. Cf. iii. 3, *walk according to man*, for which (2 Cor. x. 2) he says, *walked according to flesh*. The phrase ought not to be put in parenthesis.

I fought with beasts, ἐθηριομάχησα. St. Ignatius of Antioch, writing to the Romans, uses the same word: "All the way from Syria to Rome I have to fight with beasts, bound as I am to ten leopards, that is, a file of soldiers." This citation from almost a contemporary author, and the fact that there is no record elsewhere of St. Paul being thrown to wild beasts, nor would any magistrate have dared so to treat a Roman citizen (Acts xxii. 26)—compels us to take the phrase metaphorically of some such persons at Ephesus as those who *were hardened and believed not, speaking evil of the way of the Lord before the multitude* (Acts xix. 9). The *no small disturbance*, related in Acts xix. 23, seq., occurred after this Epistle was written.

Let us eat and drink, &c., quoted from Isaias xxii. 13, where they are the words of the Jews scoffing at God's threats to destroy them. On the logical consequence here drawn St. Chrysostom observes: " He uses this language in condescension to the weakness of those whom he addressed. He himself ran not for reward : it was recompense enow for him that his action was pleasing to God. A great reward it is, continually to please Christ ; and, apart from all other remuneration, it is a grand recompense to confront danger in His cause."

St. Paul throughout follows the same line of argu-ment as our Saviour used against the Sadducees (Matt. xxii. 23—34), taking no account of the immortality of the soul as a possibility apart from the resurrection of the body. His opponents perhaps were men like the Sadducees, who *say that there is no resurrection, neither angel, nor spirit* (Acts xxiii. 8). Hence the hypothesis of a disembodied spirit needed no discussing with them. Plato, indeed, had written : " They who have sufficiently purified themselves by philosophy, live without any bodies at all for all time to come." (*Phaedo*, 114 C). But Plato wrote for philosophers, which the Corinthians generally were not (i. 26).

33. *Evil communications.* A line from the *Thais*, a lost play of the Athenian comedian, Menander.

Good manners, ἤθη χρήσθ'. Theodoret understands it of " characters light and easily deceived," this Greek word for *good* often meaning also *goody*.

34. *Awake, ye just.* A better reading is, *awake to justice*, δικαίως. The persons addressed are not the just, but those *some* among the Corinthians *who say that there is no resurrection* (*v.* 12). They are bidden to *sin not* any more by such denial. They are told that they *have not*

the knowledge of God, as our Lord told the Sadducees: *You err, not knowing the scriptures, nor the power of God* (Matt. xxii. 29).

I speak it to your shame. Repeated from vi. 5.

36. *Not quickened except it die first.* So our Lord says: *Unless the grain of wheat falling into the ground die, itself remaineth alone: but if it die, it bringeth forth much fruit* (John xii. 24, 25). Our Lord and His Apostle speak popularly, as Holy Scripture ever does in these physical matters, not with strict scientific accuracy. Strictly speaking, of course, the grain does not die, but the life that was in it, by the process of germination—with all our science, as much a mystery as ever—gives place to the new life of the new wheat. This alteration and replacement of life by life is here, in popular language, called death.

37, 38. *Body*, the new wheat. St. Paul, in these verses, speaks of wheat in terms of the human body, as in *vv.* 42, 43, he speaks of the human body in terms of wheat.

"Of corn there arises corn, and of lentil lentil: so our bodies arise the same, but with increase of glory" (Theodoret).

39—41. The *bodies celestial* are the sun, moon, and stars, here designated (as also the grown corn, *vv.* 37, 38) by the unusual appellation σώματα, which ordinarily means living animal bodies. The reason is, because the Apostle is insisting on the analogies which all these objects bear to the bodies of men.

It seems a mistake to take *bodies celestial and bodies terrestrial* as representing *the resurrection of life* and *the resurrection of judgment* (John v. 29). Of the *celestial* and *terrestrial* each has its own *glory* (*v.* 40); but there is no glory appertaining to *the resurrection of judgment*, that is, to the wicked at the last day. The wicked are not taken into account in this chapter.

And though it be rightly gathered from these verses that there are grades of glory in the resurrection of the just, still it is not the Apostle's direct object to accentuate this gradation. Every manner of variety that he insists upon—variety of *beasts, birds,* and *fishes*—variety of *bodies celestial* and *bodies terrestrial*—variety of *sun, moon,* and *stars*—variety of *star from star*—all is meant to illustrate the one great variety which it is his purpose in this chapter to set in the strongest light, the variety of the *spiritual body* from the *natural body* (*v.* 44). It is as though he had said : ' Do not attempt to draw an argument from the condition of the human body, as we now know it, to the impossibility of a human body risen from the dead. As well might you argue that, because many animals live only on land, there can be no birds or fishes ; or because there are bodies on earth, there can be none in the sky ; or because there is the sun by day, there are no moon and stars by night ; or because a certain star is of this brightness, there can be no other star brighter.' Thus to known varieties of bodies St. Paul adds yet one more, the *reformed body of our lowliness made like to the body of his* (Christ's) *glory* (Phil. iii. 21).

42—44. *It is sown* (cf. Job xiv. 4), that is, man is begotten and, as it were, planted in this world, *in corruption, in dishonour, in weakness,* a creature corruptible, base, infirm.

A natural (or *animal,* ψυχικόν : the same word, ii. 14, is translated *sensual*) *body,* is a body animated by the soul, inasmuch as the soul is the principle of vegetative and animal life, nutrition, growth, sensation.

A spiritual body is a body animated by the soul, inasmuch as the soul is the principle of intellectual life, and, under the grace of God, lends itself also to spiritual and supernatural operations.

The life of the risen body then shall be rather

spiritual than *animal* : though it is not for us to pronounce where spirituality ends and animality begins. In particular, we cannot deny sensation to the bodies of the risen just.

From the four words, *incorruption, glory, power, spiritual,* theologians gather the four endowments of a risen body, impassibility, brightness, agility, subtlety.

45. *Man was made into a living soul,* from Genesis ii. 7. *Soul* here means *a being, animated with a soul* : as in Gen. xlvi. 27, *All the souls of the house of Jacob that went up into Egypt were seventy;* and Apoc. xviii. 13, *merchandise of . . . chariots and slaves and souls of men.* The Latins use *caput* (head) in the same sense.

The *last Adam,* Christ our Lord, *was made into a quickening spirit,* inasmuch as He has the fulness of supernatural life in Himself,—the fulness of grace, and (from the day of His resurrection) also of glory; and also is the principle of that life of grace and glory to us, for soul and body.

47. *Of the earth, earthly.* Because, as St. Augustine explains (*De Civitate Dei,* xiii. 23, 24), "the body of Adam, needing meat and drink, was only saved by the tree of life from the necessity of dying, and was not a spiritual but an animal body."

From heaven, heavenly. Before His Incarnation, our Lord pre-existed in heaven ; the materials of Adam's body pre-existed on earth. From the moment of the Incarnation, the Sacred Humanity had in the hypostatic union a natural and intrinsic title to immortality: immortality was derived to Adam from an extrinsic source. The word *heavenly* is almost certainly an addition to the text : but it is quite the meaning of St. Paul. Many MSS. read, *the Lord from heaven.*

49. *We have borne,* or *we bore* at our birth, ἐφορέσαμεν, *the image of the earthly,* but we laid it aside at our baptism (Rom. vi. 6): thenceforth *let us bear* (φορέσωμεν, *let us take*

J

up and bear) *the image of the heavenly.* A baptized man in the state of grace is a living image of Christ, soul and body, and is already potentially glorified. A less authentic reading is φορέσομεν, *we shall bear*, referring to the actual glorification of our bodies that shall be in the resurrection—if we persevere.

50. *Flesh and blood cannot possess the kingdom of God.* That is, the body *sown in corruption* (*v.* 42), the *natural body* (*v.* 44), *image of the earthly* Adam (*v.* 49). It is not the substance of flesh and blood that is excluded from heaven, but their mortal accidents, bodily needs and passions thence resulting. In the same way St. Paul speaks of *flesh and blood* (Gal. i. 16), and our Saviour Himself (Matt. xvi. 17). The body of flesh and blood, that we have now, is *changed* (*vv.* 51, 52) in quality by being glorified, but it remains the same body: even as the Body of the risen Jesus is the Body that was " born of the Virgin Mary, was crucified, dead, and buried."

It has been argued from this text that in the resurrection the body is bloodless. No doubt, but for the express declaration of our Lord (Luke xxiv. 39), we should be told that it was fleshless also, and with as good reason.

Corruption here means the corruptible body, as such, with all the train of evils attendant thereupon, both moral evils, which go by the name of *the flesh*, in the bad sense of that term (cf. Gal. v. 16, 17, 19, 24; vi. 8), and more particularly, the physical frailty and perishableness of our mortal frame.

51, 52. *I tell you a mystery.* " Something awful and secret, and a thing which not all know, he is about to tell, which showed the great honour he paid the Corinthians, telling them secrets. What then is this? " (St. Chrysostom).

According to the Latin Vulgate and the Rheims version this is the mystery, that while *all rise again, not all* shall have their bodies *changed* to *incorruption, glory,* and *power* (*vv.* 42, 43). But that was no secret to the Corinthians : all the world knew and recognised it, who had any notion of the resurrection at all. Moreover, the whole chapter is written on the theme of the resurrection of the just : the wicked are nowhere considered. The difficulty grows from the consideration of *v.* 52. There the adverbial phrases, *in a moment, in the twinkling of an eye, at the last trumpet,* have no verb to go with, unless they are attached to *rise again* in the previous verse, from which they are separated in the Vulgate by a full stop; and unless the clause, *we shall not all be changed,* is constituted a clumsy parenthesis. In the same *v.* 52, *we* who *shall be changed* stand contrasted, not with the wicked, as supposed from *v.* 51, but with *the dead,* who *shall rise again incorruptible.* Lastly, it makes an awkward juxtaposition, *we shall not all be changed, we shall be changed.* In the Vulgate reading, St. Paul lets the Corinthians into no secret : they had heard already of the resurrection of the just, and could not expect the wicked to rise to glory.

We may well ask what historical authority there is for this reading, so perplexing and unsatisfactory. It has the support of nearly all the Latin Fathers and Latin Versions from the time of Tertullian (third century); and of one Greek MS. of the sixth century. On the other hand it is countenanced by no other Greek MS., no Greek Father, no other than Latin versions, and, in the time of St. Jerome, not by all of them.

There are two variant readings. One, the less common, runs : *We shall all sleep* [die, *v.* 18], *but we shall not all be changed.* This is the reading of the Sinaitic Greek manuscript (fourth century), and of a few other MSS. and versions. It is open to all the difficulties urged against the Vulgate reading.

The other is the reading of the Vatican manuscript (fourth century) πάντες οὐ κοιμησόμεθα, πάντες δὲ ἀλλαγησόμεθα, which (generally with the addition of μὲν after πάντες in the first clause) is followed by the other Greek MSS. for the most part, and by almost all the Greek Fathers. The Vatican reading will translate: *We shall all—not sleep* [die] *—but we shall all be changed.* The question is: What does St. Paul mean by *changed*? In the next verse the meaning is clear: they who are *changed* are opposed to *the dead*, who *rise again incorruptible*: the *changed* then are the living, who *put on incorruption* without passing through death. Such then must be the meaning of *changed* in this verse also. Hence we gather that there is no antithesis between *all* and *not all*: the same collection of persons is spoken of in both clauses. The addition of μὲν therefore is an error. The *all* are *all we* (good Christians, not a word said about the wicked) who are alive at the last day: *we shall not die, but we shall be changed* to incorruption and immortality, and that, *in a moment, in the twinkling of an eye*, &c., this verse 52 following without a break upon 51.

The Vulgate reading, *Omnes quidem resurgemus, sed non omnes immutabimur*, seems traceable to the Sinaitic. Read *dormiemus* for *resurgemus*, and you have the Sinaitic rendered exactly. Then some one took on himself to alter *dormiemus* (*we shall sleep*, or die in hope of resurrection) to *resurgemus* (*we shall rise again*), a most unhappy emendation, if made.

If we take the Sinaitic reading, and put the comma after οὐ instead of before it, we have, πάντες κοιμησόμεθα οὔ, πάντες δὲ ἀλλαγησόμεθα, *we shall all—die, no, but we shall all be changed*, which gives the same sense as the Vatican reading, but is perhaps too smart and antithetical for Pauline Greek. The Vatican position of οὐ (πάντες οὐ κοιμησόμεθα) is supported by 1 John ii. 21, πᾶν ψεῦδος ἐκ τῆς ἀληθείας οὐκ ἔστι. Probably the Vatican MS. is right.

Of the meaning of St. Paul, after years of reflection, I feel confident that it is: *None of us shall die, but we shall all be changed*, the *us* and the *we* being the just who shall be found alive at the judgment day. Cf. notes on 1 Cor. iii. 14; 2 Cor. v. 2—4.

Of the authority assigned to the Latin Vulgate by the Council of Trent, see the remarks in the Preface.

The last trumpet is the last signal given to the camp or army of God, the Church Militant. Cf. Num. x. 2—10.

For the doctrine which this reading contains, see 1 Thess. iv. 14—16, on which St. Augustine writes (*Ad Dulcitium*): "As to the words of the Apostle, he seems to assert that at the end of the world, when the Lord comes and there is to be the resurrection of the dead, some are not to die, but, found alive, are suddenly to be changed to that immortality which is given also to the other saints, and are to be *taken up together with them in the clouds.* Nor has my opinion been any other, as often as I have been minded to think of these words." Such is also the opinion of Tertullian, alleging these passages and 2 Cor. v. 2—4: he adds: "The privilege of this grace awaits those whom the coming of the Lord shall find in the flesh, who for the hardships of the times of Antichrist shall deserve to join the risen by the short way of death blotted out by change" (*De resur. carn.* 41). In this view we have a ready explanation of the saying of St. Peter, repeated in the Creeds, that Jesus of Nazareth *was appointed by God to be judge of the living and of the dead* (Acts x. 42). The contrary opinion on the whole was favoured by St. Augustine, and after him by most of the Latin authorities, but only as an opinion. It went with what we have argued to be a false reading of the present passage in St. Paul.

True *in Adam all die* (*v.* 22) that is, all are in the way of death: but in this last generation death shall be anticipated by the glorious *change*. St. Thomas says of them : " Even though they die not, still there is in them the liability to death, but the penalty is taken away by God " (1a 2æ, q. 81, art. 3, ad 3).

St. Paul here uses the first person in what is called the *communicative sense*, not knowing when the coming of the Lord was to be. Here and in 1 Thess. iv. 15, 17, he associates himself with them who are to be alive at that coming ; elsewhere (vi. 14 ; 2 Cor. iv. 14) with them who are to be raised up, and consequently must have died before. Cf. 2 Thess. ii. 2 ; 2 Pet. iii. 8.

53. In *the dead* who *shall rise again, this corruptible must put on incorruption.* In us *who are alive, who remain unto the coming of the Lord* (1 Thess. iv. 14), and who *shall be changed, this mortal must put on immortality.*

54. *And when.* The best authorities here repeat the whole of the preceding verse, not the latter half only.

Shall come to pass, or simply, *shall be spoken, the saying.*

Death is swallowed up in victory. The Apostle follows a variant Hebrew reading of Isaias xxv. 8 : *He shall cast death down headlong for ever.*

55. Quotation from Osee xiii. 14, more or less according to the Septuagint, which has : *Where is thy plea, O death ? Where is thy sting, O hell ?*

" As it were, sacrificing a thankoffering for victory, and seized with ecstasy from on high, and seeing the future as though it were already accomplished, the Apostle leaps and tramples upon the prostrate form of Death, singing loud the song of triumph " (St. Chrysostom).

The victory of the grave was complete, when the man died: his decease was a total defeat, dissolution and spoliation of his humanity: but when he rises again, victory passes over to his side.

56. *The sting of death,* as it were of a scorpion (Apoc. ix. 10), *is sin,* because it is only through sin that death has been able to slay us (Rom. v. 12).

The strength of sin is the law, because *sin was not imputed when the law was not* (Rom. v. 13; vii. 7—11).

57. *Who has given.* Read, *who gives.* Cf. Rom. vii. 24, 25.

58. "Then let us sit down in religion, and make heaven to be our end" (Jeremy Taylor).

———

CHAPTER XVI.

1. Now concerning the collections that are made for the saints, as I have given order to the churches of Galatia, so do you also. 2. On the first day of the week let every one of you put apart with himself, laying up what it shall well please him; that when I come the gatherings be not then to be made. 3. And when I shall be with you, whomsoever you shall approve by letters, those will I send to carry your bounty to Jerusalem. 4. And if it be meet that I go also, they shall go with me. 5. Now I will come to you, when I shall have passed through Macedonia; for I shall pass through Macedonia. 6. And with you, perhaps, I shall make a stay, or even spend the winter, that you may bring me on my journey whithersoever I shall go. 7. For I will not see you now by the way; for I hope that I shall remain with you some time, if the Lord permit. 8. But I will stay at Ephesus until Pentecost. 9. For a gate is opened to me large and evident, and many adversaries. 10. Now if Timothy come, see that he be with you without fear: for he worketh the work of the Lord, as I also do. 11. Let no man, therefore, despise him, but conduct ye him on his way in peace, that he may come to me: for I look for him with the brethren. 12. As to our brother Apollo, I let you know that I earnestly entreated him to come to you with the brethren: and indeed it was not his will at all to come at this time; but he will come when he shall have leisure. 13. Watch ye, stand fast in the faith, do manfully, and be strengthened. 14. Let all your actions be done in charity. 15. And I beseech you, brethren, (you know

the house of Stephanas, and of Fortunatus, and of Achaicus, that
they are the first-fruits of Achaia, and have dedicated themselves to
the ministry of the saints,) **16.** That you also be subject to such,
and to every one that worketh with us, and laboureth. **17.** And I
rejoice in the presence of Stephanas, and Fortunatus, and Achaicus :
for that which was wanting on your part they have supplied.
18. For they have refreshed both my spirit and yours ; know them,
therefore, that are such. **19.** The churches of Asia salute you.
Aquila and Priscilla salute you much in the Lord, with the church
that is in their house; with whom I also lodge. **20.** All the
brethren salute you. Salute one another with a holy kiss. **21.** The
salutation of me Paul, with my own hand. **22.** If any man love
not our Lord Jesus Christ, let him be Anathema, Maran atha.
23. The grace of our Lord Jesus Christ be with you. **24.** May
charity be with you all in Christ Jesus. Amen.

1. *For the saints,* i.e. *for the poor of the saints that are at
Jerusalem,* Rom. xv. 26, according to the agreement,
Gal. ii. 9, 10. Evidently the community of goods (Acts
ii. 44, 45) was at an end, or no longer sufficed.

To the churches of Galatia, Acts xviii. 23.

2. *On the first day of the week.* Read, *Every first day of
the week,*—already a day of assembly for Christians,
Acts xx. 7 : called *the Lord's day,* Apoc. i. 10.

Put apart with himself. "Make thy house a church,
thy chest a treasury: become a keeper of sacred
moneys, a self-elected steward of the poor: love of thy
king gives thee this priesthood" (St. Chrysostom).

*What it shall well please him. Whatsoever he may be
prospered in,* represents the Greek better.

3. *By letters* should go with *send,* not with *approve.*

4. *That I also go,* as he finally did, Acts xxi. 15.

5. He had intended to come straight to Corinth,
and go thence to Macedonia (2 Cor. i. 16).

7. *Abide with you some time.* He came through
Macedonia, and stayed three months at Corinth (Acts
xx. 1—3).

8. *At Ephesus,* whence he writes this letter, about
Easter.

9. *A gate, large and evident*, a great opening to do good. We have a specimen of the *many adversaries* in Acts xix. 23, seq.

10. *If Timothy come.* Cf. iv. 17. He was coming round by Macedonia (Acts xix. 22). This Epistle was written after his start from Ephesus.

11. *Let no man despise him.* Cf. *Let no man despise thy youth* (1 Tim. iv. 12), written some seven years after this.

Him with the brethren, Timothy and his companion Erastus (Acts xix. 22), and perhaps some Macedonians.

12. *Apollo*, iii. 4—6; Acts xviii. 24—28. Apollo, like Barnabas, *was a good man and full of the Holy Ghost* (Acts xi. 23). There is no sign of his at all lending himself to those admirers of him at Corinth who set him up as greater than Paul. There was evidently a request from Corinth for his return.

With the brethren, bearers of this letter.

13, 14. An exhortation, prompted by thought of the party strife which had arisen about Apollo.

" Under this appearance of exhortation he is really reprehending their sloth. Therefore he says, *watch ye,* implying that they were asleep; *stand fast*, implying that they were shaken; *do manfully and be strengthened*, showing that they were turning soft; *let all your things be done in charity*, arguing their party strife. The one exhortation is against deceivers, *watch ye, stand fast*. The other is against the malevolent, *do manfully*. The third is against factious persons and promoters of dissension, *let all your actions be done in charity, which is the bond of perfection* (Col. iii. 14), and root and source of good. What means, *all actions in charity*? It means that, whether one finds fault, or commands, or is commanded, or learns, or teaches, all must be with charity. All the previous evils mentioned in this Epistle came about from neglect of this virtue. But

for such neglect, they would not have been *puffed up*
(v. 2); they would not have said, *I am of Paul, and I of
Apollo* (i. 12).   Had charity been among them, they
would not have *gone to be judged without* (vi. 1 : cf. v. 12),
or rather they would not have had lawsuits at all (vi. 7).
Had charity been there, that man would not have
taken his father's wife (v. 1); they would not have
despised the weak brethren (viii. 10, 11); they would
not have had divisions (xi. 18, 19); they would not
have been vainglorious of their gifts (xii. — xiv.).
Therefore he says, *let all things be done with . charity* "
(St. Chrysostom).

15. *The house of Stephanas, first-fruits of Achaia*
(Greece), i. 16.   All the best MSS. omit all mention of
Fortunatus and Achaicus in this verse.

The words *you know* to the end of the verse make a
parenthesis.

16. *Subject to such*, not as to superiors, but with the
deference due to men of merit and virtue.   A better
translation might be, *that you second such*.

17. The three persons here mentioned are generally
understood to have been the bearers of the letter of
the Corinthians to St. Paul at Ephesus, and of his
reply, this Epistle.   Fortunatus and Achaicus are not
mentioned elsewhere.

That which was wanting on your part.   Better, *the lack
of you.*   These envoys had come on behalf of all the
Corinthians, and their presence in a manner made up
for the absence of the rest.   It is not a reproach, but
a commendation.

18. *They have refreshed both my spirit and yours.*   The
letter they had carried and their oral address was a
refreshment to the spirit as well of St. Paul, who
received it, as of the Corinthians, who sent it.

Know such.   For this use of *know* (ἐπιγιγνώσκειν) see
xiii. 12.

19. *The churches of Asia* (Acts xix. 10), that is, the Mediterranean shore of Asia Minor.

For *Aquila and Priscilla* see Acts xviii. 2, 3, 18, 26; Rom. xvi. 3, 4.

The church that is in their house (Rom. xvi. 5), the Ephesian Christians who met to celebrate the holy mysteries in the house of Aquila and Priscilla, no special sanctuaries being as yet built for that purpose. The faithful who met for Mass at such places as Hindlip Castle in the days of persecution in England, might have been called *the church that is in the house* of the noble family who owned the place.

20. *A holy kiss.*   Cf. St. Chrysostom, quoted on 2 Cor. xiii. 12.   For the practice among the Jews see 1 Kings xx. 21; 2 Kings xix. 39; Matt. xxvi. 48; Acts xx. 37.   Among the first Christians, Rom. xvi. 16; 1 Thess. v. 26.   As practised in the Christian assemblies, the Apostolic Constitutions restrained it to those of the same sex.

21. *With my own hand.*   The rest of the letter was in the hand apparently of Sosthenes (i. 1), as that to the Romans was written by Tertius (Rom. xvi. 22). *The salutation of Paul with* his *own hand* was *the sign in every epistle* (2 Thess. iii. 17) of its genuineness,—a sign not wholly uncalled for (2 Thess. ii. 2).

22. *Anathema,* Greek for *a thing accursed.   Maran atha,* two Aramaic words, mean either *The Lord is come* (Phil. iv. 5), or *May the Lord come* (Apoc. xxii. 20).

SECOND EPISTLE TO THE CORINTHIANS.

INTRODUCTION.

St. Paul had sent Timothy as his envoy to the Corinthians (1 Cor. iv. 17; xvi. 10). Of the result of this mission we hear nothing. Timothy certainly returned, and was St. Paul's amanuensis in writing this Second Epistle. After Timothy St. Paul had sent another envoy to Corinth, Titus, whose return he awaited with the keenest anxiety (ch. vii.). Meanwhile, driven from Ephesus by the sedition of the silversmiths (Acts xix.), the Apostle had gone to Troas, and thence to Macedonia (ch. ii. 12, 13; Acts xx. 1), where Titus found him and reported on the partial success of the First Epistle. From some city of Macedonia (tradition names Philippi) St. Paul wrote this Second Epistle, some five months after the First, that is, about the month of September, A.D. 58, and gave the letter to Titus to carry back to Corinth.

CHAPTER I.

1. Paul, an apostle of Jesus Christ by the will of God, and Timothy our brother, to the church of God that is at Corinth, with all the saints who are in all Achaia: 2. Grace to you and peace from God our Father, and from the Lord Jesus Christ. 3. Blessed be the God and Father of our Lord Jesus Christ, the Father of mercies, and the God of all consolation; 4. Who comforteth us in all our tribulations, that we also may be able to comfort them who

are in any distress, by the exhortation wherewith we also are exhorted by God. **5.** For as the sufferings of Christ abound in us, so also by Christ doth our comfort abound. **6.** Now whether we be in tribulation, it is for your exhortation and salvation; or whether we be comforted, it is for your consolation; or whether we be exhorted, it is for your exhortation and salvation, which worketh the enduring of the same sufferings which we also suffer. **7.** That our hope for you may be steadfast, knowing that as you are partakers of the sufferings, so shall you be also of the consolation. **8.** For we would not have you ignorant, brethren, of our tribulation, which came to us in Asia, that we were pressed out of measure above our strength, so that we were weary even of life: **9.** But we had in ourselves the answer of death, that we should not trust in ourselves, but in God who raiseth the dead; **10.** Who hath delivered, and doth deliver us out of so great dangers; in whom we hope that he will yet also deliver us: **11.** You helping withal in prayer for us, that, for this gift obtained for us by many persons, thanks may be given by many in our behalf. **12.** For our glory is this, the testimony of our conscience, that in simplicity of heart and sincerity of God, and not in carnal wisdom, but in the grace of God, we have conversed in this world, and more abundantly toward you. **13.** For we write no other things to you than what you have read and known, and I hope that you shall know unto the end; **14.** As also you have known us in part, that we are your glory, as you also are ours on the day of our Lord Jesus Christ. **15.** And in this confidence I had a mind to come to you before, that you might have a second favour; **16.** And to pass by you into Macedonia, and again from Macedonia to come to you, and by you to be brought on my way toward Judæa. **17.** When, therefore, I had a mind to do this, did I use levity? or the things that I purpose, do I purpose according to the flesh, that there should be with me IT IS, and IT IS NOT? **18.** But God is faithful; for our preaching which was to you was not IT IS, and IT IS NOT. **19.** For the Son of God, Jesus Christ, who was preached among you by us, by me, and Silvanus, and Timothy, was not IT IS, and IT IS NOT; but IT IS was in him. **20.** For all the promises of God are in him IT IS: therefore also by him, Amen to God, unto our glory. **21.** Now he that confirmeth us with you in Christ, and he that hath anointed us, is God; **22.** Who also hath sealed us, and given the pledge of the Spirit in our hearts. **23.** But I call God to witness upon my soul, that to spare you I come not as yet to Corinth; not because we lord it over your faith, but we are helpers of your joy: for in faith you stand.

1, 2. The opening resembles that of the First Epistle. Timothy is now amanuensis instead of Sosthenes, as he is also in the letters to the Philippians, Colossians, Thessalonians, and to Philemon. *Achaia* of course is Greece.

3. *The God and Father of our Lord Jesus Christ.* Cf. Eph. i. 17: *the God of our Lord Jesus Christ, the Father of glory;* and John xx. 19: *I ascend to my Father and to your Father, to my God and to your God.*

4. *By the exhortation wherewith we are exhorted by God,* should be, *by the comfort wherewith we are comforted by God.* The same words are used as in the previous member, παρακλήσεως, παρακαλούμεθα, and should have the same translation, *comfort,* although in another context they might mean *exhortation* and *exhort.*

5. *The sufferings of Christ, i.e.* the sufferings which Christ bore first, and left for us to bear the like in imitation of him, as the Apostle says elsewhere, to *fill up those things that are wanting of the sufferings of Christ* (Col. i. 24).

6. The first thing to be done for this verse is to strike out the words, *or whether we be exhorted, it is for your exhortation,* which, as all the Greek MSS. show, is merely a second and mistaken version of the clause already correctly rendered, *or whether we be comforted, it is for your consolation.* See above on *v.* 4. The word *exhortation* in the first clause is also to be altered to *consolation.* For *worketh the enduring* we should read *is wrought in the enduring.*

There are difficulties even in the Greek MSS., not so much that the words are uncertain, but the clauses have been inverted, and the order of them must remain doubtful. The following translation is presented as probable: it is taken in the main from the Vatican MS.: *Now whether we be in tribulation, it is for your consolation and salvation, which is wrought out in the enduring of the same*

*sufferings which we also suffer : or whether we be comforted, it
is for your consolation.*

Which is wrought, τῆς ἐνεργουμένης. It seems better to
take this as passive. All the other passages in which
this form occurs are Rom. vii. 5; 2 Cor. iv. 12;
Eph. iii. 20; Col. i. 29; 1 Thess. ii. 13; 2 Thess. ii. 7;
James v. 16. The passive sense suits them all, except
perhaps the last.

The meaning is thus explained by St. Chrysostom :
" Your salvation comes, not by the mere fact of your
having believed, but further by your suffering the same
things as us and enduring. Just as an athlete is admired
when he appears in good condition, having his skill self-
contained in himself; but when he goes to work, and
bears blows, and strikes his adversary, then he is
especially brilliant, because then especially his fine
condition is put to act, and the proof of his skill is
shown forth ; so your salvation is then more put to act
(ἐνεργεῖται), that is, is shown, is increased, is intensified,
when it has the quality of endurance, when it suffers
and bears all bravely. And he did not say *which worketh*
(τῆς ἐνεργούσης), but *which is wrought* (τῆς ἐνεργουμένης),
showing that along with their good will grace also
contributes much, working in them."

Whether we be comforted, it is for your consolation, is
explained by *v.* 4.

7. *That our hope for you,* should be, *And our hope for
you is.* The Vatican MS., with other Greek MSS. and
Fathers, place this clause, *And our hope for you is steadfast,*
in the middle of the previous verse. But it suits the
context better here, where it is placed by equally good
authorities.

8. *In Asia,* that is, at Ephesus (1 Cor. xvi. 8, 19).
What the *tribulation* was, the Corinthians knew, but we
do not. It may have been the tumult of the silversmiths
(Acts xix.), or some grievous malady.

So that we were wearied even of life, more exactly, *so that we despaired even of life*.

Above our strength. What is said in the next verse, *that we should not trust in ourselves, but in God*, shows that the Apostle speaks of mere human strength. There is then no contradiction with 1 Cor. x. 13.

9. " What is *the answer of death ?* The sentence, the judgment, the expectation: for such was the voice of facts, such the answer returned by circumstances, that we should certainly die " (St. Chrysostom).

The latter part of the verse signifies that deliverance from so great dangers was tantamount to a resurrection from the dead. Cf. Rom. iv. 17; Heb. xi. 19.

10. *Dangers.* A better reading is *deaths. We trust,* ἠλπίκαμεν: this perfect (found, John v. 45; 1 Cor. xv. 19; 1 Tim. iv. 10; v. 5) denotes well-established and assured confidence, a *rest in hope* (Ps. xv. 9).

11. Better—*that from many* [glad] *faces thanks may be given on our behalf for this gift obtained for us by the prayers of many.* The objection to translating προσώπων *persons* here is that nowhere else in the Bible is the word so used.

12. For *carnal wisdom* see 1 Cor. i. 17, 19; ii. 1, 4, 13, 14.

We have conversed elsewhere, and more abundantly towards you, *i.e.* we have borne ourselves and taught elsewhere, and with more particular care at Corinth. There the Apostle would not accept the remuneration which he took in other churches, xi. 7—9; 1 Cor. ix. 1—15.

13. *What you have read and known.* Better, *what you read or recognise*, ἀναγινώσκετε ἢ καὶ ἐπιγινώσκετε. The former of these two words is the ordinary Greek word for *to read*, meaning properly to *recognise*. St. Paul plays upon this original meaning; and in order to show that he does so, he adds the second word, meaning also *to recognise* (cf. on 1 Cor. xiii. 12). Hence the meaning is well given by St. Chrysostom: " Reading you recognise

(ἀναγινώσκοντες ἐπιγινώσκετε) : . . . the knowledge that you had before accords with the reading (συνᾴδει τῇ ἀναγνώσει ἡ γνῶσις)." Cf. iii. 2, where there is a similar play upon *known and read*, γινωσκομένη καὶ ἀναγινωσκομένη.

The colon at the end of this verse in the English editions is a mistake : it should be only a comma, as in the Clementine Vulgate.

14. It would be clearer if this verse were made to begin at *And I hope* in the verse previous, and were printed thus : *And I hope that you shall recognise entirely (as also you have recognised us in part) that we are your glory, etc.* There is an antithesis between *in part*, ἀπὸ μέρους, and *entirely*, ἕως τέλους. The latter phrase is equal εἰς τέλος in St. John xiii. 1. The translation, *unto the end*, loses the antithesis.

In the day of our Lord, "that dread and awful day in which all things are revealed ; then shall we glory in you and you in us " (St. Chrysostom).

Thus far the Preface of the Epistle. Dividing the Epistle into three parts, Apologetic, Hortatory, and Polemic, the Apologetic portion commences at the next verse, and ends at vii. 16. It is St. Paul's defence of himself against the calumnies of false apostles.

15. *In this confidence.* "In what confidence ? In strong trust in you, in glorying in you, in being your glory, in loving you intensely, in being conscious of no evil, in assurance of our proceedings being all spiritual, and having you as witnesses thereof " (St. Chrysostom).

To come to you before I went to Macedonia. This intention the Apostle must have signified to the Corinthians, perhaps by some epistle now lost.

A second grace, i.e. a second visit.

16. *To pass by you into Macedonia.* This visit was given up. The Apostle announces his change of purpose : *Now I will come to you when I shall have passed*

K

through Macedonia (1 Cor. xvi. 5). So indeed he did
(Acts xx. 1, 2).

Thus what was to have been the *second grace* became
the only *grace* or visit he paid them on this journey.
He comforted them with the hope that he would not
see them merely *by the way*, but would *abide some time*
with them (1 Cor. xvi. 7). His stay amounted in fact
to *three months* (Acts xx. 3).

17. These interrogations amount to negations : ' I did
not *use lightness*, *i.e.* did not change my mind out of mere
fickleness. How is that shown ? By this, that my
purposes are not made *according to the flesh*, as a head-
strong self-will carries men now here now there. The
fleshly man is free and may go anywhere : the spiritual
man is governed and restrained by the Spirit. Therefore I was not able to come straight from Ephesus to
Corinth, because the Spirit would not let me.' So Paul
and Silas once before *attempted to go into Bithynia, and the
Spirit of Jesus suffered them not* (Acts xvi. 7). Thus it
rested not with the Apostle in his purposes finally to
decide *It is* and *It is not;* or better, according to the
Greek, *yea, yea,* and *nay, nay;* but his purpose was conditioned upon the Spirit approving it. It follows that
St. Paul's first purpose in regard of this journey was
not the prompting of the Spirit, but of his own fallible
human judgment. Cf. xii. 8, 9. But from this a difficulty arises, as St. Chrysostom puts it : " If there is not
with you *yea, yea,* and *nay, nay,* but what you now say,
you afterwards overturn, as you have done in the matter
of this visit, woe betide us, if perchance the like has
happened in your preaching also." To dispel this alarm
is the purpose of the next five verses.

18. *God is faithful* (repeated, 1 Cor. i. 9; *ib.* x. 13;
1 Thess. v. 24). It would be to no purpose appealing
to the faithfulness of God, and of the Son of God
(*vv.* 19, 20), unless St. Paul meant to imply, and his

hearers understood, that in his preaching he represented to them God and His Christ, and was the inspired herald of Him who *was called Faithful and True* (Apoc. xix. 11). Cf. xiii. 3; Gal. i. 8, 11, 12; Luke x. 16; John xvi. 13.

Our preaching was not, It is, and It is not. Altogether unlike the preaching of the Church of England as to the Real Presence.

19. *Silvanus*, otherwise called Silas, for whom see Acts xv. 22, to xviii. 5; also 1 Thess. i. 1; 2 Thess. i. 1.

On the text cf. Heb. xiii. 8.

20. The first part of this verse might be more intelligibly translated: *For of all the promises of God, in him is yea, i.e. the accomplishment.* All the promises of God are accomplished in Christ Jesus, the Messianic promises of the Old Law (vii. 1; Rom. ix. 4; Gal. iii. 16, 21; Heb. vi. 12; vii. 6; xi. 13, 17), and as we expect to see, the promises of the New Law, the permanence of the Church, the efficacy of the sacraments, the resurrection of the body, and life everlasting.

Amen to God. The practice of answering *amen* at the end of public prayers was already established (1 Cor. xiv. 16). The whole verse then means: 'All the promises of God for our salvation have their accomplishment through Christ: therefore through Him, in faith and in acknowledgment, be the hymn of praise ratified by the voice of the faithful to the glory of God by our ministry.'

Unto our glory. A better reading is *unto glory through us.* The *us* of this verse and of *vv.* 18, 19, 21, 22, is not all the faithful, but the select few who are *ministers of Christ and dispensers of the mysteries of God* (1 Cor. iv. 1).

21. *Confirmeth us*, the teachers, *with you*, the taught. *Hath anointed us*, χρίσας. This word, from which the name of *Christ* (the Anointed) is derived, is used only in four other places in the New Testament (Luke iv. 18;

Acts iv. 27 ; x. 38 ; Heb. i. 9), and in all four of our
Saviour Himself, who, as St. Gregory Nazianzen (Orat.
10) puts it, has " His Humanity so anointed with His
Divinity as that both are made one." Here then the
word must denote some singularly close assimilation to
Christ, such as is not affirmable of the general body of
the faithful, but of those who represent Christ and bear
His person before the rest, namely, the pastors of His
flock on earth. They are *anointed* inasmuch as they are
associated with the Supreme Shepherd, and adorned
with the graces proper to their pastoral charge. The
combination, χριστόν χρίσας, as it were *Christ* and *Christ-
making*, is not merely accidental.

There is no allusion to any material anointing with
oil. Still less can this verse be alleged in evidence of
the Sacrament of Confirmation, a sacrament proper to
all the faithful, whereas what is said here is said only of
the priests and pastors of the Church.

22. Cf. v. 5 : *God, who hath given us the pledge of the
Spirit ;*—Eph. i. 13, 14 : *You were signed with the Holy
Spirit of promise, who is the pledge of our inheritance ;*—Eph.
iv. 30 : *the Holy Spirit of God, whereby you were sealed unto
the day of redemption.* From these passages it appears
that the Spirit Himself is the *seal*, marking us for God's
own, and also the *pledge* (or *earnest*) of a still better
participation of divine gifts in the life to come.

In the three passages quoted, all the faithful are
addressed, and there appears to be a reference to the
rite which made them Christians, to wit, the two sacraments of Baptism and Confirmation. In the verse now
under consideration, St. Paul speaks of himself and his
fellow-ministers only. From the parallelism of the other
passages there is reason to think that the Apostle refers
here to the rite whereby he and they were made ministers
of Christ, which was of course the Sacrament of Order.
Cf. Acts xiii. 2, 3.

This verse should have been the conclusion of the chapter.

23. *I came not any more to Corinth.*   The Apostle first came to Corinth from Athens, and stayed there eighteen months (Acts xviii. 1, 11); then went to Ephesus (Acts xviii. 19; xix. 1).   From that city, as we have seen, he intended to go again straight to Corinth, instead of which he went to Macedonia first, and then to Corinth. During the delay of this his second visit, the Corinthians must have complained that Paul *came not any more to Corinth.*   He says that it was in mercy that he came not, *sparing you,* for there was much to correct, as indeed there was at a later time,—see xii. 20, 21.

Not because, better, *not that.*   Some words are understood, as, 'In my delay, and in writing meanwhile the First Epistle with those strong reprehensions, it was not that I wished to *lord it over your faith.*'   This phrase is like our 'abuse your generosity.'   It is probably what some at Corinth said of St. Paul: 'He finds us devout believers, and lords it over us accordingly:' to which St. Paul replies: 'Nay rather I would be a *helper of your joy,* my words and action towards you turning to the common joy of us all,'—cf. ii. 3.

For in faith you stand.   "In the construction the word μὲν is left out, so that it should be τῇ μὲν γὰρ πίστει ἑστήκατε.   He means: In the matter of faith I in no way blame you: you are sound on that point: but you do offend on other points, which need correction" (Theodoret).   The clause with *but* (δὲ), antithetical to μὲν (*indeed*), is found in the next words, *But I determined* (ἔκρινα δὲ).   Hence it appears that, *In faith you stand,* should not be separated from, *But I determined,* by a full stop, still less by the division of a verse, and less still should it be in a separate chapter.

CHAPTER II.

1. But I determined this with myself, that I would not come to you again in sorrow: 2. For if I make you sorrowful, who is he then that should make me glad, but he who is made sorrowful by me? 3. And I wrote this same to you, that I may not, when I come, have sorrow upon sorrow from them of whom I ought to rejoice; having confidence in you all, that my joy is the joy of you all. 4. For out of much affliction and anguish of heart I wrote to you with many tears; not that you should be made sorrowful, but that you might know the charity I have more abundantly toward you. 5. And if any one have caused grief, he hath not grieved me, but in part; that I may not charge you all. 6. To him who is such a one this rebuke is sufficient, which is given by many: 7. So that on the contrary you should rather forgive him, and comfort him, lest perhaps such a one be swallowed up with over-much sorrow. 8. Wherefore I beseech you, that you would confirm your charity toward him. 9. For to this end also did I write, that I might know the experiment of you, whether you be obedient in all things. 10. And to whom you have forgiven anything, I also: for what I forgave, if I have forgiven anything, for your sakes have I done it in the person of Christ, 11. That we may not be circumvented by Satan: for we are not ignorant of his devices. 12. And when I was come to Troas for the gospel of Christ, and a door was opened to me in the Lord, 13. I had no rest in my spirit, because I found not Titus my brother; but bidding them farewell, I went from thence to Macedonia. 14. Now thanks be to God, who always causeth us to triumph in Christ Jesus, and maketh manifest the odour of his knowledge by us in every place. 15. For we are unto God the good odour of Christ in them who are saved, and in them who perish. 16. To some, indeed, the odour of death unto death; but to the others the odour of life unto life: and for these things who is so sufficient? 17. For we are not as many, adulterating the word of God: but with sincerity, but as from God, in the sight of God we speak in Christ.

1. *In sorrow* and severity.

2. *Who is he then?* καὶ τίς; for which cf. Mark x. 26, καὶ τίς δύναται σωθῆναι; *who then can be saved?* Also ii. 16, καὶ πρὸς ταῦτα τίς ἱκανος; *who then is sufficient for these things?* In this verse the Apostle begins to lead up to

the case of the incestuous man (1 Cor. v. 1—5), to whom he pointedly refers in *vv.* 6, 7.

3. *And I wrote this same to you*, namely, the reprehensions contained in the first six chapters of the First Epistle.

My joy is the joy of you all. Therefore the joy mentioned in *v.* 2, which the Apostle conceived at the Corinthians' sorrow and repentance, ended in being no selfish but a common joy.

4. *I wrote to you* in that First Epistle.

5. *He hath not grieved me* alone, *but*, &c. Cf. John xii. 44 : *He that believeth in me, doth not believe in me* alone, *but in him that sent me* : also Jerem. vii. 22, 23.

But in part, that I may not charge you all. These words are unintelligible as they stand. *You all* is really the object, not of *charge*, but of the previous *grieved*. 'He has not grieved me alone, but in some sort and proportion he has grieved you all.' Thus the common grief at the sin answers to the common joy (*v.* 3) at the repentance. The words, *that I may not charge*, ἵνα μὴ ἐπιβαρῶ, are parenthetic. They answer exactly to the Attic phrase, ἵνα μηδὲν φορτικὸν λέγω, *to say nothing burdensome*, which did duty for our polite parenthesis, *if you will allow me to say so*.

6. *Which is given by many*, that is, by the Corinthian Church, joining with St. Paul in the censure of the incestuous man (1 Cor. v. 4, 5), superiors passing and promulgating the decree, inferiors obeying and executing it.

8. *Confirm your charity towards him.* "Unite the member to the body, add the sheep to the fold, show him warm affection" (Theodoret). The pronoun *your* is an addition of the English translator, not in the Latin, nor in the Greek, κυρῶσαι εἰς αὐτὸν ἀγάπην, *ratify charity towards him*, *i.e.* gave him the kiss of peace.

9. *To this end also did I write* (in the First Epistle), *that I may know*, or *in order to know, the experiment of you*,

or *the proof of you*, as in Phil. ii. 22, *know ye the proof of him* (Timothy), where the same phrase is used.

Whether you be obedient in all things.   The command to cut off the incestuous man from the communion of the faithful (1 Cor. v. 13), equally with the present command to readmit him, put to proof the obedience of the Corinthians.   The *I beseech you* of *v.* 8 is tantamount to an injunction.

10. *To whom you have forgiven.*   Read *you forgive*, χαρίζεσθε.   And then, not wishing to seem to anticipate their act, he adds : *if I have forgiven anything.*

In the person of Christ, or, *in the face*, that is, *in the presence of Christ* (ἐν προσώπῳ, iv. 6; v. 12), Christ, as it were, looking on and approving: cf. 1 Cor. v. 4.   So ἐν προσώπῳ αὐτοῦ, Prov. viii. 30, means *in his presence.* See on *v.* 17.

11. *Overreached by Satan.*   The verb here used, πλεονεκτεῖν, means *to take more than one's share.*   St. Chrysostom observes on the appositeness of the word. When Satan, he says, tempts us to fornication, or other open sin, he uses his own weapons.   But when under pretence of repentance he leads on to excessive dejection and despair, he snatches our weapons from our hands, and uses them against us : that is indeed taking more than his share.

His devices, to lead to evil by abuse and overdoing of what is good, as here by *overmuch sorrow* (*v.* 7).

From this passage of the pardon of the Corinthian, St. Thomas (Sup. q. 25, art. 1) and other theologians argue the Church's power of granting Indulgences : for it would have been a poor favour to release the man from his canonical penance, and leave him to meet those liabilities in Purgatory which he would otherwise have discharged by undergoing that penance.

12. *Come to Troas*, a second visit, the first being that mentioned, Acts xvi. 8.

A door was opened, 1 Cor. xvi. 9.

13. *No rest, because I found not Titus,* that is, because I had no tidings from Corinth, to which city Titus had been sent to report to St. Paul how his First Epistle was taken there. It was as messenger from Corinth that Titus was so desiderated. This is shown by vii. 5, seq.

14. *Maketh us to triumph,* better, *leadeth us in triumph,* θριαμβεύοντι ἡμᾶς, not as vanquished men, in which sense the verb is used, Col. ii. 15,—cf. Cleopatra's οὐ θριαμβεύσομαι, said as she took the poison,—but as associates in the victory of His Divine Son.

Observe *always . . . in every place.*

The odour of his knowledge. " In calling our present knowledge an *odour of knowledge,* he teaches us two things, first that it is a small part of perfect knowledge, and then that perfect knowledge is hidden, but shall be made manifest in time, after the likeness of incense, which, thrown on a fire in a chamber, emits its fragrance outside, so that they who come across it, enjoy the fragrance without seeing the fragrant body " (Theodoret).

15. *Are saved . . . perish,* literally, *in the way of salvation, in the way of perdition,*—an instance of the classical use of the Greek present participle.

16. *The odour of death,* as of a dead thing, *stinking before* them (Exod. v. 21), and cast aside with loathing : so some men reject the gospel *unto death,* that is, to their own spiritual death and damnation (Mark xvi. 16).

The odour of life, and sweetness, and attractiveness *unto life* everlasting. For the two different effects of the Word of God, cf. Luke ii. 34 ; John xii. 48 ; Matt. xi. 21. Nothing is more clearly contained in Holy Writ than this, that the teaching of Christ and of the envoys of Christ to men is not a teaching which it is open to mankind to reject with impunity. The message is not : ' Here is a way, one of many good ways, if you like to take it :' but, as St. Peter put it on the day of Pentecost : *Save yourselves from this perverse generation* (Acts ii. 40). Therefore a Church whose chief mark is " comprehensiveness," cannot be the Church of Christ.

Who is so sufficient ? So should be omitted. The answer is that no man of his own strength and ability is sufficient for this ministry, and no man at all anyhow except those, *whom God hath made fit ministers of the new testament*, iii. 5, 6, which verses carry the Apostle's reply to his own question. *Quis tam* (Vulg.) may be for *Quisnam*.

17. *Adulterating the word of God.* There is a verse of the Roman poet, Ennius, *non cauponantes bellum, sed belligerantes*, " not playing the huckster in war, but waging war." The Apostle's word καπηλεύοντες answers exactly to *cauponantes*, " playing the huckster." St. Chrysostom explains : " this is to play the huckster, when one adulterates the wine, when one sells for money what one ought to give for nothing." He quotes Isaias i. 22, as it is in the Greek : *Thy hucksters mingle the wine with water.* There are then two ideas in the phrase : first, that of adulterating the word of God with human conceits and inventions calculated to draw the applause of the hearers; and secondly, that of turning preaching into a mere trade and means of money-making. The *many* adulterators or hucksters are the teachers who set up to outbid St. Paul at Corinth, with whom he contrasts himself, 1 Cor. ii. 13; iii. 14, 15; iv. 19, 20; viii. and ix. See below, iv. 2, 6.

As from God, in the sight of God, in Christ. This expresses the meaning of what is rendered in *v.* 10, *in the person of Christ.*

CHAPTER III.

1. Do we begin again to commend ourselves? or do we need (as some do) epistles of commendation to you, or from you? 2. You are our epistle, written in our hearts, which is known and read by all men: 3. You being made manifest that you are the epistle of Christ, ministered by us, and written not with ink, but with the Spirit of the living God; not in tables of stone, but in fleshy tables of the heart. 4. And such confidence we have through Christ toward God: 5. Not that we are sufficient to think anything of ourselves, as of ourselves; but our sufficiency is from God: 6. Who also hath made us fit ministers of the new testament; not in the letter, but in the spirit: for the letter killeth, but the spirit giveth life. 7. Now if the ministration of death, engraven with letters upon stones, was glorious, so that the children of Israel could not steadfastly behold the face of Moses, for the glory of his countenance; which is done away; 8. How shall not the ministration of the Spirit be rather in glory? 9. For if the ministration of condemnation be glory, much more the ministration of justice aboundeth in glory. 10. For even that which was glorious in this part was not glorified, by reason of the glory that excelleth. 11. For if that which is done away was glorious, much more that which remaineth is in glory. 12. Having, therefore, such hope, we use much confidence; 13. And not as Moses put a veil over his face, that the children of Israel might not steadfastly look on the face of that which is made void: 14. But their senses were made dull: for until this day the self-same veil in the reading of the old testament remaineth not taken away, (because in Christ it is done away.) 15. But even until this day, when Moses is read, the veil is upon their heart. 16. But when they shall be converted to the Lord, the veil shall be taken away. 17. Now the Lord is a Spirit: and where the Spirit of the Lord is, there is liberty. 18. But we all, beholding the glory of the Lord with face uncovered, are transformed into the same image from glory to glory, as by the Spirit of the Lord.

1. *Epistles of commendation*, or letters of introduction, see examples in Acts xv. 25—27; xviii. 27. The word συνιστᾶν, or συνιστάνειν, here translated *commend*, means to *introduce* one person to another. St. Paul's detractors at Corinth would have it that he was always introducing, or intruding, himself and his own praises.

2, 3. St. Paul's reply is : ' You and your growth in Christian life are our letter of introduction : any one may read it ; and that letter we carry about with us everywhere, as you are written in our hearts.'   Cf. 1 Cor. ix. 2, *You are the seal of my apostleship.*

The metaphor of the *letter* is somewhat varied.   In *v.* 3 the letter is the Christianity written in the hearts of the Corinthians by Christ our Lord through St. Paul's instrumentality ; while in *v.* 2 the letter is two-fold, first, as in *v.* 3, the Corinthians and their Christianity ; secondly, the memory of the Corinthians written in the heart of the Apostle.   The metaphor would be clearer, if the author had not inserted the words, *written in our hearts.*

The fleshy tables of the heart are the hearts of the Corinthians.   Cf. Ezech. xxxvi. 26 ; and for the *tables of stone*, Exod. xxxi. 18.

4. *Such confidence,* as in the eyes of his opponents was accounted arrogance.   Cf. Rom. xi. 13, *I will honour* (or, *I magnify*) *my ministry.*

5. *To think anything,* λογίσασθαι.   St. Paul's meaning would be better given, if it were rendered, *to think of anything.*   The verb means *to reckon up, to calculate.* Theodoret explains : " Our preaching is not a web of our own ideas."   Of themselves, the ministers of the gospel cannot think of anything to say, that shall effectually move their hearers to supernatural good : but *of God* and of the divine grace *is the sufficiency* of the preacher to preach and of the hearer to hear and do anything that shall directly make for the kingdom of heaven.   Upon this text the Second Council of Orange framed its seventh canon against the Pelagians : " If any one maintains that by his natural powers he can think to the point, or choose any gift that appertains to the salvation of eternal life, or assent to the saving preaching of the gospel, without the illumination and

inspiration of the Holy Ghost, who gives all facility
in assenting to and believing the truth, he is deceived
by an heretical spirit, not understanding . . . the saying
of the Apostle, *Not that,* &c."

6. *Hath made us fit ministers.* More literally, *hath
made us suffice for ministers.* There is thus a triple
reiteration, *sufficient, sufficiency, suffice.* Observe also the
question : *And for these things who is sufficient ?* (ii. 16)—to
which this is the answer.

Not in the letter, but in the spirit. We should read,
new testament, not of letter, but of spirit. " What then,"
asks St. Chrysostom, " was not the law [the Old Law]
spiritual ? How then does he say : *We know that the
law is spiritual* (Rom. vii. 14) ? It was spiritual, to be
sure, but it did not give the Spirit : for it was not the
Holy Spirit that Moses brought, but letters, whereas
we have been entrusted with the giving of the Holy
Ghost."

The letter killeth. The explanation of these words is
given by St. Paul himself, Rom. viii. 7—13 ; iv. 15 ;
v. 20. And St. Augustine (*De spir. et lit.* 4, seq.) : " The
letter of the law killeth, apart from the quickening
(life-giving) Spirit : for it makes sin known rather than
shunned, and thereby increases rather than diminishes
it, transgression of the law coming in as an addition
to evil concupiscence."

The spirit quickeneth. Because, as we read of the
Holy Ghost in the postcommunion of Whit Tuesday,
" He is the forgiveness of all sins."

All this passage seems especially directed against
the Judaizing party at Corinth. See note on 1 Cor.
i. 12.

7. There are three points of contrast brought out
in this and the four following verses. The law was
nothing more than *letters upon stones :* the new testament is the giving of the Spirit. The law was unto

condemnation and death : the gospel is unto *justice.* The law *is done away :* the gospel *remaineth.* The whole argument shows that, though the glory of the law, when first promulgated, was sensible, while that of the gospel in the preaching of it is spiritual, yet much greater is the glory of the gospel than of the law, and of the ministers of the New Testament than of the ministers of the Old. Compare the contrast between Christ and Aaron, worked out in Heb. vii. viii. ix. x. 1—18.

The face of Moses, Exod. xxxiv. 29—35. St. Chrysostom observes that what shone, was not the tablets of the law, but the face of the lawgiver.

For an example of the setting of *the letter* above the spirit, in diametrical opposition to St. Paul's teaching here, see the Anglican Article vi., extolling the word *engraven with letters,* along with Article xix. decrying *the ministration of the Spirit* in the living teacher, in whom *the Spirit of truth abides for ever* (John xiv. 16, 17).

Which is done away, i.e. which vanished. The glory on the face of Moses was only a passing thing.

10. *That which was* formerly *glorious* about the giving of the Old Law, *in this part, i.e.* in this comparison of the Old with the New, *was not glorified, i.e.* was no glory at all, *by reason of the glory that excelleth* in the New. The greater light obscures the less.

11. *Remaineth.* See 1 Cor. xiii. 13, with note.

12. *Such hope* of the future that Christianity was to have in the world. Christianity was young and undeveloped when this was written : we have seen its maturity and the fulfilment of the Apostle's hope.

Much confidence, literally, *freedom of speech.* "We preach everywhere, hiding nothing, but speaking plainly, nor are we afraid of wounding your eyes, as Moses dazzled the eyes of the Jews " (St. Chrysostom).

13. *And not as Moses.* The clause is understood:
' We hide not the import of our message, as Moses, &c.'

Steadfastly look on the face. Face here (and *faciem* in
the Vulgate Latin) is a clerical error that has come
in from *v.* 7, *steadfastly behold the face.* All the Greek
MSS. except the Alexandrine, and all the Fathers,
Latin as well as Greek, for *face* here read *end.* Read
therefore : *might not steadfastly look on the end of that which
is made void.*

That which is made void is the Old Law, the *old
testament,* or covenant, *which is made void in Christ.* Christ
therefore is *the end of that which is made void*—cf. Rom.
x. 4, *the end of the law is Christ*—because in Him the
shadows and types of the Old Law pass into reality.
The veiling of the face of Moses was in the order of
Divine Providence a symbol and a prediction of what
happened, that the Jews as a nation *might not,* or rather
did not, steadfastly with the firm gaze of faith *look on* the
Christ; in whom the old covenant came to an *end* and
was made void by the new (Heb. viii. 8—13).

14. *The self-same veil, i.e.* the want of spiritual perception which the veil on Moses' face signified, Moses
veiled being a type of his people.

Because in Christ it is made void, ὅτι ἐν χριστῷ καταργεῖται,
means *in respect of the fact that in Christ it* (the old testament) *is made void.* In respect of this fact there is a
veil upon the heart of the Jews, so that they recognise it
not.

15. *When Moses is read.* Cf. Acts iii. 22, 23; and
xiii. 27, *not knowing him, nor the voices of the prophets, which
are read every sabbath.* The Jews of this day have a
covering for their heads when the Law is read in the
synagogue.

16. In the *New Testament faithfully translated into
English out of the authentical Latin, by the English College
then Resident in Rhemes, now set forth the second time by the*

same College now returned to Doway, printed at Antwerp, by Daniel Vervlier, 1600, this verse is rendered : *But when he shal be converted to our Lord, the vele shall be taken away :* which is "faithfully translated out of the authentical Latin," *cum conversus fuerit,* and the Greek of all the MSS., ἡνίκα δ' ἂν ἐπιστρέψῃ. Some one since then has foisted in the plural, *But when they shall be converted.* Correcting this, and taking the reading of all the Greek MSS. and Fathers, and of the early Latin editions, *is taken away,* for *shall be,* we have the verse : *But when he turneth to the Lord, the veil is taken away.* The *he* is Moses, and the verse is in effect a repetition of Exod. xxxiv. 34 : *But when he (Moses) went into the Lord and spoke with him, he took it (the veil) away till he came forth.* This statement St. Paul repeats in a mystical sense. Moses veiled is a type of the Synagogue of the Jews, whose *eyes are held that they know not Christ* (cf. Luke xxiv. 16). Moses, *when he turneth to the Lord,* is a type of the conversion of the Synagogue. When that conversion comes, *the veil is taken away, their eyes are opened and they know him* (Luke xxiv. 31 : cf. Rom. xi. 25, 26).

This is the explanation of St. John Chrysostom and Theodoret. It quite tallies with St. Paul's love of allegory, shown in such passages as Gal. iv. 22—31. The Anglican Authorized Version reads : *When it shall turn to the Lord,* namely, *their heart* (v. 15). The rendering is consonant with the Greek, but loses the allegory, which the Latin Vulgate, *cum conversus fuerit,* directs us to preserve.

17. Translate according to the Greek, ὁ δὲ Κύριος τὸ Πνεῦμά ἐστιν, *Now the Lord is the Spirit :* that is to say, *the Lord,* mentioned in the last verse, to whom the Jewish people, typified by Moses, *turns,* is the Holy Ghost, *the Spirit* mentioned in *vv.* 6, 8. The conversion of the Jews shall be a *turning to the Lord,* that is, from *the letter* that *killeth* to *the Spirit* that quickeneth. *The*

Lord then *is the Spirit of the Lord*, the Holy Ghost; *and where the Spirit of the Lord is, there is liberty*, liberty, that is, from the ceremonial precepts of the Jewish law, as is set forth, Gal. iv. 21—31; v. 1, 13. From 1 Cor. xi. 3, it appears that the veil on the head was a sign of subjection.

In this verse, as the Greek Fathers elaborately argue, the Divinity of the Holy Ghost is stated in so many words. *The Lord*, even Jehovah Himself, *is the Holy Ghost*.

18. *Beholding*, say, *reflecting*, κατοπτριζόμενοι. In the active voice the word means *to make a mirror of, to light up*. It is used by Plutarch (*De placitis philosophorum*, lib. 3, c. 5) of the sun lighting up a cloud, which reflects the solar rays. The passive, used here, refers to a burnished surface *being lit up*, i.e. *reflecting*. The one face of Moses, when unveiled, reflected the glory of God; but *all we* Christians, with the *open face* of full recognition by faith of the divine revelation, have our countenances lit up with *the glory of the Lord, reflecting* the light of the Holy Ghost shining upon us. " For, as soon as we are baptized," says St. Chrysostom, "our soul, cleansed by the Holy Spirit, shines brighter than the sun; and not only do we gaze upon the glory of God, but we also catch the splendour radiant from thence. For just as clean silver, exposed to the sun's rays, will itself emit rays, not of its own mere nature, but from the brightness of the sun, so the soul, purified and made brighter than silver, receives a ray from the glory of the Spirit, and flashes it back. Therefore he says: *Reflecting the brightness* (κατοπτριζόμενοι), *we are transformed into the same image, from glory*, that of the Spirit, *to glory*, our own, that which is produced in us, *as* was to be expected *from the Lord the Spirit*,"—so he renders κυρίου πνεύματος : it may also mean, *the Spirit of the Lord*.

L

NOTE.—The idea of κατοπτριζόμενοι is well given in the opening of *Marmion :*

> Their armour, as it *caught the rays,*
> *Flashed back again the* western *blaze*
> In lines of dazzling light.

———

CHAPTER IV.

1. Therefore, seeing we have this ministration, according as we have obtained mercy, we faint not; 2. But we renounce the hidden things of dishonesty, not walking in craftiness, nor adulterating the word of God ; but, by manifestation of the truth, commending ourselves to every man's conscience in the sight of God. 3. And if our gospel be also hidden, it is hidden to those who perish : 4. In whom the god of this world hath blinded the minds of unbelievers, that the light of the gospel of the glory of Christ, who is the image of God, should not shine unto them. 5. For we preach not ourselves, but Jesus Christ our Lord ; and ourselves your servants through Jesus. 6. For God, who commanded the light to shine out of darkness, hath shined in our hearts, to give the light of the knowledge of the glory of God in the face of Christ Jesus. 7. But we have this treasure in earthen vessels, that the excellency may be of the power of God, and not of us. 8. In all things we suffer tribulation, but are not distressed ; we are straitened, but are not destitute ; 9. We suffer persecution, but are not forsaken ; we are cast down, but we perish not ; 10. Always bearing about in our body the dying of Jesus, that the life also of Jesus may be made manifest in our bodies. 11. For we who live are always delivered unto death for Jesus' sake, that the life also of Jesus may be made manifest in our mortal flesh. 12. So then death worketh in us, but life in you. 13. But having the same spirit of faith, as it is written : I have believed, therefore I have spoken ; we also believe, and therefore we speak ; 14. Knowing that he who raised up Jesus will raise up us also with Jesus, and place us with you. 15. For all things are for your sakes, that the grace, abounding through many, may abound in thanksgiving to the glory of God. 16. For which cause we faint not ; but though our outward man is corrupted, yet the inward man is renewed day by day. 17. For our present tribulation, which is momentary and

light, worketh for us above measure exceedingly an eternal weight
of glory; **18.** While we look not at the things which are seen, but
at the things which are not seen: for the things which are seen are
temporal; but the things which are not seen are eternal.

1. *We have obtained mercy*, as Moses obtained it,
Exod. xxx. 19.

2. By *the hidden things of dishonesty*, (i.e. *of shame*,
αἰσχύνης), as opposed to *manifestation of the truth*, is meant
the policy of hiding gospel truth through shame of the
folly of the cross (1 Cor. i. 18, 21). Cf. Rom. i. 16,
*I am not ashamed of the gospel. The concealment prompted by
shame* would be a clearer translation.

Adulterating the word of God. See on ii. 17.

3. 'If our gospel is dark to any, it is not we who
have made the mystery, but the indisposition of the
hearers.' Cf. Acts xxviii. 26, 27.

Those who perish, or, *are in the way of being lost*, ἀπολλυμένοις. See note on ii. 15.

4. *The god of this world*, Satan, *the prince of this world*
(John xiv. 30), *the prince of the power of this air* (Eph. ii. 2).
Cf. what Satan says of himself (Luke iv. 6). He is a
god of the same rank as that in which the belly is a god
(Phil. iii. 19), and Mammon a lord and master (Matt.
vi. 24).

Christ, who is the image of God; and therefore minds
blinded to Him, are blinded to God (John viii. 19;
xiv. 7—10: cf. also Heb. i. 3).

5. *For, etc.* The conjunction carries us back to *v.* 2:
vv. 3, 4, being parenthetical.

Through Jesus, or, *for the sake of Jesus*, διὰ 'Ιησοῦν.

6. *Hath shined.* Read with the Vulgate (*ipse illuxit*)
and St. Chrysostom, *himself hath shined.* "Then *God
said, Let there be light; and light was made* (Gen. i. 3): but
now He does not say anything, but Himself is become
our light: therefore it is not sensible things that we see
by the shining of such a light, but God Himself through

Christ,"—*i.e.* we know God by faith through the revelation of Christ. So St. Chrysostom, who proceeds to show how the three Persons of the Blessed Trinity are mentioned with equal honour, the Holy Ghost, iii. 18; the Son, iv. 4; the Father, iv. 6.

In the face of Christ Jesus (who is the image of God, v. 4), "showing that through Him we know the Father, as through the Spirit we are brought to Him" (St. Chrysostom).

7. *This treasure* of the Christian ministry. *Earthern vessels.* "He signifies the fragility of human nature, and the weakness of the flesh: for it is no better than earthernware, so open it is to the attacks of death and diseases and variations in the air: . . . there is nothing of man in our strength" (St. Chrysostom).

That the excellence may be of the power of God. Rather, from the Greek, *that the excellence of the power may be of God.*

8. *We suffer tribulation, but are not distressed.* Literally, *being squeezed* ($\theta\lambda\iota\beta\acute{o}\mu\epsilon\nu\upsilon$, a wrestler's word, cf. Eph. vi. 12), *but not put into* (unendurably) *narrow room* ($\sigma\tau\epsilon\nu\upsilon\chi\omega\rho\upsilon\acute{\upsilon}\mu\epsilon\nu\upsilon\iota$,—$\theta\lambda\acute{\iota}\psi\iota\varsigma$ and $\sigma\tau\epsilon\nu\upsilon\chi\omega\rho\acute{\iota}\alpha$ are joined, Rom. ii. 9; viii. 35).

We are straitened, but are not destitute: more literally, *having our way blocked, but not quite barred.*

9. Taking this verse with the preceding, the Apostle says, recounting the trials of twenty-four years since his conversion: 'Having our *way blocked* ($\dot{\alpha}\pi\upsilon\rho\upsilon\acute{\upsilon}\mu\epsilon\nu\upsilon\iota$), yet not altogether *closed* ($\delta\iota\alpha\pi\upsilon\rho\upsilon\acute{\upsilon}\mu\epsilon\nu\upsilon\iota$), we get away, and when *pursued* ($\delta\iota\omega\kappa\acute{o}\mu\epsilon\nu\upsilon\iota$), and even overtaken and *cast down* ($\kappa\alpha\tau\alpha\beta\alpha\lambda\lambda\acute{o}\mu\epsilon\nu\upsilon\iota$), still we are not *forsaken* ($\dot{\epsilon}\gamma\kappa\alpha\tau\alpha\lambda\epsilon\iota\pi\acute{o}\mu\epsilon\nu\upsilon\iota$), nor apt finally *to perish* ($\dot{\alpha}\pi\upsilon\lambda\lambda\acute{\upsilon}\mu\epsilon\nu\upsilon\iota$).

10. *The dying of Jesus,* $\nu\acute{\epsilon}\kappa\rho\omega\sigma\iota\nu$, *mortificationem* (Vulg.). It is not a question of *mortification* in the ascetic sense (though there is authority for that too in St. Paul, 1 Cor. ix. 27), but of exposure to danger of death,

which exposure the Apostle calls *dying*. So in 1 Cor.
xv. 31 he says, *I die daily*, explaining himself in the
previous verse 30: I am *in danger* of death *every hour*.
Such a living ever next door to martyrdom means
something more than ordinary mortification. It is
exemplified in the life of missionaries labouring in a
pagan or persecuting country, as Japan or England
was in the seventeenth century.

11. *We who live*, and have not yet been put to death
like James (Acts xii. 2).

Are always delivered, better, are *always being delivered*.

Death for Jesus' sake explains *the dying of Jesus*:
indeed this verse is simply the preceding in other
words.

The life of Jesus is the supernatural life of grace,
which is lived even *in our mortal flesh*.

12. *Death worketh in us*, say rather, *is wrought*
(ἐνεργεῖται, passive, cf. τῆς ἐνεργουμένης, i. 5).

But life in you, that is, the above-mentioned *life of
Jesus*. The danger of martyrdom then was confined to
the Apostles: the Corinthian Church enjoyed the fruit
of supernatural life, gathered for it by the Apostles'
perils.

13. *Having the same spirit of faith* with the psalmist
who wrote : *I believed, for which cause I have spoken*
(Ps. cxv. 1). St. Paul quotes the psalm as it is in the
Septuagint. The Hebrew may be translated: *I believed,
because I spoke*. The two versions substantially agree.
In the former, the cause, faith, is shown working out its
effect in utterance. In the latter, faith is argued from
utterance, the existence of the cause from the presence
of the effect. But what was it that the psalmist believed,
and what did he speak? He believed in the watchful
guardianship of God delivering His servant's *soul from
death, his eyes from tears, and his feet from slipping* (see
Ps. cxiv., which in the Hebrew makes one psalm

with cxv.). And he uttered the psalm of thanksgiving, of which this is the first verse. In like manner the Apostles, in their tribulations and distresses, *believed* that they should never be *destitute, forsaken, perish* (*vv.* 8, 9); and they *spoke* the gospel message.

14. *Will raise up us.* Sometimes, as here and in 1 Cor. vi. 14, St. Paul speaks as though he expected to be dead before the day of judgment, and sometimes, as 1 Cor. xv. 52, and here *v.* 2—4, as though he expected to live to see that day: the fact being that he *knew not the day nor the hour* (Matt. xxv. 13), nor the condition in which it should find him.

Place us with you alive in the kingdom of God. The verb παραστήσει is the same that occurs in Acts i. 3; ix. 41 : *He shewed himself alive : He presented her alive.*

15. *May abound in thanksgiving.* Better, from the Greek, *may make thanksgiving abound.* The verb περισσεύσῃ is transitive here, as in ix. 8, where it is translated *make abound.*

16. The *outward man* is all that we have in common with brute beasts : the *inward man* is what we have in common with the angels. Cf. Rom. vii. 22. This distinction is not the same as that between *the old man and the new* (Rom. vi. 6; Eph. iv. 22, 24; Col. iii. 9, 10), or the pagan and the Christian man. Both inward and outward man in us had *sinned*, and did *need the glory of God* (Rom. iii. 23): both were unregenerate, and have been born to newness of life in Christ, albeit the outward man shall not have the benefit of this new life till the day of the resurrection. *Corrupted* here implies no moral taint, but means simply *wastes away.* *Our outward man is corrupted* is in other words, *our earthly house of this habitation* is being gradually *dissolved* (*v.* 1).

17. *Weight* is opposed to *light*, and *eternal* to *present.* *Momentary* is not in the Greek.

Above measure exceedingly, καθ' ὑπερβολὴν εἰς ὑπερβολήν,

literally, *exceedingly to excess.* St. Paul uses the strongest phrase he can invent. There may be some thought of the light grain sown, and the heavy harvest, thirty, sixty, or a hundred fold (Matt. xiii. 8). On the other hand is the contrary reckoning of the wicked in hell (Wisdom v. 4—14), small enjoyment turning to an intolerable load of pain.

This verse is quoted by the Council of Trent (sess. 6, cap. 16), in evidence of the position that the good works of the just are truly meritorious of eternal glory.

18. " He does not say, the tribulations are temporal, but *the things which are seen,* all of them, be it chastisement, be it enjoyment and repose, are temporal; so that we be neither enervated by the one, nor overpowered by the other. Therefore in speaking of the future he does not say either, *the kingdom is eternal,* but, *the things which are not seen are eternal,* be it kingdom, or be it punishment, so as to terrify us from the one, and incite us to the other " (St. Chrysostom).

1. For we know, that, if our earthly house of this habitation be dissolved, we have a building of God, a house not made with hands, eternal in heaven. 2. For in this also we groan, desiring to be clothed over with our habitation which is from heaven; 3. Yet so that we may be found clothed, not naked. 4. For we also who are in this tabernacle do groan, being burdened: because we would not be unclothed, but clothed over, that what is mortal may be swallowed up by life. 5. Now he that maketh us for this very thing is God, who hath given us the pledge of the Spirit. 6. Therefore, having always confidence, knowing that while we are in the body we are absent from the Lord: 7. (For we walk by faith, and not by sight:) 8. We are confident, I say, and have a good will to be absent rather from the body, and to be present with the Lord. 9. And therefore we labour, whether absent or present, to please him. 10. For we must all appear before the judgment-seat of Christ; that every one may receive the proper things of the body, according as he hath done, whether it be good or evil. 11. Knowing, therefore, the fear of the Lord, we persuade men: but to God we are manifest; and I trust also that in your consciences we are manifest. 12. We commend not ourselves again to you, but give you occasion to glory in our behalf, that you may have somewhat to answer them who glory in face, and not in heart. 13. For whether we are transported in mind, it is to God; or whether we are more moderate, it is for you. 14. For the charity of Christ presseth us; judging this, that if one died for all, then all were dead. 15. And Christ died for all, that they also who live may not now live to themselves, but to him who died for them, and rose again. 16. Wherefore, henceforth we know no man according to the flesh; and if we have known Christ according to the flesh, but now we know him so no longer. 17. If then any be in Christ, a new creature: old things are passed away; behold, all things are made new. 18. But all things are of God, who hath reconciled us to himself by Christ, and hath given to us the ministry of reconciliation. 19. For God, indeed, was in Christ, reconciling the world to himself, not imputing to them their sins; and he hath placed in us the word of reconciliation. 20. We are, therefore, ambassadors for Christ, God as it were exhorting by us. For Christ we beseech you, be ye reconciled to God. 21. Him, who knew no sin, he hath made sin for us, that we might be made the justice of God in him.

1. *House of this habitation*, the Vulgate *domus hujus habitationis*, does not correspond to the Greek οἰκία τοῦ σκήνους, *house of the tent*, *i.e.* house no better than a tent, which is pitched one day and struck the next. This *tent-house* is our mortal body: cf. Job iv. 19; Isaias xxxviii. 12. A tent, as St. Paul the tent-maker well knew (Acts xviii. 3), was a thing *made with hands* (1 Cor. iv. 12), and therefore perishable, as are all the works of man. Contrasted with this stands the body glorified in the resurrection, now *a building*, and no longer a *tent; a building of God, not made with hands, that is, not of this creation* (Heb. ix. 11: cf. Mark xiv. 58; Acts vii. 48; xvii. 24; Eph. ii. 11; Col. ii. 11); not belonging to this order of transitory things, but *eternal in heaven. We have* this already in the sense in which *he who heareth my word hath life everlasting* (John v. 24), in promise and potency.

Here *house of the tent*, οἰκία τοῦ σκήνους, is opposed to οἰκοδομή, *building: eternal* is the opposite of *made with hands;* and *in heaven* is opposed to *earthly* (ἐπίγειος, *upon earth*).

2. *In this*, ἐν τούτῳ, *i.e. on this account, as in* 1 Cor. iv. 4. *We groan*, Rom. viii. 19—26.

To be clothed over, ἐπενδύσασθαι, *to put on as over-clothing.* The body which in the previous verse has been called, and is again called in this, a *house* or *habitation*, οἰκία, οἰκητήριον, of the soul, is here by a change of metaphor spoken of as a garment. The Apostle says, we should like to *put on immortality*, without first putting off *this mortal* body by death: *i.e.* we should like to be found alive at the day of judgment, and so simply to be *changed* instead of having to *rise again* (cf. 1 Cor. xv. 51—53, and notes thereupon).

Our habitation which is from heaven, better, *of heaven*, i.e. *heavenly*, ἐξ οὐρανοῦ. So the glorified body is called, because it is *the image of the heavenly*, 1 Cor. xv. 49.

3. Read εἴ γε, καὶ ἐκδυσάμενοι, οὐ γυμνοὶ εὑρεθησόμεθα·
and translate : *Since, even if we are stripped* [of our bodies],
we shall not be found naked. The usual reading is
ἐνδυσάμενοι, *clothed.* But ἐκδυσάμενοι is read in three
Greek MSS., and is sanctioned by Tertullian and
St. Paulinus. St. Chrysostom, though he prefers the
other reading, had ἐκδυσάμενοι in his copy, a MS. at
least as old as the Sinaitic and the Vatican, our oldest.
Naked means *not clothed in Christ, void of grace,* as is
gathered from Matt. xxii. 11 ; Gal. iii. 27; Apoc. iii. 18;
xvi. 15: it never means *disembodied.* Nor could ἐνδυσάμενοι,
if we took that reading, mean *clothed in flesh,* of a human
soul, that was created in the body, and had no previous
existence. The similar aorist participles, ὁ ἀποθανών,
he that is dead (Rom. vi. 7), and τοὺς πεσόντας, *the fallen*
(Rom. xi. 22), are used of those who died at some time,
having been alive, and fell some time, having stood
before.

St. Paul then longed for the day of judgment. He
hoped to be alive that day, and to be straightway
glorified, without tasting death. This hope in him
was reasonable, because even if he were to die before,
the judgment would not find his soul unclothed in
sanctifying grace, or unworthy of resurrection to glory.

This verse, as it stands with the usual reading
ἐνδυσάμενοι, has been called "the cross of interpreters,"
a cross however not set up by St. Paul, but by some
misguided copyist.

For εἴ γε some read εἴπερ. If we might read εἰ δ᾽ οὖν,
the verse would translate : *But if after all we are found
stripped of our bodies, still we shall not be found naked :* which
makes the passage still simpler.

4. *In this tabernacle,* or *tent,* σκήνει, the mortal body,
so called in *v.* 1 : see note.

Not be unclothed, but clothed over, i.e. not die, but be
changed to immortality, as above, *v.* 2 ; the lot of them

who are alive, who are left at the last day, *who shall be taken up together with them* who were dead and are risen again, *in the clouds to meet Christ,* 1 Thess. iv. 16.

That which is mortal may be swallowed up, Osee xiii. 14; 1 Cor. xv. 54, with note.

5. *He that maketh us:* better, *he that wrought us,* κατεργασάμενος.

For this very thing, our habitation that is of heaven, v. 2, our glorified body.

The pledge of the Spirit, even to the outpouring of sensible miraculous gifts (1 Cor. xiv. with notes), enumerated 1 Cor. xii. 7—11.

6. *Having confidence, . . . I say, we are confident* (v. 8), θαρροῦντες . . . θαρροῦμεν δέ. All between is a parenthesis.

We are in the body, ἐνδημοῦντες, more fully, *at home in the body. Absent,* ἀποδημοῦντες, properly, *abroad.* The same words are repeated in *v.* 8. On earth we are *absent,* or *abroad, from the Lord* in this sense, that He does not show Himself to us δι᾿ εἴδους (*v.* 7), that is, in His own proper nature and appearance, according as He really is.

7. *Faith, sight,* δι᾿ εἴδους. Cf. iv. 18; Heb. xi. 1. The word here translated *sight,* means rather *visible appearance,* as in John v. 37; Luke iii. 22; ix. 29.

8. *A good will to be absent,* or *go abroad, rather from the body.* St. Paul's great desire was for the coming of Christ the Judge, even in his life-time. But if that was not to be, *rather* than live long in this world, he would *go abroad* from his body, die, and so come *to be at home,* with his Lord,—as he says elsewhere, *having a desire to be dissolved and to be with Christ* (Phil. i. 23). This *good will* and *desire* supposes, against the error of some modern Greeks, that the saints who are dead are with Christ, and have not to wait till the day of judgment to enter heaven.

9. *Whether absent or present.* The Greek order is,

whether present or absent. The verse means : We labour now to please the Lord, whether the day of judgment is to find us *present, at home in the body* (*v.* 6), or *absent, abroad from the body* (*v.* 8).

10. *For we must all, whether present or absent,* alive or dead at the judgment-day, *be manifested* (φανερωθῆναι, cf. 1 Cor. iv. 5, *will manifest,* φανερώσει, *the counsels of heart*) *before the tribunal of Christ* at the general judgment.

The proper things of the body, τὰ ἴδια τοῦ σώματος, or, *the things done through the body,* τὰ διὰ τοῦ σώματος, mean in either case the human acts done while soul and body are united on earth.

11. *The fear of the Lord,* that is, the terrors of the judgment-day.

We persuade men, to remove, as we are bound to remove, the prejudices that stand in the way of our ministry. The men to whom he uses this persuasion, are those adversaries and calumniators whom he has so often mentioned.

12. *We commend not ourselves again,* iii. 1.

Who glory in face, and not in heart, those rival preachers at Corinth (1 Cor. iii. 18—21 ; iv. 18—20, &c.), who made a brave show of words and high doctrine, but in whom *the inner man of the heart* (1 Pet. iii. 4) was not up to the outward profession,—called in this Epistle *false apostles, deceitful workmen, ministers of Satan* (xi. 13, 15).

13. *Transported in mind,* so as to *become foolish* (xii. 11), and speak our own praises, as the Apostles does (xi. 16—xii. 4), doing it however *to God* and to His greater glory.

Moderate, for you. If we hide our good gifts, and depreciate ourselves, it is for your edification. Instances of such sobriety, i. 8, 9 ; iv. 7 ; x. 13 ; xii. 6—10 ; 1 Cor. ii. 1—4 ; iv. 9—13.

14. *Presseth us,* συνέχει, literally, *besets us :* the word is used by St. Luke, viii. 45 ; xix. 43.

If one died for all, then all were dead.   Better, *if one died* (ἀπέθανεν) *for all, then all died* (ἀπέθανον) : it is the same tense in both clauses.   The meaning is : ' If Christ died for all men, then all men died in Christ vicariously : ' as though we were to say : ' If one spoke for all, then all whom he represented spoke in him.'   But that this death of Christ may be effectually the death of any individual man, and save him from the penalty of eternal death, he must be *planted in the likeness* of Christ's death, which is done by baptism, so that being *dead with Christ*, he may *live also together with Christ.*   See Rom. vi., where this doctrine is explained.

15. *That they also who live*, by the spiritual life which they received in baptism.

16. *Henceforth we know no man according to the flesh*, that is, we can no longer take a mere natural view of any man, least of all, of any Christian.   " Likely enough," says St. Chrysostom, "seeing that all have died, and all have risen again.   For what though they are in the flesh ? yet that life of the flesh has vanished, and we are born again from above of the Holy Ghost, and know another citizenship and conduct and life and constitution, that is in heaven."

Now we know him (Christ) so (according to the flesh) no longer.

Observe that our Lord is here called, not by His proper name, Jesus, but by His official name, Christ (Messiah).   St. Paul had not been acquainted, as man with man, with Jesus of Nazareth.   But the Christ of prophecy he had known well, and had gloried, as *a Hebrew of Hebrews* (Phil. iii. 5 ; Rom. xi. 1) in being of the same stock with Him (cf. Rom. xi. 4, 5).   All these national distinctions, *things that once were a gain to him*, he now *counted to be but loss for the excellent knowledge of Jesus Christ his Lord* (see Phil. iii. 4—10).   He had no longer any *confidence in the flesh*, as one born of the same race as the Messiah, for *not they that are the children of the flesh are the children of God, but they that are the children of the promise* (Rom. ix. 8). This ceasing to trust in mere carnal propinquity to the Messiah, he calls *no longer knowing Christ according to the flesh.*

17. The Latin here is deficient in punctuation. There should be a comma after *Christ,* and a colon or full stop after *creature.* The Greek is: εἴ τις οὖν ἐν Χριστῷ, καινὴ κτίσις, which translates: *If then any man be in Christ, he is a new creature.* Cf. Gal. vi. 15; Eph. ii. 10; iv. 24.

All things new, Isaias xliii. 18, 19; Apoc. xxi. 1, 5.

19. *Was in Christ reconciling, i.e.* was reconciling through Christ.

Not imputing to them their sins, Rom. iv. 6—8. The sins are not imputed, because they are entirely blotted out, and the sinner is *washed, sanctified, justified* (1 Cor. vi. 11), *holy and unspotted, and blameless before God* (Col. i. 22). So perfect is the *reconciliation* and *peace through the blood of Christ's cross* (Col. i. 20).

21. He was made *sin,* as we are made *justice,* the abstract being put for the concrete. So too was He *made a curse for us* (Gal. iii. 13). As St. Chrysostom explains: "Him that was just he made a sinner, that he might make sinners just. Or rather, this is not what the Apostle says, but something much greater; not *he made a sinner,* but *sin,* and that of Him who not merely was no sinner, but who knew not sin, that we might be made, not *just,* but *justice,* and *the justice of God, not by works* (Rom. xi. 6), but by grace, where all sin completely disappears." God allowed His most innocent Son to be condemned as a sinner, and to die as one under a curse, *laying upon him the iniquity of us all* (Isaias, liii. 6), to *bear our sins in his body upon the tree* (1 Pet. ii. 24), that they might be entirely taken away.

Chapter VI.

1. And we, helping, do exhort you that you receive not the grace of God in vain. **2.** (For he saith : In an accepted time have I heard thee, and in the day of salvation have I helped thee : behold, now is the acceptable time ; behold, now is the day of salvation.) **3.** Giving no offence to any one, that our ministry be not blamed : **4.** But in all things let us exhibit ourselves as the ministers of God, in much patience, in tribulation, in necessities, in distresses, **5.** In stripes, in prisons, in seditions, in labours, in watchings, in fastings, **6.** In chastity, in knowledge, in long-suffering, in sweetness, in the Holy Ghost, in charity unfeigned, **7.** In the word of truth, in the power of God, by the armour of justice on the right hand and on the left, **8.** Through honour and dishonour, through infamy and good name : as seducers, and yet speaking truth ; as unknown, and yet known ; **9.** As dying, and behold, we live ; as chastised, and not killed ; **10.** As sorrowful, yet always rejoicing ; as needy, yet enriching many ; as having nothing, yet possessing all things. **11.** Our mouth is open to you, O ye Corinthians, our heart is enlarged. **12.** You are not straitened in us : but in your own bowels you are straitened : **13.** But having the same recompense (I speak as to my children) be you also enlarged. **14.** Bear not the yoke together with unbelievers : for what participation hath justice with injustice ? or what fellowship hath light with darkness ? **15.** And what concord hath Christ with Belial ? or what part hath the faithful with the unbeliever ? **16.** And what agreement hath the temple of God with idols ? For you are the temple of the living God : as God saith : I will dwell in them, and walk among them ; and I will be their God, and they shall be my people. **17.** Wherefore, Go out from among them, and be ye separate, saith the Lord, and touch not the unclean thing : **18.** And I will receive you ; and I will be a father to you ; and you shall be my sons and daughters, saith the Lord Almighty.

1. *We helping*, as *ambassadors* (v. 20), *God's coadjutors* (1 Cor. iii. 9), bearing the request of a Master whom it is perilous to deny, who asks now, but one day will compel.

2. *In an accepted time*, &c., Isaias xlix. 8. The words are addressed to *my servant*, the Messiah, and in Him to His people.

Now is the acceptable time, " while still we are labouring in the vineyard (Matt. xx), while still the eleventh hour is left " (St. Chrysostom).

3. 1 Cor. x. 32.

4. *Let us exhibit ourselves.* All the MSS. read *exhibiting ourselves*, doubtless what St. Paul wrote. This and the next six verses are not an exhortation to the lay-folk at Corinth, but a description how St. Paul and his fellow-apostles bore themselves, and what they had to bear, in the sacred ministry.

In much patience. Patience first, " the foundation of all good things," says St. Chrysostom. A priest will never do a member of his flock any good, if he is not patient with him.

The Apostle then mentions nine matters of patience, the first three general, the remaining six particular, of which three are imposed by others, and three are of the Apostle's own taking up.

In tribulations, in distresses, ἐν θλίψεσιν, ἐν στενοχωρίαις (cf. iv. 8), literally, *in pressures, in close confinements*. There seems to be a gradation; *in pressures* there are many ways, all hard; *in necessities* there is but one way, and that a hard one; *in close confinements* there is no way left at all.

5. *In stripes*, xi. 24, 25.

In prisons, Acts xvi. 23, 24.

In seditions, ἐν ἀκαταστασίαις, so the word is used, Luke xxi. 9; 1 Cor. xiv. 33. But here it is more likely to mean *tossing to and fro*,—as we say, 'being hunted from pillar to post:' *e.g.* Acts xvii. 10; xx. 3.

In fastings, Mark ii. 20.

6. This verse gives a list of five other virtues, besides *patience* mentioned above, which St. Paul gave example of.

In long-suffering of persecution from without; *in sweetness* to those within the fold. The Greek word for *sweetness* denotes the habit whereby one is *easy to deal with*; it is predicated of the Lord, Ps. xxxiii. 9.

In the Holy Ghost, the Spirit of truth (John xv. 26), and love (Rom. v. 5), and power (1 Cor. ii. 4, 5).

In charity unfeigned; repeated Rom. xii. 9, in the original.

7. *In the word of truth, in the power of God.* Mark xvi. 20.

By the armour of justice on the right hand and on the left. The soldier of St. Paul's time carried his spear, or sword, in his right hand, and his shield on his left. On the right hand then were offensive arms, on the left defensive. A man takes the offensive in prosperity, and stands on the defensive in adversity. Thus the metaphor means prosperity and adversity, as particularised, and the particulars set over against each other, in the next three verses.

8. Cf. Phil. iv. 12: *I know both how to be brought low, and I know how to abound, etc.*

As unknown, and yet known, ὡς ἀγνοούμενοι καὶ ἐπιγιγνωσ-κόμενοι, i.e. *ignored and yet recognised:* cf. 1 Cor. xiv. 38; xiii. 12, with notes.

10. *Needy,* literally, *beggars. Enriching many,* spiritually and also temporally (1 Cor. xvi. 1—3).

" He collected money from all, and sent it to the poor; and *having nothing,* he was master of every pious household " (Theodoret): so much so that he says to the Galatians: *You would have plucked out your own eyes, and would have given them to me* (Gal. iv. 15).

Having, possessing, ἔχοντες, κατέχοντες, a play upon words, something like *holding* and *upholding.*

11. *Our mouth is open to you,* to speak freely as friend with friend: for, as St. Chrysostom quaintly remarks, "conversation is to minds what shaking hands is to bodies."

O ye Corinthians. This translation is too ceremonious.

M

The Apostle says simply, Κορίνθιοι, *Corinthians*, the abruptness of affection being shown by the omission of the usual ὦ. So Φιλιππήσιοι, *Philippians* (Phil. iv. 15).

Our heart is enlarged. " As it is the way of heat to expand, so it is the work of charity to enlarge, for virtue is warm and glowing. This opened the mouth of Paul, and enlarged his heart. Not with mouth alone do I love, he says, but with my mouth my heart is in concert : therefore do I speak freely with my whole mouth and my whole heart. For nothing was there wider than the heart of Paul, wherewith he loved all the faithful with a love of charity as intense as the passion of love. There was no division of his affection nor weakening of the same, but it was planted entire in every object. And what wonder in the case of the faithful, seeing that even as regards unbelievers the heart of Paul embraced the whole inhabited world" (St. Chrysostom). And if the heart of Paul, how much more the Heart of Jesus !

For St. Paul's love of his flock, Rom. i. 11 ; Gal. iv. 19 ; Phil. iv. 1 ; Col. ii. 1 ; 1 Thess. ii. 7.

12. *You are not straitened in us, i.e.* there is room enough in my heart to contain you all.

In your own bowels you are straitened, i.e. you find in your hearts no place for me.

13. *Having the same recompense.* This word *having* is not in the Greek, and perplexes the sense. It might be rendered : *By way of requital in kind, be your hearts also enlarged.*

vi. 14—18 and vii. 1 are marked by rationalist critics as an interpolation, because they interrupt the sense. They may have got out of place, or have been added as an afterthought.

14. *Bear not the yoke with unbelievers.* The word *inaequale* (unequal) seems to have dropped out of the Vulgate Latin, *jugum ducere.* We want *inaequale jugum*

ducere as a translation of ἑτεροζυγοῦντες. The word means
unequally yoked. It occurs (in the form ἑτεροζύγῳ) Levit.
xix. 19; and its meaning is illustrated by the precept :
Thou shalt not plough with an ox and an ass together (Deut.
xxii. 10). Therefore *bear not an unequal yoke with infidels.*
The principle is clear; its application difficult. Instances,
1 Cor. v. 9, 10; vii. 12, 13; x. 27 ; and the note on *marry
in the Lord*, vii. 40.

15. *Belial*, a Hebrew word, meaning literally, *inutility*,
worthlessness. It occurs in the Old Testament, Deut.
xiii. 13; Nahum i. 11 ; ii. 1 ; Job xxxiv. 18, &c., but not
as here, as a name of the devil, who is eminently *the
good-for-nothing*, ὁ πονηρός, from whom we pray to be
delivered, Matt. vi. 13.

16. *You are the temple of the living God*, 1 Cor. iii.
16, 17; vi. 19, with notes.

The quotation is from Leviticus xxvi. 12.

17. Isaias lii. 11.

18. This quotation, exactly as it stands, is not found
in the Old Testament. The substance of it appears in
Jer. xxxii. 37, 38; xxxi. 9; Deut. xiv. 1, 2; xxxii. 6, 9.

CHAPTER VII.

1. Having, therefore, these promises, dearly beloved, let us cleanse ourselves from all defilement of the flesh and of the spirit, perfecting sanctification in the fear of God. 2. Receive us: we have injured no one, we have corrupted no one, we have over-reached no one. 3. I speak not this to your condemnation: for we have said before, that you are in our hearts, to die together and to live together. 4. Great is my confidence with you, great is my glorying for you: I am filled with comfort, I exceedingly abound with joy in all our tribulation. 5. For also, when we were come into Macedonia, our flesh had no rest, but we suffered all tribulation: combats without, fears within. 6. But God, who comforteth the humble, comforted us by the coming of Titus; 7. And not by his coming only, but also by the consolation wherewith he was comforted in you, relating to us your desire, your mourning, your zeal for me; so that I rejoiced the more. 8. For although I made you sorrowful by my epistle, I do not repent; and if I did repent, seeing that the same epistle (although but for a time) did make you sorrowful, 9. Now I am glad; not because you were made sorrowful, but because you were made sorrowful unto penance; for you were made sorrowful according to God, that in nothing you should suffer damage by us. 10. For the sorrow which is according to God worketh penance unto salvation, which is lasting: but the sorrow of the world worketh death. 11. For, behold, this self-same thing, that you were made sorrowful according to God, how great carefulness doth it work in you, yea defence, yea indignation, yea fear, yea desire, yea zeal, yea revenge! In all things you have showed yourselves to be undefiled in the matter. 12. Wherefore, though I wrote to you, not on account of him who did the injury, nor of him who suffered the wrong, but to manifest our solicitude which we have for you 13. Before God: therefore we were comforted: but in our consolation we did the more abundantly rejoice for the joy of Titus, because his spirit was refreshed by you all. 14. And if I have boasted any thing to him of you, I have not been put to shame; but as we have spoken all things to you in truth, so also our boasting which was made to Titus is found a truth: 15. And his bowels are more abundantly toward you, remembering the obedience of you all, how with fear and trembling you received him. 16. I rejoice that in all things I have confidence in you.

1. *Defilement of the flesh*, sins against the cardinal virtue of temperance.

And of the spirit, the spiritual sin of idol-worship, which at Corinth readily led to *defilement of the flesh*.

2. *Receive us* into your hearts, where before the Apostle had complained that there was no room for him (vi. 12). The Greek means, *make room to contain us*.

We have corrupted, *i.e.* taught false doctrine to, *no man*. Cf. xi. 3, where the word has the same signification.

We have overreached, *i.e.* wrung money out of, *no man*. Cf. xii. 17, 18, for the same word in the same meaning. In this verse the Apostle glances at the contrary practice of the *false apostles* (xi. 13).

3. *To your condemnation—ad condemnationem vestram*. *Your* (*vestram*) is not in the Greek : we may almost say, it should be there. The Apostle means: 'I am not condemning *you* (Corinthians generally), only those false apostles.'

We have said before that you are in our hearts, iii. 2 ; vi. 12.

4. *My confidence with you, παρρησία πρὸς ὑμᾶς*, that is, my freedom of speech in speaking out to you, " as a father to his children, as a master to his scholars " (Theodoret).

My glorying for you, speaking well of you before others, at the same time desiring your still greater improvement, as he writes to the Hebrews after much rebuking of them : *But, my dearly beloved, we trust better things of you, and nearer to salvation, though we speak thus* (Heb. vi. 9).

5. *When we were come into Macedonia, our flesh had no rest*. This carries us back to ii. 12, 13, where he says that, finding no *rest in his spirit* in Troas, he went into Macedonia. What disturbed the rest and peace of his spirit, was his uncertainty and anxiety about the Corinthians. In Macedonia this anxiety of spirit continued, and his *flesh*, or body, was also harassed by external persecutions, so that he *suffered all tribulation*,

combats without with open enemies of the gospel, *fears within* for the safety of the Corinthian church. The last words are a reminiscence of Lamentations i. 20.

6. *The coming of Titus*, who reported the good reception of the First Epistle at Corinth.

8. Copyists and commentators, as Bengel observes, have wonderfully confused this verse, from failure to appreciate the idiomatic force of the thrice repeated εἰ καί. "In the day time," says Sextus Empiricus, "you can observe nothing, but only the movements of the sun, *if even that*," μόνα δέ, εἰ καὶ ἄρα, τὰς τοῦ ἡλίου κινήσεις. The phrase εἰ καὶ implies that a particular concession is the utmost that can be conceded, indeed rather more than ought to be conceded. It may be translated, *granting for argument's sake*, or *at most*. So then we should translate this verse : ' *Granting* (εἰ καὶ) *that I made you sorrowful by my epistle, I do not repent ; and granting* (εἰ καὶ) *that I once did repent* (*seeing that the same epistle did make you sorrowful but for a time at most*, εἰ καί,) *now I am glad, etc.*'

9. *That you might suffer damage by us*, that is, by our silence and connivence at the scandal, 1 Cor. v. 1.

10. *The sorrow that is according to God* arises out of the love of God, at least incipient : while *the sorrow of the world* comes of the love of the world, for which see 1 John ii. 15, 16.

11. *Yea defence*, ἀπολογίαν, the Corinthians clearing themselves before Titus of any sympathy with the incestuous man.

Indignation at his crime.

Fear of St. Paul's coming *with a rod*, 1 Cor. iv. 21 ; *desire* nevertheless of his coming, as of children for their father (1 Cor. iv. 15).

Zeal for the condign punishment of the delinquent, which is here called *revenge*, being the vengeance of the law.

You have shown yourselves to be undefiled. By *putting away the evil one from among you,* that *little leaven, old* and corrupt, you have escaped the threatened corruption of *the whole lump* (1 Cor. v. 6, 7, 13).

12. *Though I wrote to you, not on account of him.* The English makes no sense through the omission of the verb, which is readily supplied in the Greek and Latin. Translate: *Granting that* (εἰ καὶ) *I wrote to you* (somewhat severely), *it was not on account of him,* &c.

Him that suffered it, the father mentioned in 1 Cor. v. 1, whom we gather from this verse to have been alive at the time.

13. The Greek means: *We are thoroughly comforted at your consolation, but still more abundantly did we rejoice for the joy of Titus, because his spirit is quite refreshed by you all.*

16. *I have confidence in you,* even to rebuke and censure you, knowing your docility; and when again I praise you, Titus is my witness that you do not belie my praises.

These last verses are the introduction to a charity sermon, which takes up the next two chapters.

Chapter VIII.

1. Now we make known to you, brethren, the grace of God that hath been given in the churches of Macedonia: 2. That in much experience of tribulation they have had abundance of joy, and their very deep poverty hath abounded unto the riches of their simplicity: 3. For according to their power, I bear them witness, and beyond their power, they were willing; 4. With much entreaty begging of us the grace and communication of the ministry that is done toward the saints: 5. And not as we hoped; but they gave their own selves first to the Lord, then to us by the will of God; 6. Insomuch that we desired Titus, that as he had begun, so also he would finish in you this same grace: 7. That as in all things you abound in faith, and word, and knowledge, and all carefulness; moreover, also, in your charity toward us; so in this grace also you may abound. 8. I speak not as commanding, but by the carefulness of others approving also the good disposition of your charity. 9. For you know the grace of our Lord Jesus Christ, that being rich, he became poor for your sakes, that through his poverty you might be rich. 10. And in this I give counsel: for this is profitable for you, who have begun not only to do, but also to be willing the year before. 11. Now, therefore, perform ye it also in deed; that, as your mind is forward to be willing, so it may be also to perform, out of that which you have. 12. For if the will be forward, it is accepted according to that which it hath, not according to that which it hath not. 13. For I mean not that others should be eased, and you burdened; but by an equality. 14. In this present time let your abundance supply their want, that their abundance also may supply your want; that there may be an equality: as it is written: 15. He that had much had nothing over; and he that had little had no want. 16. And thanks be to God, who hath given the same carefulness for you in the heart of Titus. 17. For indeed he accepted the exhortation; but, being more careful, of his own will he went unto you. 18. We have sent also with him the brother, whose praise is in the gospel through all the churches; 19. And not that only, but he was also ordained by the churches companion of our travels, for this grace, which is administered by us to the glory of the Lord, and our determined will: 20. Avoiding this, lest any man should blame us in this abundance which is administered by us. 21. For we foresee what may be good, not only before God, but also before men. 22. And we have sent with them our brother also, whom we have often proved diligent in many things, but now

much more diligent, with much confidence in you, **23.** Either for
Titus, who is my companion and fellow-labourer toward you, or
our brethren, the apostles of the churches, the glory of Christ.
24. Wherefore show ye to them, in the sight of the churches, the
evidence of your charity, and of our boasting on your behalf.

It hath pleased them of Macedonia and Achaia [modern
names, Albania and Greece] *to make a contribution for the
poor of the saints that are in Jerusalem. For it hath pleased
them ; and they are their debtors. For if the gentiles have
been made partakers of their spiritual things, they also ought
in carnal things to minister to them* (Rom. xv. 26, 27).
Such was the understanding arrived at, when St. Paul
received his commission as Apostle of the Gentiles
(Gal. ii. 10). Already a year ago (viii. 10; ix. 2) he
had commenced this collection, and had made some
advances towards it even at Corinth (1 Cor. xvi. 1—3).
He now urges it there more earnestly. Titus is to be
the collector.

1. *The grace of God*, the offering (τὴν χάριν, *vv.* 1, 4,
6, 7, and 1 Cor. xvi. 3) made to God in His poor.

The churches of Macedonia, as Philippi (Acts xvi. 12),
Thessalonica (Acts xvii. 1), Beroea (Acts xvii. 10).

2. *Experience* (δοκιμῇ, *trial*, or *testing*) *of tribulation :*
cf. Rom. v. 3, 4 ; *tribulation worketh patience, and patience
trial* (δοκιμήν). For the tribulation of the Philippians,
Phil. i. 29, and of the Thessalonians, 1 Thess. ii. 14,
cf. Heb. x. 34.

The riches of their simplicity, i.e. the abundant alms
which they have contributed with singleness of heart,
not considering themselves and their own poverty, but
only the need of their brethren. Simplicity makes men
liberal: cf. ix. 11, and Rom. xii. 8: *he that giveth, with
simplicity.*

3—5. These three verses in the original make one
sentence, which may be outlined in English thus: *Of
their own free choice, with much entreaty begging of us, did*

they give the offering and share of the ministry that is done toward the saints,—yea their own selves they gave. It is one sentence, but the English idiom requires the verb, ἔδωκαν, to be taken twice over. The words δέξασθαι ἡμᾶς in the received Greek text are here unnoticed. They have been put in by some one who did not understand the sentence. The Latin shows no trace of them.

Almsgiving is *the ministry*, and *the saints* are the Christian poor at Jerusalem (Rom. xv. 26).

Not as we hoped, rather, *expected.* The Apostle had every reason to expect good will of the Macedonians; but seeing they had been spoiled of their goods by their persecutors, he could not expect any large sum to be raised. The sum contributed surpassed his expectations.

They gave their own selves. He gives himself, who imitates the widow, who, *casting in two brass mites, cast in all the living that she had* (Luke xxi. 2—4). The Macedonians were *with much entreaty begging* the Apostle to accept all that they had.

To us by the will of God ministers of the Lord. That these words are to be supplied, appears by 1 Cor. i. 1; 2 Tim. i. 1. It is the equivalent of the phrase that bishops and kings use now, *by the grace of God*, or again, *by the mercy of God*,—who *hath mercy [on whom he will* (Rom. ix. 18).

6. *This same grace.* St. Paul here rather plays on two meanings of χάρις, *grace* and *offering*. He wishes the Corinthians not to come short of the *grace* that has been given in Macedonia, and to make an *offering* as the Macedonians have offered.

7. *That . . . you may abound*, a defective translation. The phrase ἀλλ' ἵνα περισσεύητε, *sed ut abundetis*, ought to be rendered, *come, see that you abound.* For this imperative use of ἵνα cf. Eph. v. 33, ἡ δὲ γυνὴ ἵνα φοβῆται τὸν ἄνδρα, *let the wife fear her husband.*

The Corinthians seem to have been loth to part with their money, and on that point St. Paul used special forbearance in dealing with them (1 Cor. ix. 1 —18 ; 2 Cor. xi. 8, 9; xii. 13). He exhorts them here to add the grace of liberality to their other virtues.

Carefulness, here and *v.* 8, rather, *fervour, earnestness* (σπουδή).

8. *By the carefulness*, &c. This is clearer from the Greek ; *by occasion of the fervour of others* [the Mace-donians] *testing the sincerity of your love.* It is not unlikely that *ingenium*, now read in the Vulgate, is the error of an early copyist for *ingenuum*, which would be exactly the γνήσιον (sincerity) of the Greek.

9. *He became poor*, had not *where to lay his head* (Matt. viii. 20).

You might be rich with *the unsearchable riches of Christ* (Eph. iii. 8), told in Eph. i., ii. In all our Lord's sufferings the contrary good was obtained for us (1 Pet. ii. 24). "He was a little child that you may be a perfect man : He was wrapped in swaddling-clothes that you may be loosened from the snares of death : He was in the manger that you may be at the altar : He was on earth that you may be in heaven. That poverty therefore is my patrimony, and my Lord's weakness is my strength " (St. Ambrose on Luke ii. 41).

10. *In this I give counsel*, as he said above (*v.* 8), *I speak not as commanding* your alms.

Not only to do, but also to be willing, i.e. not only to do something [ποιῆσαι, aorist of instantaneous act], but also to stand in readiness [θέλειν, present] for doing more. This readiness had been checked by the dis-sensions that had broken out at Corinth, and no further step had been taken in the way of a collection, until perhaps quite recently (*v.* 6).

A year ago, before the First Epistle was written, which answers some questions about the collection

(1 Cor. xvi. 1). This Second Epistle was written in September, A.D. 58: the First about Easter in the same year.

11. *Out of that which you have.* St. Paul does not ask of the Corinthians the heroism of the Macedonians, to give *beyond their power* (*v.* 3), nor the perfection which Christ proposed to the young man, *go sell what thou hast, and give to the poor* (Matt. xix. 21).

14. *Your abundance* of temporals, *their abundance* of spiritual goods (Rom. xv. 27; xi. 17, 18).

15. Exod. xvi. 18, said of the manna, and applied by St. Paul here in an "accommodated sense," for which see on Rom. ix. 6—8.

16. *The same carefulness for you,* the same interest (σπουδὴν) in you that I have.

17. *Being more careful,* σπουδαιότερος, specially interested.

He went unto you, i.e. he is going to you with this letter. It is the ancient epistolary style to use past tenses for what will be past when the letter is read, *e.g. scribebam,* 'I wrote.'

18. *The brother,* according to some, is St. Luke. But *in the gospel* has no reference to St. Luke's gospel, which was not yet written. It means *in the preaching of the gospel.*

19. *He was ordained by the churches companion of our* travels. St. Chrysostom takes the person spoken of to be St. Barnabas, referring to Acts xiii. 2; Gal. ii. 9, 10. This would satisfy *v.* 18, which seems to indicate some distinguished man. On the other hand St. Barnabas was not *ordained for this grace,* namely, *the grace* (offering, collection) *that hath been given in the churches of Macedonia* (*v.* 1), which seem to be the *churches* referred to in this verse. If they are referred to, they would probably have appointed one of their own countrymen, it may be Sopater of Beroea, or

either of the Thessalonians, Aristarchus and Secundus
(Acts xx. 4), who afterwards went with St. Paul, carrying the collection to Jerusalem. Of these, Aristarchus
(mentioned also Acts xix. 29; xxvii. 2; Coloss. iv. 10;
Philem. 24) is the most likely. It may however have
been Silas (Acts xv. 40), otherwise called Silvanus
(i. 19), who was well-known at Corinth (Acts xviii. 5),
and also at Philippi (Acts xvi, 25, 29), and at Thessalonica (1 Thess. i. 1). The choice seems to lie
between Aristarchus, Silas, and St. Luke, who was
also known in Macedon, and went with St. Paul
to Jerusalem (Acts xx. 6; xxi. 15). St. Barnabas's
companionship with St. Paul had ended as mentioned,
Acts xv. 39, long before this collection was set on foot.

He was ordained, ἐχειροτονήθη. This verb only occurs
in one other place in the New Testament, Acts xiv. 22,
they (Paul and Barnabas) *had ordained to them priests in
every church.* Meaning in classical Greek 'to elect by
show of hands,' in later ecclesiastical Greek this verb
was the regular word used for sacramental ordination
by imposition of hands. Whether in St. Paul's time
it already had that meaning of itself, apart from
context, we must remain in doubt. As for context
here, we know that from early times (cf. Acts vi. 6),
deacons were appointed to look after the temporal
affairs of the church. It may be therefore,—we cannot
say for certain—that this *brother* was a deacon, *ordained
by the churches,* that is, by the election of the churches
and imposition of the Apostle's hands, to be his
coadjutor in temporals. That a deacon was empowered
to preach (*v.* 18), we know by the example of St. Stephen
(Acts vi. 8, 10) and Philip (Acts viii. 40). But this
touches on matter of much erudition and great uncertainty.

Our determined will, τὴν προθυμίαν ἡμῶν, means simply
our ready will in the matter of this contribution. Some

read *your ready will.* But St. Paul identifies himself with the enterprise.

20. *This abundance,* this large contribution.

21. *We foresee,* προνοοῦμεν, *we make provision for.* Rom. xii. 17. St. Paul took care to have companions and colleagues in conveying the money to its destination, that his administration of it might be beyond all challenge. " Cæsar's wife should be above suspicion," and a priest's integrity: therefore it is well to have witnesses.

22. This *brother* again is an uncertainty. Theodoret suggests Apollo (1 Cor. xvi. 12).

With much confidence goes with *we have sent.*

23. This runs in the Greek: *Whether* [I write] *of Titus, he is my companion and fellow-labourer towards you, or* [as to] *our brethren* [the two mentioned, *vv.* 18, 22, they are] *the apostles of the churches,* &c. For this use of *apostle,* cf. Phil. ii. 25, *Epaphroditus, your apostle.*

The glory, or image, *of Christ,* as woman is the glory and image of man (1 Cor. xi. 7).

24. *In the sight of the churches* of Macedonia, which have sent them (*v.* 19).

Our boasting on your behalf—cf. vii. 14.

1. For concerning the ministry that is done towards the saints, it is superfluous for me to write to you : 2. For I know your ready mind, for which I boast of you to the Macedonians, that Achaia also was ready a year ago ; and your emulation hath provoked a great many. 3. Now I have sent the brethren, that what we boast of concerning you be not made void in this behalf, that (as I have said) you may be ready : 4. Lest, when the Macedonians shall come with me, and find you unprepared, we (not to say ye) should be ashamed in this matter. 5. Therefore I thought it necessary to desire the brethren that they would go to you before, and prepare this blessing before promised, to be ready, so as a blessing, not as covetousness. 6. Now this I say : He who soweth sparingly shall also reap sparingly ; and he who soweth in blessings shall also reap of blessings. 7. Every one as he hath determined in his heart, not with sadness, or of necessity : for God loveth a cheerful giver. 8. And God is able to make all grace abound in you ; that ye always, having all sufficiency in all things, may abound in every good work ; 9. As it is written : He hath dispersed abroad ; he hath given to the poor : his justice remaineth for ever. 10. Now he that ministereth seed to the sower will both give you bread to eat, and will multiply your seed, and increase the growth of the fruits of your justice : 11. That being enriched in all things, you may abound unto all bountifulness, which causeth through us thanksgiving to God. 12. For the administration of this service doth not only supply the want of the saints, but aboundeth also by many thanksgivings in the Lord. 13. By the proof of this ministry, glorifying God in the obedience of your confession to the gospel of Christ, and for the liberality of your communicating to them, and to all, 14. And in their praying for you, having an affection for you because of the eminent grace of God in you. 15. Thanks be to God for his unspeakable gift.

1. 'I have praised the ministers' (the collectors, Titus and the other two), *for concerning the ministry* (the collection itself) *it is superfluous for me to write.*

2. The punctuation of the Latin is misleading, and the word *also* is not in the Greek, nor in the earlier editions of the Vulgate. Rewrite : *I boast of you to the Macedonians,* saying *that Achaia is ready from the year past ;*

and your emulation [the emulation created by you] *hath provoked very many.* St. Paul was writing in the Roman Province of Macedonia. Greece was the Province of Achaia. By Achaia here St. Paul means particularly Corinth. That *Achaia is ready from the year past*, was true inasmuch as the Corinthians had begun *not only to do* something, *but also to be willing* to do more, *a year ago* (viii. 10).

4. *Lest when the Macedonians.* The Greek is put more delicately, *lest if* (any) *Macedonians came with me*, ἐὰν ἔλθωσι Μακεδόνες.

In this matter, ἐν τῇ ὑποστάσει ταύτῃ, rather, *in this firm assurance*, which is the meaning of ὑπόστασις in Ps. xxxviii. 7; Ezech. xix. 5; Heb. xi. 1.

5. *This blessing*, i.e. the contribution, *as a blessing*, " for," as St. Chrysostom observes, " no one gives a blessing unwillingly."

Not as avarice, πλεονεξίαν, better, *extortion*, which is the meaning of the verb in vii. 2; xii. 17, 18.

6. *In blessings, of blessings.* The Greek is the same for both, ἐπ' εὐλογίαις, the preposition used signifying the terms or conditions *on* which the thing is done. ' He who sows on the terms of scattering abundantly, shall reap on the conditions of an abundant harvest.'

God loveth a cheerful giver. The quotation is from Prov. xxii. 9, according to the Greek: *God loveth a man cheerful and a giver.* Cf. Ecclus. xxxv. 11.

8. *All grace* and *all sufficiency in all things* includes things both spiritual and temporal.

9. Ps. cxi. 9. *Justice* here is the general virtue, of which St. Thomas speaks, 2a 2æ, q. 58, art. 5. " The acts of all the virtues may belong to justice, as that directs a man to the general good; and in this sense justice is called a *general* virtue " (*Aquinas Ethicus*, ii. 14).

10. Isaias lv. 10, we read, *until it* (the rain) *giveth seed to the sower and bread for eating*, σπέρμα τῷ σπείραντι καὶ

ἄρτον εἰς βρῶσιν, which is exactly the Greek of St. Paul, evidently a quotation from the prophet. This shows that the stop should be put after βρῶσιν (*manducandum*), is unnecessary after σπείραντι (*seminanti*), and should be removed after χορηγήσει (*praestabit*). Translate accordingly : *And he that ministereth seed to the sower and bread to eat, will both give and multiply your seed,* &c.

The fruits of your justice, from Osee x. 12, in the Greek : *Sow to yourselves in justice, reap in the fruit of life, kindle to yourselves the light of knowledge, seek the Lord until fruits of justice* (γεννήματα δικαιοσύνης) *come to you.* The phrase signifies that *all sufficiency in all things* (*v.* 8), which, however frustrated or deferred, is the ordinary reward of virtue, as is so often inculcated in the Book of Proverbs.

11. The Greek has simply, *being enriched unto all simplicity,* *i.e.* open-hearted liberality (viii. 2). The participle, *being enriched,* goes with the verb *abound* in *v.* 8.

Thanksgiving on the part of those who are the objects of the liberality.

12. *The administration of this office* of almsgiving, ἡ λειτουργία τῆς διακονίας ταύτης. The noun λειτουργία (whence *liturgy*), with its derivatives, occurs in these places of the New Testament : Luke i. 23 ; Acts xiii. 2 ; Rom. xv. 16, 27 ; xiii. 6 ; 2 Cor. ix. 12 ; Phil. ii. 17, 25, 30 : Heb. i. 7. 14 ; viii. 2, 6 ; ix. 21 ; x. 11. In most of these places it has reference to some act of religious service or worship. The other substantive, διακονίας, is also a religious term,—whence *deacon.* Terms of religion are used to express offices of charity.

Aboundeth by many thanksgivings in the Lord : more correctly : *overfloweth by the channel of many thanksgivings to the Lord : i.e.* has a further effect in causing the recipients of the bounty to thank God for it.

13, 14. These two verses are very obscure : indeed

N

they can scarcely be said to exemplify the ordinary rules of language. The participle δοκιμάζοντες (*glorifying*) hangs loose, and there is a difficulty about καὶ αὐτῶν δεήσει ὑπὲρ ὑμῶν ἐπιποθούντων, the opening words of *v.* 14. Taking αὐτῶν ἐπιποθούντων for a genitive absolute, and resolving δοκιμάζοντες into an indicative verb, we have : *By the proof of this ministry* [*i.e.* upon the proof of your virtue which this almsgiving affords], *they* [the recipients] *glorify God for the obedience of your confession unto the gospel of Christ, and for the simplicity of your communicating* [liberality of your gifts] *unto them and unto all, they themselves also in prayer for you being desirous of you* [affectionate towards you] *because of the excellent grace of God in you.*

15. *The unspeakable gift* is *the excellent grace of God* just mentioned (*v.* 14). St. Paul does what in *vv.* 12, 13, he paints the Jewish Christians as doing, glorifying God for the faith and Christian charity of the Corinthians.

Here ends the charity sermon. The remainder of the Epistle is the Apostle's defence of himself against his adversaries at Corinth. Nowhere more than in these four next chapters do we feel with St. Jerome (Ep. 48, *ad Pamm.*). " Whenever I read Paul, I seem to hear not so much words as peals of thunder."

Chapter X.

1. Now I Paul myself beseech you, by the meekness and gentleness of Christ, who in presence indeed am lowly among you, but being absent am bold toward you: 2. But I beseech you, that I may not be bold when I am present with that confidence wherewith I am thought to be bold against some, who think of us as if we walked according to the flesh. 3. For walking in the flesh, we do not war according to the flesh. 4. For the weapons of our warfare are not carnal, but powerful through God to the destruction of fortifications, subverting counsels, 5. And every height that exalteth itself against the knowledge of God, and bringing into captivity every understanding to the obedience of Christ; 6. And having in a readiness to revenge all disobedience, when your obedience shall be fulfilled. 7. See the things that are according to outward appearance. If any man trust to himself that he is Christ's, let him think this again with himself, that as he is Christ's, so are we also. 8. For if I also should boast somewhat more of our power, which the Lord hath given us for edification, and not for your destruction, I should not be ashamed. 9. But that I may not be thought as it were to terrify you by epistles: 10. (For his epistles, indeed, say they, are weighty and strong; but his bodily presence is weak, and his speech contemptible:) 11. Let such a one think this, that such as we are in word by epistles, when absent, such are we also in deed, when present. 12. For we dare not rank or compare ourselves with some that commend themselves: but we measure ourselves by ourselves, and compare ourselves with ourselves. 13. But we will not glory beyond our measure, but according to the measure of the rule which God hath measured to us, a measure to reach even to you. 14. For we stretch not ourselves beyond our measure, as if we reached not to you; for we are come as far as to you in the gospel of Christ: 15. Not glorying beyond the measure in other men's labours; but having hope of your increasing faith, to be magnified in you according to our rule abundantly, 16. Yea, to those places that are beyond you to preach the gospel, not to glory in another man's rule in those things that are made ready to our hand. 17. But he that glorieth, let him glory in the Lord. 18. For not he that commendeth himself is approved, but he whom God commendeth.

1. *Now I Paul myself.* For the solemn mention of his own name cf. Gal. v. 2. *Behold, I Paul tell you;* and Philem. 9: *as Paul an old man.*

Who in presence, etc.   St. Paul repeats here what his
adversaries said of him, as again in *v.* 10, not as saying
it of himself.   Hence ταπεινός is better translated in this
place *mean* (its classical sense) rather than *lowly*.

2. *But I beseech you*, δέομαι δέ, *well then, I beseech you*.
The δέ takes up the *I beseech you*, παρακαλῶ, of the previous
verse.   A similar use of δέ will be noted elsewhere.
In this verse he tells his adversaries : ' Take care that,
when I come, you do not find me bold with that boldness which I am credited with possessing only when
not confronted with you.'   Cf. *vv.* 10, 11, and 1 Cor.
iv. 21.

As if we walked according to the flesh, *i.e.* as if our
behaviour were worldly and unchristian.   *To walk* in
the New Testament is *to behave*.   For the whole phrase
as here used cf. Rom. viii. 1, 4, 5, 12, 13 ; 1 Cor. i. 26 ;
2 Cor. i. 17.

3. There is no antithesis between *walk* and *war*, only
a rapid change of metaphor.   The antithesis is between
in the flesh and *according to the flesh*, in the same sense as
between *in the world* and *of the world* (John xvii. 11, 16).
St. Paul was *in the flesh*, as Christ our Lord was *in the
days of his flesh* (Heb v. 7), *of the seed of David according to
the flesh* (Rom. i. 3).

4. *Powerful through God*, not an *arm of flesh* (Jerem.
xvii. 5).   *Fortifications*, the obstacles put in the way of
faith and the gospel by *the wisdom of this world* (1 Cor.
i. 20).   *The weapons of our warfare* are still with the
Church *unto the destruction of* these *fortifications*, which are
multiplied around us daily : we need men of the stamp
of St. Paul to use the weapons.

Subverting counsels, ought to be the beginning of *v.* 5.
The participle καθαιροῦντες is masculine, going with
περιπατοῦντες (*walking*) in *v.* 3, and agreeing with *we*.

Counsels, λογισμούς, *reasonings*, — such philosophy as
that against which St. Paul warns the Colossians (ii. 8).

5. *Every height*, not of intellect, but of pride. *The knowledge of God*, *i.e.* the *recognition* of God as the Lord, and *obedience* to Him. For *knowledge* meaning *obedience*, see Isaias liii. 11. There is always a connection of thought in Scripture between *knowing* God and *obeying* Him as God, cf. Rom. i. 21 : hence the one is put for the other, *e.g.* Ps. lxxviii. 6 ; xciv. 10 ; Jer. iv. 22.

Bringing into captivity every understanding [or *every thought*, πᾶν νόημα] *to the obedience of Christ*, called in Rom. i. 5, *the obedience of faith*. There are two lines of thought, *free thought* and *captive*, or *chastened*, *thought*. On the line of free thought, travel as far as you will, you will never find God and His Christ. To be a Christian, a man must admit some authority in matters of religious specu-lation, an authority which it is a sin to question, challenge, doubt, disbelieve, or disobey. In this most important particular, religion differs from the subject-matter of any physical science, as chemistry. No chemical theory can ever be tendered to any one on chemical grounds, as something which it is wicked and immoral to reject: nor is there such a thing as a chemical revelation, to be believed on authority on pain of damnation (cf. Mark xvi. 16; Gal. i. 8, 9). And therefore the methods of physical science are not the methods of religious truth. Such at least has been the persistent teaching of the Catholic Church from the time of St. Paul. This teaching is the first stone to be laid in building up an argument with non-Catholics.

Against the captivity of faith we must set the capti-vity of being run away with by free thought. It is like the alternative of the two servitudes, to sin and to justice, of which Rom. vi. 19—23.

6. *To revenge all disobedience*, not of the heathen outside the Church, over whom St. Paul claimed no jurisdiction (1 Cor. vi. 12, 13), but of the makers of schism within the Christian community at Corinth.

When your obedience shall be fulfilled. 'When I see the rest of you obedient, I will punish the incorrigible.' For, as St. Augustine says (*Ep. Parmen.* 3, 2), "the severity of discipline is applied without prejudice to peace and unity, when the multitude of the congregation in the church holds aloof from the crime that is anathematised."

7. *See the things that are according to outward appearance, i.e.* see what is staring you in the face.

If any man, and (*v.* 11) *let such a one.* The Apostle appears to have had some particular individual in his mind. If the supposition is correct of a fourth party at Corinth, made up of those who had actually seen our Lord in the flesh (see on 1 Cor. i. 12), this individual will have belonged to that party. Then *as he is Christ's, so are we also*, will be a repetition of 1 Cor. ix. 1 : *Am I not an apostle? have I not seen Christ Jesus our Lord?* Otherwise *Christ's* must mean Christ's minister. The Apostle then says less here than he says afterwards (xi. 23): *They are the ministers of Christ : I am more.*

8. *Unto edification, and not for your destruction*, to build you up, not to pull down the spiritual edifice of your church, 1 Cor. iii. 9—17. "This is the text so often quoted about ecclesiastical power, that it can do nothing against good morals, nay nor even against things of better good, as are the counsels of Christ" (Cajetan).

I should not be ashamed, οὐκ αἰσχυνθήσομαι, *non erubescam* (Vulg.), which is the future tense. Translate therefore, *I shall not be brought to the blush*, understand, 'by my boasting being shown to have no grounds.' The Apostle in fact was about to boast *somewhat more of our power*, and does so, xii. 11, 12. "Since he was about to make some high speech, see how he prepares men's minds for it" (St. Chrysostom).

10. *His bodily presence is weak.* The tradition of the

Greek Church represents Paul as small, pale, shrivelled, and somewhat stooping.

His speech contemptible. See on 1 Cor. ii. 1.

12. This and the next four verses, as Theodoret says, seem to be designedly obscure. The individuals at whom they are aimed would be sufficiently reached by them: upon us the point of the allusion is lost.

The end of this verse is quite altered by the omission in the Vulgate of two words, that occur in almost every Greek MS., and continually in the citations of St. Augustine and the other Fathers. The words are, οὐ συνιᾶσιν, or (what is the same thing) οὐ συνιοῦσιν, meaning, *they do not understand* (cf. Mark viii. 17; Matt. xv. 16, in the Greek). The clause then must be translated thus: *They measure themselves by themselves, and compare themselves with themselves, and* (so doing) *are wanting in understanding.* The general sense is: 'They make fools of themselves, measuring themselves by their own standards,—but we,' &c. (*v.* 13). And this reading is to be preferred.

Several MSS. and Fathers however omit four words, the last two of *v.* 12, and the two first of *v.* 13, οὐ συνιᾶσιν, ἡμεῖς δὲ. The result of the omission would be expressed by the following translation: *But we measuring ourselves by ourselves, and comparing ourselves with ourselves, will not glory beyond our measure,* an improvement on the Vulgate reading, but not equal to the other in manuscript authority. It is observable that by the reading here preferred the process of measuring oneself by oneself is marked as something reprehensible: in the other readings it stands for something commendable.

13. Cf. Eph. iv. 7. Taking the better reading, οὗ ἐμέρισεν, the latter part of this verse would translate more accurately from the Greek: *according to the measure of the rule, the measure that God hath assigned to us, to reach even to you, i.e.* to carry our preaching as far as Corinth.

St. Paul was no unsent teacher, but was specially appointed apostle of the Gentiles, Gal. ii. 7—9 ; Eph. iii. 7, 8 : his going about here and not there was directed by Heaven, Acts xvi. 6—9 ; and his preaching was borne out *by the virtue of signs and wonders, in the power of the Holy Ghost*, Rom. xv. 16, 18, 19 : moreover he was careful to preach *not where Christ was named*, lest he should *build upon another man's foundation*, Rom. xv. 20. On all which points he stands contrasted with his adversaries, those false apostles (xi. 13) of Corinth.

14. The meaning is simply : ' Our coming to Corinth was not a stretching out of ourselves beyond the measure of the rule which God hath assigned us.'

15. *Your increasing faith*, αὐξανομένης τῆς πίστεως ὑμῶν. This is a genitive absolute, not depending on *hope*. The construction is, *hope to be magnified*. Translate : *having hope, as your faith increases* (when the faith is firmly established in Corinth), *to be magnified in you* (to make great advances, using Corinth as a point of departure) *according to our rule* (still within the measure assigned to us), *abundantly, even to those places that are beyond you* (v. 16). The Apostle hoped to make the seaport of Corinth a missionary centre for carrying the faith further westward, to Italy and Spain (Rom. xv. 24).

16. *Not*—to do what those *false apostles* are doing at Corinth—*to glory in another man's rule* (*i.e.* within another man's district) *in those things which are made ready to hand*, *i.e.* in conquests to the faith already secured.

17. Cf. Jerem. ix. 23, 24. The Apostle implies that his adversaries are not glorying in the Lord.

18. *Commendeth himself*, or *introduceth himself*. The verb is the same as in iii. 1, where see note. The *false apostles* had introduced themselves to the Corinthians : God had not introduced them there.

After all, these men were not heretics, scarce even schismatics : they were ministers of the Church, who

had intruded themselves from motives of vanity and
without a call.   What would St. Paul have said of an
heretical or schismatical teacher ?   Cf. Ezech. xiii.

Chapter XI.

1. Would to God you could bear with some little of my folly :
but do bear with me.   2. For I am jealous of you with the jealousy
of God : for I have espoused you to one husband, that I may
present you as a chaste virgin to Christ.   3. But I fear lest, as the
serpent seduced Eve by his subtlety, so your minds should be
corrupted, and fall from the simplicity which is in Christ.   4. For
if he that cometh preacheth another Christ, whom we have not
preached ; or if you receive another spirit, whom you have not
received ; or another gospel, which you have not received ; you
might well bear with him.   5. For I suppose that I have done
nothing less than the great apostles.   6. For though I be rude in
speech, yet not in knowledge : but in all things we have been made
manifest to you.   7. Or did I commit a fault, abasing myself, that
you might be exalted ? because I have preached to you the gospel
of God gratis ?   8. I have taken from other churches, receiving
wages of them to serve you.   9. And when I was present with you,
and wanted, I was burdensome to no man : for that which was
wanting to me the brethren supplied who came from Macedonia ;
and in all things I have kept myself without being a burden to you,
and so I will keep myself.   10. The truth of Christ is in me, that
this glory shall not be stopt in me in the regions of Achaia.
11. Wherefore ? because I love you not ? God knoweth it.   12. But
what I do, that I will do, that I may cut off the occasion from them
that desire occasion ; that in what they glory, they may be found
even as we.   13. For such false apostles are deceitful labourers,
transforming themselves into apostles of Christ.   14. And no
wonder ; for Satan himself transformeth himself into an angel of
light.   15. Therefore it is no great thing if his ministers be transformed as ministers of justice, whose end shall be according to
their works.   16. I say again, (let no man think me to be foolish,
otherwise take me as one foolish, that I also may glory a little,)
17. That which I speak, I speak not according to God, but as it
were in foolishness, in this matter of glorying.   18. Seeing that
many glory according to the flesh, I will glory also.   19. For you

gladly suffer the foolish, whereas you yourselves are wise. **20.** For
you suffer, if a man bring you into bondage, if a man devour you, if
a man take from you, if a man be extolled, if a man strike you on
the face. **21** I speak according to dishonour, as if we had been
weak in this part. Wherein if any man is bold (I speak foolishly)
I am bold also. **22.** They are Hebrews: so am I. They are
Israelites: so am I. They are of the seed of Abraham: so am I.
23. They are ministers of Christ (I speak as one less wise):
I am more: in many more labours, in prisons more frequently, in
stripes above measure, in deaths often. **24.** Of the Jews five times
did I receive forty stripes save one. **25.** Thrice was I beaten with
rods, once I was stoned, thrice I suffered shipwreck, a night and a
day I was in the depth of the sea; **26.** In journeys often, in perils
of rivers, in perils of robbers, in perils from my own nation, in
perils from the gentiles, in perils in the city, in perils in the wilderness, in perils in the sea, in perils from false brethren; **27.** In
labour and painfulness, in watchings often, in hunger and thirst, in
many fastings, in cold and nakedness. **28.** Besides those things
that are without, my daily instance, the solicitude for all the
churches. **29.** Who is weak, and I am not weak? who is scandalized, and I do not burn? **30.** If I must needs glory, I will glory
of the things that concern my infirmity. **31.** The God and Father
of our Lord Jesus Christ, who is blessed for ever, knoweth that I
lie not. **32.** At Damascus, the governor of the nation under Aretas
the king guarded the city of the Damascenes, to apprehend me;
33. And through a window in a basket I was let down by the wall,
and so escaped his hands.

1. *My folly*, explained by *vv.* 16, 17; xii. 6, 11.
Boasting is folly; and to utter one's own praises has
the appearance of boasting, even when it is done for
grave cause, and, as here, under divine inspiration:
therefore St. Paul calls it by the name of that which
it always resembles, and ordinarily is, a name no doubt
which his enemies would be ready enough to apply to
what he is going to say.

2. *The jealousy of God.* As of old God was *jealous
with great jealousy* of any false divinity coming in between
Him and the people of Israel, whom He had espoused
to Himself (Ezech. xvi. 8; Zach. i. 14; viii. 2); so is
He now jealous of the purity of faith in His Church,

which He has espoused to Himself in the Incarnation
(Eph. v. 25—32), according to His promise (Osee ii.
19—24 ; Isaias liv.).

I have espoused you, ἡρμοσάμην, literally, *I have seen you
espoused,* the work of the *shosben,* or *friend of the bridegroom,*
mentioned in John iii. 29.   The Apostle went out on
his mission to the Gentiles to woo this bride for Christ,
as he says : *For Christ we are ambassadors* (v. 20) : even
as Abraham dispatched his faithful servant (Gen. xxiv.
—nameless, all that he says of himself is, *I am the servant
of Abraham, ib. v.* 34, cf. Heb. vii. 3), to bring home a
foreign bride for his son.

A chaste virgin.   The only chastity here referred to
is the chastity of faith.   The *false apostles* at Corinth
were not indeed heretical in their teaching, but they
were vainglorious and fleshly : now among the *works of
the flesh* are *sects* (Gal. v. 19, 20).

3. *The serpent,* Gen. iii. 4 ; cf. Apoc. xii. 9 ; xx. 2.

The simplicity that is in Christ.   Read according to
the Greek of the best MSS., *the simplicity and chastity
that is unto Christ.*   Once more, the chastity of faith,
from which it was possible for such a local church as
Corinth to fall.   From 1 Cor. xv. 12 we see that the
minds of some Corinthians had been *corrupted* upon the
article of the resurrection of the body.

4. Between this and the previous verse there is an
ellipsis of words something to this effect : ' After all,
what fresh boon can these new teachers confer upon
you ? '   Then the Apostle continues in this sense : ' If
they could tell you of a new Jesus, pour out upon you
a new Spirit, preach you a new gospel, you would do
well to suffer them.   But the gospel, the Spirit, the
Saviour, you have already received through my ministration : they can add nothing to what you already
have of me.'

Thus this verse in no way clashes with Gal. i. 6—9 :

rather it is borne out by what is said there (*v.* 7), that there is no other gospel than the gospel which St. Paul preached.

5. *I have done nothing less than the great apostles.* A better translation is given, xii. 11,—*I have in no way come short of them that are above measure apostles:* the Greek being the same in both places. If Peter, James, and John, were referred to, we should compare 1 Cor. xv. 10: *I have laboured more abundantly than all they:* but it is more likely that St. Paul refers ironically to his adversaries, who claimed apostolic gifts superior to his.

6. *Although* (εἰ δὲ καὶ) *I be rude in speech.* On this form of concession see note on vii. 8. We cannot gather from it that St. Paul was *rude* (ἰδιώτης, *devoid of professional training*) *in speech.* Whatever we may think of his Greek, no one who reads this and the following chapter can contest his eloquence.

Knowledge, 1 Cor. i. 5.

7. In this verse, it would be better to put a comma instead of the mark of interrogation after *exalted*, and to change *because* to *in that.*

Abasing myself to labour with my hands (1 Cor. iv. 12 ; Acts xviii. 3).

Gratis. Read again 1 Cor. ix. 7—15.

8. *I have taken from*, ἐσύλησα, *plundered.* The churches in Macedonia, of whom he took alms, were in *very deep poverty* (viii. 2).

9. *The brethren who came from Macedonia*, Silas and Timothy (Acts xviii. 5), apparently from Philippi (Phil. iv. 15).

Supplied, προσανεπλήρωσαν, *supplied in addition* to what I could get by my own labour.

10. This verse means: *As the truth of Christ is in me, this glorying shall not be broken off:* an asseveration. *Broken off* (*infringetur*, Vulgate) is some misconception

of the Greek φραγήσεται, *shall be checked*, the metaphor
taken, as St. Chrysostom says, from interference with
the course of rivers.

Achaia, Greece.

12. From *v.* 20 and 1 Cor. ix. 12 we gather that the
false apostles did accept of recompense for their services.
From this verse it appears that they even gloried in
the amount they received, measuring thereby the appreciation in which they were held, as other preachers
ere now have gloried in "a great take" at a collection.
They would gladly have had St. Paul for an example
to quote and a rival to meet on this ground; and that
is the occasion which he says he is resolved to cut off.

13. This verse is better rendered: *Such men are false
apostles, deceitful workmen, transforming themselves into apostles
of Christ*.

14. *An angel of light*, whereas his is *the power of darkness* (Luke xxii. 53; Col. i. 13).

16. *Again I say*. What he says is the rest of the
verse, as all the Fathers agree; the marks of parenthesis
therefore ought to be removed. The verse is virtually
a repetition of *v.* 1.

17. *Not according to God*, or, as the Greek has it, *not
according to the Lord*, that is, not according to the general
rule of our Lord's teaching, which is, *Sound not a trumpet
before thee* (see Matt. vi. 1—6): which general rule
however fails to apply, when such a motive as the good
of the Church requires a man, as it required St. Paul,
to speak his own praises. Yet in so doing, by way of
deprecating censure, he calls his language what such
language generally amounts to, *folly* and *not according to
the Lord*. Thus a clergyman, disguised as a layman
to save his life, might say to a friend: 'You see me in
this uncanonical costume:' because it is contrary to
canon law for a clergyman ordinarily to dress as a
layman, though it be no violation of the canons in an

emergency.   St. Paul then is far from denying his own
inspiration in this passage.

In this matter of glorying, ἐν ταύτῃ τῇ ὑποστάσει τῆς
καυχήσεως, the same phrase as ix. 4, which see.
Translate, *in this assurance of glorying*.

18. *According to the flesh*, " in exterior things, birth,
wealth, learning, circumcision, Hebrew parentage,
reputation " (St. Chrysostom).   The phrase is explained
by Phil. iii. 4, 5.

19. *The foolish*, *i.e.* those who speak in their own
praise, *vv.* 1, 16, 17.   It is not without irony that the
Corinthians here are called *wise*, as appears by the
strange proof of their wisdom given in the next verse.
The tone is similar to that of 1 Cor. iv. 8, 10.

20. The general meaning of this verse is: ' You
suffer the tyranny of those false apostles, who '—he
goes on to say in particular—' *bring* you '—*i.e.* try to
bring you, old English, *are a-bringing of you*, cf. note on
ii. 15—' *into bondage*,' that of the Jewish law (Gal. ii.
4; v. 1); 'who *devour* you by the large remunerations
which they *take* for their services '—for *devouring* in this
sense see Mark xii. 40; Luke xx. 47; 'who are *extolled*,
or pride themselves, as *Hebrews*, *Israelites*, &c. (*vv.* 22,
23); who browbeat you and offer even to *strike you on
the face*.'

21. *I speak according to dishonour*, *i.e.* as one who quite
loses caste in comparison with these brave bragadoccios,
as if we had been weak in this part, *i.e.* as if it were mere
weakness that prevented our bullying you as they
did.   The words *in this part* are absent from the best
MSS.

Wherein if any man is bold is a mistranslation as well of
the Greek, ἐν ᾧ δ᾽ ἄν τις τολμᾷ, as of the Latin, *in quo quis
audet*.   The original Rheims version (ed. 1583 and 1600)
has: *Wherein any man dare*, which is correct.   The *if*
has been inserted by some one who did not understand

the English, did not look at the Latin, and possibly took the Greek ἄν here to mean *if*.

Is bold to launch out into his own praise.

Foolishly, as explained on *vv*. 1, 16, 17, 19. It had been better for the sense, if *Wherein any man is bold* had begun a new verse.

22. *Hebrews*, so called not from Abraham's ancestor, Heber (Gen. xi. 14—17), but from Abraham himself, to whom the name was first given, meaning *one who comes from across the water* (τῷ περάτῃ, Gen. xiv. 13). The word here denotes the nationality of Abraham's descendants; as the term *Israelites* denotes their being the peculiar people of God (Exod. xix. 5, 6; Rom. ix. 4); while *seed of Abraham* points to them as inheriting the Messianic promises (Rom. ix. 5, 7, 8; Gal. iii. 16). From this verse it appears again that St. Paul's principal opponents at Corinth were the Judaizing faction (cf. Phil. iii. 2).

St. Paul's own standing as a Jew is stated, Phil. iii. 5.

23. *They are ministers of Christ:* that is, so they called themselves; but according to St. Paul they were *false apostles* and served another master (*vv*. 13—15). Of their exact status in the Church of Corinth we cannot now be sure.

I speak as one less wise, see above on *vv*. 1, 17.

In many more labours, not exactly the Greek, which is, *in labours more abundantly* (περισσοτέρως), not yet the Latin, *in laboribus plurimis, in labours very many*.

In prisons more frequently: the Greek has *more abundantly* (περισσοτέρως, again). One instance antecedent to this Epistle is related in Acts xvi. 23—36.

In deaths often, cf. i. 8—10.

24. *Of the Jews five times forty stripes save one.* We have no other record of these scourgings. *Save one*, to be on the safe side of the law: *Yet so that they exceed not the number of forty, lest thy brother depart shamefully torn*

before thy eyes (Deut. xxv. 3). The culprit was scourged with thongs of leather, thirteen blows on his bare breast, and thirteen on each shoulder. During the operation verses of the Law were read to him, Deut. xxviii. 58, 59; xxix. 9; concluding with Psalm lxxvii. 38.

25. *Thrice was I beaten with rods*, by the Gentiles, as was our Blessed Lord Himself (John xix. 1). There was no legal limit to the number of blows here. One of these occasions, at Philippi, is recounted by St. Luke (Acts xvi. 22).

Once I was stoned, and taken up for dead, at Lystra (Acts xiv. 18).

Thrice I suffered shipwreck, when and how we do not know. The shipwreck recounted in Acts xxvii. took place three years after this was written.

A night and a day, twenty-four hours, *I was in the depths of the sea*. " The hull of the vessel went to pieces, and all the night and the day I spent, carried hither and thither by the waves " (Theodoret), clinging, we may suppose, to some fragment of the wreck. We know nothing more of this incident.

26. *In journeys often*. This is best illustrated by a map of the (known) voyages of St. Paul, and reflecting what travelling meant in those days for a man poorly supplied with money.

27. *In many fastings*, voluntary afflictions over and above the *hunger and thirst* which came perforce.

The whole passage *vv.* 23—27 is parallelled by vi. 4—10. There is none more characteristic of St. Paul.

28. *Those things which are without* (τῶν παρεκτός, a rare word occurring only Matt. v. 32; Acts xxvi. 29), the external and bodily troubles above mentioned, as distinguished from the distresses of mind mentioned in this and the next verse.

My daily instance (ἐπίστασις, the reading of the best MSS., supported by the Vulgate *instantia*, not ἐπισύστασις), attention, anxiety (φροντίδων ἐπιστάσεις, Sophocles, *Antig.* 225), the state of mind of a commander in the field, like Wellington at Torres Vedras, or (cf. x. 4) St. Paul at Ephesus.

The solicitude for all the churches of the Gentiles, by the appointment of Heaven and the agreement specified in Gal. ii. 7—9. There is this difference among others between St. Peter and St. Paul, that St. Paul has had no successors.

29. *Who is weak, and I am not weak?* So St. Paul imitated his Master, of whom it was written : *He took our infirmities and bore our diseases* (Isaias liii. 4; Matt. viii. 17). *To the weak*, he says, *I became weak* (1 Cor. ix. 22), *i.e.* 'I accommodated myself to their *weak conscience*' (1 Cor. viii. 10). For an instance of St. Paul being *on fire*, when one was *scandalized*, see 1 Cor. viii. 9—13. As St. Chrysostom says : "As though he were in himself the Church throughout the world, so did he grieve for every single member."

30. The whole tale of his glorying, *vv.* 23—29, is a tale, not of miracles, not of eloquence, not of successes, but of sufferings. This he calls *my infirmity.*

32. *At Damascus*, &c., Acts ix. 23—25. This was at the opening of St. Paul's missionary career, three years after his conversion. Flight has always an air of weakness, even an escape like this, which reminds us of the daring escape of St. John of the Cross from his confinement at Toledo.

Aretas the Arab was the father of Herod's first wife, whom he divorced to marry Herodias (Mark vi. 17), for which outrage Aretas made war on him with success, and became master of Damascus.

o

Chapter XII.

1. If I must glory, (it is not expedient indeed :) but I will come to visions and revelations of the Lord. 2. I know a man in Christ above fourteen years ago, (whether in the body I know not, or out of the body, I know not : God knoweth,) such a one caught up to the third heaven. 3. And I know such a man, (whether in the body, or out of the body, I know not : God knoweth,) 4. That he was caught up into paradise, and heard secret words, which it is not granted to man to utter. 5. Of such a one I will glory : but for myself I will glory nothing, but in my infirmities. 6. For even if I would glory, I shall not be foolish ; for I shall say the truth : but I forbear, lest any man should think of me above that which he seeth in me, or any thing he heareth from me. 7. And lest the greatness of the revelations should puff me up, there was given me a sting of my flesh, an angel of Satan to buffet me. 8. For which thing I thrice besought the Lord, that it might depart from me. 9. And he said to me : My grace is sufficient for thee ; for power is made perfect in infirmity. Gladly, therefore, will I glory in my infirmities, that the power of Christ may dwell in me. 10. Therefore I take pleasure in my infirmities, in reproaches, in necessities, in persecutions, in distresses for Christ's sake : for when I am weak, then I am powerful. 11. I am become foolish ; you have compelled me to it : for I ought to have been commended by you ; for in nothing have I been inferior to those who are above measure apostles, although I am nothing. 12. Yet the signs of my apostleship have been wrought on you in all patience, in signs, and wonders, and mighty deeds. 13. For what is there that you have had less than the other churches, but that I myself was not burdensome to you ? pardon me this injury. 14. Behold, now the third time I am ready to come to you ; and I will not be burdensome to you : for I seek not the things that are yours, but you : for neither ought the children to lay up for the parents, but the parents for the children. 15. And I most gladly will spend and be spent myself for your souls ; although, loving you more, I be loved less. 16. But be it so, I did not burden you : but being crafty, I caught you by guile. 17. Did I circumvent you by any of those whom I sent to you ? 18. I desired Titus, and I sent with him a brother. Did Titus circumvent you ? did we not walk with the same spirit ? did we not in the same steps ? 19. Of old, think you that we excuse ourselves to you ? we speak before God in Christ ; but all things, my dearly beloved, for your edification. 20. For I fear,

lest, when I come, I shall not find you such as I would, and that I shall be found by you such as you would not : lest perhaps contentions, envyings, animosities, dissensions, detractions, whisperings, swellings, seditions, be among you : **21.** Lest again, when I come, God humble me among you, and I bewail many of them that sinned before, and have not done penance for the uncleanness, and fornication, and lasciviousness that they have committed.

1. The best Greek reading has: *Must I glory? It is not expedient indeed, but I will come to the visions,* &c.

Not expedient, as a rule : " for it is not in the nature of good deeds in themselves to cause elation : elation comes of the testimony and knowledge of the multitude " (St. Chrysostom)

2. *I know a man.* Evidently himself.

Above fourteen years ago. This was written A.D. 58, twenty-four years after St. Paul's conversion. There is therefore no reference to the events recorded in Acts ix.; but to the year A.D. 44, in which Paul was sent with Barnabas from Antioch to Jerusalem, Acts xi. 27—30; xii. 25. The rapture next mentioned may be the one mentioned as occurring in the Temple (Acts xxii. 17 —21), though that is far from certain.

Whether in the body, I know not, or out of the body, I know not. " If Paul knew not," says St. Chrysostom, " much less do we." We do not even understand the alternatives proposed. Was he caught up, body and soul, to heaven? Or did his soul quit his body and fly to heaven? Or did his soul all the while remain in his body, the activity of it only being raised to heaven, but not the substance? Lastly, what is *the third heaven?*

4. *Paradise* seems somehow distinct from *the third heaven.* " To the third heaven, and thence to paradise," says Clement of Alexandria (*Strom.* v. 12).

Secret words, cf. John iii. 12 ; Apoc. x. 4. " Some say that these words were things ; and that he saw the beauty of paradise, and the bands of the Blessed

therein, and heard the full chorus of their song " (Theodoret). St. Thomas (2a 2æ, q. 175, art. 3) argues that
he saw the face of God as the Blessed see it in heaven.

5. *For such a one . . . but for myself.* This St. Paul's
distinction of himself from himself is explained by the
words of St. Thomas (2a 2æ, q. 129, art. 3, ad 4): " In
man there is found something great, which he possesses
by the gift of God; and some shortcoming which
attaches to him from the weakness of his nature. Magnanimity makes a man deem himself worthy of great
honours in consideration of the gifts that he possesses
of God; while humility makes him think little of himself
in consideration of his own shortcomings."

6. The meaning is: ' If I had a mind to glory, there
would be no folly in my so doing, seeing that, whatever
I said in my own commendation, I should not pass the
bounds of truth. But I refrain from all further glorying:
rather let me be judged by what is visible and apparent
about me, in my person and in my preaching.'

7. *A sting of my flesh.* That this was some strong
motion of impurity, either physical or excited by the
Evil One, is the favourite explanation of modern
ascetical writers. They adopt it themselves without
suspicion, and have made it generally accepted among
the people, so successfully as to have determined the
English phrase to this special meaning. Yet such
certainly was not the meaning of St. Paul.

The Greek Fathers wholly ignore this explanation.
No Latin Father of the first six centuries gives it any
clear support. St. Thomas approves of it, but assigns
another explanation as the literal meaning of the text.
So much for authorities. The intrinsic arguments against
this explanation are: (*a*) St. Paul is evidently speaking
of something extraordinary, peculiar, and personal to
himself, not of any incident of ordinary humanity, as
such temptations are, as he describes, Rom. vii. 23.

(*b*) Nor could he lawfully have *gloried* (*v.* 9), or *taken pleasure* (*v.* 10) in such an infirmity as is supposed. (*c*) The interpretation has been countenanced by the Latin *stimulus carnis*, which however is not a very accurate rendering of σκόλοψ τῇ σαρκί, *a thorn to the flesh*. The word σκόλοψ means a *pointed piece of wood*, used not as a *goad* or *sting* (*stimulus*, κέντρον, Ecclus. xxxviii. 25; Acts ix. 5; xxvi. 14; 1 Cor. xv. 55, 56), to be thrust in and pulled out again, but as a *skewer* remaining in the flesh and causing continual pain (Num. xxxiii. 55; Ezech. xxviii. 24; Ecclus. xliii. 19).

The older opinion remains therefore in possession, that the *sting of the flesh*, or rather, *the thorn to the flesh*, was some sort of bodily ailment,—what, we cannot say, but it was probably known to the Corinthians, and St. Paul spoke clearly enough for them to whom he was writing. He mentions it again, Gal. iv. 13, where see note. This ailment is likewise called *an angel of Satan;* as in Luke xiii. 11, 16, we read of *a woman who had a spirit of infirmity eighteen years, and she was bowed together, neither could she look upwards at all,* whom our Lord speaks of as *this daughter of Abraham whom Satan hath bound these eighteen years;* as Job was smitten by Satan with a grievous ulcer (Job ii. 7: cf. Ps. lxxvii. 49); as the excommunicate Corinthian was *delivered to Satan for the destruction of the flesh* (1 Cor. v. 5). On this connection of Satan with bodily sickness, we may observe that sickness and death, in the present order, are consequences of sin, and *it was by the envy of the devil that death entered into the world* (Wisd. ii. 24).

Bearing in mind however how St. Antony and other saints were tormented by the physical and sensible action of evil spirits—we remember in modern times the conflicts of the Cure d'Ars with *le grappin*—it may be that St. Paul also was tormented by Satan visibly and corporeally, and to that he refers.

Anyhow the affliction was chronic and continual. St. Chrysostom observes that the phrase for *to buffet* is not ἵνα κολαφίσῃ, the aorist of transient action, but ἵνα κολαφίζῃ, the continuous present.

8. *Thrice I besought the Lord that it might depart*, as the Lord Himself prayed on Olivet, Matt. xxvi. 44.

9. *Power is made perfect in infirmity.* The power of God sustaining is brought out in human weakness.

Gladly will I glory. The word *rather*, μᾶλλον, has fallen out before *glory*. 'Far from being dejected over my *infirmities*,' he says, '*I will rather glory* in them.'

Dwell in me, ἐπισκηνώσῃ, the word is used of soldiers *billeted* or *quartered* upon a civilian.

10. Here St. Paul's *glorying* (begun at xi. 1) all ends in what St. Ignatius of Loyola in his *Spiritual Exercises* describes as "the most perfect humility, . . . when I choose poverty with Christ poor rather than riches, reproaches with Christ laden with them rather than honours, and I desire to be counted a good-for-nothing and a fool for Christ, who was first held for such, rather than pass for a wise and prudent man in this world."

So St. Paul in this verse. Cf. Acts v. 41.

11. *I am become foolish*, γέγονα ἄφρων,—better, *I have done making a fool of myself* (boasting). For this use of γέγονα cf. Apoc. xvi. 17; xxi. 6.

I have no way come short of them that are above measure apostles. The Greek is a repetition of xi. 5, where see note.

Although (εἰ καί, see note on vii. 8) *I be nothing.*

12. *The signs of my apostleship :* in the Greek, *the signs of the apostle.* *Patience* is mentioned before *signs and wonders* (joined together as in fifteen other places in the Old and New Testament) and *mighty deeds*, as the first of the signs of the true Apostle. Cf. Luke xxi. 19.

13. Cf. xi. 9. *Pardon me this injury*, the wrong I have done to myself (cf. 1 Cor. ix. 14), if you are at all hurt thereby. .

14. *Now the third time.* These words must be taken with *I am ready*, not with *to come.* The Apostle did actually visit Corinth only twice, once before (Acts xviii. 1), and once after (Acts xx. 2) the writing of these two Epistles. The *second grace*, or second visit, as he intended it to be, that between the First and Second Epistle, was never paid: see on i. 15, 16.

Children ought to support their parents, but they are not expected to *lay up* for them, but rather the *parents for the children*, who are naturally the survivors and more concerned in the future. St. Paul puts in this remark to shield the Corinthians from the odium of not supporting him their spiritual father.

16. *But be it so* introduces an objection, that at any rate he put the Corinthians to the charge of supporting his envoys, which he shows he did not do.

18. *I desired Titus* to go to you (viii. 6, 16, 17).

A brother, τὸν ἀδελφόν, *the brother*, possibly the same whom he was sending again, *the brother whose praise is in the gospel through all the churches* (viii. 18), whoever that was. Titus at any rate had come under their observation already, as the medium of communication between them and St. Paul (ii. 13; vii. 6, 7).

19. *Of old* (πάλαι, a better authorised reading than the received Greek πάλιν) *think you that we excuse ourselves to you?* The sense appears better without the interrogation: *You have been thinking some time that we are on our defence before you.* 'Not so,' the sense of the Apostle continues, 'God is our judge: *we speak before God in Christ;* and all that we have said in our own behalf is *for your edification*, that you be not scandalized in us, but not as though we were amenable to your tribunal.' Cf. 1 Cor. iv. 3.

20. *For*, far from your judging me, *I fear lest when I come*, I shall have to sit in judgment and pass severe sentence upon some of you.

Contentions, &c., such as those spoken of, 1 Cor. i. 11; iii. 3. *Contentions, envyings, animosities, dissensions:* the Greek of these four words is repeated in Gal. v. 20.

21. *Humble me among you*, as a teacher is humbled when he finds that his scholars have not learnt of him.

Uncleanness, &c. Corinth, it must be remembered, was the city of Aphrodite, the Greek Venus: its gaieties were proverbial. The sins here spoken of would have been committed after baptism. That the first Christians were far from immaculate, see on 1 Cor. xi. 20.

Chapter XIII.

1. Behold, this is the third time I am coming to you: In the mouth of two or three witnesses shall every word be established. 2. I have told you before, and foretell, as present, and now absent, to them that sinned before, and to all the rest, that, if I come again, I will not spare. 3. Do you seek a proof of Christ who speaketh in me, who toward you is not weak, but is mighty in you? 4. For though he was crucified through weakness, yet he liveth by the power of God: for we also are weak in him, but we shall live with him by the power of God toward you. 5. Try your ownselves if you be in the faith; prove ye yourselves. Know you not your ownselves, that Christ Jesus is in you? unless perhaps you be reprobates. 6. But I trust that you shall know that we are not reprobates. 7. Now we pray God that you may do no evil; not that we may appear approved, but that you may do that which is good, and that we may be as reprobates. 8. For we can do nothing against the truth, but for the truth. 9. For we rejoice that we are weak, and you are strong. This also we pray for, your perfection. 10. Therefore I write these things being absent, that, being present, I may not deal more severely, according to the power which the Lord hath given me to edification, and not to destruction. 11. For the rest, brethren, rejoice. Be perfect, take exhortation, be of one mind, have peace; and the God of peace and of love will be with you. 12. Salute one another with a holy kiss. All the saints salute you. 13. The grace of our Lord Jesus Christ, and the charity of God, and the communication of the Holy Ghost be with you all. Amen.

1. *This is the third time I am coming.* See on xii. 14.

In the mouth of two or three witnesses, &c. (Deut. xix. 15), "counting for witnesses his visits and denunciations" (St. Chrysostom). His thrice intended visit to Corinth, and his actually going there now for the second time, reminds St. Paul of this text of the Law. We must not press the application too closely, as it is only quoted in an "accommodated sense." For another instance of such quotation see viii. 15.

It has been proposed to take the quotation literally, as though St. Paul was going to open a spiritual court of justice at Corinth. There is a nineteenth century plainness about the suggestion, but it fails of being in touch with the manner of St. Paul, who like his countrymen and contemporaries delighted to allege the words of the Old Testament in other than their obvious measuring. For examples see iii. 16; Gal. iv. 24; Heb. vii. 3; 1 Cor. ix. 9; xiv. 21.

2. *As present and now absent.* This text has suffered a curious mutilation, even to the effacement of the sense. St. Paul undoubtedly wrote, ὡς παρὼν τὸ δεύτερον καὶ ἀπὼν νῦν. The received Greek text adds γράφω (I write) but the word is absent from the three best MSS., and is well away. The old Latin versions had *sicut præsens secundo*, or, less well, *ut præsens bis*. The *bis* got into *vobis*, and the superfluous *vobis* was struck out of the Clementine Vulgate. The Greek words mean literally, *as present the second time, even absent now.* The meaning is none of the clearest, but taking it (see on *v.* 1) that St. Paul so far had only been once actually to Corinth, we draw this sense: even *now in my absence, you may already consider me as present for the second time.* St. Paul was actually present in Corinth for the second and last time shortly after writing this Epistle (Acts xx. 2, 3).

3. *Do you seek?   An quæritis?* but the Greek ἐπεὶ ζητεῖτε is undoubtedly the original: ἐπεὶ has passed into εἰ, represented by *an.* In a classical Greek author, the verb would be the imperative, *come, seek;* but it may be doubted whether this construction is used by St. Paul. Taking then ζητεῖτε for the indicative, we have the sentence thus: *Since you seek a proof of Christ speaking in me,* (v. 5) *try your own selves, prove ye yourselves.* The intervening words are all a parenthesis.

Is mighty in you, in miraculous graces, 1 Cor. xiv.; 2 Cor. xii. 12.

4. *Crucified through weakness,* of His own choosing (John x. 18; Phil. ii. 6, 8).

By the power of God, His Father's and His own (John v. 17—21; x. 30; xvii. 10).

Weak in him, in the likeness of Him, as set forth in 1 Cor. iv. 9—13.

We shall live with him. This does not refer to heaven and the resurrection, but to the *power of God towards you,* that is the power of ruling and judging which the Apostles, as mouthpieces of the risen Christ, exercise over the faithful. This text by implication warrants not only that power, but also the ecclesiastical pomp and splendour which are the ensigns of that power in the Pope and Bishops, the successors of the Apostles, to this day. Individually, like other Christians, and more than other Christians, they must *bear in their bodies the dying of Jesus:* but, officially, *the life also of* the risen and glorified and reigning *Jesus must be made manifest in their mortal flesh* (2 Cor. iv. 4).

The future, *we shall live,* is used in reference to his coming visit to Corinth.

5. To understand this verse, we must observe that it is the premise to a conclusion, *a proof of Christ that speaketh in me* (v. 3), an argument of the Apostle's official power, not of his personal sanctity. We are not to look

in the premise for an element quite foreign to the conclusion. Therefore the *faith* spoken of in this verse is
not the theological faith, whereby we are justified (Rom.
v. 1). There is no question in the whole passage of any
justification, not of St. Paul, nor of the Corinthians;
but St. Chrysostom is right in his surmise: "To me he
seems here to speak of the faith of miracles: for believers
in those days wrought miracles." For "the faith of
miracles," see on 1 Cor. xii. 9; xiii. 2. Consequently,
Christ Jesus is in you, means that He works wonders by
you, according to His promise (John xiv. 12). It does
not refer to that union of grace and love elsewhere
mentioned (John vi. 57; xv. 4).

Nor is this interpretation to be set aside for the
concluding words of the verse, *unless perhaps you be repro-*
bates. The meaning of that term must be decided by
the meaning that it bears in the next verse. There
(*v.* 6) it does not mean *marked for damnation*, but simply
rejected, set aside and suspended from power; in St. Paul's
case, the power of the ministry. Here then it means
set aside (doubtless for some fault so deserving it) from
the miraculous powers then common among Christians.
The Greek would be better translated, *unless in some thing*
(μή τι, not μή πως) *you be set aside.*

From the explanation given it appears how entirely
without foundation in this verse of St. Paul is the
Lutheran doctrine of justification by believing that you
are justified, the doctrine condemned by the Council of
Trent (Sess. vi. cap 9, and cann. 12—15).

7. For *not that*, οὐχ ἵνα, St. Chrysostom reads ἵνα μή,
that not, which shows the sense better. It may be
Englished: *that it may not be a case of our appearing clad*
in power (δόκιμοι), *but that, while you do right* (ὑμεῖς for the
classical ὑμεῖς μὲν), *we may appear as though set aside from*
office (ἀδόκιμοι). Theodoret well explains: "We pray
that we may not receive from you any occasion to show

the active exercise of the apostolic charge: rather I
pray that you may be resplendent in all good deeds,
and that we may hide our power."

8. *Against the truth*, the cause of truth and justice,
which is the cause of the innocent.

9. *We rejoice that*, &c., read, *we rejoice when*. The
present Vulgate *quoniam* is against all Greek authority,
and against that of the early Latin versions, which
have *quum*, or *quando* (*when*).   *Weak* is *powerless to punish ;*
and *strong* means *strong in faith and good works.*

10. *Unto edification, and not unto destruction*, that is, to
the building up of the good rather than to the destruction and punishment of the wicked.   *Not* here is equal
to *not so much*, a usual Hebrew idiom (cf. Jerem. vii.
22, 23; Osee vi. 6; John vii. 16; xii. 44).   For the
matter, see Luke ix. 54—56; John iii. 17; xii. 47.   For
the rest, the Apostle, like the prophet Jeremy (Jer. i. 10),
and every ruler of the Church, was *set to pluck up and
destroy*, as well as *to build and plant*; and he knew his
work (x. 4—6).

11. *Take exhortation*, rather, *take comfort*, παρακαλεῖσθε,
for which word see on i. 4, 6.

12. *A holy kiss*, in eastern fashion (cf. on 1 Cor.
xvi. 20), on which St. Chrysostom further writes : " We
are the temple of Christ.   We kiss the porch and
entrance of this temple in kissing one another.   See
you now how many kiss the porch of this temple in
which we are met, some stooping down for the purpose,
others touching it with their hand and applying their
hand to their mouth ?   Through these gates also, the
gates and doors of our body, Christ has entered in, and
does enter in to us, whenever we communicate.   Ye
who partake of the mysteries know my meaning.   In
no common way is our body honoured, receiving the
Body of the Lord.   Let them hear this who speak
foul language ; let them hear who give immodest

kisses; and shudder to think what a mouth they dishonour."

All the saints, the Christians where St. Paul was writing (1 Cor. i. 2; Col. i. 2), probably at Philippi. Salutations are not added in detail, as elsewhere, because the Apostle was shortly to visit Corinth.

13. In this verse St. Paul gives his blessing, like a bishop as he was (Acts xiii. 2, 3; 2 Tim. i. 6), to the Corinthians, in the name of the three Persons of the Blessed Trinity. " Let us also pray to be made worthy of the apostolic benediction, and to attain to the good things of the promise " (Theodoret).

THE EPISTLE TO THE GALATIANS.

INTRODUCTION.

GALATIAN, Γαλάτης, was the Greek name for the people, otherwise known as Gauls or Celts, who once inhabited France and the British Isles. The Greeks had experience of an invasion of them, B.C. 279. Repulsed from Greece, this Celtic people overran Asia Minor. Gradually they were confined to a strip of land, 200 miles long, in the interior, of which Ancyra was the capital. But the Roman province of Galatia at the time of St. Paul was wider than Galatia proper. It included these places mentioned in the Acts, Antioch in Pisidia (xiii. 14), Iconium (xiii. 51), Lycaonia with its cities of Lystra and Derbe (xiv. 6), and part of Phrygia (xviii. 23). This is the Galatia spoken of by St. Peter (1 Pet. i. 1). On the other hand St. Luke twice only mentions *the Galatian country*, τὴν Γαλατικὴν χώραν (Acts xvi. 6; xviii. 23); and both times he evidently means Galatia proper. St. Luke knew and lived in Asia Minor: St. Peter wrote at a distance. It was natural therefore for St. Peter to speak of the official Galatia; while St. Luke used the word of what in Asia Minor was popularly called Galatia, namely, the country of the Galatians proper. It must ever

remain a moot point whether St. Paul addresses the
larger and official Galatia, all within the Roman
province of that name, or the much smaller country
of the Galatians proper, who alone in Asia Minor
would commonly be called Galatians. We shall
assume that St. Paul's use of the term is that of his
fellow-voyager St. Luke, the local and narrower
sense. The objections to this view will appear as
we proceed to be by no means insurmountable.

St. Paul twice visited Galatia proper. " When
they (Paul and Silas) had passed through Phrygia
and the country of Galatia " (Acts xvi. 6) : " he went
through the country of Phrygia and Galatia in order,
confirming all the disciples " (Acts xviii. 23) : this is
all the information that St. Luke affords us concerning these visits. *The churches of Galatia* are men.
tioned (1 Cor. xvi. 1) as having had *order given* them
by St. Paul *concerning the collections that are made for
the saints* at Jerusalem. The rest of our information
about the Galatians must be drawn from the Epistle
itself.

The date of the Epistle turns as well on the
previous question, to what Galatians precisely the
Epistle is addressed, as also on the interpretation
put upon i. 6. Conformably to the view already
taken, and the interpretation to be given presently,
the Epistle must be subsequent to the two visits to
Galatia above related by St. Luke (see on iv. 13—16),
subsequent that is to A.D. 54. On the other hand
we have clear intrinsic grounds for supposing this
Epistle to have been in close conjunction with that
to the Romans, of which it is a sort of first edition,

the theme of both being the same : *we account a man to be justified by faith without the works of the law* (Rom. iii. 28 : cf. Gal. ii. 16). To compare things sacred to things profane, the *Gorgias* of Plato is in the same way a first edition of his *Republic*. Of the two epistles we may fairly suppose that which is the more incomplete and rapid outline to have been first written. So St. Chrysostom (Preface to *Romans*) : " In my judgment the epistle to the Galatians is prior to that to the Romans." The Epistle then to the Galatians stands in order of composition between the Second to Corinthians and that to the Romans. This is the hypothesis of Lightfoot (cf. 2 Cor. xii. 20, 21 ; Gal. v. 19—21 ; Rom. xiii. 13) and others. The date then would be the winter of A.D. 58-9.

Our Lord had instructed His Apostles to preach the gospel to the entire world (Matt. xxviii. 19 ; Mark xvi. 15). The Gentiles then were to be members of the Christian Church. This was shown in vision to St. Peter, and recognised by the rest of the disciples (Acts x. ; xi. 1—18). But was the Synagogue to go wherever the Church went ? Did the taking up of the yoke and burden of Christ mean the taking up therewith of the yoke of the law of Moses, as the first Christians, being Jewish converts, bore it, and as it continued to be borne at Jerusalem till close upon the destruction of the city ? Three questions in fact arose in this matter.

1. Must all Christians absolutely keep the law of Moses ?

2. Are not the Christians who keep the law of Moses better Christians than the rest : or at least

is not circumcision necessary to the perfection of the Christian man ?

3. Is the observance of the Mosaic law, is circumcision itself, so much as permissible in a Christian ?

The first question was answered in the negative by the Council of Jerusalem (Acts xv. ; Gal. ii.).

The main purpose of the Epistle to the Galatians is to enforce the negative also to the second question: see especially ii. 4 ; iii. 24—29 ; v. 6 ; vi. 15.

The answer to the third question we shall investigate upon ii. 17 ; v. 2, 4: cf. Acts xvi. 3, and again Gal. v. 6 ; vi. 15.

CHAPTER I.

1. Paul, an apostle, (not from men, neither by man, but by Jesus Christ, and God the Father, who raised him from the dead,) 2. And all the brethren who are with me, to the churches of Galatia: 3. Grace be to you, and peace, from God the Father, and from our Lord Jesus Christ, 4. Who gave himself for our sins, that he might deliver us from this present wicked world, according to the will of God and our Father: 5. To whom is glory for ever and ever. Amen. 6. I wonder that you are so soon removed from him who called you to the grace of Christ, to another gospel: 7. Which is not another; only there are some that trouble you, and would pervert the gospel of Christ. 8. But though we, or an angel from heaven, preach a gospel to you beside that which we have preached to you, let him be anathema. 9. As we said before, so I say now again: If any one preach to you a gospel beside that which you have received, let him be anathema. 10. For do I now persuade men, or God ? or do I seek to please men ? If I did yet please men, I should not be the servant of Christ. 11. For I give you to understand, brethren, that the gospel which was preached by me is not according to man. 12. For neither did I receive it from man, nor did I learn it, but by the revelation of Jesus Christ. 13. For you have heard of my conversation in time past in the Jews' religion; how that beyond measure I persecuted the church of God, and laid it waste: 14. And I made progress in the Jews' religion above many of my equals in my own nation, being more

P

abundantly zealous for the traditions of my fathers.   **15.** But when it pleased him, who separated me from my mother's womb, and called me by his grace,   **16.** To reveal his Son in me, that I might preach him among the gentiles; immediately I condescended not to flesh and blood: **17.** Neither went I to Jerusalem to the apostles who were before me; but I went into Arabia, and again I returned to Damascus.   **18.** Then, three years after, I came to Jerusalem to see Peter, and stayed with him fifteen days.   **19.** But other of the apostles I saw none, except James the brother of the Lord.   **20.** Now the things which I write to you, behold, before God, I lie not.   **21.** Afterwards I came into the regions of Syria and Cilicia;   **22.** And I was unknown by face to the churches of Judæa which were in Christ.   **23.** But they had heard only: He, that persecuted us in times past, doth now preach the faith which once he impugned: **24.** And they glorified God in me.

1. *Paul, an apostle,* in the strict sense of the word, as being (*a*) a witness of the resurrection (Acts i. 22; iv. 33; Luke xxiv. 48; 1 Cor. ix. 1; xv. 8); (*b*) immediately appointed by Christ, Gal. ii. 8; and consequently (*c*) a peer of the original twelve (Mark iii. 13—19; Acts i. 25, 26).

Not of men. This distinguishes him from mere pretenders to the Christian ministry, men unsent of God either mediately or immediately, like the false prophets of old (Jer. xiv. 14).

Neither by man, as the lawful preachers of the word of God at this day are sent *by man,* that is, by an ecclesiastical superior, although their mission is not *of men.* As St. Chrysostom says: "The being *not of men* was common to all, for the gospel-preaching has its beginning and root from above: but the being *not by men* [so he reads] was proper to the apostles: for our Lord called them not by men, but Himself by Himself." St. Paul was baptized by Ananias (Acts ix. 17, 18), ordained by the *prophets and doctors* at Antioch (Acts xiii. 1, 3), but designated Apostle by Christ Himself, as a Catholic bishop in England is designated by the Pope, but consecrated by some other bishop.

Who raised him from the dead. The resurrection is mentioned because it was the special function of Apostles to *preach Jesus and the resurrection* (Acts xvii. 18).

2. *The brethren who are with me*, possibly, Timothy and Erastus (2 Cor. i. 1 ; Acts xix. 22), Titus and the two brethren (2 Cor. viii. 16—24), and others mentioned in Acts xx. 4, including St. Luke himself (*ib.* 5).

To the churches of Galatia. Plain address, without epithet of commendation. " He writes not to one city, but to the entire nation, for the disease [of Judaizing] had crept everywhere " (Theodoret).

4. *Who gave himself for our sins.* The idea is that *we shall be saved from wrath through him*, not by the Mosaic law, which rather *worketh wrath* (Rom. v. 9 ; iv. 15).

This present wicked world, present as distinguished from the future *new heavens and new earth in which justice dwelleth* (2 Pet. iii. 13): this world *seated in wickedness* (1 John v. 19), or more properly, *in the power of the Evil One* (ἐν τῷ πονηρῷ) ; this world, of which Satan is *the prince* (John xii. 14), and even *the god* (2 Cor. iv. 4), maintaining his dominion over all who wilfully reject the gospel and salvation of Christ.

Theodoret explains it : " By *wicked world* he means this temporal estate of men, in which sin has place: for, so long as we are clad in mortal nature, some of us venture on greater offences, others on less : but when we are transferred to that immortal life, we shall be superior to sin : this hope Christ our Lord has given us." Which incomplete explanation is completed by St. Jerome : " Not only in the life to come, according to the promised hope wherein we believe, but also from this present world has He delivered us, inasmuch as *being dead with* Christ (2 Tim. ii. 11), we are *transformed in the newness of our mind* (Rom. xii. 2), and are *not of this world*, by which deservedly we are not loved (John xv. 18—20)."

6. *I wonder*, &c.   A rebuke more abrupt and stern than the Apostle's wont.

So soon, οὕτω ταχέως, not *so soon after your conversion*, but *so soon after the temptation came upon you.* We may well translate it *so lightly*, cf. 1 Tim. v. 22 : *Impose not hands lightly* (ταχέως) *upon any man ;* or *so easily*, cf. 2 Thess. ii. 2 : *that you be not easily* (ταχέως) *moved.*

Are removed, a poor rendering of μετατίθεσθε (middle voice).   Say *shift your side.*   A man who went over from one philosophical sect to another was called ὁ μεταθέμενος. *Transfugitis* would be a better translation than the Vulgate *transferimini.*

To the grace of Christ, ἐν χάριτι χριστοῦ, should be *in* (i.e. *through*) *the grace of Christ.*   As St. Chrysostom observes : " The calling is of the Father (*him that called you*), but the cause of the calling is of the Son."

6, 7.   *Unto another gospel, which is not another.*   Rather, *unto a different* (ἕτερον) *gospel, which* (different gospel) *is not one gospel more* (ἄλλο).   " It is not another gospel, for there cannot be two gospels ; and as it is not the same, it is no gospel at all " (Lightfoot).

8.   *Beside that*, παρ' ὅ, i.e. *contrary to that*, the Greek preposition παρά having both meanings.

Anathema, see on 1 Cor. xii. 3.

The text is strong meat for those pliant heralds of the gospel who, when any one contradicts them, meekly avow that they are only airing their own opinions, and have no idea of imposing them upon others.   St. Paul was the minister of a Church which, like her Founder, teaches what it is sin to disbelieve (John xvi. 9), and takes no pleasure, where dogmas are concerned, in the attribute of " comprehensiveness."

9.   *As we said before*, my companions and myself in our previous preaching (Acts xviii. 23), *so now I say again.*

If any one preach, εἴ τις εὐαγγελίζεται, better, *if any one is preaching,* the use of the indicative mood in this verse, not in *v.* 8, hinting that such preaching is actually going on.

10. *Persuade,* πείθω, *try to gain to my side,* cf. Acts xii. 20, *having gained Blastus,* πείσαντες Βλάστον.

To please men. Hence the compound *man-pleasers,* ἀνθρωπάρεσκοι, used Eph. vi. 6; Col. iii. 22. The best commentary on this verse is 1 Thess. ii. 4—6. St. Paul means that he did not make it his primary object to please men. But whoever seeks supremely and above all things the glory and good pleasure of God is sure, not in all things but upon the whole, to please men of good will, and to be feared and respected even by the wicked and malicious. Moses was *beloved of God and men* (Ecclus. xlv. 1), and the Divine Child *advanced in grace with God and men* (Luke ii. 52).

11. *I give you to understand, brethren.* A favourite form of expressing the writer's earnestness (1 Cor. xii. 3; xv. 1; x. 1; xii. 1; 2 Cor. viii. 1).

According to man, see on 1 Cor. xv. 32.

12. *By the revelation of Jesus Christ,* cf. Acts xxvi. 16. St. Paul then was equal to the Twelve in being *with Jesus,* and by Him *sent to preach* (Mark iii. 14). The antithesis in this verse implies the divinity of our Saviour.

13. *The Jews' religion.* St. Paul uses one word, *Judaism,* meaning of course not the religious belief of the Jews, but the observances of their law, and particularly *the traditions of my fathers,* or *tradition of the ancients,* human additions to the Mosaic Law, for which see Mark vii. 3—13.

And laid it waste, ἐπόρθουν. The same word is spoken of Saul in Acts ix. 21, where our translation has *persecuted.*

14. *Of my equals* in age, συνηλικιώτας, *the young men of my time,* youth being the age for zeal. The young Saul was more *abundantly zealous*—literally, *more abundantly a*

zealot—than the rest. *Zealot* was a name given to the Jews of stricter observance. It was borne by the Apostle St. Simon (Luke vi. 15: cf. Acts xxi. 20). St. Paul gives many testimonies to his early thorough-going Judaism (Acts xxii. 3; xxvi. 7; Phil. iii. 5, 6). The object in testifying to it here is to show that no mere word of man could ever have won him to the gospel of Christ; and again to give point to his coming denunciation of Judaism from the fact that he had himself been born a Jew and heir to all the prejudices of his race.

15. *Separated me from my mother's womb. Set me apart* would be less ambiguous than *separated*. So (Rom. i. 1) he says he is *separated* (*set apart*) *unto the gospel*.

From my mother's womb, cf. Ps. lxx. 6; Isaias xlix. 1, 5; Judges xvi. 17. Long *before the child knew how to reject evil and choose good* (Is. vii. 16), he was marked by the gratuitous providence of God as His future apostle.

Called me by his grace, on the road to Damascus, at once to the faith and to the apostolate (Acts xxvi. 16—18).

16. *I condescended not, non acquievi*, οὐ προσανεθέμην. The same word occurs in ii. 6, where it is rendered *contulerunt, added*. The simple verb, ἀνεθέμην, in ii. 1, is rendered *contuli, conferred;* and in Acts xv. 14, *indicavit, told*. What the verb really means is to *impart* a matter to another to get his advice about it. St. Paul then, full of the revelation of Christ, *immediately* made it his policy not to *impart* to men what he had learned, or to *confer* with men about it, as though he needed human guidance or instruction, when he was replete with that which was divine.

Flesh and blood in Scripture (cf. Ecclus. xiv. 19; xvii. 30; Eph. vi. 12; and especially Matt. xvi. 17, and 1 Cor. xv. 50, with note) means, not anything evil, but simply human nature apart from any special favour of

God, or supernatural endowment. Here it is pretty well equivalent to *kith and kin.* St. Paul took no counsel with men of his own race and kindred, his natural advisers, in the matter of his conversion and of the revelation vouchsafed to him.

17. *I went into Arabia.* This visit is not mentioned by St. Luke. It must be placed either immediately before or immediately after what is narrated in Acts ix. 22. Arabia, like other terms of ancient geography, *e.g.* India, is a sufficiently vague expression. It included the regions east and south-east of Palestine. From the way that *Sina, a mountain in Arabia,* is presently mentioned (iv. 25), it has been concluded that St. Paul's sojourn was in that region, where the Law was given (Exod. xix.), which his preaching was in substance and essence to fulfil, and in its accidental minutiæ to set aside; where also Elias had his vision (3 Kings xix. 8—15). It was no missionary journey, as some have supposed, but a long retreat, in which the new convert seems to have received the favours mentioned, 2 Cor. xii. 2—4, and to have been formed to the Apostolate by repeated apparitions of our Lord Himself (Gal. i. 12).

18. *After three years*, the *many days* of Acts ix. 23. The Acts go on to inform us why and how he left Damascus, a detail on which St. Paul here is silent, but refers to it, 2 Cor. xi. 32, 33, showing how poor an argument silence is of discrepancy.

To see Peter. "He says not *to see* (ἰδεῖν) *Peter*, but *to take note of* (ἱστορῆσαι) *Peter*, the word used by those who make a study of great and illustrious cities. Though he needed no human teaching, as having received his lesson from the God of all, he pays the proper honour to the Coryphæus [or *chief*, usual name given to St. Peter by the Greek Fathers]. Therefore did he come to him, not to learn anything of him, but only to set eyes on him " (St. Chrysostom).

So much for St. Paul's respect for St. Peter, though he had nothing to learn from him. We however are not Pauls: divine revelations are not given to us, and we need to learn the truth of God from the successor of Peter.

Fifteen days, at the end of which time the visit had to be broken off, owing to the violence of the Jews (Acts ix. 29; xxii. 17—21). Thus its very shortness furnishes an argument for what is asserted in *v.* 12.

19. *Other of the apostles I saw none, except James.* If for *other of the apostles*, ἕτερον δὲ τῶν ἀποστόλων, we had had, *of the other apostles*, τῶν δὲ ἄλλων ἀποστόλων, we might not have been able—considering the use of *except*, εἰ μή, in Matt. xii. 4; Luke iv. 26, 27; Gal. ii. 16; Apoc. xxi. 27—to argue that *James* here is the Apostle, *James of Alpheus* (Luke vi. 15). "But," as Lightfoot acknowledges, "the sense of ἕτερον (*other*) naturally links it with εἰ μή (*except*), from which it cannot be separated without harshness, and ἕτερον carries τῶν ἀποστόλων (*of the apostles*) with it. It seems then that St. James is here called an Apostle." And that, we may add, means inclusion in the Twelve: for the recorded fact that St. Paul on this occasion saw a good deal of St. Barnabas (Acts ix. 26), shows that the word *apostle* is here used in its strictest sense, of the Twelve and them alone.

The brother of the Lord, but *the son of Alpheus* (Ἰάκωβον τὸν τοῦ Ἀλφαίου, Luke vi. 15), which shows that *brother* here has not the ordinary English meaning. As Theodoret explains: "He was called the brother of the Lord, but was not so by nature. Nor yet as some [Origen, St. Epiphanius, and others] have supposed, was he the son of Joseph by a previous marriage, but he was the son of Clopas [or Cleophas, otherwise Alpheus], and cousin of the Lord: for his mother was the sister of the Lord's mother." See note on 1 Cor. ix. 5.

21. *Syria and Cilicia.* To save his life, *the brethren* at Jerusalem *sent him away to Tarsus* (Acts ix. 30), his native city, the capital of Cilicia, whither Barnabas *went to seek* him, and *brought him to Antioch*, the metropolis of Syria (Acts xi. 25).

Chapter II.

1. Then fourteen years after, I went up again to Jerusalem with Barnabas, taking Titus also with me. 2. And I went up according to revelation, and communicated to them the gospel which I preach among the gentiles, but apart to them who seemed to be something; lest, perhaps, I should run, or had run, in vain. 3. But neither Titus, who was with me, being a gentile, was compelled to be circumcised: 4. But because of false brethren unawares brought in, who came in privately to spy our liberty which we have in Christ Jesus, that they might bring us into bondage: 5. To whom we yielded not by subjection, no, not for an hour, that the truth of the gospel might continue with you. 6. But of them who seemed to be something, (what they were some time, it is nothing to me: God accepteth not the person of man;) for to me they that seemed to be something added nothing: 7. But on the contrary, when they had seen that to me was committed the gospel of the uncircumcision, as to Peter was that of the circumcision; 8. (For he who wrought in Peter to the apostleship of the circumcision, wrought in me also among the gentiles:) 9. And when they had known the grace that was given to me, James, and Cephas, and John, who seemed to be pillars, gave to me and Barnabas the right hands of fellowship; that we should go to the gentiles, and they to the circumcision: 10. Only that we should be mindful of the poor; which same thing also I was careful to do. 11. But when Cephas was come to Antioch, I withstood him to the face, because he was blameable. 12. For before that some came from James, he did eat with the gentiles; but when they were come, he withdrew, and separated himself, fearing those who were of the circumcision. 13. And to his dissimulation the rest of the Jews consented; so that Barnabas also was led by them into that dissimulation. 14. But when I saw that they walked not uprightly unto the truth of the gospel, I said to Cephas before them all: If thou, being a Jew, livest after the manner of the gentiles, and not of the Jews,

how dost thou compel the gentiles to follow the way of Jews?
15 We by nature are Jews, and not of the gentiles sinners.
16. But knowing that a man is not justified by the works of the
law, but by the faith of Jesus Christ, we also believe in Christ
Jesus, that we may be justified by the faith of Christ, and not by
the works of the law: because by the works of the law no flesh
shall be justified. 17. But if, while we seek to be justified in
Christ, we ourselves also are found sinners, is Christ then the
minister of sin? God forbid. 18. For if I build up again the
things which I have destroyed, I make myself a transgressor.
19. For I, through the law, am dead to the law, that I may live to
God. With Christ I am nailed to the Cross: 20. And I live; now
not I, but Christ liveth in me: and that I live now in the flesh,
I live in the faith of the Son of God, who loved me, and delivered
himself for me. 21. I cast not away the grace of God: for if
justice be by the law, then Christ died in vain.

1. *After fourteen years* from his coming into Syria
and Cilicia (i. 21), seventeen from his conversion, *i.e.*
A.D. 51.

I went up again to Jerusalem. This is the journey
related in Acts xv. The intermediate journey, mentioned
in Acts xi. 29, 30, is not here alluded to.

2. *According to revelation*, and also at the sending of
the Christians of Antioch (Acts xv. 2), just as Peter
went to Cæsarea, Cornelius sending for him, and the
Spirit bidding him go (Acts xi. 11, 12). Other instances
of Heaven directing St. Paul on his courses are Acts
xxii. 17; xvi. 6, 9; xviii. 9, 10; xx. 22, 23; xxiii. 11.

Who seemed to be something. This is a misleading
translation of τοῖς δοκοῦσιν, which means simply *those in
position*, namely, *the apostles and ancients* (Acts xv. 23) of
the church of Jerusalem.

Lest perhaps, in the eyes of my calumniators, *I should
run or had run in vain.* Cf. 1 Thess. iii. 5. He wanted
no assurance for himself, but a testimonial against his
adversaries: " not that I may learn aught myself, but
that I may teach the harbourers of these suspicions
that I run not in vain," as St. Chrysostom paraphrases.

3. *Being a gentile*, apparently on the side of both his parents, in that differing from Timothy, whose mother was a Jewess (Acts xvi. 1). The reason why St. Paul circumcised Timothy (Acts xvi. 3), and yet would not consent to the circumcision of Titus, will appear presently.

4. *But because of false brethren. Id autem propter* would here be a better rendering of δὶα δέ than the Vulgate *sed propter*. Translate: *and that on account of the false brethren.* That is to say, it was on account of the false brethren (St. Luke, Acts xv. 5, says they were *some of the sect of the Pharisees*) that the authorities of the Church at Jerusalem, following St. Paul, stood out and refused to order the circumcision of Titus. St. Augustine explains: —" Though Titus was a gentile, and there was no custom or kindred to compel his circumcision, as there was with Timothy, yet Paul would readily have allowed even Titus to be circumcised. For his doctrine was that such circumcision was no bar to salvation: but if the hope of salvation was fixed upon the rite, that view of the matter he showed to be against salvation. He could very well therefore tolerate circumcision as a superfluity, according to the judgment that he delivered elsewhere (1 Cor. vii. 19): *Circumcision is nothing, and uncircumcision is nothing ; but the observation of the commandments of God.* But *on account of the false brethren unawares brought in* Titus was not compelled to be circumcised: that is to say, Paul's consent could not be extorted to his circumcision, because they who *came in privately to spy our liberty*, he says, were keeping a keen look out in eager desire of the circumcision of Titus, that they might straightway preach circumcision as necessary to salvation by the witness and consent of even Paul himself."

False brethren, cf. 2 Cor. xi. 13 ; Jude 4 ; 2 Pet. ii. 1.

Unawares brought in, παρεισάκτους, literally, *smuggled in, contraband*.

To spy our liberty, that is, our freedom from the Jewish law, presently called a *servitude*. Cf. v. 1, 3. *To spy* of course is to act as spies, who come into a city only to ensure its capture and enslavement.

5. *No, not for an hour*. King Charles's final answer, when the Long Parliament bargained with him for the command of the militia. The phrase πρὸς ὥραν means the same as πρὸς καιρὸν (*for awhile*) in Luke viii. 13. The exact meaning here is *for the nonce*. St. Paul would not yield to the circumcisionists even for this one occasion. Otherwise *an hour* would have been time enough and more for the circumcision of Titus.

The truth of the gospel. Such truths as that of there being *in Christ a new creature: the old things are passed away, all things are made new : in Christ Jesus neither circumcision availeth anything, nor uncircumcision, but faith that worketh by charity* (2 Cor. v. 17; Gal. v. 6).

Might continue with you, the Gentile churches.

6. *Of them who seemed to be something*—then a long parenthesis, ending at *but on the contrary;* then a temporal clause, *when they had seen* (v. 7); then another parenthesis (v. 8) ; then a second temporal clause, *and when they had known ;* and finally the apodosis, *James and Cephas* (v. 9). Thus *vv.* 6—10 are all one long sentence.

What they were some time. It seems better for the previous context to give ὁποῖοί ποτε its classical meaning, *whatever they were*, *i.e.* however high in authority.

God accepteth not the person of man in bestowing his revelations (i. 12). For the idea of *accept the person*, cf. Deut. i. 17; x. 17; xvi. 19; 2 Par. xix. 7; Job xxxii. 22; Ecclus. xxxv. 15, 16; Matt. xxii. 16, and often in the New Testament.

They that seemed to be something added nothing. Here· is a false antithesis, not intended by the writer, between *something* and *nothing*. The words *to be something* are not in the Greek, nor in the old editions of the Vulgate. For the meaning of *they that seemed* see on *v.* 2.

Added nothing, οὐδὲν προσανέθεντο. On the meaning of the verb see on i. 16. The meaning here is, that the authorities of the Church at Jerusalem, so vaunted by the Judaizing party among the Galatians, *imparted* no new knowledge of the gospel to St. Paul: they read him no lesson upon the relations of Christianity to Judaism, but acquiesced in the understanding of the matter that he had *by the revelation of Jesus Christ* (i. 12).

7. *But on the contrary*, ἀλλὰ τοὐναντίον; translate, *but quite the reverse*. Join these words to the previous verse, from which they should be separated only by a comma; and put a colon after them. The words mean: *they rather learned of me than I of them.* What they learned doubtless was how the Gentile converts should be treated, a lesson repeated at Antioch with some emphasis (*vv.* 11—14).

8. Innocent X., 29 Jan. 1674, condemned as heretical the doctrine that "St. Peter and St. Paul are two supreme pastors and governors of the Church, who make one head,—understood as asserting an all-round equality between St. Peter and St. Paul, without sub-ordination and subjection of St. Paul to St. Peter in the supreme command and government of the Universal Church." Such "subordination and subjection" of St. Paul to St. Peter is certainly not apparent in these two verses, but nothing to the contrary is apparent there either. It is merely a question of a division of spheres of action, St. Peter to go on addressing himself mainly to the Jews, and St. Paul mainly to labour for the Gentiles. As the conversion of the Jews in Palestine became more and more hopeless, St. Peter too (cf. Acts xxviii. 28) left them for Antioch and for Rome. As St. Peter had *the apostleship of the circumcision*, so our

Lord was *minister of the circumcision* (Rom. xv. 8), without prejudice to His universal pastorate. A Pope is none the less Pope for being Bishop of Rome and Patriarch of the West. So long as there appeared any human hope of our Lord's design upon Jerusalem being fulfilled, that it should be the first city in His Kingdom, it was reasonable that His Vicar should remain ministering principally to the Jews in Palestine.

That St. Paul held his commission and jurisdiction as Apostle not of St. Peter, is clear (i. 1, 12, 17; ii. 7); but neither did John, nor James, nor any of the Twelve. But St. Peter alone had successors as an Apostle: the special apostolic powers of St. Paul and the rest lapsed with their death.

Wrought in *v.* 8 means *wrought miracles* (iii. 5; 1 Cor. iv. 20; xii. 10).

9. Join together *when they had seen* (*v.* 7), *and when they had known.*

James the Less, *the brother of the Lord* (see on i. 19), bishop of Jerusalem. He is mentioned first because the Judaizers, whom St. Paul was opposing, sheltered themselves most under his authority and example. St. James the Greater had been martyred by Herod some years before (Acts xii. 2). *Cephas* of course is Peter (John i. 42).

Who seemed to be pillars (οἱ δοκοῦντες, see on *v.* 2), better, to modern understandings, *the recognised pillars*.

10. *Which same thing also I was careful to do*, bearing alms from the Gentile converts to the poor in Jerusalem (Rom. xv. 26, 27; 1 Cor. xvi. 1—4; 2 Cor. ix.; Acts xxiv. 17).

11. *When Cephas was come to Antioch*, and Paul and Barnabas were also there (Acts xv. 30—40).

I withstood him to the face. St. Paul speaks as though he had done something very bold, that might well amaze the Galatians, in withstanding Peter. The

Fathers are profuse with their explanations, even extraordinary and quite untenable explanations, as that Cephas was not the Apostle Peter (Clement of Alexandria), or that the error and the reprehension was a little piece of acting, previously arranged between St. Peter and St. Paul as a lesson to the faithful (St. Chrysostom and St. Jerome): all this solicitude to save the dignity of St. Peter! Protestant commentators are not so solicitous. A parallel instance would be, if some Pope wished to take up his residence again at Avignon; and the College of Cardinals, with the evils of the fourteenth century before their eyes, *withstood him to his face.* Certainly no Catholic would take that for a denial of Papal infallibility.

To be blamed, κατεγνωσμένος, *condemned,* not for any error of doctrine, but for the unwisdom of his personal conduct.

Infallibility is no guarantee of a uniformly wise policy either in Peter or in the successors of Peter. Infallibility in doctrine and wisdom in policy move in different spheres.

12. *Some came from James :* more exactly, *some of James's people came,* no doubt, *all zealots for the law* (Acts xxi. 20).

He did eat with the gentiles, neglecting the Mosaic distinction between meats clean and unclean, as he had learned to do by revelation (Acts xi. 2—9).

He withdrew and separated himself. If we can suppose this withdrawal to have been at the *agapæ* (for which see on 1 Cor. xi. 20, seq.), it would have involved a separation of St. Peter and *those of the circumcision, i.e.* the converted Jews, from the rest of the faithful even in the celebration of the Holy Eucharist, a deplorable division of the head from the members, enough to justify the strong remonstrance of St. Paul. Still there is no shadow of an indication that St. Peter here varied from the teaching of the Council of Jerusalem (Acts xv. 5 —29). It was not his purpose to compel the Gentile converts to take up Jewish rites : but he over indulged the prejudice of his countrymen against worshipping in common and eating in common with Christians who would not add to their Christianity the extra observance of the Jewish law,—as if the Pope, intimidated by teetotalism, were weak enough to yield to a demand that he should not grant an audience to any one who was not a teetotaler. He might not purpose to compel Catholics to total abstinence. His conduct would not amount to a doctrinal declaration that alcohol is *malum in se*. But the effect of his conduct would go rather towards compelling his flock to be total abstainers.

13. This verse should be more accurately rendered. The Greek means : *And with his pretence* (or *pretended scruple*) *the rest of the Jews fell in, so that Barnabas also was carried away with their pretence.* The verb συναπήχθη (*was carried away* as by a flood) occurs 2 Pet. iii. 17, where it is again less accurately rendered *being led aside*.

14. *They walked not uprightly unto the truth of the gospel.* More exactly and more intelligibly, *they acted not straight-forwardly in accordance with the truth of the gospel*, or, as a modern would say, ' they had not the courage of their convictions.' Peter, Barnabas, and those who imitated them, were as convinced as St. Paul that the Mosaic rule of meats was neither a command nor a counsel in the Christian Church : yet they returned to the observance of it, not from fear of any persecution, but from a too scrupulous and here injudicious sense of that same charity which made St. Paul explaim : *If meat scandalize my brother, I will never eat flesh* (1 Cor. viii. 13) ; and which prompted him afterwards, at St. James's recom- mendation, to sanctify himself with the four other men, and have an oblation offered for him in the Temple (Acts xxi. 20—26).

The verb ὀρθοποδοῦσιν (ὀρθός, straight, and πούς, foot) is found only here in St. Paul, and in some late imitators. It means *to walk straight*, ' to walk' being the Hebrew idiom for ' to behave.' St. Peter's denial was a much more lamentable instance of not *walking straight*, or *behaving straightforwardly*.

His faith failed not then (Luke xxii. 32), nor his teaching on this occasion, but there was weakness in his conduct, and *pretence* (ὑπόκρισις), putting on another character than that which belonged to him, and not daring for the nonce to proclaim himself as he really was and really thought.

If thou, being a Jew, &c., well amplified by St. Jerome: " If, O Peter, thou, by birth a Jew, circumcised from tender age and guarding all the precepts of the Law, now by the grace of Christ knowest that these observances have no utility of themselves, but are patterns and images of things to come, and so thou takest food with them who are of the Gentiles, and art nowise living as before under religious scruples, but freely and indifferently; how dost thou compel those who from Gentiles have become believers to live as do the Jews, withdrawing from them, and separating and setting thyself apart from them, as though their company were contamination? For if they are unclean from whom thou withdrawest, and thy withdrawal is on the ground that they have not circumcision, thou compellest them to be circumcised and become Jews, though thou thyself, a born Jew, livest after the manner of the Gentiles." " But the great Peter by his silence ratifies what is said," adds Theodoret.

The address to Peter ends here. He stood in no need of a doctrinal homily from his fellow-apostle, such as follows, *vv.* 15—21. " For similar instances of the intermingling of the direct language of the speaker and the after comment of the narrator, see John i. 15—18,

Q

where the testimony of the Baptist loses itself in the thoughts of the Evangelist, and Acts i. 16—21, where St. Peter's allusion to the death of Judas is interwoven with the after explanations of St. Luke " (Lightfoot).

At the same time there is nothing to prevent our supposing St. Paul to have delivered an address something of this tenor at Antioch, not to St. Peter, but to the assembled multitude (*before them all*, v. 14), for the instruction of the converts from Judaism.

15. *We by nature are Jews. We*, himself and St. Peter and the rest, not of course the Galatians. *By nature, i.e.* by birth, cf. Phil. iii. 5. " He is by nature a Jew," says St. Jerome, " who is of the race of Abraham, and was circumcised by his parents on the eighth day : he is not by nature a Jew, who has become one after being of the Gentiles." The Jews habitually called the Gentiles *sinners* (cf. Matt. xxvi. 45, *shall be betrayed into the hands of sinners*, the *band of soldiers*, Roman soldiers, mentioned by St. John xviii. 3), as being *strangers to the testament, having no hope, and without God in this world* (Eph. ii. 12). With *of the gentiles sinners*, the phrase of the Old Law, contrast that of the New Law, *the brethren of the gentiles* (Acts xv. 23).

16. *The works of the law.* The precepts of the Old Law were some 'ceremonial,' as circumcision, the sabbath, meats clean and unclean ; and some ' moral,' as the ten commandments, the third excepted (*Aquinas Ethicus*, i. 309). The heresy of Pelagius in St. Augustine's time turned upon the observance of the ' moral precepts,' which of course are obligatory upon Christians and upon all men. But the solicitude of the Judaizers, against whom St. Paul wrote, was for the observance of the ' ceremonial precepts,' as *days and months and times and years* (iv. 10), and principally *circumcision* (v. 2—11). The observance then of these ' ceremonial precepts ' constitutes the *works of the law* here spoken of. The Epistle

is available against the Pelagians by the inferences that it affords, rather than by its express statements. Cf. however iii. 10. See note on Rom. iii. 20.

We also believe, should be, *came to believe*, ἐπιστεύσαμεν. See on Rom. xiii. 11.

By the works of the law no flesh shall be justified, a quotation (repeated Rom. iii. 20) from Psalm cxlii. 2: *no living man shall be justified in thy sight*. *No living man* includes the Hebrew people, for all their observance of ceremonial precepts, *the works of the law*.

17. *We ourselves are found sinners*. That is what the Judaizers objected, that by seeking justification in Christ, or in the Christian dispensation alone, without observance of the ceremonial precepts of Judaism, St. Paul and others like him become as *gentiles, sinners* (*v.* 15). To which his reply is: *Is Christ then the minister of sin?* Have we been betrayed into sin by our conversion to the faith of Christ? Is a Christian, who, taking the grace of Christ to be all-sufficient for his justification, has departed from the Mosaic rites, no better than a mere heathen? *God forbid.*

It may be objected on behalf of the Judaizing Christian: *These things*, faith in Christ and baptism in His Name, *you ought to have done, and not to leave those* works of the ceremonial law of Moses *undone* (Matt. xxiii. 23). 'True,' he might say, '*justice* is not *by the law* (*v.* 21): a man is *justified by the faith of Christ*, and *not by the works of the law*: still it was never Christ's intention that you should part with the law in order to go to Him: there is an utter lack of proof of the baptized man being exempted from the ceremonial precepts, as he certainly is not exempted from the moral precepts of the law of Moses.'

This is a real difficulty. It is not met by St. Paul in the present passage, but it is met fully and explicitly in the Epistle to the Hebrews, vii. 18—ix. 18: *There is indeed a setting aside of the former commandment because of the weakness and unprofitableness thereof. . . . In saying a new (covenant), he hath made the former old. . . . The law having a shadow of the good things to come,* &c. The argument is briefly, that types and shadows, such as the Mosaic ritual, must yield to the substance and fulfilment, which is come in Christ; and that he who still clings to the shadow as a thing of necessity to salvation, virtually denies that the substance has yet come,—in other words, he denies that Jesus is the Messiah. And such is the argument urged in this very epistle, iii. 24, 25; iv. 1—9.

If we might add to the imagery of St. Paul, we might say that the Jewish rites were to the Christian economy as is a scaffolding to the arch which is erected upon it: to insist upon retaining the scaffolding as a thing that must not be touched, after the arch was complete and set, would be to impugn the sufficiency of the arch.

And this, we may as well remark once more, explains the different practice of the Church at Jerusalem and the Gentile Churches, of St. James and St. Paul, and even of St. Paul himself at various times (cf. Gal. ii. 3 with Acts xvi. 3), the one preserving, the other repudiating the Mosaic observances. Such customs were things indifferent in themselves (1 Cor. vii. 18, 19), and might well be permitted for a time to those who were used to them, to bury the Synagogue with honour; but the moment they were made essentials to Christianity, that was heresy and denial of our Redemption.

18. *The things which I have destroyed* are the ceremonial *works of the law* which I have quitted.

A transgressor. A retort upon the Judaizers. They said that whoever quitted the Jewish observances to join Christ, made himself *a gentile, a sinner* (*vv.* 17, 15). ' No,' says St. Paul, ' you are the sinner, you the *trans-*

gressor, you the gentile fallen away from *the Israel of God* (vi. 16: cf. Rom. ix. 6), who after believing in Christ, have gone back as to things of necessary observance to those works and ceremonies of the law, which the coming of the Messiah has superseded and rendered nugatory. You call me a false Jew: I say you are no true Christian, and therefore no genuine son of Abraham (iii. 29; v. 22, 31), but a *stranger to the testament* (Eph. ii. 12), like one lapsed into heathendom.'

19. *I through the law am dead to the law*, literally, *I through law died to law.* The best commentary on this is Rom. vii. 8—11, and 1 Cor. xv. 56. Syllogistically it would stand thus:—What gave me knowledge of con-cupiscence and sin, what gave occasion to sin, what quickened sin, what is the strength of sin, through that I died (morally and spiritually). But law did this and is this. Therefore *through law I died*, and *to law*, or so far as law was concerned, I became as one dead morally and spiritually. In this state of spiritual death the grace of Christ found me, and gave me life, and a new law with strength to keep it, not the mere law of Moses, graven on tables of stone, nor a mere natural law written in the conscience of humanity, but a law of love, promulgated by Christ and carried out through His grace, which law of love does not carry with it the ceremonial observances of the Old Law. Such is the explanation given by St. Chrysostom:—" *Through law I died to law:* for the law commands men to do all that is written in it, and chastises him who does it not. At that rate we have all died to it, for no one has fulfilled it [*i.e.* apart from the grace of Christ, there has been no thoroughly law-observing man]. As then it is impossible for a corpse and a dead man to obey the commands of the law, so neither is it possible for me who have died under the curse of the law. Let it not then dictate to the dead man, whom itself has slain."

Law here (νόμος without the usual article) is law in general, particularly the Mosaic law in all its extent, but including also the natural law; all mere law away from the grace of Christ.

With Christ I am nailed to the cross.   Explained by Rom. vi. 6.

20. *And I live, now not I,* ζῶ δὲ οὐκέτι ἐγώ, *and no longer do I live.*

Christ liveth in me.   This is the new life of baptism, by which I am dead to sin, and live in the image of Christ my Saviour (Rom. vi. 4; 2 Cor. v. 15; Col. ii. 12; iii. 1—3).

And that I live now in the flesh means, ' And the life that I live now, since my baptism, still a mortal man among other men.'   St. Paul speaks in the first person, uttering the innermost sentiment of his own heart, but in the name of all Christians as such.

21. *I cast not away the grace of God,* the grace of baptism, described in the two previous verses, as they do, who by clinging to Mosaic observances, and placing their hopes of salvation in them, make Christ to have died *gratuitously* (δωρεάν, *gratis*), it being enough for salvation in their view to be *disciples of Moses* (John ix. 28).   This view was not expressed formally and fully by the Judaizers, as that would have meant sheer apostasy from Christianity, but St. Paul, it seems, was thinking of the effect which their teaching would have on minds which accepted it.   We must remember the fanatical attachment of the Jews of that date to the ceremonial precepts as well of Moses as of the later Rabbis, and the sense of self-righteousness engendered by the observance of those rules.   Cf. Luke xviii. 10—12; Matt. xxiii. 5, 16—23.   Formalism took the place of *the weightier things of the law,* even of the Old Law.   It threatened to arrest the transition from the Old Law to the New (Heb. viii. 7—13); to make men

forget God their Saviour (Isaias xvii. 10), the merits of His death, the value of His ordinances, and rank no higher than Elias or Jeremias Him who was the Christ (Matt. xvi. 14, 16); and at the same time to *put a yoke upon the necks of the disciples*, sure to prevent any wide acceptance of the Gospel among the heathen (Acts xv. 10). That is why St. Paul spent great part of his energies in combating the Judaizers, whose system, be it observed, presents several curious analogies with Puritanism and with Jansenism.

CHAPTER III.

1. O senseless Galatians, who hath bewitched you, that you should not obey the truth, before whose eyes Jesus Christ hath been set forth, crucified among you? 2. This only would I learn of you: Did you receive the Spirit by the works of the law, or by the hearing of faith? 3. Are you so foolish that, whereas you began in the Spirit, you would now be made perfect by the flesh? 4. Have you suffered so great things in vain? if yet in vain. 5. He therefore who giveth to you the Spirit, and worketh miracles among you, doth he do it by the works of the law, or by the hearing of the faith? 6. As it is written: Abraham believed God, and it was reputed to him unto justice. 7. Know ye, therefore, that they who are of faith are the children of Abraham. 8. And the Scripture, foreseeing that God justifieth the gentiles by faith, told Abraham before: In thee shall all nations be blessed. 9. Therefore, they who are of the faith shall be blessed with the faithful Abraham. 10. For as many as are of the works of the law are under a curse: for it is written: Cursed is every one that continueth not in all things which are written in the book of the law, to do them. 11. But that by the law no man is justified with God, it is manifest: because, The just man liveth by faith. 12. But the law is not of faith: but, He that doeth these things shall live in them. 13. Christ hath redeemed us from the curse of the law, being made a curse for us; for it is written: Cursed is every one that hangeth on a tree: 14. That the blessing of Abraham might come on the gentiles through Christ Jesus; that we may receive the promise of the Spirit by faith. 15. Brethren,

(I speak after the manner of man,) yet a man's testament, if it be confirmed, no man despiseth, nor addeth to it. **16.** To Abraham were the promises made, and to his seed. He saith not : And to his seeds, as of many ; but as of one : And to thy seed, who is Christ. **17.** Now this I say, that the testament, which was confirmed by God, the law, which was made after four hundred and thirty years, doth not disannul, to make the promise of no effect. **18.** For if the inheritance be of the law, it is no more of promise : but God gave it to Abraham by promise. **19.** Why then was the law ? It was set because of transgressions, till the seed should come to whom he made the promise, being ordained by angels in the hand of a mediator. **20.** Now a mediator is not of one, but God is one. **21.** Was the law, then, against the promises of God ? God forbid : for if there had been a law given which could give life, verily justice should have been by the law. **22.** But the Scripture hath concluded all under sin, that the promise by the faith of Jesus Christ might be given to them that believe. **23.** But before that faith came, we were kept under the law, shut up unto that faith which was to be revealed. **24.** Wherefore the law was our pedagogue in Christ, that we might be justified by faith. **25.** But after that faith is come, we are no longer under a pedagogue. **26.** For you are all the children of God by faith in Christ Jesus. **27.** For as many of you as have been baptized in Christ have put on Christ. **28.** There is neither Jew nor Greek, there is neither bond nor free, there is neither male nor female : for you are all one in Christ Jesus. **29.** And if you be Christ's, then you are the seed of Abraham, heirs according to the promise.

1. In this verse the words, *that you should not obey the truth*, as the best MSS. show, are a gloss from v. 7 : also the *among you* is doubtful : so that the verse as St. Paul wrote it probably ran : *O senseless Galatians, who hath bewitched you, before whose eyes Jesus Christ has been set forth crucified.*

From this point of the Epistle, as St. Chrysostom observes, the Apostle, "having established his own credit as a teacher, discourses with greater authority."

Who hath bewitched you? The reference is to the 'evil eye,' which Italians still believe in. St. Paul merely draws a metaphor from the notion, as one might call a house rebuilt after a fire 'phœnix-like,' without

pledging oneself to the fabulous history of that bird.
He says: 'One would think that the evil eye of a
sorcerer had caught and fascinated you,' the sorcerer
being he who insisted upon the necessity, or at least the
high expediency, of Jewish observances for Christians.

Before whose eyes Jesus Christ has been set forth (προεγράφη,
written up in public) *crucified.* The power of the 'evil
eye' was defeated by the intended victim fixing his
gaze on something else, and not catching the eye of the
sorcerer. St. Paul then, keeping up the metaphor,
says: 'Why did you not keep your eyes on that public
notice of Jesus Christ crucified, which I had set clearly
before you?' He means that if they had kept well in
view the sufficiency of the atonement that Christ made
for us upon the cross, they would never have thought
of eking that atonement out by the now exploded
observances of the Jewish ceremonial law.

2. *Receive the Spirit*, the Holy Ghost, whom we also
receive in Baptism and Confirmation, but whose reception in those days was rendered sensible by a profusion
of miraculous gifts, for which see 1 Cor. xiv. To these
miraculous powers, which the Galatians must also have
enjoyed, St. Paul now appeals in evidence.

The hearing of faith, ἀκοὴ πίστεως, like ὑπακοὴ πίστεως,
Rom. i. 5; xvi. 26, *the hearing*, or *obedience*, *that comes of
faith*.

3. The Greek has two interrogations: *Are you so
foolish? Having begun in the spirit, are you now being made
perfect by the flesh?* The same two verbs *to begin* and *to
make perfect* are conjoined in 2 Cor. viii. 6, and Phil. i. 6.
They are used especially of the beginning and the
completion of a religious rite. *In the spirit* means by
the grace of the Holy Ghost, with all its miraculous
accompaniments then given in baptism. *By the flesh*
means by circumcision.

4. *Suffered so great things*, persecution for the faith.

The age of martyrs had not yet set in : Christianity was safe by its obscurity : but there were local annoyances, cf. Heb. x. 33, 34.

In vain, if yet in vain. The last words are added to show that all is not lost : the Apostle hopes that the past sufferings of the Galatians for the faith will not be in vain. We are not to conceive of the Galatians as apostates, or people fallen from grace (*v.* 5), or as having generally submitted to circumcision (v. 2, 3). They were wavering, but yet unrouted soldiers of Christ.

5. This verse is a repetition of *v.* 3. *The hearing of the faith* is a mistake for *the hearing of faith*, explained above.

6. *It is written* ought to be away. The sentence runs, *the hearing of faith, as Abraham believed*, or *had faith*, &c., a quotation from Gen. xv. 6, enlarged upon in Rom. iv., which see.

7—9. Rom. ix. 6—8.

The Scripture foreseeing, that is, the Holy Ghost, the Author of Scripture, foreseeing.

Told before, προευηγγελίσατο, *told the glad tidings before*. The quotation that followed is a fusion of two passages, Gen. xii. 3 ; xviii. 18.

Therefore they that are of faith, &c. The argument is this :—All nations shall be blessed in Abraham, in his person, as being contained in him and springing from him,—in other words, as his children. But the nations, the Gentiles, are not children of Abraham by nature, nor again by any adoption, coming of their receiving the covenant of circumcision (Gen. xvii.) and keeping the Jewish law. Therefore nothing is left for them but to be adopted children of Abraham, solely as sharing his faith, and thereby inheriting the blessing which that faith drew down.

The Apostle goes on to argue that for those who will not have faith as Abraham had faith, born Jews though they be, there is reserved not a blessing, but a curse.

10. *As many as are of the works of the law* is opposed to *those who are of faith* (*v.* 9), and means persons who putting aside faith in Christ as unnecessary, or at least insufficient, seek their justification by the works of the Mosaic law, by which we are to understand especially, though not exclusively, the ceremonial observances of that law,—not exclusively, as appears by reading the series of maledictions, Deut. xxvii. 15—26, the last of which is here quoted.

But the Judaizer might reply: 'True we are *under a curse*, inasmuch as we are threatened with one, if we disobey: but we are not actually *cursed*, for we have kept the law.' St. Paul's argument assumes that they have not kept the law, as well for its difficulty (Acts xv. 10), as also on this account, that the law shows sin (Rom. iii. 20; iv. 15), but does not afford strength to overcome sin : that comes only of faith and the grace of Christ (Rom. viii. 2, 3).

11. *The just man liveth* (ζήσεται, *shall live*) *by faith.* Quoted from Habacuc ii. 4, here, and again Rom. i. 17; Heb. x. 38. The Hebrew has, *shall live in his faith*; and the Greek, *shall live of faith in me.* The prophet promises deliverance from the Chaldean invader, after a period of waiting, during which time the incredulous will sin by his incredulity, but the just man, having faith in the promise made on the part of God, shall live through the trial.

12. *The law is not of faith.* As St. Thomas explains : " The precepts of the law are not of things to believe, but of things to do, although it does announce something for belief; and therefore its virtue is not of faith, but of works. And he proves this, because God wishing to confirm the law did not say, *He that believeth*, but, *He that doeth these things* (Lev. xviii. 5): but the New Law is

of faith, for, *He that believeth, and is baptized, shall be saved*
(Mark xvi. 16)." The Old Law, as such, afforded no
grace of faith for men to believe in the God who gave
it. Such grace was indeed afforded under the Old
Law, but not by the Law, by anticipation of the merits
of Christ our Saviour; and on these merits, and on
faith and hope in Christ to come, it depended whether
observance of the Old Law, in the days when it was in
force, should avail a man for life everlasting.

13. *Christ hath redeemed us from the curse of the law*,
incurred by non-observance, as explained under *vv.* 10,
11. From this *curse of the law* Christ was exempt, as
being of Himself the *Lamb unspotted and undefiled* (1 Pet.
i. 19). And yet he is said to have been *made a curse*, as
also to have been *made sin* (see on 2 Cor. v. 21). Taking
upon Himself the sins of the whole world, He chose to
appear not so much a sinner as *sin* itself; and taking
upon Himself the curse incurred by all, He willed to
appear not so much accursed as *a curse*.

Cursed is every one that hangeth on a tree (Deut. xxi. 23).
Crucifixion or impalement was not a Jewish method of
execution, except under circumstances quite unusual,
e.g. Num. xxv. 4. The Gabaonites, who crucified the
sons of Saul (2 Kings xxi. 9), *were not of the children of
Israel*. But the dead body of a criminal was sometimes
fastened up. This was to be taken down and buried
the same day, lest it should pollute the land, the Holy
Land, the suspended body of the malefactor being an
accursed thing. This legal curse our Saviour incurred in
His crucifixion; and His Body was taken down before
sunset in accordance with the prescription of Deuter-
onomy, especially urgent in His case, as that sunset
ushered in the great sabbath-day (John xix. 31). This
scandal of the cross (*v.* 11; 1 Cor. i. 23) was often in the
mouths of the Jews to taunt the Christians. St. Paul
glories in it (vi. 14), and shows cause.

14. *The blessing of Abraham*, promised to Abraham for his faith (*vv.* 8, 9), thanks to the curse that our Saviour bore upon the cross, has descended upon Jews, who were under the curse of the law, and upon Gentiles also, as many as will imitate Abraham *by faith*.

The promise of the Spirit means the promised Spirit.

15. *Brethren.* After the abrupt addresses of i. 6, and iii. 1, St. Paul is come back to his habitual kindliness.

I speak after the manner of man, i.e. I borrow an example from human life, as in 1 Cor. ix. 7.

Yet a man's testament ; ὅμως ἀνθρώπου διαθήκην, *though it be but a man's covenant, yet,* &c. : see 1 Cor. xiv. 7 for a similar use of ὅμως. The word διαθήκη in classical Greek generally, though not quite always, means a *last will and testament* ; and so it does in Heb. ix. 16, 17. But the corresponding Hebrew word *berith* means simply *a covenant*. In the present passage we shall translate *testament* or *covenant*, according as we consider the Apostle's mind to have been swayed by the ordinary meaning of the Greek word he used, or by the meaning of its Hebrew original. The argument holds well enough either way. In favour of the rendering *testament* is the verb in the same verse, ἐπιδιατάσσεται (*addeth to it*), if we observe that διατάσσομαι means *I make a will*, and ἐπιδιαθήκη means *a codicil*.

Despiseth, an inadequate translation of ἀθετεῖ (in the Vulgate *spernit*), *setteth aside*. A *covenant* is not to be cancelled, nor re-written ; a *will* is neither to be set aside nor modified by a codicil ; once the *covenant* is *confirmed*, or *ratified*, κεκυρωμένην, or the *will made final* by the death of the testator (Heb. ix. 17).

16. *To Abraham were the promises made and to his seed.* The promises referred to are : *All the land that thou beholdest, I will give to thee and to thy seed for ever* (Gen. xiii. 15) ; and, *I will give to thee and to thy seed the land of*

thy sojourning, all the land of Chanaan for an everlasting possession, and I will be their God (Gen. xvi. 8).

The word *seed* in all this context is the exact Hebrew and Greek equivalent of the English word *issue*, which may be conveniently substituted for it. We do not speak of *issues* in the sense of *sons*, nor is the Hebrew word used in the plural in this sense. But the cognate Chaldee word is ; and the Greek plural σπέρματα, *seeds*, *i.e. sons*, is found in Plato, *Laws*, 853 C ; Sophocles, *Œd. Col.* 600 ; and approaches to that sense in Josephus, *Antiq.* viii. 7, 6, and in the apocryphal Fourth of Maccabees, xvii. Still the argument from the non-employment of the exceedingly rare plural *issues*, instead of the usual singular form *issue*, is not of itself very strong. Its strength lies in its association with the tradition of the Jewish schools, of which it is an outcome. It is a Rabbinical argument, and points to the continuous belief of the Rabbis, who under the Old Law were the authorised interpreters of Scripture, that the *seed*, or *issue* of Abraham, to which the promises of the land were made, was not a multitude of separate individuals, but one person, Christ, the King of Israel. His was to be the land of promise, and His people's, for that they were His people.

The land of promise, which is literally the country of Palestine, is taken by St. Paul in the spiritual sense for *the kingdom of heaven* (Matt. xxv. 1), the Church on earth ; and further for *the kingdom of Christ and of God* (Eph. v. 5), the Church in heaven (cf. Heb. iv. 8—11). So the descendants of Abraham, who share spiritually in the promises made to him, are not his mere carnal posterity, but the inheritors of his faith in Christ (iii. 9, 29).

17. The verse means that *the law*, given to Moses, *does not disannul the testament*, or *covenant*, made with Abraham. It is an application to Divine conduct of

what is said *after the manner of man* in v. 15. God Himself
cannot set aside His *testament*, or *covenant*, when made in
the form of an express *promise to Abraham and to his seed,
Christ* (cf. Ps. lxxxviii. 35, 36). Nor can He load His
promise with conditions, which were not put in when
the promise was first given and accepted. But the
observance of the Mosaic law would have been the
laying on of a huge condition (cf. Acts xv. 10, 11) to
the promise, centuries after the pact was complete.
Therefore *the works of the law*, its ceremonial observances,
are in no manner of way to be brought forward as
conditions for the fulfilment of the promises made of
old to Christ, and to us in Christ, *the promise of eternal
inheritance* (Heb. ix. 15). Such is St. Paul's argument
in this place.

There is a difficulty, which however does not touch
the argument, a chronological difficulty about the *four
hundred and thirty years*, which seems to be all the time
that St. Paul allows between the promise made to
Abraham and the giving of the law on Mount Sina;
whereas from the ages of the patriarchs it is manifest
that some two hundred years must have elapsed between
this promise and the going of the Israelites into Egypt;
while from Gen. xv. 3; Acts vii. 6; Exod. xii. 40, it
appears that their stay in Egypt was of four hundred,
or in exact numbers, four hundred and thirty years.
Why then does not St. Paul say *six hundred and thirty
years?*

One solution of the difficulty is by correcting the
Hebrew text of Exod. xii. 40 from the Greek of the
Septuagint, where after *in the land of Egypt* is added
and in the land of Chanaan, thus reducing the sojourn in
Egypt to some two hundred and thirty years. Another
solution is suggested from Matt. i. 9, where three
generations are omitted between Joram and Ozias, as
appears from 4 Kings viii. 25; xi. 2; xiv. 1, 21; and

yet in *v.* 17 we read: *From David to the transmigration of Babylon are fourteen generations.* The Bible is an Oriental book, written to Oriental, not European standards of historical accuracy. Understatement of itself is not falsehood. To an understated number our fastidious ears require the prefix of an *at least,* which St. Paul and St. Matthew and the people they lived with were very willing to forego, except perhaps in money matters (Luke xvi. 7). If four hundred and thirty years, the duration of the Israelites' stay in Egypt, were abund· antly enough for St. Paul's argument of the law being at a much later date than the promise, why should we insist on his adding in the other two hundred years? They made nothing to his purpose.

It is also possible that the fact of the promise made to Abraham having been renewed to Isaac (Gen. xxvi. 3—5) and Jacob (Gen. xxviii. 13—15; xxxv. 12; xlviii. 4), may have moved St. Paul deliberately to omit these years in which these patriarchs and their race dwelt in the land of Chanaan.

18. Read Romans iv. for another statement of the case here concluded. The conclusion now arrived at is that the inheritance promised to Abraham, the promised land, taken for that which it spiritually repre· sented, *the unsearchable riches of Christ* (Eph. iii. 8, set forth in Eph. i.—iii.), was not of the nature of wages for the observance of the Mosaic law. Hence the question naturally arises, which is asked in the next verse :

19. *Why then was the law?* The answer to this question takes us up to iv. 7.

It was set because of transgressions, τῶν παραβάσεων χάριν, literally, *because of the transgressions* (which were to take place) *until the seed should come, i.e.* Christ, *v.* 16: *for where there is no law, neither is there transgression* (Rom. iv. 15). The law then was to *conclude all under sin, i.e.*

as St.Chrysostom explains, "to convict them and show them their own offences: for since the Jews did not perceive their own sins, and not perceiving them had no desire of the remission of them, He gave the law revealing their wounds, that they might long for the physician."

The law given on Sina, *being ordained,* ordered, set forth in detail, *by angels* (Heb. ii. 2; Acts vii. 53). The angels may have been the immediate authors of the prodigies on Mount Sina: nay an angel there may have spoken in the place of God (Exod. xix. 16, seq.).

In the hand of. A Hebraism for *by the agency of.* So Acts vii. 35; Num. iv. 37, seq.

A mediator. Moses. Cf. Exod. xx. 19; Deut. v. 23—27. A world of confusion has been created about this passage, by the commentators who have taken the *mediator* here to be Christ. The verse that follows has been explained in some four hundred different ways.

20. *Now a mediator is not of one,* but of two contracting parties, whom he brings together, and who make through him what is called a 'bilateral,' or two-sided contract, of the form, 'I do or give this, on condition that you do or give that,' under which conditional form the parties are reciprocally bound.

The Mosaic Law was a covenant of this nature: *he that doeth these things shall live in them* (*v.* 12): read the celebrated chapter, Deut. xxviii. Consequently the Mosaic covenant might fail and come to nought, through the infidelity of one of the two contracting parties, the Jewish people. Not so the promise made to Abraham, which was no bilateral contract,—not a thing *ordained in the hand of a mediator,* bringing two parties together, and binding them on condition of mutual good faith; —but there was only one contracting party in that promise, and He was God, promising gratuitously and

R

absolutely. This is the significance of St. Paul's somewhat abrupt addition, *But God is one.*

The verse is a sort of last touch to the argument
begun at *v.* 6, to show that the law, with its conditions
of works, can be no substitution for the promise made
to Abraham, simply for his faith. Rather it might
seem that, such a promise having been made, the law
ought never to have been superadded. This difficulty
St. Paul proceeds to consider.

21. *If there had been a law given which could give life*
eternal, *justice*, or supernatural holiness, *should have been
by the law*, not by faith, and then the law would have
been against the promises (Rom. iv. 13, 14). But, the
argument goes on, the law could not give life. This
seems inconsistent with the text quoted in *v.* 12: *He
that doeth these things shall live in them :* till we remember
that this was just the weakness of the law, that it could
not get itself kept (Rom. ii. 17—24; iii. 9—20),—it
made no provision for securing its own observance;
it was barren of grace, without which man cannot
steadily resist sin, which grace comes only of faith in
the Redeemer promised to Abraham, and since sent
into the world.

22. *The Scripture*, ἡ γραφή, rather, *the text :* this word
in the singular means, not the Scriptures generally
(αἱ γραφαί), but some special text. St. Paul may here
refer, as in ii. 16, to Ps. cxlii. 2.

Hath concluded all under sin. For the sense cf. Rom.
iii. 9; and for the word *concluded*, συνέκλεισεν, Rom. xi. 32.
The Scripture marks the fact, that all mankind are
brought into and held under the category of sinners,
as fish might be driven into and caught in a net,
and, so to speak, *concluded* there.

That the promise, i.e. the spiritual inheritance promised
to Abraham, *might be given to them that believe*, not for
their observance of the Jewish law, which was powerless

to justify, but *by the faith of Jesus Christ, who is made unto us justice and sanctification and redemption* (1 Cor. i. 30). For the Jewish law substitute the exigences and decencies of modern civilised society, and St. Paul's words have their application to this day. These decent observances are all insufficient before God without faith, hope, and charity. And there is no faith without a creed: there is small hope and charity without sacraments; and creed and sacraments find no custodian except in a divinely preserved and divinely guided Church.

23. *Before the faith came*, that is, the object of our faith, Christ.

Shut up, as captives and prisoners under the bonds of the law.

Unto that faith that was to be revealed, i.e. waiting for the coming of Christ, who *has made us free* (iv. 31).

24. *The pedagogue* (παιδαγωγός, child-leader) was not a schoolmaster, but a slave who took the boy to school, saw that he went, and guarded him from danger on the way.

In Christ, εἰς χριστόν, *unto Christ.* The law led us like children to the school of Christ, the acceptance of whose teaching is called *faith*.

25. *We are no longer under a pedagogue.* The pedagogue leaves the child when he passes in at the school door.

26. *You are all the children of God.* The emphasis is on the word *all*, which stands first in the Greek. *All*, both Gentiles and Jews. The Galatian converts were principally of the Gentiles, which may be the reason why the Apostle passes from *we* to *you*. The argument is developed in the beginning of the next chapter. The Christian, whoever he be, and of whatsoever race and belief before his conversion, stands to the Jew under the Mosaic law, **as the grown up** son to the child, and

is consequently emancipated from the state of tutelage, which is the essence of that law.

Faith in Christ Jesus. The Latin Vulgate takes these words together : but the construction is more probably : *You are all children of God in Christ Jesus by faith.* Cf. iv. 4, 5 ; Eph. i. 5.

27. *Baptized in Christ,* εἰς χριστόν, *unto Christ,* dedicated to Him, and made part of His mystical body. See on Rom. vi. 3, 4.

Have put on Christ. " For if Christ is the Son of God, and you have put Him on, having the Son in yourself and being likened to Him, you are brought to one kindred and one form with Him " (St. Chrysostom). All this is very inadequately expressed by saying that we are conformed to Christ in the imitation of His virtues. The Fathers say much more than that : *e.g.* St. Cyril of Jerusalem : " You are made of the same form with the Son of God. God has made us of the same form with the glorious Body of Christ. Being then made partakers of Christ, you are rightly called other Christs " (*Catech.* 21). And again, St. Chrysostom in the verse next following : " You have all one form, one impress, that of Christ. What could be more awful than these words ? Greek and Jew, even the slave of yesterday, goes about in the form, not of angel or archangel, but of the very Lord of all."

28. All these differences of nationality, condition, and sex, are merged in the Christian character. *You are all one* (*one man,* εἷς, though the Vulgate has *unum, one thing*) *in Christ Jesus.*

29. Well explained by Theodoret :—" If we are the body of Christ, and He is our head, at the same time that He is called the seed of Abraham, then through Him we are allied to Abraham by faith, and reap the blessing of the promise : for it is impossible for the head to be of Abraham, and the body to be of any other."

Chapter IV.

1. Now I say: As long as the heir is a child, he differeth nothing from a servant, though he be lord of all; **2.** But is under tutors and governors until the time appointed by the father. **3.** Even so we, when we were children, were in bondage under the elements of the world. **4.** But when the fulness of the time was come, God sent his son, made of a woman, made under the law; **5.** That he might redeem those who were under the law; that we might receive the adoption of sons. **6.** And because you are sons, God hath sent the Spirit of his Son into your hearts, crying: Abba, Father. **7.** Therefore now he is no more a servant, but a son: and if a son, an heir also through God. **8.** But then, indeed, not knowing God, you served them who by nature are no gods. **9.** But now, after that you have known God, or rather are known of God, how turn you again to the weak and poor elements which you are desirous to serve again? **10.** You observe days, and months, and times, and years. **11.** I am in fear for you, lest perhaps I have laboured in vain among you. **12.** Be ye as I; for I also am as you; brethren, I beseech you: you have not injured me at all. **13.** And you know how through infirmity of the flesh I preached the gospel to you heretofore and your temptation in my flesh. **14.** You despised not nor rejected; but received me as an angel of God, even as Christ Jesus. **15.** Where is then your blessedness? For I bear you witness, that, if it could be done, you would have plucked out your own eyes, and would have given them to me. **16.** Am I then become your enemy in telling you the truth? **17.** They are zealous in your regard not well; but they would exclude you, that you might be zealous for them. **18.** But be zealous for that which is good in a good thing always; and not only when I am present with you, **19.** My little children, of whom I am in labour again, until Christ be formed in you. **20.** And I would willingly be present with you now, and change my voice: because I am ashamed for you. **21.** Tell me, you that desire to be under the law, have you not read the law? **22.** For it is written: that Abraham had two sons, the one by a bond-woman, and the other by a free-woman. **23.** But he that was by the bond-woman was born according to the flesh; but he by the free-woman was by the promise. **24.** Which things are said by an allegory: for these are the two testaments; the one indeed on Mount Sina, which bringeth forth unto bondage, which is Agar. **25.** For Sina is a mountain in Arabia, which hath an affinity with that which now is Jerusalem, and is in bondage with her children. **26.** But that Jerusalem which is above is free, which is our mother. **27.** For it is written : Rejoice, thou barren, that bearest not ; break forth and cry out, thou that travailest not : for many are the children of the desolate, more than of her that hath a husband. **28.** Now we, brethren, as Isaac was, are the children of the promise. **29.** But as then he who was born according to the flesh persecuted him who was born according to the Spirit, so also now. **30.** But what saith the Scripture ? Cast out the bond-woman and her son : for the son of the bond-woman shall not be heir with the son of the free-woman. **31.** Therefore, brethren, we are not the children of the bond-woman, but of the free : by the freedom wherewith Christ hath made us free.

1. There are three stages of divine sonship (by adoption): (*a*) the Jew under the Old Law, cf. Rom. ix. 4, ὧν ἡ υἱοθεσία ; (*b*) the Christian under the New Law ; (*c*) The Saint in heaven. St. Paul says that the first stands to the second as the heir, still a minor, to the heir of full age. The same proportion may also be instituted between the second and the third.

The father of this child is supposed to be dead. But every comparison halts : Our Father in heaven never dies.

2. *Tutors and governors*, ἐπιτρόπους καὶ οἰκονόμους, the former being controllers of his person, the latter of his property.

Until the time appointed by the father, or more usually by the law, for the termination of his minority.

3. *When we were children*, under the Old Law.

The elements of the world. This expression occurs three times in St. Paul, here, and in Col. ii. 8, 20, to which we may add *v.* 9, below, *weak and needy elements.* It is always in connection with some observance of a calendar, as below, *v.* 10, *days and months and times and years ;* and Col. ii. 16, *in respect of a festival day, or of the new moon, or of the sabbaths. The elements of the world* then are the sun and moon, as determining sabbaths, new moons, and the other recurring festivals of the Jewish calendar. As late as the fifth century, the observance of Jewish feasts by Christians drew down the strong animadversions of the pastors of the Church.

4. *Made of a woman, made under the law.* The word γενόμενον, twice repeated, lends itself equally well to the translation, *born of a woman, born under the law,* and the sense is the same. The reading γεννώμενον in the first clause is absurd, as that would mean *in the act of being born.*

5. *He was born under the law,* and bore the curse of the law (iii. 13), *that he might redeem them that were under the law.* Again, Son of God as He was, He was *born of a woman,* and became our brother, *that we might receive the adoption of sons.*

6. *God* (the Father) *hath sent the Spirit of his Son.* This is one of the texts quoted to prove the procession of the Holy Ghost from the Father and the Son.

Crying, i.e. as explained in the parallel text, Rom. viii. 15, 16, *whereby we cry.*

Abba, Father. Abba was the very word used by our Lord (Mark xiv. 16), and was joined by the first Christians in affectionate remembrance with the corresponding Greek word for *Father.*

7. *He is not now a servant.* A better reading is, *Thou art not.* The conclusion is that, as a son come of age, you are free from the servile state of pupillage, which was the Jewish law.

8. Taken out of its Greek dress, this sentence would be Englished : *Formerly, when you served those who by nature are not gods, it was because you did not know God.*

9. *After that you have known God,* more literally, *have recognised God.*

Or rather, are known by God. Say, *are recognised by God* and owned by Him for His own, a very common phrase, *e.g.* Ps. i. 6 ; 1 Cor. viii. 3 ; xiii. 12. For the doctrine,

1 John iv. 10: *Not as though we had loved God, but because he hath first loved us.*

Weak and needy elements. On *elements* see note on *v.* 3. The *elements* are the sun and moon, which the pagans worshipped as gods, and the relative positions of which to the earth determined the feasts in the Jewish calendar. These elements are called *weak*, because the rites celebrated upon observation of them in the Jewish law had no power to justify : they are called *needy*, or *beggarly*, because those rites even at their best were but shadows of good to come. Cf. Heb. vii. 18: *the weakness and unprofitableness thereof.*

Which (*elements*, sun, moon, and stars) *you desire to serve again.* Well explained by Theodoret : " He goes about to show that the observance of days according to the law is idolatry. Before you were granted your call to the faith, he says, you served them that were not by nature gods, making gods of the elements ; but from this error Christ our Lord delivered you ; now, strangely enough, you are going back to the same error : for in keeping sabbaths and new moons and the other days, and fearing to transgress these observances, you are like those that make gods of the elements."—The law, in its own proper period, was *holy and just and good* (Rom. vii. 12): but now that Christ has come and fulfilled what the law foreshadowed, to take the ceremonial law for a binding obligation, or even for a better good, is a superstitious and soul-destroying idolatry.

10. *You observe days*, recurring weekly, sabbaths ; *and months*, new moons (cf. Isai. lxvi. 23); *and times*, the annual festivals of the Passover, Pentecost, and Tabernacles (John vii. 2—on the Jewish feasts generally read Levit. xxiii.) ; *and years*, the sabbatical year (Levit. xxv. 4).

This text may have given some colour to the old Puritan objection against Christmas Day and other feasts of the Church's calendar—though, be it noted, it is not less applicable against the sabbath. But the reproach of the Apostle falls, not on Christian feasts, which were yet in their infancy, but on Jewish celebrations, from the keeping of which the Judaizing teachers hoped gradually to lead on the Galatians to circumcision and the rest of Jewish observances. Cf. Col. ii. 16.

12. This passage, *vv.* 12—21, is one of the most touching expressions of personal feeling in St. Paul, and makes amends to the Galatians for the somewhat stern tone of the earlier portion of the Epistle.

Be ye as I, because I also am as you. More literally, *become ye* (γίνεσθε) *as I, because I also* am become *as you.* It means: 'put aside Jewish observances, as I have done, because I, born a Jew, have become a stranger to such observances as much as you native Gentiles.'

You have not injured me. ' I have no personal complaint against you: quite the contrary ' (*v.* 14).

13. *Through infirmity of the flesh I preached the gospel to you heretofore*, rather, *on the first occasion*, τὸ πρότερον, referring to *the former* of his two visits to Galatia (Acts xvi. 6; xviii. 23). He preached then δι' ἀσθένειαν σαρκός, *per infirmitatem carnis* (Vulg.), or as St. Jerome rightly has it, *propter infirmitatem carnis*, i.e. *by reason of infirmity of the flesh*, not *in infirmity*, which would be δι' ἀσθενείας, a distinction which is maintained no less in Hellenistic than in classical Greek, as examination of the uses of διὰ in the Old and New Testament proves. The plain meaning of the words then is that it was some illness, not mentioned by St. Luke, that detained St. Paul in his first passage through Galatia, and led to his preaching where he would otherwise have simply travelled through to what seemed more promising ground. See the passage, Acts xvi. 6.

And your temptation in my flesh. In all other texts but the Latin Vulgate, and in the earlier editions of the

Vulgate itself, there is no stop after *flesh*. The words really belong to *v.* 14, and we should read: *And your temptation in my flesh you did not despise.* The first edition of the Rheims version, in 1583, reads: *And your tentation in my flesh you despised not.* The phrase is indeed harsh, but the meaning is clear: 'Shocked as you were at my bodily ailment,'—the mysterious thorn in the flesh of 2 Cor. xii. 7, apparently a recurring thing, and painful to behold—'and tempted as you were to despise me and reject my teaching, still *you despised not nor rejected me.*' Some have thought St. Paul's ailment to have been epilepsy. It has been well compared to the strange malady that haunted King Alfred upon his own petition. See Father Knight's *Life of King Alfred*, Quarterly Series, pp. 30, 31.

15. *Where then is your blessedness?* μακαρισμός, *your felicitation* of yourselves at having gotten me for your teacher?

16. *Your enemy.* We gather from the Clementine Homilies that the later Judaizers actually called St. Paul "the enemy."

The truth, so unpleasant to Galatian ears, must have been told them on the second visit (Acts xviii. 23), to which he refers, i. 9; v. 21.

17. *They*, the teachers who insist on Jewish observances.

But they would exclude you. The *but* takes up the *not* well. *Exclude you*, or *shut you off* from all other teaching than their own.

Be zealous for them, pay regard to them, look up to and admire them, of course to the exclusion of St. Paul.

18. *Be zealous for what is good in a good thing always.* It is difficult to attach any meaning to these words. They represent in fact a wrong reading, ζηλοῦσθε (*be zealous*), the imperative, for the infinitive, ζηλοῦσθαι. The imperative is found indeed in the Sinaitic and Vatican

manuscripts, as well as in the Latin Vulgate, but the weight of manuscript and patristic evidence is against it. It represents also an impossible formation, the verb ζηλῶ not being used in the middle voice. Lastly, it scarcely makes sense.

What St. Paul says is: *It is good to be regarded and admired* (ζηλοῦσθαι, infinitive passive) *on good ground always.* For ζηλοῦσθαι we might have had in classical Greek ζηλωτοὺς εἶναι, the adjective ζηλωτός, in frequent use, meaning *enviable, looked up to with emulation.* There is a well known description of ζῆλος (emulation) in Aristotle's *Rhetoric,* bk. ii. ch. 11.

Theodoret paraphrases the whole verse: " I wish you to shine conspicuous in all good gifts, that alike in my presence and absence you may have good credit."

19. *My little children,* a favourite phrase of St. John (1 John ii. 1, 12, 18, 28, &c.), but by St. Paul only used in this place, where, says St. Chrysostom, " he imitates a mother trembling for her little ones."

Of whom I am in labour again. His first labour was the trouble he had originally in converting them to Christ; his second, the anxiety and fear he now has of their perversion. *Until Christ be formed in you,* Eph. iv. 13, 14.

20. *And change my voice, i.e.* weep over you. So St. Chrysostom explains it, quoting Acts xx. 31 : *I ceased not with tears to admonish every one of you ;* and remarks: " When overcome by difficulties starting up unexpectedly, we find there is nothing for it but a flood of tears." To *change one's voice* then is the same thing as to *change one's countenance,* 1 Kings i. 18; Ezech. xxvii. 35.

I am ashamed for you, a mistranslation of *confundor,* ἀποροῦμαι : it means, *I am in perplexity over you.* The word occurs 2 Cor. iv. 8, where it is rendered, *we are straitened.* " I know not what to say or what to think.

How is it that you who were mounted to the height of heaven, as well through the dangers that you underwent for the faith, as through the signs which you wrought by the faith, are now on a sudden fallen to such mean estate as to be dragged into circumcision and sabbath-keeping, and hang on to Jewish customs?" (St. Chrysostom).

21. *Have you not read the law?* A better reading has, *Hear you not the law?* The law (here the Pentateuch, but cf. 1 Cor. xiv. 21) was read in the synagogues (Acts xiii. 27; xv. 21), and doubtless in the Christian assemblies.

22. *It is written*, Gen. xvi.; xxi. 1—12. *Two sons*, Ismael *of the bond-woman*, Agar; Isaac *of the free-woman*, Sara.

23. *According to the flesh*, in the ordinary course of nature.

By promise, Gen. xvii. 16, 19; xviii. 10; and contrary to the course of nature, Rom. iv. 18—21; Heb. xi. 11, 12.

24. *Which things are said by an allegory*. The best commentator on this is St. Paul himself, 1 Cor. x. 1—11. See also what is said of the two sons of Rebecca, Rom. ix. 10—13. Philo and the Alexandrine Jews dwelt so much on the allegorical meaning of the Old Testament narratives, as to set aside their historical truth. But St. Paul, as Theodoret observes, " does not take away the history, but teaches what was prefigured in the history." Parables were the favourite vehicles of Our Lord's teaching. Some of His parables, *e.g.* those in Luke xvi., appear to be relations of actual occurrences. As the daily events of life symbolise spiritual realities, much more does this symbolic character attach to the operations of a special and miraculous Providence, recounted in the Old Testament, and also to the miracles of Our Lord, recounted

in the New. The Old Testament history, while it is a real history, is also one great drama, prefiguring the Christian dispensation. St. Paul here, inspired by the Holy Ghost, explains to us the meaning attached in the counsels of God to one episode of that drama.

These are the two testaments, i.e. these two women, allegorically or typically understood, are the two covenants, of the Old and of the New Law. In sharp contrast with Matthew xxvi. 26, this passage is fixed to a figurative sense by the word *allegory*, as a similar passage, 1 Cor. x. 4, is by the word *spiritual*.

The one, the Old Testament, given *from Mount Sina* (Exod. xxxiv.), *engendering unto bondage*, notwithstanding the Jews' proud boast (John viii. 33), for the Jewish law was a bondage.

Which is Agar, or, *such as is Agar*: cf. 1 Cor. iii. 17, which may be rendered, *such as you are*.

25. *Sina is a mountain in Arabia.* So the Sinaitic MS. and the Vulgate, and no doubt they are right. The Alexandrine and Vatican MSS., and the Greek Fathers generally, read, *Agar is Sina, a mountain in Arabia.* This reading is explained by a statement, which we find first in St. Chrysostom, and which modern commentators and travellers have endeavoured to make good, to the effect that Agar, the name of Abraham's handmaid, was also and still is a name given by the Arabs to Mount Sina. No reliance can be placed on this story, as Lightfoot shows. The words *in Arabia* are not superfluous. They go to show the connection of Sina with Agar, the posterity of her child Ismael being the Arabians (cf. Gen. xxi. 18, 21; xxv. 12—18; Baruch iii. 23). The fact then of the Law being given in the land of the sons of Ismael was typical of the Law being a bondage, as compared with the Gospel.

Hath affinity, συστοιχεῖ, *is in the same line.* There is no question of contiguity of place, for Sina is far enough

from Jerusalem. The word is used of a file of soldiers,
one behind the other. Then it means in philosophy a
column of names of similar qualities. All these names
would be said συστοιχεῖν. They would be opposed by
another column of names of opposite qualities, which
two columns in their several members would be said
ἀντιστοιχεῖν. Two such columns, illustrative of St. Paul's
meaning, might be drawn up, one against the other,
thus :—

Agar.	Sara.
Sina.	Sion (Heb. xii. 18, 22).
Ismael.	Isaac.
Old Covenant.	New Covenant.
Earthly Jerusalem.	Heavenly Jerusalem.
Bondage of the Law.	Liberty in Christ.

The antithesis is further set forth, Heb. xii. 18—24.

26. *That Jerusalem which is above, coming down out
of heaven* (Apoc. xxi. 2), wherein is our *conversation*,
or rather our *citizenship* (πολίτευμα, Phil. iii. 20), the
mother to whom *we are* already *come* (Heb. xii. 22), in
some sort in reality and to a still further extent in hope
(1 Cor. xiii. 9—12), in *our assembly* (Heb. x. 25), which
is the Christian Church on earth.

27. From Isaias liv. 1. By the *barren* and *desolate*
woman the prophet denotes the then state of the Jewish
people. Fertility and prosperity is announced to come
with the Messias, when the kingdom of Israel is to
embrace the Gentiles (*v.* 3). But as the prophet has
previously mentioned Abraham and Sara (li. 2), the
Apostle takes occasion therefrom to make a more
definite application of the text, within the same scope.
Sara then herself is the *desolate* woman, and *she that hath
a husband*, during the time of the barrenness of Sara, is
Agar (Gen. xvi.). Further, Agar is the Old Covenant,
the Synagogue, fruitful and prosperous in its day ; and

Sara is the New Covenant, the Church founded by the Messias. Thanks to St. Paul, an inspired commentator, we are enabled to draw a fuller meaning from the utterance of the inspired prophet.

28. Repeated in other words, Rom. ix. 8. *We*, both Jews and Gentiles (Rom. x. 12). Some MSS. read *you*, which makes St. Paul address the Galatians as Gentiles taken to be sons of Abraham in the spirit.

29. *Persecuted.* All that we read in Genesis xxi. 9, is that *the son of Agar played with Isaac;* but from Sara's indignation, as also from the tradition of the Jews, we gather that "that playing was a mockery," as St. Augustine observes. A reference to Concordances, Hebrew and Greek, will show that the verb has a bad sense elsewhere. We should also take into account the hostilities which went on between the Ismaelites, *sons of Agar*, as they are called, and Isaac's descendants (Ps. lxxxii. 7; 1 Paral. v. 10, 19).

30. Gen. xxi. 10, which saying of Sara is immediately ratified by the Almighty, *v.* 12; and afterwards by our Saviour, John viii. 35.

31. Literally, *not children of any bond-woman* (παιδίσκης without the article), *but of her who is free* (τῆς ἐλευθέρας), the Church Catholic.

By the freedom wherewith Christ has made us free. By the Greek Fathers, and in the best Greek MSS., these words are joined on, with sundry variations of reading, to the first verse of the next chapter: so that the sense should be, *Stand firm to the freedom*, &c. But the construction in that case required is harsh. The Vulgate collocation seems as likely as any other.

CHAPTER V.

1. Stand firm, and be not held again under the yoke of bondage. 2. Behold, I, Paul, tell you, that if you be circumcised, Christ will profit you nothing. 3. And I testify again to every man that circumciseth himself, that he is a debtor to do the whole law. 4. Christ is become of no effect to you, whosoever of you are justified by the law; you are fallen from grace. 5. For we in spirit, by faith, wait for the hope of justice. 6. For in Christ Jesus neither circumcision availeth anything, nor uncircumcision; but faith, which worketh by charity. 7. You did run well; who hath hindered you, that you should not obey the truth? 8. This persuasion is not from him who calleth you. 9. A little leaven corrupteth the whole mass. 10. I have confidence in you in the Lord, that you will not be of another mind: but he that troubleth you shall bear the judgment, whosoever he be. 11. And I, brethren, if I yet preach circumcision, why do I yet suffer persecution? The scandal of the cross is therefore made void. 12. I would they were even cut off who trouble you. 13. For you, brethren, have been called unto liberty; only use not liberty for an occasion to the flesh, but by charity of the Spirit serve one another. 14. For all the law is fulfilled in one sentence: Thou shalt love thy neighbour as thyself. 15. But if you bite and devour one another, take heed that you be not consumed one by another. 16. I say, then: Walk in the Spirit, and you shall not fulfil the lusts of the flesh. 17. For the flesh lusteth against the Spirit, and the Spirit against the flesh: for these are contrary one to another; so that you do not the things that you would. 18. But if you are led by the Spirit, you are not under the law. 19. Now the works of the flesh are manifest; which are, fornication, uncleanness, immodesty, luxury, 20. Idolatry, witchcraft, enmities, contentions, emulations, wraths, quarrels, dissensions, sects, 21. Envy, murder, drunkenness, revellings, and such like: of the which I foretell you as I have foretold to you, that they who do such things shall not obtain the kingdom of God. 22. But the fruit of the Spirit is charity, joy, peace, patience, benignity, goodness, longanimity, 23. Mildness, faith, modesty, continency, chastity: against such there is no law. 24. And they who are Christ's have crucified their flesh, with the vices and concupiscences. 25. If we live in the Spirit, let us also walk in the Spirit. 26. Let us not become desirous of vain-glory, provoking one another, envying one another.

2. *I, Paul, tell you*, speaking with the authority of an apostle (i. 1, 12). Cf. 2 Cor. x. 1 : *I, Paul, myself beseech you ;* and 1 Cor. vii. 40.

If you be circumcised. The supposition is put in the present tense, ἐὰν περιτέμνησθε, *if you go about to get circumcised*, not, *if you have been circumcised.* The text is aimed at any Gentile Christian who should think of circumcision as a complement to baptism, as though he would superimpose the Old Covenant upon the New.

Christ will profit you nothing, for the reason assigned in notes on ii. 17, 21.

3. Circumcision was to the Jewish law as Baptism is to the commandments of the Church, or as profession in a religious order is to the rule of the order, an engagement to fulfil it. The Judaizing teachers, while they insisted on circumcision, were ready to divest it of this onerous consequence (vi. 13).

4. Translate : *You are severed from Christ as useless, as many of you as go about to be justified by the law : you are cast out from grace.* These words do not imply that the Galatians actually had fallen away from Christ and His grace, but they show the necessary and immediate consequence of seeking circumcision as though baptism were not enough for full justification. Cf. John xv. 6 : *If any one abide not in me*, ἐβλήθη, *he is cast forth.* So the aorists κατηργήθητε, ἐξεπέσατε, are here to be translated as presents. For καταργεῖν cf. 1 Cor. xiii. 10, 11 ; Rom. vii. 2, 6.

Are justified, i.e. seek to be justified.

As ἐκπίπτειν is the virtual passive of ἐκβάλλειν, this ἐξεπέσατε answers to ἔκβαλε of iv. 30, and is well translated, *you are cast out*, according to the sentence passed on the bondwoman Agar, into whose lineage you have entered.

5. *We in spirit*, under the grace of the New Law, which *quickeneth*, as opposed to the bare *letter* of the

S

Old Law, *which killeth* (2 Cor. iii. 6, see notes), which the Judaizers were endeavouring to enforce.

By faith, not by the works of the Old Law (ii. 16, 20, 21 ; iii. 2, 3, 5, 7, 9, 25, 26 ; iv. 9).

Wait for, ἀπεκδεχόμεθα, the word used in Rom. viii. 19, 23 ; where the intense longing that it implies is expressed by ἀποκαραδοκία, *waiting with outstretched neck.*

The hope of justice is the hoped for *crown of justice* (2 Tim. iv. 8), the justice in question being not the *justice which is of the law, but that which is of the faith of Jesus Christ, which is of God, justice in faith* (Phil. iii. 9 : cf. Gal. ii. 21 ; iii. 6, 21).

6. 1 Cor. vii. 18, 19; Gal. vi. 15. "As in the choice of athletes," says St. Chrysostom, "the shape of the nose and the colour of the skin goes for nothing : the one thing regarded is their strength and their training : so, when one is enrolled under the new covenant, these bodily conditions hurt him not by their absence, nor aid him by their presence."

Faith that worketh by charity : ἐνεργουμένη is probably passive (see on 2 Cor. i. 6) : hence we should translate, *faith set going by charity*, or *faith astir with charity*. But the sense is the same. "These words," as Lightfoot writes, "bridge over the gulf which seems to separate the language of St. Paul and St. James. Both assert a principle of practical energy, as opposed to a barren, inactive theory."

7. *You did run well*, the same metaphor from the games as in 1 Cor. ix. 24.

8. *Him that calleth you*, above i. 6, 15 ; 1 Thess. v. 24 ; 1 Cor. i. 2. The Gentile Galatians were not called to Judaism.

9. "Then, that none might say : 'Why dost thou make so much of the matter and aggravate it by talk? we have kept but one precept [circumcision], and dost thou raise this clamour?'—hear how he frightens them,

not by the present, but by the future, saying thus : *A little leaven corrupteth* [leaveneth] *the whole lump :* 'so,' he argues, 'this little error, not corrected, avails to draw you into entire Judaism.'" (St. Chrysostom.) Cf. *v.* 3.

10. *Whosoever he be.* A reference to 2 Cor. x. 7 (where see notes) may throw some light on this unknown person, or the party to which he belonged.

11. *If I yet preach circumcision, why do I yet suffer persecution?* It was objected to St. Paul that he was inconsistent with himself, preaching and inculcating at sundry times and places that very Mosaic Law which here he disallows. St. Paul certainly did at times publicly conform to the Law (Acts xvi. 3; xxi. 26), becoming to the Jews a Jew, that he might gain the Jews (1 Cor. ix. 20). But he never preached the Law as a commandment in the Church : he would not have it even as an evangelical counsel. Had he consented to that, as he says here, all his persecution from the Jews might have ended. They hated and persecuted him precisely as a despiser of their Law (Acts xxi. 28). Once he had accepted Judaism as a necessary part of Christianity, all this opposition would have ceased. But where should we Gentiles have been? (Cf. notes on ii. 21.)

Then is the scandal of the cross made void. The *stumbling-block* (1 Cor. i. 23) ceases to be a stumbling-block, when we accept the argument: *Justice is by the law : therefore Christ died in vain* (ii. 21 ; see notes on ii. 17 ; iii. 1).

12. *I would they were even cut off,* ἀποκόψονται, *abscindantur* (Vulg.). The Greek word means what it means in Deut. xxiii. 1 : so it is understood by all the Greek Fathers; and so the Latin word is taken by the Latin Fathers. As Lightfoot observes: " The remonstrance is doubly significant as addressed to Galatians; for Pessinus, one of their chief towns, was the home of the

worship of Cybele, in honour of whom these mutilations were practised." It is no expression of a wish, but of strong abhorrence, such as is expressed again Phil. iii. 2, 3. There was no more salvation to be had now of the characteristic rite of Judaism than of the abominable practice of the heathen.

Who trouble you, οἱ ἀναστατοῦντες, they who would turn you out of house and home, from *that Jerusalem which is above, which is our mother* (iv. 26 : cf. Heb. xii. 22), and bring you into *bondage* (iv. 24).

13. *You have been called unto liberty*, freedom from the ceremonial precepts of the Jewish law, freedom also from the temporal penalties which under that law formed the sanction of the moral precepts, but not freedom from the obligation of those moral precepts themselves, which are of nature, pre-existent to the law given on Sina (Rom. ii. 14, 15), and were confirmed by Christ (Matt. xix. 17). Only, these moral precepts which in the Old Law were enforced by threats of temporal punishment, are in the New Law facilitated by grace. This is St. Paul's witness against Anti-nomianism, for which also read Rom. vi.

By charity serve one another, δουλεύετε, *be in bondage to one another*. The bondage of charity to replace the bondage of fear and of the law.

14. Expanded into three verses, Rom. xiii. 8—10. The quotation is from Levit. xviii. 19, where for *friend* the Septuagint has *neighbour*. The Jewish doctors were prone to limit the extension of this term *neighbour* to Jews, a limitation which Our Saviour sets aside in the parable of the Good Samaritan (Luke x. 29—37).

" Since the perfection of charity involves two precepts, the love of God and the love of our neighbour, why does the Apostle make mention only of the love of our neighbour ? Why but because men can lie concerning the love of God, seeing that temptation

comes less frequently to try it, but in the matter of
the love of their neighbour they are more easily convicted of not possessing it, when they deal unjustly
with men?   Besides, who can love his neighbour, that
is, every man, unless he love God, by whose precept
and gift he is enabled to compass the love of his
neighbour?   Since then such is the nature of either
precept that the one cannot be kept without the other,
it is generally sufficient to mention merely one of them,
when there is question of the works of justice: but that
one is more aptly mentioned, on which a transgressor
is more easily convicted " (St. Augustine).   Cf. 1 John
iv. 20.

15. *If you bite and devour one another.* It is St. Jerome's
remark, that the Apostle has described each province
by its own special features; and that the same vestiges
of errors or virtues as he described were to be met with
in the same places three centuries afterwards.   Galatia
attained to unhappy notoriety as a nest of wrangling
heresies, particularly of outrageous forms of Montanism
and Manichæism.

16. *The spirit—the flesh.*   " By the flesh he means
the inclination of the mind to the worse: by the spirit,
the indwelling grace " (Theodoret).   So St. Chrysostom
explains the flesh to be " the earthy view of things."
The flesh in fact is the whole man, both in his intellectual and in his animal faculties, but in his animal
faculties particularly, inasmuch as he feels an inclination to break away from God and set up his rest in the
goods of this life.

The Apostle says of it: *There dwelleth not in my flesh
that which is good* (Rom. vii. 18); and again, *the wisdom of
the flesh is not subject to the law of God, neither can it be*
(Rom. viii. 7).   The flesh endures in every man, even
in a saint on earth, till his dying day.   Only in Our
Saviour and in His Blessed Mother there was flesh,

but not technically *the flesh*. In the day of the
resurrection, *the flesh*, as here spoken of, shall be no
more.

Still the theological maxim, quoted by the Council
of Trent (sess. 5, can. 5) holds good, that "in the
regenerate (by baptism) there is nothing that God
hates." The flesh is not wicked, though it prompts to
wickedness : it is not sin, nor sinful, though it tempts
us to sin. As St. Chrysostom says : " Though the
passions give trouble, their ravings go for nothing,"
in the man who *walks by the spirit*, that is, leads a supernatural life of faith, hope, and charity. That is why
St. Paul writes here, not *you shall not feel*, but *you shall
not fulfil*, that is, carry out into human act, *the lusts of the
flesh*.

In all that has been written, be it clearly understood
that by *the flesh* is not meant *the body*, a point which
St. Chrysostom elaborates with great care.

17. *So that* (ἵνα, equivalent to ὥστε according to a
later Greek usage, expressing not purpose but result,
cf. 1 Thess. v. 4) *you do not the things that you would.*
That is : ' So that either way you do not all your
inclination : for if you follow the spirit, you do not the
inclination of the flesh ; and if you follow the flesh, you
deny the prompting of the spirit : you have thus some
manner of self-renunciation either way.' Cf. Rom. vi. 16.

18. *Not under the law* that threatens slaves, but under
the spirit that leads the children of God. Cf. Rom.
vi. 14 ; viii. 2.

19. *The works of the flesh, which are*, ἅτινά ἐστι, *of which
sort are*. The Apostle is not enumerating all the works
of the flesh, but some specimens.

Fornication, uncleanness, luxury. The same words
appear in a different order in 2 Cor. xii. 21, as *uncleanness
and fornication and lasciviousness. Immodesty* (*impudicitia*,
Vulg.) is merely another suggested rendering of ἀσέλγεια

(*luxury*), the proper meaning of which is *shameless sensuality*.

20. *Idolatry, witchcrafts. Sorcerers and idolaters* are joined together in Apoc. xxi. 8.

Contentions, emulations, wraths, quarrels. The same Greek words in the same order reappear in 2 Cor. xii. 20 as *contentions, envyings, animosities, dissensions.* The word ἐριθεῖαι, variously rendered *quarrels* and *dissensions*, means *intrigues* for place and power, or *party-spirit.*

The word διχοστασίαι, here rendered *dissensions*, means *standings aloof*, of a less permanent kind than *sects*, αἱρέσεις (heresies), which are *abiding religious quarrels.*

21. *Envies, murders*, φθόνοι, φόνοι: likeness of sound has brought the two words together.

Revelling, or *rioting* (Rom. xiii. 13), κῶμος, was a Greek custom. After a feast, followed by heavy drinking, the company would sally out and parade the streets with music, frequently in the end bursting into the house of a friend, and rousing the inhabitants to more drinking.

Shall not obtain (*inherit*) *the kingdom of God.* No, they shall not, however intense their persuasion that they have found Christ, the Saviour.

22. *The fruit of the spirit*, but *v.* 19, *the works of the flesh*, because, as St. Chrysostom says, "evil works come of ourselves alone, therefore he calls them works: but good ones need not only our care, but likewise the kind aid of God."

Charity, which contains all the rest, and from which all the rest spring, as shown 1 Cor. xiii. 4—7. They are enumerated, as "the twelve fruits of the Holy Ghost," but only nine are mentioned by St. Paul, *patience* being a second rendering of μακροθυμία (*longanimity*), *modesty* of πραΰτης (*mildness*), and *chastity* of ἐγκράτεια (*continency*). These three are omitted in the early Latin versions, and in all the Greek MSS., except that ἁγνεία (*chastity*) appears in some of inferior type.

Longanimity (μακροθυμία), *benignity* (χρηστότης). The two Greek words occur in 1 Cor. xiii. 4: *Charity is patient* (μακροθυμεῖ), *is kind* (χρηστεύεται). *Benignity* is in the disposition, *goodness* to our neighbour is in the act. The words might be rendered *kindliness* and *bounty* respectively.

23. *Mildness.* Charity *is not provoked to anger* (1 Cor. xiii. 5). *Faith.* Not here faith in God, for such faith does not follow upon charity, but precedes it ; besides the virtues here enumerated regard rather our behaviour as men to men. *Faith* then is *fidelity*, or *honesty*, as in Matt. xxiii. 23 ; Tit. ii. 10.

Against such there is no law. Cf. v. 18 above, and 1 Tim. i. 9. As *Moses was instructed in all the wisdom of the Egyptians* (Acts vii. 22), so was Paul of Tarsus in all the wisdom of the Greeks. He here, consciously or unconsciously, is quoting Aristotle, who says of men of transcendent virtue : " Against such there is no law; for they are a law of themselves " (*Politics*, iii. 13, nn. 13, 14), a saying that may easily have become proverbial.

24. *They that are Christ's have crucified their flesh, with the vices and concupiscences,*—more exactly, *passions and desires.* The reference is to what was done in baptism, as Theodoret explains : " They who were buried with Christ (in baptism), rendered their body dead to sin." Cf. above, ii. 19, 20 ; Rom. vi. 3—11.

25. In modern theological language : ' If we are in sanctifying grace (the state in which our baptism placed us), let us live up to the actual graces which wait upon such a state.'

26. *Vainglory* is somewhat abruptly introduced. Evidently St. Paul saw it to be a special danger to the grace of God in the Galatians, leading to rivalries

(*envying one another*), and challenges (*provoking one another*), and ending in *biting and devouring one another* (*v.* 15).

————

CHAPTER VI.

1. Brethren, and if a man be overtaken in any fault, you who are spiritual instruct such a one in the spirit of mildness, considering thyself, lest thou also be tempted. 2. Bear ye one another's burdens, and so shall you fulfil the law of Christ. 3. For if any man think himself to be something, whereas he is nothing, he deceiveth himself. 4. But let every one prove his own work, and so he shall have glory in himself only, and not in another. 5. For every one shall bear his own burden. 6. And let him who is instructed in the word communicate to him who instructeth him in all good things. 7. Be not deceived; God is not mocked. 8. For what things a man shall show, those also shall he reap. For he that soweth in his flesh, of the flesh also shall reap corruption; but he that soweth in the Spirit, of the Spirit shall reap life everlasting. 9. And in doing good let us not fail: for in due time we shall reap, not failing. 10. Therefore, whilst we have time, let us do good to all men, but especially to those who are of the household of the faith. 11. See what a letter I have written to you with my own hand. 12. For whosoever desire to please in the flesh, they constrain you to be circumcised, only that they may not suffer the persecution of the cross of Christ. 13. For neither they themselves who are circumcised keep the law; but they will have you to be circumcised, that they may glory in your flesh. 14. But God forbid that I should glory, but in the cross of our Lord Jesus Christ, by whom the world is crucified to me, and I to the world. 15. For in Christ Jesus neither circumcision availeth any thing, nor uncircumcision, but a new creature. 16. And whosoever shall follow this rule, peace be upon them, and mercy, and upon the Israel of God. 17. From henceforth let no man be troublesome to me: for I bear the marks of the Lord Jesus in my body. 18. The grace of our Lord Jesus Christ be with your spirit, brethren. Amen.

1. The connection of this verse with the preceding is that the Galatians justified their bickerings by a pretended zeal for the correction of an erring brother. *You, who are spiritual*, or take yourselves to be such.

Instruct, καταρτίζετε, in provincial English, *fettle up*. The word is used of *setting* a broken limb.

In the spirit of meekness. "Never," says St. Augustine, "should we undertake the business of reproving another's sin, except when upon examination of our conscience and inward enquiries we have returned ourselves a clear answer before God that we do it in love."

Considering thyself, lest thou—come to need correction in thy turn, which of course one would wish to be done gently. The Apostle passes from the plural, *you, who are spiritual*, to the singular *thou*, to bring home the weakness inherent in every man, as man, with whom suddenly *to be tempted* is so often the same thing as to be *overtaken in fault.*

2. *Bear ye one another's burdens, and so ye shall fulfil the law of Christ*, well explained by Theodoret : "You have this fault, but not that : he contrariwise has not what you have, but has another fault : you bear his, and let him bear yours : for so is fulfilled the law of charity : for by *the law of Christ* he means the law of charity : for these are Christ's own words : *A new commandment I give unto you, that you love one another* (John xiii. 34).''

3. *For if any man thinketh himself to be something.* This is a caution for *you who are spiritual.*

Whereas he is nothing, "has nothing of himself but lying and sin," as the Second Council of Orange says, can. 22 : cf. 1 Cor. iv. 7. *He deceives himself*, φρεναπατᾷ, *is the sport of his own fancies*, a word first used by St. Paul, here and Tit. i. 10.

4. *In himself* (*in semetipso*, εἰς ἑαυτόν), and *not in another* (*in altero*, εἰς τὸν ἕτερον). Here, as so often in the Latin Vulgate, *in* with the ablative is put for *in* with the accusative (*e.g.* Matt. xxviii. 19; Phil. ii. 11). The meaning is *looking to himself*, and not *looking to another*. The example of the man who had glory *looking to another* is the Pharisee in the gospel (Luke xviii. 11). In

allowing a man to *have glory looking to himself*, the Apostle is speaking ironically, knowing that whoever examines his conscience himself by himself alone before God will find scant matter for self-glorification.

5. *Every one shall bear his own burden*, meet his own liabilities at the judgment-seat of Christ (1 Cor. iv. 4, 5). This verse is in no contradiction with *v.* 2: for here is question of what shall be in the next world, there of what ought to be done in this: here the *burden* (φορτίον, a man's *load*) is responsibility before God: there *the burdens* (βάρη, *encumbrances*) are faults considered as things grievous and annoying to the community.

6. This verse, on the duty of supporting pastors, for which see 1 Cor. ix. 4—14; 2 Cor. xi. 7, 8; Phil. iv. 14—18; 1 Tim. v. 17, 18,—has no connection either with what goes before or with what follows. It is the way, at the end of a letter, to string together disconnected remarks.

Instructed, κατηχούμενος, *being catechized*, or *orally taught*, not however a *catechumen;* the direction is to baptized Christians. Cf. on Rom. ii. 18.

Communicate to him in all good things, *i.e.* share all his worldly goods with his instructor. Tithes (Exod. xxii. 29) are an institution of the Old Law that St. Paul did not wholly reprobate.

7, 8. These two verses are a caution against Antinomianism, on the lines of v. 13, 16, 21. Grace does not make us free of good works. Grace may be lost. The soul, justified in baptism, must still, as the Psalm has it (Ps. xxxiii. 15), *turn away from evil* (*v.* 8), *and do good* (*vv.* 9, 10).

God is not mocked, as the wicked learn in hell.

He that soweth in his flesh, he that gratifies the evil desires of his nature. For *the flesh* see on *v.* 16. The Apostle speaks of *sowing* and *reaping*, because human acts carry consequences with them both for this world and for the next.

Shall reap corruption. Whatever is given to the body ends in corruption, sooner or later : in like manner every gratification of lust has its connatural result in the defilement of the soul, and spoiling of the body also at the last day. And conversely, of what is *sown in the spirit,* that is, of works of grace.

9. The sense of this verse might have been more apparent, had the words run in this order : *In doing good, let us not fail : for, not failing (i.e.* on condition of not failing), *in due time we shall reap.* There are two Greek words here both translated *fail.* Literally we might render : *In doing good, let us not be fainthearted : for, not relaxing,* &c.

10. Imitating in our conduct *God, who is the Saviour of all men, especially of the faithful* (1 Tim. iv. 10).

11. *See what a letter I have written to you with my own hand.* This translation is apt to convey the opinion of St. Chrysostom and others, that St. Paul wrote this whole letter with his own hand, not using an amanuensis as he did in writing to the Romans (Rom. xvi. 22), the Corinthians (1 Cor. i. 1 ; 2 Cor. i. 1) and the rest. It is however not an accurate translation. From the Greek it should run thus. *See in what large letters* (πηλίκοις γράμμασι) *I write to you with my own hand.* I *write* is ἔγραψα, the epistolary aorist, used where we use the present. Nor is there anything in πηλίκοις γράμμασι to compel us to accept St. Chrysostom's paraphrase : " It seems to me to indicate not the size but the ugliness of the letters, as though he said : Not knowing how to write very well, nevertheless I am forced to write by myself, to close the mouth of the calumniators." We must presume that Greek characters came readily enough from the hand of Paul of Tarsus. The better explanation is that St. Paul, having used the

customary amanuensis up to this verse, here takes the
pen into his own hands and writes in *large letters*, to be
more emphatic, the rest of the epistle, gathering up in
seven forcible verses the main gist of all that he had
said before. For his habit of adding something in his
own hand cf. 2 Thess. iii. 17 ; 1 Cor. xvi. 21 ; Col. iv. 18.

12. *For* is not in the Greek, and should be away.
St. Paul is, as it were, starting afresh.

To please, εὐπροσωπῆσαι, *to put on a good face, in the flesh,*
i.e. in outward observances, notably in such a carnal
thing as circumcision.

They constrain you, ἀναγκάζουσι, *they are putting pressure*
on you. The word does not imply that they had
succeeded.

That they may not suffer persecution. From *v.* 11 it
appears that conformity with the Jews in the main rite
of their Law ensured toleration, as well from the Jews
themselves, as also from the Romans, with whom the
Jews, and all who could be classed as Jews, had a legal
standing and protection.

13. *Who are circumcised.* There are two readings of
equal authority, the perfect περιτετμημένοι, *who are actually*
circumcised, and the present περιτεμνόμενοι (as we should
say in familiar English), *who go in for circumcision.* Either
way it refers to the Judaizing teachers, against whom
the Epistle is written.

Glory in your flesh, glory in having brought you over
to this fleshly observance. On the inconsistency of
this proceeding, above, *v.* 3.

The following verses, written with St. Paul's own
hand, are the quintessence of his spirit. One should be
a saint to explain them.

14. *The cross of our Lord Jesus Christ.* For the shame
of the cross see on iii. 13. It was *despising the shame*
(Heb. xii. 2) to profess, and still more to *glory* in the
profession, that He who suffered that death was the

Messias, the Deliverer, and the death itself the deliverance, of *the Israel of God* (v. 16); and that before this
reality there passed away like a shadow *the covenant of
circumcision* (Acts vii. 8). For St. Paul's glorying in the
cross, see 1 Cor. i. 18—24; ii. 2; Gal. iii. 1. " Truly
the thing seems to be shameful," says St. Chrysostom,
" but only before the world and in the eyes of infidels;
but in heaven and in the eyes of the faithful it is the
greatest glory. So is poverty matter of reproach, but
to us a glory. So is abjection ridiculous in the eyes
of the many, but we make a darling of abasement. So
also is the cross our glory." To St. Paul, as St. Cyril
of Jerusalem says, it was "the glory of glories."

To understand what St. Paul was surrendering for
the shame of the cross, we should appreciate the intense
pride which every Jew took in belonging to the covenant
of circumcision, and his corresponding horror and
disdain of the Gentile world, evinced by such phrases
as *this uncircumcised Philistine* (1 Kings xvii. 36), and to *die
the death of the uncircumcised* (Ezech. xxviii. 10). The
Mohammedan horror of Christians is an illustration.
That St. Paul entered fully into this sentiment we see
from Rom. ix. 4, 5, and from Phil. iii. 4—10, which is a
perfect echo of this present passage.

By whom, rather, *by which* (cross), δι' οὗ (σταυροῦ).

The world. " What he calls the world, are the things
of this life, honour, glory, wealth " (Theodoret): understand, such things in their abuse, as they are made ends
in themselves, and lived for, apart from God our Lord
and the world to come; also understand, all men who
live for such things as above specified. Cf. on i. 4.
The world in short is Naturalism, or Secularism, and its
votaries. To this *world* St. Paul in his baptism (Rom.
vi. 4, 6), and in the full carrying out of his Christian
and Apostolic calling (Eph. ii. 2—5; 2 Cor. iv. 6, 10, 11;
John xvii. 14, 16) *is crucified*, he is as one dead, he is a

horror to it; and it is *crucified to him*: it is to him as
a dead thing, its works are *dead works* (Heb. vi. 1 ; ix. 14)
ghastly and abominable.

15. The Vatican manuscript reads: *Neither circumcision is anything, nor uncircumcision, but a new creature.* The
other words may have been put in from v. 6.

A new creature, or *a new creation*, a *new birth* (Tit. iii. 5 :
John iii. 5). See on 2 Cor. v. 17; also Col. iii. 9, 10.
Baptism is a *new creation* in the order of grace. The *new
heaven* and the *new earth*, which we are promised (Apoc.
xxi. 1), are also a *new creation*. The one is a first instal-
ment of the other. And both to baptism and to the
general resurrection the same term is applied, παλιγγενεσία
regeneration, new birth (Tit. iii. 5 : Matt. xx. 28). In the
day of baptism and in the day of the resurrection it
matters not in the least whether one be or be not
circumcised.

16. *This rule*, of the *cross* and of the *new creation*
(*vv.* 14, 15).

The Israel of God, as opposed to *Israel according to the
flesh*; true Christians, whether Jew or Gentile, in contrast
with unbelieving Jews (Rom. ix. 6—8 ; Phil. iii. 3 ; Gal.
iii. 29).

17. *Let no man be troublesome to me*, raise further difficulties, require further answering on the points of this
Epistle. The Master intimates that he has spoken once
for all. Similarly a discussion is broken off, 1 Cor. xi. 16.

I bear the marks of the Lord in my body. Marks, στίγματα,
but there is no question of any *stigmata* such as were
imprinted on St. Francis, " by a singular privilege,
not granted in past ages," as St. Bonaventure writes.
St. Paul refers to the marks left on his body from the
scourgings and stonings he had endured (2 Cor. xi.
23—25; Acts xiv. 18). We read in Herodotus, ii. 113,
of a temple : " If any man's domestic flies there, and
gets the sacred brand put upon him, and gives himself

over to the god, no one is allowed to touch him." And in the same author, vii. 233, we are told of certain Greeks who submitted to the King of Persia, on whom by his command "they branded the royal brand," to mark them as his slaves. Cf. Gen. iv. 15; Ezech. ix. 6; Apoc. vii. 3—9; ix. 4. St. Paul then says of the weals and scars on his body (2 Cor. iv. 10), that they mark him as the servant of Christ, and consequently as free from the Jewish law (iv. 31).

The Greek for *I bear* is βαστάζω, which means often, as St. Chrysostom points out, *I bear exultingly and lovingly, I cherish*. So Luke xiv. 27; John xix. 17; Acts ix. 15.

18. The same benediction concludes the Epistle to Philemon. The word *brethren*, put last, but wholly omitted in the sternness of the opening (i. 6), gives a dying fall of tenderness.

THE EPISTLE TO THE ROMANS.

INTRODUCTION.

THE last chapter of the First Epistle to the Corinthians is *concerning the collection that is being made for the saints*, for the needy Christians at Jerusalem. St. Paul, writing from Ephesus, says he will stay there till Pentecost; that then he will pass over to Macedonia, there to collect (2 Cor. viii. 1—4), and would thence come for the same purpose to Corinth and winter there, and would himself, if need be, take the contributions to Jerusalem next spring (1 Cor. xvi. 1—8). He did actually come, and stayed at Corinth three months (Acts xx. 2, 3). According to the chronology that we have followed, this event took place in the years 58, 59, A.D. St. Paul wrote the First Epistle to the Corinthians from Ephesus in the spring of 58; the Second to Corinthians from Philippi in the September of 58; the Epistle to the Galatians from Corinth that same winter. The Epistle to the Romans followed close upon that to the Galatians, and must have been written from Corinth quite in the early months of 59, before St. Paul started on that journey to Rome which is narrated in Acts xx. 4—xxi. 17. This is evident from Rom. xv.

T

25, 26 : *But now I shall go to Jerusalem, to minister unto the saints : for it hath pleased them of Macedonia and Achaia to make a contribution for the poor of the saints that are in Jerusalem.*

The traditional adscript at the end of the Epistle is to this effect : " To the Romans was written from Corinth through the hands of Phœbe the deaconness of the church at Cenchreæ," mentioned as such Rom. xvi. 1.   Cenchreæ was the port of Corinth. In connection with Cenchreæ, "the city " must mean Corinth, as at the Piræus it would mean Athens.   *Erastus, the treasurer of the city* then was the treasurer of Corinth.   We read in 2 Tim. iv. 20 : *Erastus remaineth at Corinth.*   Finally, *Gaius, my host* (xvi. 23), as we know from 1 Cor. i. 14, was a Corinthian.

Four great Epistles were thus written in these two years, from Ephesus, from Philippi, and from Corinth.   Living in Greece, and surrounded by Greeks, the Apostle was full of thought, of anxiety, of wonderment, as to the blending of Jew and Greek into one Christian civilization.   We may wonder too at the fertility of his mind, who amid the cares of the Apostleship, *in journeyings often, in perils, in labour and painfulness* (2 Cor. xi. 26, 27), could have given birth to such works.   Especially the rapidity with which the Epistle to the Romans must have followed upon that to the Galatians, may move our surprise.   But we must consider what has been already remarked, that the former Epistle is a first sketch and outline of the latter.   Having written what he had to say to the Galatians, a church in danger and needing a warning, the Apostle found his mind full of great thoughts, that called for a more ample development than he had been able to give them in an Epistle, written perhaps hurriedly to meet a pressing emergency. He fixed his eye therefore on another church, the rising "mother and mistress of all the churches," a church with which he had no fault to find, for which he had nothing but praise (Rom. i. 7, 8), the church of Rome, and to this church he dedicated his fuller lucubrations, to strengthen the flock of his brother Peter, and to be comforted by that which was common to them both, the faith of Peter and of Paul (i. 11, 12). He writes to the Romans, not for their need, but for their dignity, as one dedicates a book to a man of great name. Notwithstanding the numerous salutations with which it concludes, it is rather a treatise than a letter. There is a certain ceremoniousness and formality, as of one addressing a people whom he has not seen. We miss those traits of personal feeling and human sympathy, which are the charm of the Epistles to the Corinthians and the Galatians. Still it is a grand treatise, and in many ways the author's greatest work—a burst of inspiration breathing upon an apt instrument, the soul of Paul.

CHAPTER I.

1. Paul, a servant of Jesus Christ, called to be an apostle, separated unto the gospel of God, 2. Which he had promised before, by his prophets, in the holy Scriptures, 3. Concerning his Son, who was made to him of the seed of David according to the flesh, 4. Who was predestinated the Son of God in power, according to the spirit of sanctification, by the resurrection of our Lord Jesus Christ from the dead : 5. By whom we have received grace and apostleship, for obedience to the faith in all nations for his name; 6. Among whom are you also the called of Jesus Christ : 7. To all that are at Rome, the beloved of God, called to be saints : Grace to you and peace from God our Father, and from the Lord Jesus Christ. 8. First I give thanks to my God through Jesus Christ for you all, because your faith is spoken of in the whole world. 9. For God is my witness, whom I serve with my spirit in the gospel of his Son, that without ceasing I make a commemoration of you 10. Always in my prayers ; beseeching that by any means I may at length have a prosperous journey by the will of God in coming to you. 11. For I long to see you, that I may impart unto you some spiritual grace to strengthen you ; 12. That is to say, that I may be comforted together in you, by that which is common to us both, your faith and mine. 13. And I would not have you ignorant, brethren, that I have often purposed to come to you, (and have been hindered hitherto,) that I might have some fruit among you also, even as among other nations. 14. To the Greeks and to the barbarians, to the wise and to the unwise, I am a debtor : 15. So (as much as is in me) I am ready to preach the gospel to you also that are at Rome. 16. For I am not ashamed of the gospel : for it is the power of God unto salvation to every one that believeth ; to the Jew first, and to the Greek. 17. For the justice of God is revealed therein from faith to faith : as it is written : The just man liveth by faith. 18. For the wrath of God is revealed from heaven against all impiety and injustice of those men that detain the truth of God in injustice ; 19. Because that which is known of God is manifest in them ; for God hath manifested it to them. 20. For the invisible things of him, from the creation of the world, are clearly seen, being understood by the things that are made, his eternal power also and divinity ; so that they are inexcusable : 21. Because that, when they had known God, they have not glorified him as God, nor gave thanks ; but became vain in their thoughts, and their foolish heart was darkened :

22. For professing themselves to be wise, they became fools.
23. And they changed the glory of the incorruptible God into the
likeness of the image of a corruptible man, and of birds, and of
four-footed beasts, and of creeping things. 24. Wherefore God
gave them up to the desires of their heart, to uncleanness, to dishonour their own bodies among themselves: 25. Who changed
the truth of God into a lie, and worshipped and served the creature
rather than the Creator, who is blessed for ever. Amen. 26. For
this cause God delivered them up to shameful affections: for their
women have changed the natural use into that use which is against
nature: 27. And in like manner the men also, leaving the natural
use of the women, have burned in their lusts one toward another:
men with men doing that which is filthy, and receiving in themselves the recompense which was due to their error. 28. And as
they liked not to have God in their knowledge, God delivered them
up to a reprobate sense, to do those things which are not con-
venient; 29. Being filled with all iniquity, malice, fornication,
covetousness, wickedness; full of envy, murder, contention, deceit,
malignity; whisperers, 30. Detractors, hateful to God, contumelious, proud, haughty, inventors of evil things, disobedient to
parents, 31. Foolish, dissolute, without affection, without fidelity,
without mercy: 32. Who, having known the justice of God, did
not understand that they who do such things are worthy of death;
and not only they who do them, but they also who consent to them
that do them.

1. *Paul, a servant of Jesus Christ,* a title not taken at
the opening of any of the three previous epistles, but
lately much in the Apostle's thoughts, as appears from
Gal. vi. 17. It would be better to read either *Paul,
servant,* or *Paul, the servant.*

Separated unto the gospel of God. Cf. Acts xiii. 2:
*The Holy Ghost said to them: Separate me Saul and Barnabas
for the work whereunto I have taken them.* Cf. also Gal. i.
15, 16. The apostleship is of a nature to absorb all a
man's energy, life, and love.

2. *Promised by his prophets.* The prophets were the
apostles (men *sent* by God, Isaias vi. 8) of the Old
Testament, as the Apostles were the *prophets* (God's
spokesmen, Luke x. 16) of the New. The faithful are

built upon the foundation of the apostles and prophets (Eph. ii. 20).

3. *Made to him.* The *to him* is not in the Greek. *Made*, or *born*, γενομένου.

Of the seed of David. The genealogy in St. Luke iv. 23—31, is probably that of Mary ; *Joseph, who was of Heli*, meaning *son-in-law of Heli*, otherwise called Heliachim, or Joachim. The difficulty arising from Luke i. 5, 36 ; Exod. ii. 1 ; iv. 14, joined with Num. xxxvi. ; Tob. vi. 11, 12, is surmounted by supposing the prohibition of intermarriage between the tribes to have been confined to the case of females who were left heiresses by the failure of male issue. Thus Elizabeth on the mother's side may well have been of the tribe of Juda, and so related to Mary.

According to the flesh, that is, in His human nature, as Man : cf. ix. 3, 5. The phrase bears another sense in viii. *passim ;* 1 Cor. i. 26 ; 2 Cor. i. 17 ; x. 2, 3 ; xi. 18 ; Gal. iv. 23, 29 ; John viii. 15 : cf. i. 13. It occurs remarkably in 2 Cor. v. 16, where see notes.

4. *Who was predestinated the Son of God.* The Vulgate *prædestinatus* points to a Greek reading, προορισθέντος (the word occurs in Acts iv. 28 ; Rom. viii. 29, 30 ; 1 Cor. ii. 7 ; Eph. i. 5, 11), which is not found in any Greek MS., but appears in St. Epiphanius (*Hær.* 54, 6). All the Greek MSS. read ὁρισθέντος (*marked out*), without the preposition. St. Hilary (*De Trin.* 7, 24) has *destinatus*, and Tertullian (*Adv. Prax.* 28) *definitus.* The Greek is the more received and likely reading. The Greek Fathers explain it to mean *shown forth and manifested.* Such is the sense required by the words that follow, as will be evident. If we keep the reading *predestinated*, we must understand it to mean *predestinated to be shown forth, i.e.* marked out beforehand from eternity to be shown forth in time as the Son of God.

In power according to the spirit of sanctification means

exactly what we read in xv. 19, *in* (i.e. *by*) *the power of
the Holy Ghost*. So *the justice which is by faith*, literally,
justice according to faith (Heb. xi. 7), is equivalent to *the
justice of faith* (Rom. iv. 13).

*By the resurrection of our Lord Jesus Christ from the
dead*. We have here a double mistranslation. A literal
rendering of what St. Paul wrote would run thus: *Who
was marked out Son of God in power according to the Spirit of
sanctification by resurrection of dead, Jesus Christ our Lord*.
The words *Jesus Christ our Lord* are in apposition with
Son of God: they are not the genitive after *resurrection*.
True, they are genitive in the Greek, but so is *Son of
God*, τοῦ ὁρισθέντος υἱοῦ θεοῦ. The Latin translator has
put this participle as a relative clause, changing υἱοῦ
into *filius*, and has failed to change what was in apposition with υἱοῦ into the nominative also. This is
one error—of no dogmatic consequence, but a loss of
forcibleness and grammatical accuracy.

The second error is peculiar to our English trans-
lators, who have translated *ex resurrectione mortuorum*,
ἐξ ἀναστάσεως νεκρῶν, *by the resurrection from the dead*,
instead of *by resurrection of dead*. The phrase ἀνάστασις
νεκρῶν, or τῶν νεκρῶν, occurs eleven times in Scripture
(Matt. xxii. 31; Acts xvii. 32; xxiii. 6; xxiv. 21;
xxvi. 23; 1 Cor. xv. 12, 13, 21, 42; Heb. vi. 2, and
here); and it invariably means the same as the eleventh
article of the Creed, *the resurrection of the body*, that is, of
all dead bodies at the day of judgment. On the other
hand, *resurrection from the dead* is ἀνάστασις ἐκ νεκρῶν,
resurrectio ex mortuis (Phil. iii. 11; Luke xx. 35; 1 Pet.
i. 3, &c.)

The literal then is the right rendering, ἐξ ἀναστάσεως
νεκρῶν, *ex resurrectione mortuorum*, *by rising of the dead*. The
preposition ἐξ, *ex*, is rightly rendered *by*, as appears
from James ii. 18; Apoc. viii. 11,—showing the source
of the demonstration.

But how can the Divine Sonship of Jesus Christ be
marked out and manifest by the resurrection of the
dead, an event which has not yet taken place? The
answer is that it has taken place already, in promise
and potency, by the resurrection of Christ Himself.
So St. Paul says: *But now Christ is risen from the dead,*
the first-fruits of them that sleep: for by a man came death,
and by a man the resurrection of the dead (ἀνάστασις νεκρῶν):
and as in Adam all die, so also in Christ all shall be made
alive (1 Cor. xv. 20—22). Nor is the phrase irrespective
of our resurrection in baptism (vi. 4, 5, 11).

5. *By whom we have received*, that is, ' of whom I have
received.' It refers to the special call to the apostleship that St. Paul had from Jesus Christ Himself. See
on Gal. i. 1. Cf. also 1 Tim. i. 12 ; and for the use of
the preposition (δι' οὗ) to denote the chief agent, 1 Cor.
i. 9 ; 1 Pet. ii. 14.

Grace and apostleship, i.e. a gratuitous gift of apostleship: *freely have you received* (Matt. x. 8).

For obedience to the faith, to win men's obedience to
the faith, that is, to the gospel. Cf. Acts vi. 7, *obeyed*
the faith, meaning exactly *obey the gospel* (Rom. vi. 16).
For another possible explanation see on Gal. iii. 2.

For his name, on his behalf, Acts v. 41 ; ix. 16.

6. *The called of Jesus Christ.* Cf. John v. 25, *the dead*
there spoken of being those dead in sin, as the Ephesians
(Eph. ii. 1) and Romans were before their conversion.
Called in the New Testament (*e.g.* Matt. xxii. 14) means
always those who have been called and have come to
the faith and fold of Christ. Thus it means *called by*
Jesus Christ, through the Apostles speaking in His name.

7. In the New Testament generally, as here, the
Father is called *God*, the Son *Lord:* in which phraseology the names are given, not " essentially," but
" notionally," as theologians speak. That is to say,
the Father is *God*, the fountain of divinity, as He is the

First Person of the Holy Trinity: the Son is *Lord* by
the title of redemption. But if therefore the Son is not
God, neither is the Father Lord.

8. *Your faith is spoken of in the whole world.* Cf. for
similar praises 1 Thess. i. 7, 8; 2 Thess. i. 3, 4; Eph.
i. 15, 16, &c. But, spoken to the Romans, these words
are specially significant. For first, as St. Leo says,
"what nations anywhere could be ignorant of what
Rome had learned?" Then the flourishing state of the
Roman church here implied affords a probable indication of some great apostolate working at Rome. Whose
that apostolate was we learn from Catholic tradition,
of which tradition suffice it here to quote two witnesses.
"Peter had preached there, but he (Paul) regarded his
(Peter's) work as his own: so free was he from all
envy" (St. Chrysostom in v. 8). "Since the great
Peter had been the first to bring them the gospel, he of
necessity added, *to strengthen you :* for he says, it is not
a different teaching that I wish to bring you, but to
strengthen the teaching already brought, and to water
the plants already planted" (Theodoret in v. 11). Here
St. Paul might have said (cf. 1 Cor. iii. 6): ' Peter has
planted, I water.' Lastly, these words are an honourable testimony, from the mouth of the Holy Ghost
Himself, to the faith of that church which is by divine
appointment the "mother and mistress of all churches."

9. *In my spirit*, that is, according to the grace given
me.

A commemoration of you always in my prayers, Eph. i. 16;
1 Thess. i. 2; Phil. i. 4; 1 Tim. ii. 1.

10. *I may have a prosperous journey,* εὐοδωθήσομαι, *in
coming.* More simply and exactly, *I may succeed in coming.*
The Greek word occurs, 1 Cor. xvi. 2; 3 John 2; Gen.
xxxix. 3, 23; 2 Paral. xiii. 12.

11, 13. *I long to see you, and have been hindered hitherto.*
Cf. xv. 22—24.

14. *I am a debtor.* What had Paul received from *Greeks and barbarians*, that he should be in their debt? Nothing, but he had received of God the gratuitous graces of the apostolate to communicate to others. Cf. 1 Cor. ix. 16, 17; Matt. xxv. 26.

16. *I am not ashamed of the gospel*, a phrase that reads rather tame as compared with that written a little before to the Galatians (vi. 14): *God forbid that I should glory, save only in the cross of our Lord Jesus Christ:* unless we remember the wealth and glory of Rome, the city to which the Apostle wrote, and the honour paid to the Roman emperors alive and dead. Jesus Christ was a Leader of another sort, *the carpenter, the son of Mary* (Mark vi. 3), the *crucified* (Mark xvi. 6). The first step to glorying in such a Lord was not to be ashamed of Him in the high places of the earth. *Blessed is he that shall not be scandalized in me* (Matt. xi. 6).

It is the power of God unto salvation. Cf. 1 Cor. i. 18, **23**, *The word of the cross . . . is the power of God.* And Simon Magus's admirers said of him (Acts viii. 10): *This man is the power of God.*

To the Jew first and to the Greek. The word *first* has been questioned: cf. vi. 12. But it is sufficiently explained by Acts xiii. 46; xxviii. 23, 28; besides what we read in this Epistle, iii. 1, 2; ix. 4, 5. The Jew is the *natural branch* of the *olive-tree* (xi. 17, 21): the *elder brother* of the prodigal (Luke xv. 25—32).

17. *The justice of God.* Justice in a general sense is observance of law (see Aristotle, *Ethics*, v. c. 1, nn. 12 —14). It is also used of the vindication of law, either by the punishment of the transgressor, who is said to be 'brought to justice,' or by his submission and pardon. From the latter use comes the theological phrase of the 'justification' of a sinner. *The justice of God* is so called as coming from God and being recognised of God. It is distinguished from the *justice which*

is of the law (Phil. iii. 8) of which we have an admirable
example in the Pharisee who set himself before the
Publican (Luke xviii. 11, 12). *The justice of God* is
something coming from God to the sinner and resting
on him and in him. It is no mere imputed justice. To
declare just or righteous a man who still remained
a sinner, would be simply to tell a lie. To impute
righteousness where righteousness was none, would be
at least to make a mistake. But God is truthful and
unerring. There is therefore an intrinsic change wrought
in the soul of him who is justified. That change is by
the infusion of what theologians call ' sanctifying grace.'
Sanctifying grace, like the ' light of glory ' in heaven, to
which it prepares the way, is much more than we
mortals can describe in specific detail : one main element
however of it, much insisted upon by St. Paul (*e.g.* viii.
9—11), is the indwelling of the Holy Ghost.

Is revealed from faith unto faith, means that the justice
of God, which comes of faith, or has faith for its root,
is revealed unto the faith, or for the belief, of believers.
Cf. iii. 22.

The just man liveth by faith. See notes on Gal. iii. 11.

18. *For the wrath of God is revealed from heaven.* At
this point the Apostle abruptly quits the subject, which
he had just introduced, of the justice of God, to speak
of the wrath of God, provoked by the prevarications of
Gentile and Jew. Of this wrath is born the sore need
in which all men stand of the *justice of God*, that is, of
justification and sanctification, to which subject the
Apostle returns, iii. 21.

Is revealed, in the gospel, not yet written, but
preached, *e.g.* Acts xxiv. 25.

Detain the truth of God in injustice. Detain, κατεχόντων,
hold back, restrain, prevent from going forth at liberty
(so the word is used in 2 Thess. ii. 6 ; Luke iv. 42), or
as we say, *suppress* truth. It is question of people

suppressing truth within themselves *in injustice*, that is, by leading wicked lives, as we read (John iii. 19, 20): *Men loved darkness rather than the light, for their works were evil : for every one that doeth evil hateth the light, and cometh not to the light that his works may not be reproved.* The anger of God against such men is revealed in many pages also of the written gospel, *e.g.* John xii. 35—48; Matt. xi. 20—24.

19. *That which is known of God* by natural knowledge from the evidence of creation. The argument that follows in the next verse turns upon such natural knowledge.

Manifest, manifested, φανερόν, ἐφανέρωσεν, of a conclusion discerned (*clearly seen*) by the light of reason. Such is the conclusion of the existence of God, worked out by a reasoning process, which will be more or less scientific according to the capacity of the reasoner. The validity of this reasoning process is ruled by the Vatican Council in the following canon : "If any one says that God, one and true, our Creator and Lord, cannot with certainty be known by the natural light of human reason through the things that are made, let him be anathema" (sess. 1, *De Revelatione*, can. 1). This canon is simply an enforcement of St. Paul's words, *v.* 20. This knowledge is not faith, but is one of the 'preambles,' or previous conditions, of faith. Of matter of faith, as such, it is not said that it is *manifest* (cf. 2 Cor. v. 7 ; Heb. xi. 1), but that it is *revealed* (ἀποκαλύπτεται, *vv.* 17, 18). *Manifest in them, i.e.* in their minds.

20. *His eternal power also and divinity.* For *also* read *to wit*, the Greek τε, Latin *que*, for which the Vulgate *quoque* seems to be a clerical error. The particle explains what the invisible things above mentioned are.

So that they are inexcusable, goes better with the next verse.

21. Cf. Eph. iv. 18; and Wisdom xiii. 1—10, which passage St. Paul evidently had in view.

23. Cf. Ps. cv. 20: *And they changed their glory into the likeness of a calf eating grass. Four-footed beasts* and *creeping things* and *birds* were worshipped in Egypt. The Greek deities were all *in the likeness of man.* All cults, at the time the Apostle wrote, were to be met with in Rome, " where with most diligent superstition was held gathered together whatever had been set on foot by vain errors anywhere," as St. Leo says. The Apostle does not mention nature-worship, referred to Wisd. xiii. 2.

24. This verse might be turned more accurately from the Greek: *Wherefore also God gave them up in the desires of their hearts unto uncleanness, to the end that they should dishonour their own bodies one with another.* Read ἐν αὑτοῖς, and make ἀτιμάζεσθαι reciprocal middle.

This word *gave them up* means more than that God permitted the sin with what is called a ' permission of fact,' *i.e.* did not hinder it. Such mere absence of hinderance on the part of God may be predicated of any sin that ever is actually committed. But in regard of these sins of uncleanness in the heathen of old, God acted, not positively putting anything to cause them, but by way of privation withholding those gracious thoughts and pure visions, that sense of shame and feeling of dignity, whereby man is usually kept back from going all lengths in the gratification of sensuality. With the idea of God, Maker and Lord of man, which these heathen wilfully flung away, or refused ever to take up, they lost also by the just ordinance of God what Plato calls the " vision of Beauty with Modesty standing on holy pedestal" (*Phaedrus*, 254 B), and rushed headlong into sin. So Theodoret and St. John Chrysostom, the former of whom likens them to a boat left without ballast, the latter to an army abandoned by its general, not however till they have first gone away from him.

This is not one universal condemnation of all the men and women in the Gentile world. The Apostle presently uses almost as severe language of the Jews; and yet we know there was the host of saints of Israel, of whose deeds the Old Testament is the record, the *great cloud of witnesses;* whose praise is in the eleventh chapter to the Hebrews. There was a certain measure of genuine goodness in the old Gentile world (recognised, ii. 14—16). There was accumulated in time a huge mass of invincible ignorance (recognised by St. Paul speaking on the Areopagus, Acts xvii. 30; see notes on iii. 25; v. 13). Lastly, as there was no obligation on a Gentile to become a Jew, we are not to suppose that, remaining a Gentile, a man was necessarily cut off from those supernatural graces and that supernatural holiness, which obtained even under the Old Law through the anticipated merits of the Redeemer, and made saints among the children of Israel. Christ died for men of all nations and men of all times, for all the sons of Adam.

25. *Changed the truth of God into a lie, i.e.* exchanged the worship of the true God for the worship of idols. *A lie* means an idol, Jer. xvi. 19.

To *worship and serve the creature rather than the Creator* is the essential note of all paganism, Hellenism, secularism, —call it what you will—in every age of the world.

27. The sin that drew down the rain of fire on Sodom (Gen. xix.), in Greece amounted to an institution, commended by economists, as Aristotle tells us (*Politics*, ii. 10. 9), restricted, but not suppressed by legislation, connived at by philosophy,—only in his old age did Plato see his way to an entire condemnation of it (*Laws*, vii. 836—841): it was in Hellas, and wherever the Hellenes went, the national sin.

Receiving in themselves the recompense due to their error,
i.e. to their idolatry. So above, 23, 24: cf. Wisdom
xiv. 22—31.

28. "But, when God is abandoned," says St.
Chrysostom, commenting on the above mentioned fact,
"everything goes topsy-turvy." And so says St. Paul
in this verse.

A reprobate sense, ἀδόκιμον νοῦν, *a castaway mind, a mind*
rejected of God: so the word ἀδόκιμος is used five times
by St. Paul, *e.g.* 1 Cor. ix. 27; 2 Cor. xiii. 5—7. There
is a play of words, οὐκ ἐδοκίμασαν and ἀδόκιμον, which is
lost in translation.

29. *Iniquity,* or *injustice,* in the general sense, as in
v. 28, opposed to the *justice of God* (*v.* 17), and including
all the species, next enumerated.

Malice, πονηρία, "the mind of a wild beast," says
Theodoret: it means all disposition to injure others.
The devil is eminently ὁ πονηρός, *the malicious one* (Matt.
vi. 13; 1 John ii. 13).

Fornication, probably an interpolation here.

Avarice, the desire of money, the root of all evil (1 Tim.
vi. 10).

Wickedness, κακία, *vice* as opposed to virtue.

As virtue, ἀρετή, is *manliness* of soul, so vice, as Plato
says, is "disease and disfigurement and weakness"
(*Rep.* iv. 444 E). Or possibly κακία stands here for
κακουργία, *wicked cunning,* as it may in 1 Cor. xiv. 20.

Envy, murder, φθόνου, φόνου, alliteration as in Gal.
v. 21. The example primeval of both sins is Cain
(1 John iii. 12; Gen. iv.). Among his imitators come
those who envy and murder innocence.

Contention, that our Lord prayed against for His
Church (John xvii. 21—23). See however St. Thomas,
2a 2æ, q. 29, art. 3, ad 2.

Malignity is defined by Aristotle, "the putting the
worse construction on all things" (*Rhet.* ii. 13).

Whisperers, i.e. mischief-makers between friends, described by St. Thomas, 2a 2æ, q. 74. *Be not called a whisperer* (Ecclus. v. 14 : cf. 2 Cor. xii. 20). This word should have headed the next verse.

30. *Detractors,* James iv. 11. One of the lighter sins of heathendom, common enough in Christendom.

Hateful to God. Informers (Tacitus, *Annals,* vi. 7), perjurers (Plato, *Laws,* xi. 916 E), and other such enemies of the human race bore this appellation. But from a passage of St. Paul's disciple St. Clement, imitating and almost quoting this passage, the word bears an active sense, *haters of God* (Clem. 1 Cor. 35).

Contumelious, ὑβριστάς, wantonly violent, adding injury to insult. St. Paul applies the term to himself before his conversion (1 Tim. i. 13), on account of the *unprovoked violence* (ὕβρις) that he did to the Christians.

Proud, haughty, both these are renderings of the same word ὑπερηφάνους, which appears in the well known passages, Luke i. 51 ; James iv. 6.

The next term ἀλάζονας does not answer to the Vulgate *elatos* (haughty). The ἀλάζων (Aristotle, *Ethics,* iii. 10) is one who pretends to brilliant qualities which he does not possess. It may be Englished *pretentious.*

Inventors of evil things, "those who are not content with the vices common in society, but invent new ones" (Theodoret), as the reigning emperor Nero did. Antiochus, King of Syria, is called *inventor of all vice* (2 Macc. vii. 31).

Disobedient to parents. According to the received morality of the Greeks themselves, to ill-treat a parent was the very acme of wickedness. See Plato, *Rep.* 569, 574. Nero's treatment of his mother is a noted example.

31. *Foolish,* ἀσυνέτους, destitute of *spiritual understanding* (Col. i. 9). *Their foolish heart was darkened (v.* 21).

Dissolute. The word ἀσυνθέτους, well rendered by

the Vulgate *incompositos*, does not mean *dissolute*, but *uncombinable*, or we might say, *uncompanionable*, or as Dr. Johnson phrased it, *unclubbable*. It is exactly expressed by a phrase of Plato's (*Gorgias*, 507 E), κοινωνεῖν ἀδύνατος, *unable to be a partner in social life*. Of such a one Aristotle (*Politics*, i.) says he must be "either a brute or a god." Clearly in this context we have the " brute."

The words *without fidelity* (ἀσπόνδους, *absque foedere*, Vulg.) are not in the best MSS., and are evidently a gloss to explain ἀσυνθέτους, which in some measure they do.

Without (natural) affection between parent and child.

Without mercy, for the beaten, for the offending, for the suffering, for the needy, for the weak.

So much for the old paganism, not unlike to which will be the new paganism of the last days, as foretold, 2 Tim. iii. 2—4.

32. Though the general sense of this verse is clear, the structure is uncertain, and amid the various readings of the MSS. it is impossible to be sure what exactly St. Paul wrote. The following is the more probable : *Who having known the just doom of God, that they who do such things are worthy of death, not only do them, but also consent to them that do them.*

Worthy of death, that is, generally, of the severest punishment. Cf. David's saying (2 Kings xii.): *As the Lord liveth, the man who hath done this thing is a son of death.*

The men in question, not only yielded to sin themselves, as it were perforce and in secret, but applauded and abetted and maintained the cause of sin in the world around. We must remember that in the ancient world religion often, so far from being a check upon vice, was an incentive to it : its legends were tales of lust, and its rites filthiness.

U

CHAPTER II.

1. Wherefore thou art inexcusable, O man, whosoever thou art that judgest : for wherein thou judgest another, thou condemnest thyself; for thou doest the same things which thou judgest. 2. For we know that the judgment of God is according to truth against them that do such things. 3. And thinkest thou this, O man, that judgest them who do such things, and doest the same, that thou shalt escape the judgment of God ? 4. Or despisest thou the riches of his goodness, and patience, and long-suffering ? Knowest thou not that the benignity of God leadeth thee to penance ? 5. But according to thy hardness and impenitent heart, thou treasurest up to thyself wrath against the day of wrath and reve- lation of the just judgment of God ; 6. Who will render to every man according to his works : 7. To them indeed who, according to patience in good work, seek glory, and honour, and incorruption, life everlasting ; 8. But to them who are contentious, and who obey not the truth, but give credit to iniquity, wrath and indignation, 9. Tribulation and anguish, upon every soul of man that doeth evil ; of the Jew first, and also of the Greek : 10. But glory and honour and peace to every one that worketh good ; to the Jew first, and also to the Greek : 11. For there is no respect of persons with God. 12. For whosoever have sinned without the law shall perish without the law ; and whosoever have sinned under the law shall be judged by the law, 13. For not the hearers of the law are just before God, but the doers of the law shall be justified. 14. For when the gentiles, who have not the law, do by nature those things that are of the law, these, having not the law, are a law to them- selves : 15. Who show the work of the law written in their hearts, their conscience bearing witness to them, and their thoughts within themselves accusing them, or else defending them, 16. In the day when God shall judge the secrets of men by Jesus Christ, according to my gospel. 17. But if thou art called a Jew, and restest in the law, and makest thy boast of God, 18. And knowest his will, and approvest the things that are more profitable, being instructed by the law, 19. Art confident that thou thyself art a guide of the blind, a light of them that are in darkness, 20. An instructor of the foolish, a teacher of infants, having the form of knowledge and of truth in the law. 21. Thou, therefore that teachest another, teachest not thyself: thou that preachest that men should not steal, stealest : 22. Thou that sayest, men should not commit . adultery, committest adultery : thou that abhorrest idols, committest

sacrilege: **23.** Thou that makest thy boast of the law, by the transgression of the law dishonourest God. **24.** (For the name of God through you is blasphemed among the gentiles, as it is written.) **25.** Circumcision profiteth indeed if thou keep the law: but if thou be a transgressor of the law, thy circumcision is made uncircumcision. **26.** If then the uncircumcised keep the ordinances of the law, shall not his uncircumcision be reputed for circumcision? **27.** And shall not that which by nature is uncircumcision, if it fulfil the law, judge thee, who by the letter and circumcision art a transgressor of the law? **28.** For it is not he is a Jew who is so outwardly; nor is that circumcision which is outwardly in the flesh: **29.** But he is a Jew that is one inwardly; and the circumcision is that of the heart, in the spirit, not in the letter; whose praise is not of men, but of God.

1. *O man, whosoever thou art that judgest.* The expression is general, but St. Paul already has the Jew in view, and passes soon from this generality to him in particular. Verses 21—23, addressed to the Jew, are but an expansion of what we have here : *Thou doest the same things which thou judgest.*

2. *According to truth, i.e.* a judgment rigorously just and surely executed.

3. *And thinkest thou that thou shalt escape?* Again pointed at the Jews, who considered themselves safe without repentance, because they were children of Abraham (Matt. iii. 7, 9).

4. *Goodness, benignity*, χρηστότης, the same word. The χρηστός is one who makes himself *useful* to others, one who lays himself out to do them good. *Goodness* is a more active quality than *patience* and *long-suffering*, and therefore it alone is mentioned as leading men to penance. God truly *leads, i.e.* tries to lead, even those who will not go.

5. *Wrath against the day of wrath*, ἐν ἡμέρᾳ, *in die* (Vulg.): it should be *wrath in the day of wrath*. The preposition does not refer back to *treasurest*.

The day of wrath, dies iræ: the day of judgment is so called here, and Sophon. i. 15; ii. 3; Apoc. vi. 17.

In that day *the just judgment of God shall be revealed* and shown forth in its fulness, which has place imperfectly and obscurely in this life, and fully but most secretly, for the individual, when he passes out of this life into the next.

6. *Who will render to every man according to his works.* Taken from Ps. lxi. 13, and repeated, Matt. xvi. 27; Apoc. xxii. 12; ii. 23. The Apostle speaks alike of all works: but evil works merit damnation: therefore good works (understand, supernaturally good works, done in the state of grace and under the prompting of actual grace) merit heaven. Of course no one is in the state of grace who has not the habit of faith; nor does any one act under the prompting of grace without an implicit exercise of faith.

7. *Patience in good work*, inculcated so often, Luke viii. 15; xxi. 19; Heb. x. 36; James i. 4; Matt. x. 22 (in the Greek, *he that shall be patient to the end*). And still to be inculcated, and failing it, patience in reiterated repentances.

Glory and honour and incorruption are not merely the reward that is in the life to come; they are more immediately in this life, the habit of soul and body that prepares for that reward. They are the strong contraries of the *uncleanness*, the *shameful affections*, the *reprobate sense*, and all the base qualities enumerated in ch. i. On *incorruption* in particular cf. 1 Cor. xv. 50; Gal. vi. 8; 2 Pet. ii. 19.

8. *To them that are contentious*, τοῖς ἐξ ἐριθείας, *qui sunt ex contentione.* The word ἐριθεία however has nothing to do with ἔρις, *contention*, but is from ἐριθεύομαι, *I intrigue for power.* It occurs in Aristotle's *Politics*, v. 3, where it means *canvassing*. Also twice in St. Paul, 2 Cor. xii. 20, and Gal. v. 20, where it is rendered, not happily, *dissensiones* (*dissensions*) and *rixæ* (*quarrels*). It means here *self-seeking*. With τοῖς ἐξ ἐριθείας, *the party of self-*

seeking, cf. οἱ ἐκ περιτομῆς (Acts x. 45), *the party of cir-cumcision.* Understand *self-seeking* to the contempt of God.

Obey not the truth, in the same sense in which they are said to *detain the truth of God in injustice*, i. 18.

Give credit to iniquity, rather *obey* (πειθομένοις) *iniquity*, as explained vi. 12, 13, 16, 19; 2 Pet. ii. 19.

Wrath and indignation, ὀργὴ καὶ θυμός, in the nominative case, as are the other substantives that follow in *vv.* 9, 10, whereas eternal life (ζωὴν αἰώνιον, *v.* 7) is in the accusative.

9. There should be no full stop at the end of the previous verse, only a comma.

Wrath and indignation, tribulation and anguish, go together. For the two latter words see note on 2 Cor. iv. 8.

Of the Jew first, for he sinned against greater light. Cf. Luke xii. 47, 48; Acts xvii. 30.

10. *To the Jew first*, see on i. 16.

11. Job xxxiv. 18, 19; Wisd. vi. 7—9; Acts x. 34, 35.

12. *Without the law, in the law*, understand, *of Moses.* Cf. what our Lord says of *the word* of the gospel, John xii. 48.

13. *The hearers of the law*, portions of which were read aloud every sabbath in the synagogue.

The doers of the law shall be justified, understand from the previous clause, *before God.* And yet, *by the works of the law no flesh shall be justified before him* (iii. 20). None indeed, if the works of the law are separated from faith and the grace of Christ, which here they are not, but the meaning is, *the doers of the law shall be justified before God*, if they fulfil the other conditions of justifi-cation. Observe that one cannot be a *doer of the law*, that is, a steady observer of its moral precepts, without the grace of Christ. The law is insufficient to get itself done.

14. *For*, γάρ. It will be observed that this is the fourth verse in succession introduced by this conjunction. On the connection here see Canon Cholmondeley's work, *The Four ΓΑΡ* (Williams and Norgate, 1880). The connection is immediate with the words preceding, and is put by St. Thomas thus: " He shows that the doers of the law, even if they are not hearers, are justified." The *for* therefore introduces an instance, making good the last statement of the previous verse.

The sense is: ' When gentiles (ἔθνη without article), they who have not the law of Moses read to them, do by the light of nature (though not by the mere strength of nature) the works enjoined by the moral precepts of that law, such persons are (as Aristotle says, see note on Gal. v. 23) *a law to themselves*, that is, without external coercion they are of their own choice a living embodiment of the law.'

By nature, that is, as St. Thomas explains, " by the natural law, showing what is to be done, as the text has it, Psalm iv. 6; and yet there is not excluded the necessity of grace to move the will." Nay, we must suppose the presence of grace in these Gentiles ; for from *v.* 13, of which this verse is an exemplification, there is question of being *justified before God*. See St. Augustine, *De spiritu et litera*, cc. 36—38.

Thus, as St. Chrysostom says, "in answer to the enquiry why Christ came so late, and where Providence was in previous ages, the Apostle shows that even in early times, and before the giving of the law, mankind had the benefit of a perfect Providence." That was not only by the light of reason, but also by some assistance of grace ; for the grace of Christ was given in anticipation of His coming, nor was it confined to the people of whose stock He was born.

Canon Cholmondeley, with Bengel, would punctuate, *gentiles who have not the law by nature*, τὰ μὴ νόμον ἔχοντα φύσει : cf. Gal. ii. 15, *by nature Jews*, φύσει 'Ιουδαῖοι, and Eph. ii. 3, *by nature children of wrath*, τέκνα φύσει ὀργῆς,— quite a tenable collocation, still not necessary for the explanation given.

15. *Who show the work of the law written in their hearts*, not on tables of stone, Exod. xxxi. 18; cf. 2 Cor. iii. 3; Heb. viii. 10, two parallel passages also referring to supernatural justice. It is more to have *the work of the law* written in your heart than the word of the law.

Their conscience bearing witness to them. Conscience is every man's household exponent of the law, applying it to his particular acts.

Their thoughts within themselves, μεταξὺ ἀλλήλων, *between one another*, a sort of disputation between thought and thought.

Accusing them or else defending them. Some of the Rheims versions have *accusing or defending one another*, a mis-translation, which makes nonsense. When we debate whether we have done well or ill, our thoughts do not accuse or defend one another, they accuse or defend us.

St. Thomas writes (1a—2æ, q. 79, art. 13):—"Conscience is said to testify, to bind, and also to accuse; and all these acts follow on the application of a certain knowledge in us to our acts, and that in three ways. In one way, as we recognise that we have done something or not done it; and to this extent conscience is said to testify. In another way, as we judge that something is to be done or not to be done; and in this way conscience is said to bind. In a third way, as we judge that something which has been done was well or ill done; and thus conscience is said to excuse or accuse."

16. This verse is a continuation of *v.* 13. The two intervening verses, 14, 15, make a parenthesis. *According to my gospel*, simply, the gospel which I preach.

17. *But if thou art called a Jew*, &c. This *if* affects
all to the end of *v.* 20, where we should put a colon:
then comes the second part of this long, compound
sentence: *well then, thou that teachest another*, &c. (*v.* 21).
There is an inferior reading, ἰδὲ for εἰ δὲ, *lo, thou art called
a Jew.*

18. *Approvest the more profitable things*, δοκιμάζεις τὰ
διαφέροντα, of which *testest the things that differ* is a more
accurate translation. It does not refer to the legal
differences of meats (Levit. xi.), since the apostle prays
that the Philippians may have the same gift (Phil.
i. 9, 10) ; but to the power of drawing a clear line in
moral and spiritual matters, between "contraries, as
justice and injustice, temperance and licentiousness,
piety and impiety," as Theodoret says, not *calling evil
good, and good evil ; putting darkness for light, and light
for darkness ; turning bitter to sweet, and sweet to bitter*
(Isaias v. 20).

Being instructed by the law, κατηχούμενος ἐκ τοῦ νόμου,
literally, *being orally taught religion out of* [the books of]
the law. The word, whence comes our *catechize*, means
to teach orally, the master saying a thing, and the
scholar repeating it. The word occurs in five other
places in the New Testament,—Luke i. 4 ; Acts xviii. 25 ;
xxi. 21, 24 ; 1 Cor. xiv. 19 ; Gal. vi. 6—always in reference to the teaching of religion, except in Acts xxi.,
where it means simply *to din into.*

19, 20. *Guide of the blind, light of them in darkness,
instructor (educator, chastiser) of fools, teacher of babes*, all so
many titles that the Jews, the Pharisees especially,
arrogated to themselves in reference to the Gentiles.

The form of knowledge, μόρφωσιν, the word occurs elsewhere only in 2 Tim. iii. 5, where it means the *outward
show :* here we might say, the *delineation*, or the *lineaments.*

22. *Thou that abhorrest idols, committest sacrilege*, ἱερο-
συλεῖς, better, *robbest temples* (of idols), cf. Acts xix. 37.

" The Jews were severely forbidden to touch the wealth
lying in temples of idols, as being an abomination
(Deut. vi. 25, 26; 2 Macc. xii. 4): but the tyranny of
love of money induced them to trample on this law"
(St. Chrysostom). An allegation which posterity will
readily believe.

24. The quotation is from Isaias lii. 5, according to
the Septuagint. The sentiment is in Ezechiel xxxvi.
20—23.

25. *Circumcision* was the mark of a man being of the
seed of Abraham; what that implied, see ix. 4, 5. To
follow the Apostle in what he is about to say, we should
read again the covenant of circumcision, as related in
Genesis xvii.

Circumcision profiteth. See iii. 1, 2. As Baptism is
the door of the Christian covenant, so by Circumcision
a man was admitted to the covenant of the Old Law.
All who know and can are bound to pass through the
door of Baptism : there was no corresponding obligation for a Gentile to be circumcised, and so be aggre-
gated to the people of Israel. Still, such aggregation
brought with it many spiritual advantages, a more exact
knowledge of God, and a more approved mode of
religious ritual.

If thou keep the law, the whole law (see on Gal. v. 3) of
Moses, both in its moral and in its ceremonial precepts;
for the person addressed is the Jew under the Old
Covenant, upon whom that law was binding in its
entirety.

26. *If the uncircumcised* Gentile *keep the ordinances of the
law, i.e.* the moral precepts of the Mosaic law, the ten
commandments, for he was not bound to the rest.

We have seen on *v.* 14 that this supposition can
have no place except in the case of Gentiles borne up
and supported by the anticipated grace of Christ.

27. *Who by the letter and circumcision art a transgressor.*

A Greek way of speaking, τὸν διὰ γράμματος καὶ περιτομῆς παραβάτην, of the Jew who, in literal observance of the covenant, inasmuch as he is actually circumcised, still transgresses the law. We might say of a validly ordained priest, living wickedly, that by the letter and ordination he was a transgressor.

28. *Outwardly* is explained by the words that follow, by *that circumcision which is outward in the flesh*. It means '*outwardly* merely, and not *inwardly*.' St. Paul would not have denied that the man belonged to the Jewish community as a visible member of a visible body, and as such came in for the prayers and sacrifices offered for that body. All he means is that the man is not a Jew unto salvation. In like manner the Catholic Church on earth consists of all baptized professing Catholics, not as the Wicliffites and Jansenists would have it, of the elect only, or only of the just and holy.

29. *The circumcision of the heart.* The *uncircumcised of heart* are spoken of by the prophets, Jerem. ix. 26; Ezech. xliv. 7, 9; and by St. Stephen, Acts vii. 51. The sum of it is as St. Chrysostom says : " Everywhere there is need of a good life," πανταχοῦ βίου χρεία.

1. What advantage then hath the Jew, or what is the profit of circumcision? 2. Much every way. First indeed, because the words of God were committed to them. 3. For what if some of them have not believed? shall their unbelief make the faith of God without effect? God forbid. 4. But God is true, and every man a liar; as it is written: That thou mayest be justified in thy words, and mayest overcome when thou are judged. 5. For if our injustice commend the justice of God, what shall we say? Is God unjust who executeth wrath? 6. (I speak according to man.) God forbid: otherwise how shall God judge this world? 7. For if the truth of God hath more abounded through my lie unto his glory; why am I also yet judged as a sinner? 8. And not rather, (as we are slandered, and as some affirm that we say,) let us do evil, that there may come good? whose damnation is just. 9. What then? Do we excel them? By no means. For we have charged both Jews and Greeks, that they are all under sin; 10. As it is written: There is not any man just: 11. There is none that understandeth, there is none that seeketh after God. 12. All have turned out of the way, they are become unprofitable together; there is none that doeth good, there is not so much as one. 13. Their throat is an open sepulchre: with their tongues they have dealt deceitfully: the venom of asps is under their lips: 14. Whose mouth is full of cursing and bitterness: 15. Their feet are swift to shed blood: 16. Destruction and misery are in their ways: 17. And the way of peace they have not known: 18. There is no fear of God before their eyes. 19. Now we know that what things soever the law speaketh, it speaketh to them that are in the law; that every mouth may be stopped, and all the world may be made subject to God: 20. Because by the works of the law no flesh shall be justified in his sight: for by the law is the knowledge of sin. 21. But now without the law the justice of God is made manifest; being witnessed by the law and the prophets, 22. Even the justice of God by faith of Jesus Christ, unto all and upon all them that believe in him; for there is no distinction: 23. For all have sinned, and do need the glory of God: 24. Being justified gratis by his grace, through the redemption that is in Christ Jesus; 25. Whom God had set forth to be a propitiation through faith in his blood, to the showing of his justice, for the remission of past sins, 26. Through the forbearance of God, for the showing of his justice in this time; that he himself may be just, and the justifier of him

who is of the faith of Jesus Christ. **27.** Where is then thy
boasting? It is excluded. By what law? of works? No; but by
the law of faith. **28.** For we account a man to be justified by faith
without the works of the law. **29.** Is he the God of the Jews only?
is he not also of the gentiles? Yes, of the gentiles also; **30.** For
it is one God who justifieth circumcision by faith, and uncircumcision through faith. **31.** Do we then destroy the law through
faith? God forbid: but we establish the law.

1. The second member of this interrogation is only
a repetition under another form of the first.

2. *First indeed.* The abruptness of St. Paul's style is
conspicuous in the first eight verses of this chapter.
After mentioning the first advantage enjoyed by the
Jews under the old dispensation, he breaks off and
enumerates no more. He supposes us acquainted with
Deut. iv. 7, 8; vii. 6; Ps. cxlvii.; and returns himself
to the subject, ix. 4, 5.

The words of God, called *words of life* (Acts vii. 38),
principally the promise of the Messiah, by faith in
whom the Jews were justified, like their father Abraham
(iv. 1, seq.; Gal. iii. 6—9). The Greek is ἐπιστεύθησαν
τὰ λόγια τοῦ θεοῦ, *they were entrusted with the oracles of God.*

3. *Some of them have not believed.* As well the Jews of
old (cf. Ps. lxxvii.; Ps. xciv. 8—11), as also the Jews
in our Lord's time and in that of His Apostles.

Shall their unbelief, &c. means: Shall God break His
word because they have broken theirs? Cf. 2 Tim.
ii. 13. The promise of the Messiah was an absolute
promise (Ps. lxxxviii. 31—35), not conditional, like that
of the good things of earth promised to the Israelites
(Deut. xxviii.).

4. *But God is true.* So the Vulgate: *Est autem Deus
verax.* But the Greek is γινέσθω, and should be Englished:
But let God prove true, though every man (according to
the text, Ps. cxv. 11) *be a liar.*

And mayest overcome when thou art judged (Ps. l. 6).
St. Paul quotes the Septuagint. The Hebrew is: *and*

mayest be pure in thy judging, i.e. be recognised as such. It is probable that κρίνεσθαι is not passive (*to be judged*), but middle (*to go to law*). We may then translate the Greek : *That thou mayest be justified* (i.e. *acknowledged just*) *in thy words, and mayest be victorious in thy suit.* For the idea cf. 1 Kings xii. 7, seq. ; Jer. ii. 9, seq. ; Isaias v. 3, 4.

5—8. These four verses are some of the most difficult in St. Paul, not for the matter, which is tolerably plain, but for the style, the abruptness of which, like that of Gal. iii. 20, suggests a *lacuna*, or loss of words, in the text as it has come down to us. Verse 5 suggests an idea, which is repudiated in *v.* 6, is then taken up again in *v.* 7, and is finally condemned in *v.* 8 as leading to a monstrous conclusion in morals. The said idea is this, that man's injustice and man's false-hood is a useful commodity to God, and serves as a means to bring out by contrast God's justice and God's truthfulness : whence it would follow that God was unjust in *executing wrath* upon and punishing the man who in sinning was thus doing Him a service. The idea was adopted by a certain John Eckard in the fourteenth century, the author of this proposition : " In every work, however evil, whether of fault or of penalty, the glory of God is equally manifest and shines forth ; " condemned by John XXII. as heretical. In *v.* 6, which is parenthetic, this idea is scouted. St. Paul explains that he has been speaking, not as an inspired Apostle, but *according to man*, that is, as St. Peter spoke, when he drew upon himself the name of *satan* and *scandal*, for *savouring not the things of God, but the things that are of men* (Matt. xvi. 23). *God forbid*, says St. Paul : such a view would make the last judgment an impossibility (*v.* 6). Then he recurs to the idea which he has repudiated, and restates it as an objection : this fills the whole of *v.* 7. He further develops the objection in *v.* 8, showing that it involves the principle that the end justifies the means. 'Let us sin,' he says, playing the part of the objicient, 'to the end that the attributes of God may be more manifest by means of our sin.' This principle, that the end justifies the means, was slanderously imputed by the Gentiles to the first Christians: so we gather from St. Paul. With equal slander has it been imputed by Jansenists and Protestants to the Society of Jesus. For St. Paul it is enough that the idea which he is struggling against lands us in that principle: such an issue he considers a *reductio ad absurdum*.

Whose damnation is just, that is the damnation of those *some*, who ascribed the said abominable principle to the Christians, and likewise embodied it in their own practice.

9. *What then? Do we excel them? By no means.* This is explained to mean: 'Do we Jews excel the Gentiles in point of morality?' But this leaves much to be understood, which is not easily gathered from the context. It also involves quite an unparalleled use of the middle voice of the verb προέχειν, which in the active means to *excel*, but is never found in the middle voice. Theodoret reads, τί οὖν κατέχομεν περισσόν; προῃτιασάμεθα γὰρ κ.τ.λ.: *What superiority then do we possess? for we have charged*, &c., a remarkable variation. And St. Chrysostom (Hom. 8 in Rom. iv. 1) quotes this text nearly in the same form, τί οὖν προκατέχομεν περισσόν; The Vulgate reads *praecellimus?* (*do we excel?*), agreeing fairly with St. Chrysostom and Theodoret, but hardly a valid rendering of the reading προεχόμεθα. Modern commentators are much divided. If one conjecture more may be allowed in a matter so uncertain, we may take προεχόμεθα, as many do, for the passive voice; indeed it can hardly be anything else. We may then punctuate and translate as follows: τί οὖν προεχόμεθα; οὐ πάντως;

In what then are we surpassed? Is it not in every way?
This makes at least unexceptional Greek, which other
versions do not. Now for the meaning. In *v.* 4 (on
which see note) we have, *that thou mayest overcome when
thou art judged*, or *that thou mayest be victorious in thy suit.*
It is question of a judgment, plea and counterplea
between God and man, God's justice and man's
iniquity, and man is cast in the suit. The double
question, as above put, implies a double answer, that
we, all mankind, are *surpassed* by God, and that *in every
way*. Man's defence in point of justice against God
breaks down entirely. We have no case. *For we have
charged* (that is, *I*, the writer to the Romans, *have already
preferred an indictment*, προῃτιάσαμεθα, a forensic term) *both
Jews and Greeks that they are all under sin: for* (*v.* 23) *all
have sinned, and do need the glory of God*, where the verb
ὑστεροῦνται (*do need*), from ὕστερος. *behind*, forms some
antithesis to προεχόμεθα (*we are surpassed*), from πρό, *before.*

10—18. These quotations are principally from
Psalm xiii. 3. They are not to be taken absolutely
and universally, but as emphatic denunciations of a
widespread depravity.

19. *The law speaketh.* So (in John x. 34) Our Lord
cites a Psalm to the Jews as *your law.*

It speaketh to them that are in the law. Thus if the
Pope in an Encyclical were to complain of the avarice
of men, without specifying men out of the Church, his
reproaches would be supposed to fall also on the faithful
whom he addressed.

Subject to God, ὑπόδικος τῷ θεῷ. The word ὑπόδικος,
followed by a dative of a person, is a law term, meaning
liable to a legal penalty upon the action of that person. Its
use here helps out the interpretation that we have put
upon *v.* 9.

20. *By the works of the law no flesh shall be justified before
him.* Men are not justified by the works of the law,

whether the law of the ten commandments, given
through Moses, or the same law as known by nature
(ii. 14, 15; Gal. ii. 19, with note), for this sufficient
reason among others, that they have not done those
works, but have broken the law generally (*vv.* 9—18).
If it be pleaded against this that such persons as
Zachary and Elizabeth were *just before God, walking in
all the commandments of the Lord without blame* (Luke i. 6),
St. Paul would reply that all such just persons, whether
Jews or Gentiles before the coming of Christ, were just
by having something besides the law to support them,
namely, the anticipated grace and merits of Christ.
Cf. on ii. 14.

By the law is the knowledge of sin (cf. vii. 7), but not
thereby the grace to avoid sin.   Hence the law is called
the strength of sin (1 Cor. xii. 56).

The argument of this Epistle is the moral law : the
argument of the Epistle to the Galatians is rather the
ceremonial law.   See on Gal. ii. 16.

21. *But now without the law the justice of God is made
manifest.   Without the law*, or *apart from the law*, χωρὶς
νόμου, means first, *apart from observance of the law* in past
time (cf. Eph. ii. 1—9).   Neither Jews nor Gentiles
have kept the law binding on them, and yet they are
justified by faith and baptism (vi. 3), whereby all their
sins are forgiven.   So much for the past.   But their
justification will not be lasting and enduring, apart
from observance of the law (the moral law, that is) in
the future, after baptism.   *The unjust shall not possess
the kingdom of God*, . . . *nor the effeminate* (see 1 Cor.
vi. 9, 10), be he Jew or Greek or Christian.   St. Paul
was not the man to issue licenses to sin.   Cf. Eph.
ii. 10.

A secondary meaning of *without the law* might be
' apart from the sacrifices of the Old Law,' which were
insufficient to take away sin, as shown, Heb. ix. 9;

x. 1—11. But this meaning can only be secondary and implied, as the Apostle here is dealing with the moral, not with the ceremonial law.

Being witnessed by the law and the prophets, as shown *e.g.* Acts iii. 22—26; Heb. viii. 8—12.

22. *Unto all and upon all*, a mere repetition for emphasis. Good MSS. omit *upon all*.

For there is no distinction. See x. 12. Mercy for all, as all equally require mercy, *for* (*v.* 23) *all have sinned.*

23. *Do need the glory of God*, ὑστεροῦνται, literally, *do run short of the glory* (grace) *of God*. The verb occurs in the same form in Phil. iv. 12, *to abound and to suffer need*, ὑστερεῖσθαι. The substantive is ὕστερος, *hinder*, or *secondmost, e.g.* in a race. In Attic Greek they would have said λείπεσθαι.

The glory of God here is *glory before God*, (iv. 2), that is, grace. Thus *the riches of his glory* (ix. 23) means *the riches of his grace*. Also Eph. iii. 16.

24. *Justified freely*, because the Jews and Gentiles brought no merits to baptism, but rather, as has been shown, many demerits.

This Epistle to the Romans is really a glorification of the sacramental system, not of free grace away from sacraments, though God of course can give grace without sacraments. The contrast is between Circumcision and Baptism, and the state formally ensuing upon each.

25. *A propitiation*, ἱλαστήριον, which word elsewhere in the Bible means always the *propitiatory*, or *mercy-seat* (described Exod. xxv. 17—22; Heb. ix. 5), and so it is explained by Theodoret here. But the sense of *propitiatory sacrifice* (the same as ἱλασμός, 1 John ii. 2; iv. 10; so ἱλαστήριον is used by Dion Chrysostom, *Orat.* ii. p. 184: cf. σωτήρια, *peace-offerings*, Exod. xx. 24) suits the context much better.

In his blood, the blood of Christ. The *his* is emphatic,

v

as the construction ἐν τῷ αὐτοῦ αἵματι shows. There should be no comma after *propitiation*, and the words *faith in his blood* are not to be taken together, but *propitiation-through-faith* is to go together. It means that Christ is an expiatory victim, in whom men must believe, that He may be expiatory for them.

To the showing of his justice. The justice here spoken of is an attribute of God Himself, that holiness whereby God hates sin, punishes it, and blots it out. On the other hand, the *justice of God*, said in *v.* 21 to be *made manifest*, is an attribute put by God in men, whom He makes just and holy by grace, forgiving their sins.

For the remission (*remissionem*, Vulg.) *of former sins,* διὰ τὴν πάρεσιν τῶν προγεγονότων ἁμαρτημάτων ἐν τῇ ἀνοχῇ τοῦ θεοῦ. Translate, *owing to the letting pass of former sins through the forbearance of God.* The sense of the clause is given by St. Paul's words to the Athenians (Acts xvii. 30): *God indeed having winked at the times of this ignorance.* Cf. also Acts xiv. 15.

The word πάρεσις, which occurs nowhere else in Scripture, does not mean *remission* (*remissio*),—that is always ἄφεσις (Matt. xxvi. 28; Eph. i. 7; Heb. ix. 22, &c.), but *letting go by, letting pass unpunished, or unatoned for.* So God let the sins of men go by unatoned for for 4,000 or more years, till the coming of His Son; and that is what St. Paul here refers to. The words, *through the forbearance of God,* should not be preceded by any stop, much less transferred to the next verse, but joined on immediately to the words preceding, as shown above. God does not *remit* sins by *forbearing* to punish them.

26. *For the showing of his justice* means neither more nor less than *to the showing of his justice* in the previous verse. Why then the repetition? On account of what is put in between. We might paraphrase thus: ' God hath put forward Christ in the sight of all, a sacrifice

of atonement by the shedding of blood, to the showing forth of His justice : yes, I say, owing to His forbear- ance in letting pass, unatoned for, the sins of former times, He was anxious at last to have atonement made, and so put forward Christ's atonement for the showing forth of His justice in this time.' The words *in this time* are emphatic, standing in antithesis to the word *former* in *v.* 25.

That he himself may be just and the justifier, &c.: *i.e.* thus God shows Himself to be just, exacting atonement for sin, and at the same time He justifies, that is, forgives and sanctifies, him who believes in Jesus Christ and is baptized (Mark xvi. 16).

27. *Where then is thy boasting*, O Jew? thy boasted superiority over the Gentiles? seeing that Christ at His coming finds both Jew and Gentile on one dead level of sin. *It is shut out*, not by any law *of works*, or enjoining of exterior observances on Jew and Gentile for the forgiveness of their sins, but by *the law of faith*, enjoining faith in Jesus Christ, yet so that that faith be accompanied by *penance towards God* (Acts xx. 21, called by theologians *attrition*), and that he who has faith be washed in *the laver of regeneration* (Titus iii. 5). No one can *boast* of having believed and been baptized, and so justified gratuitously.

28. *Justified by faith*, cf. Acts xv. 9, *purifying their hearts by faith*, said of the baptized Gentiles.

Without the works of the law. This is explained by St. Paul's words to Titus (Tit. iii. 5): *Not by the works of justice which we have done, but according to his mercy, he saved us by the laver of regeneration and renovation of the Holy Ghost.* Without works going before to merit it, man is justified from grievous sin: but without works following after his justification, the said justification will die away, as faith without works is dead (James ii. 26).

The emphatic words in this verse are *without the*

works of the law, not the words *by faith*. So the three
best MSS. read δικαιοῦσθαι πίστει ἄνθρωπον (*justified by
faith is man*), not as the received text, πίστει δικαιοῦσθαι
ἄνθρωπον (*by faith is man justified*).

29. This verse simply argues that *a man* (in *v.* 28) is
to be taken universally, *any and every man*.

30. *By faith* (ἐκ πίστεως), *through faith* (ἐκ τῆς πίστεως,
i.e. ἐκ τῆς αὐτῆς πίστεως), that is, through the same faith.
Otherwise, as Gal. ii. 16; iii. 8 shows, the difference of
the two prepositions is not to be pressed.

For *justifieth* the Greek has *will justify*.

31. *We establish the law*, the ceremonial law, as the
substance may be said to establish the shadow; and
still more the moral law, as grace is the forgiveness
of transgression past, and strength for future observance.
Cf. above, *v.* 21; also x. 4; Gal. iii. 24; Heb. x. 1;
and our Lord's well-known words, Matt. v. 17.

CHAPTER IV.

1. What shall we say then that Abraham hath found, who is our father according to the flesh? 2. For if Abraham were justified by works, he hath glory, but not in the sight of God. 3. For what saith the Scripture? Abraham believed God, and it was reputed to him unto justice. 4. Now to him that worketh the reward is not reckoned according to grace, but according to debt. 5. But to him that worketh not, yet believed in him who justifieth the impious, his faith is reputed to justice according to the purpose of the grace of God. 6. As David also termeth the blessedness of a man, to whom God reputeth justice without works: 7. Blessed are they whose iniquities are forgiven, and whose sins are covered. 8. Blessed is the man to whom the Lord hath not imputed sin. 9. This blessedness then, doth it abide in the circumcision only, or in the uncircumcision also? For we say that faith was reputed to Abraham unto justice. 10. How then was it reputed? When he was in circumcision, or in uncircumcision? Not in circumcision, but in uncircumcision. 11. And he received the sign of circumcision, a seal of the justice of the faith which is in uncircumcision: that he might be the father of all the believers uncircumcised, that to them also it may be reputed to justice: 12. And might be the father of circumcision, not to them only that are of the circumcision, but to them also who follow the steps of the faith that our father Abraham had, being as yet uncircumcised. 13. For not through the law was the promise to Abraham, or to his seed, that he should be the heir of the world, but through the justice of faith. 14. For if they who are of the law be heirs, faith is made void, the promise is made of no effect. 15. For the law worketh wrath: for where there is no law, there is no transgression. 16. Therefore it is of faith, that according to grace the promise might be firm to all the seed: not to that only which is of the law, but to that also which is of the faith of Abraham, who is the father of us all, 17. (As it is written: I have made thee a father of many nations) before God, whom he believed, who quickeneth the dead, and calleth those things that are not as those that are. 18. Who against hope believed in hope, that he might be made the father of many nations, according to that which was said to him: So shall thy seed be. 19. And he was not weak in faith: neither did he consider his own body now dead, whereas he was almost a hundred years old, nor the dead womb of Sara. 20. In the promise also of God he staggered not by distrust; but was strengthened in faith

giving glory to God ;   21. Most fully knowing that whatsoever he
has promised, he is able also to perform.   22. And therefore it was
reputed to him unto justice.   23. Now it is not written only for
him, that it was reputed to him unto justice;   24. But for us also,
to whom it shall be reputed, if we believe in him that raised up
Jesus Christ our Lord from the dead ;   25. Who was delivered up
for our sins, and rose again for our justification.

1. There is much more difficulty about this verse
than the Rheims version shows. First, some of the
best critics, following the Vatican manuscript, omit
the verb *hath found*, and read : *What then shall we say of
Abraham our forefather according to the flesh ?* where it is
evident that *according to the flesh*, though it goes naturally
enough with *forefather*, may also be taken with the verb
say. Secondly, the best of the remaining Greek MSS.,
and the Latin Vulgate, have the words in this order :
What then shall we say that Abraham found (*invenisse Abraham*)
our father according to the flesh ? where the words, *according
to the flesh*, may be taken with *found*. Lastly, the
common Greek text reads in this order : *What then shall
we say that Abraham our father found according to the flesh ?*
which Theodoret thus paraphrases : " Before Abraham
believed God, what justice do we hear of in him accru-
ing from works ? " " *According to the flesh*," Theodoret
continues, " means justice in works, seeing that it is
through the body that we accomplish works," or, more
likely, inasmuch as the body is opposed to the spirit,
the natural to the supernatural.

St. Chrysostom, although the common Greek text is
printed at the head of his Homily viii., evidently from
his comments had before him the same text as the
Vatican MS., with εὑρηκέναι (*hath found*) omitted. That
disturbing verb has every mark of a spurious inser-
tion. With its removal the likelihood of Theodoret's
explanation is impaired, and we may acquiesce in
St. Chrysostom's interpretation : " He calls him *our*

father according to the flesh, casting the Jews out of genuine kindred with him and preparing the way for the Gentiles to claim the connection." Cf. *v.* 11.

2. *If Abraham were justified by works.* One form of justice is conformity to law, as Aristotle (*Ethics,* v. 1) says: " The just is the law-observing man, and that is just which is legal." St. Paul has been arguing that this justice was wanting both to Jews and Gentiles generally, both having broken the divine law. But it might be argued that individuals such as Abraham had kept it, and that these at least had no need to be justified by faith in Christ and acceptance of His gospel. To this St. Paul replies that if Abraham can be called just as having observed the law, that is a mere natural justice, and matter of glory in the mere natural order of human history, but is no matter of glory in the super-natural order of grace; for grace alone is *glory before God :* see on iii. 23. As a matter of fact, Abraham was justified in the supernatural order of faith and grace, and not by works done in mere human strength and on motives of natural reason. For so we read in the next verse,—

3. *Abraham believed God*, &c., Gen. xv. 6, quoted on Gal. iii. 6. No argument is drawn, and none can be drawn, from the mere word *it was reputed* (ἐλογίσθη, *it was set down to his credit*). Such *setting down* of itself may be gratuitous, or it may be an acknowledgment of service done, or good paid down. Still less does the word imply that Abraham's justice, or righteousness, was not a quality real and intrinsic in Abraham himself. But St. Paul's argument is this, that as faith alone is mentioned as the cause of Abraham's justification, and not good works, whereof Abraham did so many, justifi-cation must begin in faith, and faith must go before and animate all good works ere they can count as works of justice before God. And thus St. Paul is

conciliated with St. James ii. 21—24, a passage which he had probably before him as he wrote. The best modern criticism holds that St. James wrote prior to St. Paul.

From the passage in Genesis we are not to suppose that Abraham was then for the first time justified, having been in sin throughout the transactions recounted in chapters xii. xiii. xiv., but on occasion of this signal display of his faith the Scripture takes opportunity to observe that through faith he was originally justified, and in this instance received a notable increase of justification and supernatural holiness.

It is unfortunate that in these three verses, 3, 4, 5, the same verb, λογίζεσθαι, is rendered *reputed*, *reckoned*, *reputed* (*reputatum*, *imputatur*, *reputatur*). It would much conduce to clearness, if we read *reckoned* throughout the chapter, here and *vv.* 6, 8, 9, 10, &c. Besides, the word *reputed* favours Lutheranism.

4, 5. St. Paul distinguishes two reckonings; one of a free gift made, *according to grace ;* the other of payment made for service done, *according to debt.* He implies that Abraham did not keep a debtor and creditor account with the Almighty, so that for so much good work done for God by Abraham of his mere natural strength so much justice stood to his credit in the books of divine judgment. On the contrary, Abraham being still *ungodly* (he was an idolater, Josue xxiv. 2 ; Isaias xliii. 27, and at least in original sin), and having no good works that could merit justification, believed in God revealing Himself to him (Josue xxiv. 3 ; Gen. xii. 1—4), and thereupon was justified gratuitously. Cf. 2 Tim. i. 9.

St. Paul tacitly supposes, though he nowhere expressly states, that faith itself is a gift of God, a work of grace. Otherwise his whole argument comes to the ground, for faith being a natural work, indeed the greatest of natural works, would challenge a *reward according to debt*.

His faith, whether of Abraham, or of any *ungodly* man coming to the Sacrament of Baptism (Titus iii. 5), or to the Sacrament of Penance either, *is reputed to justice*, evidently gratuitously, or *according to grace*, since he *worketh not*, *i.e.* has no supernatural works condignly meritorious of justification. So teaches the Council of Trent on justification (sess. vi. cap. 8): "Nothing of those things which precede justification, whether faith or works, merits the grace itself of justification."

According to the purpose of the grace of God. For these words there is no Greek original anywhere, nor are they in all the Latin texts. They are intended to be equivalent to *according to grace* (*v.* 4), *i.e.* gratuitously.

6. *Justice without works*. This, as above explained, refers to the first justification of a convert from a state of sin to the state of grace. It occurs when a man in mortal sin makes an act of perfect contrition, or is baptized, or validly absolved.

7. *Sins are covered*. Sins are here spoken of as historical facts, of which the proverb holds, 'What is done, cannot be undone' (*factum non potest fieri non factum*). St. Peter's denial remains an historical fact for all time, else it would have to be blotted out of the gospel as a story that had ceased to be true. In this sense sin is not undone, it is only *covered* by pardon extended to it. Sin and pardon are two facts, each abiding separately, though, taken together, the latter *covers*, or cancels the former. Thus God is said to *cast our sins into the depths of the sea* (Mich. vii. 19), to *cast them behind his back* (Isaias xxxviii. 17), to *remember them no more* (Heb. x. 17), and yet as facts, or things once done, they can never fade from His eternal vision.

On the other hand, the guilt of the sin, its stain and loathsomeness upon the soul (see St. Thomas, *Summa*,

1a 2æ, q. 86), is not merely *covered*, but entirely removed and taken away, so that the *reconciled* are *holy and unspotted and blameless before God* (Col. i. 22), and have *renovation of the Holy Ghost* (Titus. iii. 5).

8. *Hath not imputed sin, i.e.* to whose account God has reckoned the sin that he has committed no longer to stand. The best commentary is Col. ii. 14 : *Blotting out the handwriting that was against us, he hath taken the same out of the way, fastening it to the cross.* Sin once forgiven is no longer *imputed, reckoned*, or *scored* against the sinner. The debt is paid through the merits of Christ's Passion, and the guilt of that sin and consequent liability to punishment are no more.

10. The interval between the time at which we are assured that Abraham's faith was already reckoned unto justification, and his circumcision, cannot have been less than fourteen years, may have been twenty-five (Gen. xv. 6 ; xvii. 24—26).

11. *The sign of circumcision, a seal,* &c. The sign, consisting of circumcision, is likened to the sign or figure on a seal. We put wine or other liquor into bottles and then seal them up. The seal does not put the liquor there, but denotes that it is there. So circumcision in Abraham's case did not infuse justice and sanctity into his soul, but marked the justice that was in him already, which had been in him for years.

On the other hand, when St. Paul tells the Ephesians : *You were signed with the holy spirit of promise,* . . . *the holy Spirit of God, whereby you are sealed unto the day of redemption* (Eph. i. 13 ; iv. 30) : he speaks of the Holy Ghost, given in baptism, as a sign and seal and likewise a cause of sanctity and justice. Such is the difference between circumcision and baptism : for the New Law, as compared with the Old, has a *better ministry*, is a *better testament*, and is *established on better promises* (Heb. vi. 8).

12. *Father of the circumcision, i.e.* father of the circumcised.

There are two troubles in this verse. First, the *not*
has gone astray in the Vulgate and Rheims versions,
which makes Abraham *the father of circumcision*, to all
that *follow in the steps of his faith*, whether circumcised or
not. But there is an awkwardness also in the Greek,
καὶ τοῖς στοιχοῦσιν τοῖς ἴχνεσιν, *to them also that follow the
steps*, where the article καὶ τοῖς mars the sense. Westcott
and Hort suppose it to be " probably a primitive error
for καὶ αὐτοῖς." Accepting this suggestion we translate:
*And might be the father of circumcision to them that are not of
circumcision only, but also do themselves walk in the footsteps
of the faith of our father Abraham, which was in uncircumcision*
(τῆς ἐν ἀκροβυστίᾳ).

" If he is the father of the uncircumcised, not
because he is uncircumcised (albeit he was justified in
uncircumcision), but inasmuch as they have imitated
his faith, much more must we say that he will not be
the ancestor of the circumcised because of circumcision,
unless they have faith also. If circumcision is a
venerable rite, because it declares justice, no small
precedence attaches also to uncircumcision, as having
been the first to receive justice. Then will you have
Abraham for your father, when you walk in the steps
of his faith, and are not contentious, nor factiously
endeavour to bring in the Law " (St. Chrysostom).

13. See notes on Gal. iii. 17, 18.

Heir of the world, Gen. xii. 3 ; xxii. 18 ; Psalm ii. 8.
These are Messianic promises, Gal. iii. 16.

14. *Faith is made void, the promise is of no effect.* These
two clauses coincide in meaning, the faith spoken of
being the *faith* of Abraham—and of all who by imitation
of his faith are children of Abraham—in the *promise* of
a Messiah and of the blessings which accompany the
coming of Christ. The promise is gratuitous. It is

not a contract to pay wages for the observance of any law. As a matter of fact, argued in chapters i.—iii., mankind generally had not observed any law, neither the law of nature, nor the law given to Moses long after Abraham's time, and then very indifferently kept. The argument of this verse is the same as of *vv.* 4, 5, on which see notes.

15. *The law worketh wrath* upon transgressors, such as most of mankind have been, apart from Christ. They sinned more grievously on account of the law, natural or revealed, teaching them the evil they were doing. But what worked wrath, certainly did not work justification: therefore justification and the blessing promised to the just (*because thou wilt bless the just*, Psalm v. 13) is not of the law.

No law, no transgression; and less law, less transgression (Luke xii. 47, 48).

16. *Therefore is it* [the inheritance, implied in *v.* 13] *of faith.*

What follows should be punctuated according to the Greek, and according to the old Latin versions, thus: *that it may be according to grace, that the promise might be firm,* &c. The inheritance is of faith, not of works, that it may be gratuitous, as argued *vv.* 4, 5.

17. *Father of many nations,* Gen. xvii. 4, by carnal generation, but of many more as he is *the father of all them that believe* (*v.* 11).

Who quickeneth the dead, explained by *v.* 19.

Calleth the things that are not as those that are, more literally, *calleth the things that are not, as being,* ὡς ὄντα, *i.e.* as if they were. The Vulgate and Rheims versions would require τὰ ὄντα. *Calleth* here does not mean calling into being, or the act of creation, but simply God's speaking in His promises to Abraham of the seed that was to be born of him as already existing, while yet it was not.

18. *Who against hope*, of the natural possibility of his having a child by Sara, *believed in hope*, resting *upon the hope*, ἐπ' ἐλπίδι, which the divine promise inspired in him.

The full text, Gen. xv. 5, is: *Look up to heaven, and count the stars, if thou canst : so shall thy seed be.*

19. According to the best Greek MSS. this verse should be read : *And without being weak in faith did he consider his own body now dead, whereas he was almost a hundred years of age, and the dead womb of Sara.* The οὐ before κατενόησε should be omitted.

In the Rheims version, the *neither* represents the *nec* of the Vulgate, and the οὐ of the received Greek text : the *nor*, as a rendering of *et*, καί, is simply a mistake of the modern editions. The first edition has, *and the dead matrice of Sara.*

The occasion referred to is that narrated, Gen. xvii. 15—21. Evidently there Abraham did consider that himself and Sara were past the natural age for having children : he was ninety-nine years old (Gen. xvii. 1) : still he had faith in the word of God ; and if he laughed, it was as St. Chrysostom says, that "he was delighted:" "it was the laugh not of one doubting, but of one believing " (St. Augustine) : "an indication not of incredulity, but of exultation " (St. Ambrose).

In later years Abraham had six children by Cetura (Gen. xxv. 1, 2), the miraculous gift enduring even after Sara's death.

20. *In the promise also of God.* Read with all the Greek MSS., *But in the promise of God*, εἰς δὲ τὴν ἐπαγγελίαν. This tallies with the omission of the negative in the previous verse.

He staggered not, οὐ διεκρίθη, literally, *he did not fight out an issue between two opposites.* The word occurs in this sense, Matt. xxi. 21 ; Acts x. 20 ; xi. 12 ; and below, xiv. 23, where see note.

From the whole passage, *vv.* 13—22, we gather the act, the motive, the object, and the dignity of faith. The act of faith is an assured assent (*he staggered not, v.* 20), a firm assent (*not weak, v.* 19), a full assent (*most fully knowing, v.* 21), an assent above the suggestions of sense (*against hope, v.* 18). The motive of faith is the authority of God speaking (*according to that which was said, v.* 18). The object of faith is the good things of God to be communicated to us (*that he should be heir, v.* 13): hence faith and hope go together (Heb. xi. 1). Lastly, the dignity of faith appears in the glory that it gives to God by confession of His attributes (*giving glory to God, v.* 20), and receives from God, as it is written, *whoever shall glorify me, I will glorify him* (1 Kings ii. 30).

25. It is to be noticed in this verse that the same preposition, διά, *for*, is used twice, but in two different senses. First it expresses the motive cause, *for*, i.e. *on account of our sins* (Isaias liii. 4—8). Then it expresses the final cause, *for*, *i.e.* in view of our justification as an end to be realised.

Rose again for our justification, because though the meritorious cause of our justification is the crucifixion and death of Our Lord, *who was delivered up for our sins* (cf. 1 Pet. ii. 24), yet that justification actually becomes ours only upon our believing and being baptized (Mark xvi. 16; Acts ii. 32—41). Now the central dogma of Christian faith, as the Apostles preached it, is *Jesus and the resurrection* (Acts xvii. 18; iv. 33). Jesus then *rose again for our justification*, that we might be justified by faith in His resurrection, even as Abraham, to whom *all these things happened in figure* (1 Cor. x. 11), was justified by faith in the miraculous birth of Isaac out of a *dead womb*, the type of the new birth of our Lord from the womb of death on the day of His resurrection, of which day it is written: *Thou art my son, this day have I begotten thee* (Psalm ii. 7; Acts xiii. 33).

Another view. If Christ had merely died, not risen again, God might merely have held His hand from punishing our sin, accepting that satisfaction, but not justifying and sanctifying us. That might have sufficed for a certain analogy between us and Christ. But now the analogy stands as stated below, vi. 4—11. Hence explain, *rose again for our justification*, to mean, 'rose again to be the model of our justification,' as set forth in the passage cited. Cf. also note on 1 Cor. xv. 17.

———

CHAPTER V.

1. Therefore being justified by faith, let us have peace with God through our Lord Jesus Christ: 2. By whom also we have access through faith into this grace wherein we stand, and glory in the hope of the glory of the sons of God. 3. And not only so, but we glory also in tribulations, knowing that tribulation worketh patience; 4. And patience trial; and trial hope: 5. And hope confoundeth not; because the charity of God is poured out into our hearts by the Holy Ghost, who is given to us. 6. For why did Christ, when as yet we were weak, according to the time, die for the ungodly? 7. For scarce for a just man will one die; yet perhaps for a good man some one would venture to die. 8. But God commendeth his charity towards us, because when as yet we were sinners, according to the time, 9. Christ died for us: much more, therefore, being now justified by his blood, shall we be saved from wrath through him. 10. For if, when we were enemies, we were reconciled to God by the death of his Son; much more, being reconciled, shall we be saved by his life. 11. And not only so, but also we glory in God, through our Lord Jesus Christ, by whom we have now received reconciliation. 12. Wherefore as by one man sin entered into this world, and by sin death; and so death passed upon all men, in whom all have sinned. 13. (For until the law sin was in the world: but sin was not imputed when the law was not. 14. But death reigned from Adam unto Moses, even over them that had not sinned after the similitude of the transgression of Adam, who is a figure of him that was to come. 15. But not as the offence, so also is the gift: for if by the offence of one many have died; much more the grace of God, and the gift in the grace of

one man Jesus Christ, hath abounded unto many. **16.** And not as it was by one sin, so also is the gift ; for the judgment indeed was by one unto condemnation, but the grace is of many offences unto justification. **17.** For if by one man's offence death reigned through one; much more they who receive abundance of grace, and of the gift, and of justice, shall reign in life through one Jesus Christ.) **18.** Therefore as by the offence of one, unto all men to condemnation : so also by the justice of one, unto all men unto justification of life. **19.** For as by the disobedience of one man many were made sinners ; so also by the obedience of one many shall be made just. **20.** Now the law entered in, that sin might abound : but where sin abounded, grace hath abounded more ; **21.** That as sin hath reigned unto death, so also grace might reign by justice unto everlasting life, through Jesus Christ our Lord.

1. *Being justified therefore by faith* and baptism. See on iii. 27, 28. Justice, according to Aristotle (*Ethics*, v.), involves a certain "equality," and " conformity to law." A man is just by being up to standard. A man is just before God by being up to God's standard. But God's standard for man in the present order of things is a supernatural standard. Cf. note on i. 17. A man is just before God by being in the state of sanctifying grace. That state cannot be merited by natural works going before : *otherwise grace is no more grace* (xi. 6). Of this state of justice and holiness faith is " the beginning, foundation, and root " (Council of Trent, sess. 6, cap. 8).

Let us have peace. Habeamus, the Vulgate reading, is supported by ἔχωμεν in the best Greek MSS., and in the Greek Fathers. It means, as St. Chrysostom explains, 'let us live at peace with God, to whom we were reconciled in baptism.' There is another reading, ἔχομεν, *we have peace.*

2. *We have, we stand*, ἐσχήκαμεν, ἐστήκαμεν, two present perfects, rhyming with and balancing one another, the one meaning, *we have fully*, the other, *we stand firm.* Cf. 1 Tim. iv. 10 ; *we hope*, ἠλπίκαμεν (perfect, *hope firmly*) *in the living God.*

Through faith, absent from some MSS. Though faith is the beginning and a part of justification, still we are rightly and appropriately said to have access and entrance thereby to justification, as we are said to enter a house by the door, though the door itself is part of the house.

Unto this grace, the state of sanctifying grace conferred by baptism.

Almost certainly, the reading is, *and glory in the hope of the glory of God. Of the sons of God* has come in from viii. 21. It is the glory of heaven that is spoken of, which is of course the glory of the sons of God.

3. The Apostle goes on to say that we not only glory in the hope of heaven, but also in the tribulations by which we merit heaven,—not only in the term, but in the way,—not only in the crown, but in the cross (Gal. vi. 14). Theodoret sees in the Apostle's words a profession of what is called in the Spiritual Exercises of St. Ignatius the Third Degree of Humility. "We think ourselves come to great condition and high estate, in that we share the sufferings of our Master." "This," adds Theodoret, "he does not say clearly, for it was only for Paul and the like of Paul to be of that mind: but other souls he leads on and allures with hopes of future blessedness."

Tribulation worketh patience, i.e. the habit of patience, like any other acquired virtue, is formed by repeated acts corresponding; and the acts corresponding to the habit of patience are acts of steady endurance of tribulation.

4. *And patience trial*, δοκιμήν, the word means the state of one who is approved and tried, of one who is up to examination standard, or of one who by frequent practice of any athletic exercise has attained to what is called *form*, so as to pass muster in that particular. Here it refers to the state of those whom God *has tried*

W

and *proved like gold in the furnace* of tribulation, and *has found them worthy of himself*. (Wisd. iii.). This state of trial stood is a ground of hope of reward: thus *trial worketh hope*.

5. *Hope confoundeth not.* This is the statement which is argued in these seven verses, 5—11, that God will not disappoint the hope that we place in Him. How do we know that? Because God loves us. And what proof have we of God loving us? First, the Spirit of His love, which He poured abroad into our hearts, when we were justified in baptism : secondly, the death that God died for us, when we were still in our sins,— whence arises a further *a fortiori* argument, that He who loved us so much as to die for us, when we were His enemies by sin, must love us much more now that we are sanctified and made His friends by grace and the indwelling of His Spirit ; and loving us, He will not fail to grant the grace and glory that we hope of Him.

The charity of God, here and in *v.* 8, is the friendship of God, which means mutual love, of God for us, and of us for God.

The Holy Ghost who is given to us. " The greatest gift of all, that He gave us, was not heaven and earth and sea, but something more precious than all these, something that made us of men angels and sons of God and brothers of Christ. What is that gift ? The Holy Ghost. Now if He did not wish to present us with great crowns after our labours, He would not before those labours began have given us gifts so great. But now He shows us the warmth of His charity in this, that not by quiet progress and little by little has He endowed us, but He has poured forth upon us in one effusion the source of all good, and that before we entered on the conflict " (St. Chrysostom).

6. *For why ?* The opening of this verse is vexed by various readings, εἰς τί γάρ ; (which the Vulgate, *ut quid enim ?* follows), ἔτι γάρ, εἰ γάρ, εἴ γε, over which the best

authorities are in conflict. Most suitable to the context is the received Greek reading, ἔτι γὰρ χριστὸς ὄντων
ἡμῶν ἀσθενῶν κατὰ καιρὸν ὑπὲρ ἀσεβῶν ἀπέθανεν,—*For still
when we were yet weak* (or *sick* with the sickness of sin),
Christ in season died for us ungodly.

According to the time, κατὰ καιρόν, *in season.* *When the
fulness of the time was come, God sent his Son,* &c. (Gal.
iv. 4, 5).

8. *Commendeth, i.e.* shows, συνίστησιν, as in 2 Cor.
vii. 11; Gal. ii. 18.

According to the time, foisted in from *v.* 6.

When we were enemies, Christ died for us. At the time
of the death of Christ, the world that He died for was
generally lost in sin (iii. 9—18). And to this day *the
world is seated in wickedness* (1 John v. 19). Yet Christ
died for the world (1 John ii. 2), for all mankind (1 Tim.
ii. 6), for all wicked men that are wicked at any moment
of the world's history (1 Tim. i. 15).

10. *We were reconciled to God by the death* (διὰ τοῦ
θανάτου, *per mortem*) *of his Son,* but how *shall we be saved
by his life?* This difficulty arises solely out of a corruption that has crept into our Rheims version. Not *by
his life,* but *in his life,* is the rendering of ἐν τῇ ζωῇ αὐτοῦ,
in vita ipsius. The Rheims Testament of 1600 reads
correctly: *For if, when we were enemies, we were reconciled
to God by the death of his Sonne : much more being reconciled,
shal we be saved in the life of him.* The Authorised Version
has, *we shall be saved by his life.* The preposition *in*
sometimes means *by,* but not here, where it is used in
antithesis to the proper word for *by,* διά, *per.* *We shall
be saved in his life* then when His promise shall be fulfilled:
I live and you shall live (John xiv. 19). His life, risen
and glorified, involves our glory, resurrection and life,
as the life of the Head involves the saving of the
members, and the exaltation of the Head the exaltation
of the members. Cf. iv. 25.

12. There should not be a full stop at the end of this verse, else there is no apodosis to the sentence. There are many abruptnesses in the Apostle's language, but nothing so abrupt as that. It would be the abruptness of a man who did not want to be understood. On the other hand a long parenthesis is quite in the Apostle's manner (*e.g.* ii. 13—16; Gal. ii. 6, seq.). Taking *vv.* 13—17 to be parenthetic, a characteristic burst of Pauline thought overflowing the bounds of style, we have at length the apodosis in *v.* 18, introduced by ἄρ' οὖν, *well then*, *as I was saying*, quite a classic use of οὖν to pick up the thread of a broken sentence. *Igitur*, the word in the Vulgate version, is used to exactly the same effect.

As this verse is punctuated in our modern Rheims editions, it is scarcely English. Better thus: *Wherefore as by one man sin entered into this world, and by sin death, and so death passed upon all men; in whom*, or *in which one man* [Adam], *all have sinned;*—— But it is pretty certain that *in whom* is a mistranslation of St. Paul's ἐφ' ᾧ, and even of the Vulgate *in quo*. In classical Greek ἐφ' ᾧ (more usually ἐφ' ᾧτε), with the future indicative, means *on condition that*, *e.g.* Herodotus, vii. 158. In Hellenistic Greek it is used with the present and past tenses of the indicative to mean *inasmuch as*. So it is clearly used by St. Paul, 2 Cor. v. 4, where the Vulgate has *eo quod*, and our version *because*. Again in Phil. iii. 12, Vulgate *in quo*, Rheims *wherein*, should be *inasmuch as*. The third and only other place in the New Testament where ἐφ' ᾧ occurs is Phil. iv. 10, where the Vulgate has *sicut*, the Rheims Version *as :* it should be *quatenus*, *inasmuch as.*

This verse is dogmatically explained by the Council of Trent, sess. 5, cans. 2 and 4, to teach that Adam's sin lost not for him only but for his posterity the sanctity and justice which he had received from God, and that it transfused upon all mankind not only death and bodily penalties, but sin likewise, which is the death of the soul, so that new-born babes have of Adam the guilt of original sin, which must be taken away by baptism for them to attain to eternal life.

Original sin, we may observe, is the privation of sanctifying grace (see note on v. 1), that ensues in Adam's children, as they come into existence, and ensues in consequence of the act of their father and head of their race. Actual (mortal) sin, considered as a state, is the like privation of sanctifying grace ensuing upon one's own act. Sanctifying grace is a gratuitous gift, a bounty of God, not due to human nature as such. It may be compared to a patent of nobility issued to a commoner: the patent makes him a nobleman, but he is a man without the patent. But there is this difference, that a commoner's services may deserve a patent of nobility: whereas nothing that man, as man, can ever do can deserve the conferring upon him of sanctifying grace. In bestowing this gratuitous favour upon Adam and upon mankind God was free, like any other benefactor or founder, to attach conditions to His foundation and benefaction. He founded human nature then in sanctifying grace, so that all men should be conceived and born in that grace, on condition that Adam did not forfeit it by a certain transgression. This condition was not in the nature of things, but was instituted by the positive ordinance of God, an ordinance presumably made known to Adam himself. The effect of the transgression was something like an attainder, falling upon an offender whose peerage had been granted him to remain with him and his heirs for ever only on condition of his personal loyalty. We are born commoners for our ancestor's treason, not however mere commoners, but commoners who should be nobles and are not for their father's offending. In that our original sin consists.

At the same time it must be borne in mind that the Apostle is not here explaining the doctrine of original sin, but assuming it as a thing known, to illustrate what he has been saying, that *by Jesus Christ we have received reconciliation* (*v.* 11). The point of the illustration, and the key to the understanding of all this difficult passage, *vv.* 12—19, is this. We are justified in Christ (by baptism) through no meritorious works of our own (iv. 4—9), even as we sinned in Adam through no demeritorious doing of our own. Of Adam true sin, indwelling in every child of Adam's race: of Christ true justice, indwelling in every one who becomes a member of Christ by baptism.

It is clear that nothing short of the Catholic doctrine of original sin, as laid down above by the Council of Trent, will serve the Apostle's purpose in this illustration and parallelism ; and therefore the Council rightly asserts that doctrine to underlie the Apostle's words.

We have then these statements in *v.* 12 :—

(1) By the sin of one man, Adam, sin *entered into this world*, *i.e.* came upon the human race.

(2) All men have incurred the guilt of this sin.

(3) In consequence of having incurred this guilt, all men die.

The sin here spoken of is original sin. But the death here spoken of is, primarily at least, the death of the body, as will appear by the next two verses.

13. *Until the law* of Moses was given, *sin was in the world, but was not imputed.* The sin here spoken of cannot be original sin, for the imputability of that does not depend upon the promulgation of any law : it is the actual sin that men themselves commit. Now *when the law was not*, or (*v.* 14) *from Adam unto Moses, sin was in the world*, inasmuch as men broke the natural law on all sides (ii. 14, 15 ; iii. 9, 23), but these trans-gressions were *not imputed*, *i.e.* not so much imputed (*not*

by a common Hebraism standing for *not so much, e.g.* Osee vi. 6) on account of their not being against any law positively revealed and externally promulgated. The memory of revelations made to Adam soon became fragmentary and incoherent amongst the mass of his children. See note on iii. 25, on *the remission*, or rather *the letting pass, of former sins.* This verse, by the way, affords ground for the conjecture of modern theologians, that a great deal of the sin of the ancient world was only material, not formal sin.

There is a variant reading, *sin is not imputed, when law is not :* but it makes no difference to the argument.

14. This verse, taken with the two previous, composes an argument thus :—

' Without sin, no death, *v.* 12.

But death prevailed everywhere all the time from Adam to Moses, *v.* 14.

Therefore not without sin.

But the actual sins of at least some men during that time were not sufficiently imputable to account for their dying, *vv.* 13, 14.

Therefore we must refer the cause of the death of these men to the original sin which they had contracted in Adam.'——

The explanation is difficult : but a difficult verse— and there is none more difficult in St. Paul—is precisely a verse which is not susceptible of any easy and manifestly satisfactory explanation.

From Adam unto Moses. The time from Moses unto Christ is spoken of in *v.* 20.

To *sin after the similitude of the transgression of Adam,* is to sin in some grave matter with full consent and full knowledge of the law prohibiting your act, or as theologians say, to sin *formally and mortally.* The Apostle supposes that some at least of the men who lived between Adam and Moses did not sin formally and mortally, so as to deserve death for what they did; and yet they too died, evidently therefore for original sin.   On the other hand we must suppose that the bulk of those who were drowned in the deluge (Gen. vi.). or who perished in Sodom (Gen. xix.), or of the Canaanites (Josue xi.) and Amalecites (1 Kings xv.), died, as they deserved to die, for their own formal mortal sins.

Who is a figure of him who is to come, of Christ, *the last Adam* (1 Cor. xv. 45), not here in reference to the resurrection (of which 1 Cor. xv. 21, 22), but in reference to justification, as explained *v.* 19.   " As Adam to his posterity, though they had not eaten of the tree, was the cause of death [both of body and of soul], induced by that food, so Christ to His own, though they had not done works of justice, was the agent of justification, which He graciously gave us all through the cross " (St. Chrysostom).   And this, as we observed on *v.* 12, is the burden of the whole passage.   Understand this, and you will not miss the main mind and purpose of St. Paul in these verses, although they do contain *certain things hard to be understood* (2 Pet. iii. 16).

15. *Many died, hath abounded unto many.*   The Greek has *the many*, οἱ πολλοί, τοὺς πολλούς, meaning the whole multitude of mankind.   The Vulgate for *unto many* has *in plures (unto more)*, which is open to misconstruction, as St. Augustine observed in his day.   *Græcum attende codicem* (look at the Greek), he told Julianus.   And this has ever been the mind of the Church in its approval of the Latin Vulgate text.

(The) *many died* both temporally and spiritually. The Apostle's thought gradually passes from the former death to the latter.   Cf. vii. 19.   The spiritual death here in question is the being dead to God by original sin.   With regard to this spiritual death, it would be just as unfair to force this phrase, *the many*, to include the Blessed Virgin Mary, as with regard to the death

of the body it would be unfair to force it into a contradiction of 1 Cor. xv. 51 (see notes on the passage),
2 Cor. v. 2—4 ; 1 Thess. iv. 16, where St. Paul teaches
that some shall escape death, being found alive at the
Last Day.

By the grace, ἐν χάριτι, *in gratia,* should be *in the grace.*
The grace of God and *the gift in the grace (i.e.* the gracious
gift) *of one man Jesus Christ,* are the same thing. All
the grace of God that we have is the gracious gift of
Jesus Christ. The second designation is added for the
sake of the antithesis, which is not between God and
Adam, but between Christ, as Man, and Adam.

16. To understand this verse, we must re-translate
it from the Greek, *And not as if it was a case of one sinner*
[δι' ἑνὸς ἁμαρτήσαντος, or taking the Vulgate reading, *per
unum peccatum, as though it were a case of one sin,* which
comes to the same thing], *so also is the gift. For the one*
[*the offence* of *v.* 15, which caused the condemnation, the
cause being put for the effect] *was a condemnation passing
from one individual to a general condemnation* [of the race]:
but the other [*the gift* of *v.* 15] *was a boon from many
transgressions to justification and acquittal.*

In the phrase ὡς δι' ἑνὸς ἁμαρτήσαντος, the δια is the
δια of circumstance, like δι' ὀργῆς, *in anger:* cf. διὰ
γράμματος, ii. 27; and the note on Gal. iv. 13. The
preposition might have been left out, and the simple
genitive absolute, ὡς ἑνὸς ἁμαρτήσαντος, used to express
the same sense, by a common classical idiom.

The general sense is that given by St. Chrysostom :
" One sin availed to bring in death and condemnation :
but the grace of Christ took away not that sin only, but
all the sins that came in after it. After the endless sins
that followed that sin committed in paradise, the matter
found issue in justification. Now where justice is, life
necessarily follows ; as where there is sin, death comes.
For justice is more than life, seeing it is the root of life."

Our version, made from the Latin, makes *judgment* and *grace* the subjects of the clauses in which they stand; and the Greek may be taken so. But the τὸ μὲν and the τὸ δὲ rather suggest that *judgment* and *grace* are predicates, as rendered above. Thus we are carried back to the first words of *v.* 15 : τὸ μὲν meaning *what we had of Adam :* τὸ δὲ, *what we have of Christ.* Thus, *what we had of Adam was condemnation, passing from one* (Adam) *to a general condemnation of the race : what we have of Christ is a gift of grace, from many transgressions to justification.* For *judgment* and *condemnation*, the words in the Rheims version, the Greek words are κρίμα and κατάκριμα. The word κρίμα means more than *judgment :* it means *condemnation,* cf. ii. 2, 3 ; iii. 8 ; xiii. 2 ; 1 Cor. xi. 29. What then does κατάκριμα mean ? The κατά is intensive : κατάκριμα then means *thorough condemnation, i.e.* as explained in *v.* 18, εἰς πάντας ἀνθρώπους εἰς κατάκριμα, *unto all men unto ·condemnation.* So then κρίμα is of the individual, κατάκριμα of the race.

Justification, δικαίωμα, not as in *v.* 18, where it means a *just and righteous deed,* but for δικαίωσις, the *act of pronouncing,* or *making, just and righteous.* As it is here in opposition to κρίμα, it may be rendered also *acquittal* (cf. vi. 7), but acquittal not on the score of previous innocence, but of present satisfaction tendered and accepted.

17. A reiteration of *v.* 15. Instead of *the gift and justice*, the received Greek reading, *the gift of justice*, has better authority.

Shall reign does not refer to the resurrection and the life of glory immediately, but to the triumph over sin of Christ's members on earth, who are called *a kingly priesthood.* (1 Pet. ii. 9).

18. *Therefore,* ἄρα οὖν, *well then, as I was saying.* See on *v.* 12.

So by the justice (δικαιώματος, *just deed*) *of one man.* Here is the true apodosis to *v.* 12.

All men . . . all men. " As all men who are born in the flesh of Adam incur condemnation by his sin, so all who are reborn spiritually of Christ gain the justification of life. The justification of Christ extends to the justification of all men in point of sufficiency, but in point of efficiency it reaches only the faithful " (St. Thomas).

19. This verse is a summing up of the doctrine of the last seven verses.

(The) *many* . . . (the) *many*, οἱ πολλοί, is exactly equivalent to *all men . . . all men* of the previous verse.

Disobedience, Gen. iii. 17—19.

Obedience, Phil. ii. 8.

Adam's disobedience was our disobedience, without any act of ours, as he was the head of our race, and our wills were contained in his: Adam's loss of justifying and sanctifying grace, our loss of justification and holiness: Adam's sin, our sin. In like manner, Christ's obedience becomes our obedience, through no merit of any actual obedience of ours, when by baptism we are incorporated in the Body of which He is the Head; and through Him and in Him we are made sinless, just and holy, not by any mere extrinsic justice of Christ imputed to us, but by justice, grace, and sanctity formally indwelling in us, even as the original sin in which we were born was no mere extrinsic sin, belonging to Adam and put down to us, but was through Adam our sin, making us formally *sinners*, as we are here called, worthy of death for our sin (*vv.* 12, 14), *by nature children of wrath* (Eph. ii. 3).

20. In *v.* 14 the Apostle has spoken of the time *from Adam to Moses*, showing how death, and original sin, of which death is the effect and symptom, reigned in the world. What then of the time since Moses? Has the Mosaic Law saved the observers of it from entering this world in sin? On the contrary, as he

argues at greater length, vii. 7, seq., the Law, as such, has done nothing to efface original sin ; and its indirect effect has been to aggravate actual sin.

The law entered in, παρεισῆλθεν, *entered in besides*, besides sin, which *entered*, εἰσῆλθεν, first (*v.* 12). This meaning of παρά better suits the context than its other meaning, *by stealth*, which is rather implied by the Vulgate, *subintravit*.

Sin might abound, say *offence*, παράπτωμα, which here means, not as in *vv.* 15, 17, 18, the sin of Adam, but as in *v.* 16, the actual transgressions whereby Adam's children have imitated their sire.

On the other hand, in the phrase, *sin abounded, sin*, ἁμαρτία, as in *vv.* 12, 13, and *v.* 21 following, is original sin, here considered as resulting in death, in concupiscence, and in many actual sins.

That sin might abound. This is explained by St. Paul himself, vii. 10—13. The preposition *that*, ἵνα, is to be taken according to the Hebrew and later Greek idiom, to represent result rather than purpose. So in Gal. v. 17.

21. *Sin* (original) *reigned to death,*—say, *in death*, ἐν τῷ θανάτῳ, *i.e.* showed its dominion in producing death : it is the death of the body that is primarily spoken of, as in *vv.* 12, 13.

Grace might reign by justice, i.e. supernatural holiness, the gratuitous gift of God through Christ, should reign by the expulsion of sin.

1. What shall we say then? shall we continue in sin, that grace may abound? 2. God forbid. For how shall we, that are dead to sin, live any longer therein? 3. Know you not that all we who are baptized in Christ Jesus are baptized in his death? 4. For we are buried together with him by baptism unto death; that as Christ is risen from the dead by the glory of the Father, so we also may walk in newness of life. 5. For if we have been planted together in the likeness of his death, in like manner we shall be of his resurrection. 6. Knowing this, that our old man is crucified with him, that the body of sin may be destroyed, and that we may serve sin no longer. 7. For he that is dead is justified from sin. 8. Now if we be dead with Christ, we believe that we shall live also together with Christ: 9. Knowing that Christ, rising again from the dead, dieth now no more, death shall no more have dominion over him. 10. For in that he died to sin, he died once; but in that he liveth, he liveth unto God. 11. So do you also reckon yourselves to be dead indeed to sin, but alive to God in Christ Jesus our Lord. 12. Let not sin therefore reign in your mortal body, so as to obey the lusts thereof. 13. Neither yield ye your members as instruments of iniquity unto sin: but present yourselves to God as those that are alive from the dead, and your members as instruments of justice unto God. 14 For sin shall not have dominion over you: for you are not under the law, but under grace. 15. What then? Shall we sin, because we are not under the law, but under grace? God forbid. 16. Know you not, that to whom you yield yourselves servants to obey, his servants you are whom you obey, whether it be of sin unto death, or of obedience unto justice? 17. But thanks be to God, that you were the servants of sin, but have obeyed from the heart unto that form of doctrine into which you have been delivered. 18. Being then made free from sin, you are become the servants of justice. 19. I speak a human thing, because of the infirmity of your flesh: for as you have yielded your members to serve uncleanness and iniquity unto iniquity, so now yield your members to serve justice unto sanctification. 20. For when you were the servants of sin, you were free from justice. 21. What fruit, therefore, had you then in those things, of which you are now ashamed? for the end of them is death. 22. But now, being made free from sin, and become servants to God, you have your fruit unto sanctification, and the end everlasting life. 23 For the wages of sin is death: but the grace of God, everlasting life, in Christ Jesus our Lord.

1. The Apostle warns us against such reasoning as this: 'Where sin hath abounded, grace hath super-abounded (v. 20): therefore let sin abound still further, that grace may still further superabound.' Much sin forgiven in baptism is no warrant for more sin to follow. He shows that such false reasoning as the above is a misunderstanding of the essential nature and symbolism of baptism.

To make the doctrine of this chapter practical for Christians of our time, we must observe that the Sacrament of Penance is a restoration of baptismal grace.

Shall we continue? ἐπιμενοῦμεν; the less supported Greek reading, gives the same sense as the two better readings, ἐπιμένωμεν; *are we to continue?* and ἐπιμένομεν; *continue we?*

Continue in sin. We might have expected, *relapse into sin*, for the persons spoken of are the baptized, whose sin has been all taken away in baptism. But the word ἁμαρτία is the same as in the second part of v. 20, to which it refers, and means, as there, *original sin in its effects*. Original sin is taken away by baptism, but not that particular effect of it which is called concupiscence. In this chapter and in the next, if for the continually recurring word *sin*, ἁμαρτία, we read *concupiscence*, we shall generally have the Apostle's meaning. Concupiscence, as the Council of Trent tells us (sess. 5, cap. 5), is sometimes called *sin* by the Apostle, " not because in the regenerate it is truly and properly sin, but because it comes of sin and inclines to sin." Where note that concupiscence is an accident of our animal nature, and is so far forth natural; but had it not been for Adam's sin, this natural defect, so far as it is a defect, would have been obviated by the special providence of God in all Adam's posterity, as it was originally in Adam himself. Therefore concupiscence " comes of sin " in the order of history, although it is a thing

natural in the order of nature. Martha said to Jesus:
Lord, if thou hadst been here, my brother had not died (John
xi. 32); and yet Lazarus died a natural death.

To *continue in sin* therefore, for a baptized man, is to
continue yielding to concupiscence, doing *the works of
the flesh* (enumerated, Gal. v. 19—21), and so to go on
sinning anew.

2. *Dead to sin*, cf. 1 Pet. ii. 24, such is the essential
idea of baptism, as he goes on to show. "What is it
to be dead to sin? Henceforth to obey it in nothing"
(St. Chrysostom). The Greek aorist, ἀπεθάνομεν, might
be more literally translated, *we who once died to sin, i.e.*
when we were baptized.

3. Cf. 1 Cor. vi. 15—20; xii. 13; Gal. iii. 27, with
notes.

Baptized in Christ, in his death, εἰς χριστὸν, εἰς τὸν θάνατον,
it should be, *unto Christ, unto his death*. See on xi. 36.
It means that by baptism we are dedicated to Christ,
remade (*a new creature*, Gal. vi. 15) in His likeness,—
and more than that, inserted into and ingrafted upon
Him, made members of that Body, without which He
as Head is imperfect and incomplete, and which is
therefore called His *fulness*, or *complement*, πλήρωμα (Eph.
i. 23). Cf. John xv. 1—5; Gal. ii. 20; Eph. ii. 5, 6;
v. 30; Col. ii. 10—12, &c. These expressions are not
mere figures of speech, any more than is the language
used about the Holy Eucharist, to which they are
closely allied. They mean a good deal more than that
we are to be copies of Christ's innocence, Christ's
gentleness, and Christ's kindness to suffering humanity.
What they further do mean is a *great sacrament*, or
mystery (Eph. v. 32), which, like the mystery of the
Holy Eucharist, we shall understand better when our
union with Him is perfect in another life.

Baptized unto his death means *unto the likeness of his death*,
which is represented in baptism, as presently explained.

4. *We are buried together with him.* Baptism in the
Apostolic age was commonly by immersion; and the
Church still insists that the water shall flow over
the head of the child. St. Chrysostom explains the
rite: " When our head is plunged into the water, as
into a tomb, the old man is buried and entirely sub-
merged: then, as we emerge, the new man rises."
Thus, alike by the external rite and by the inward
spiritual change wrought by that rite, on the principle
that "sacraments effect what they signify," baptism
represents in us the death, burial, and resurrection of
Christ. It is a resurrection, and therefore a regeneration, or new birth (John iii. 5; Titus iii. 5).

Baptism unto death, these words are to be joined
together, like *baptized in* (unto) *his death* above.

By the glory of the Father, διὰ τῆς δόξης, is simply, *in the
glory of the Father.* This διά with the genitive is the διά
of circumstance, adverbial διά, noticed above, *v.* 16 and
Gal. iv. 13. Cf. Phil. ii. 11. *The glory of the Father* is
one with *the glory of the Only-begotten of the Father.*
(John i. 14).

Newness of life is just the opposite of *continuation in sin*
(*v.* 1), which is *abiding in death* (1 John iii. 14).

5. *Planted together, complantati,* is not a good translation of σύμφυτοι (not συμφύτευτοι), which means simply
grown together.

In the likeness, τῇ ὁμοιότητι, probably the instrumental
dative, *by the likeness.*

The whole phrase then is: *For if we have been blended
with* (him, Christ) *by the likeness of his death, yet also*
(ἀλλὰ καὶ) *shall we be* (*blended with him by the likeness*) *of his
resurrection.* The meaning is: ' Baptism unites us with
Christ, representing in our persons His death and
resurrection. We must keep up that union and that
representation in our subsequent lives. We must live
with Christ, dead to sin, a hard matter, but along with

that we shall also be alive with Christ in our new life of grace on earth, the parallel to His life after His resurrection.' There is no immediate reference here to the resurrection of our bodies. The future, *we shall be*, merely signifies logical sequence. Cf. 2 Cor. v. 14, 15.

Learn from this verse that the innocence of a Christian man is not a mere negative quantity, like the innocence of a corpse. He positively walks the earth, a divine being, in some sort like Christ after His resurrection, so long as he keeps in the state of grace.

There should be no full stop at the end of this verse.

6. *Knowing this*, καὶ τοῦτο γινώσκοντες, *hoc scientes*, Vulg., better *et id quidem scientes*, *and that* (we shall be), *knowing*. The pronoun refers, not to what comes after, but to what goes before. Cf. xiii. 11, καὶ τοῦτο.

Our old man. See Eph. iv. 22, 24, for *the old man, who is corrupted according to the desire of error*, and *the new man, who according to God is created in justice and holiness of truth*. Read also Col. iii. 1—10, a parallel passage. There the works of *the old man* are described, as indeed they are above, i. 29—31. *The old man* lives in the corruption of the first Adam and original sin, a slave to his *flesh with its vices and concupiscences* (Gal. v. 24), often in sound health and high intellectual culture.

Is crucified with· him (see on Gal. v. 24) inasmuch as by baptism we are conformed to Christ's death, even His death on the cross, the *tree* whereon *his own self bore our sins in his body* (1 Pet. ii. 23), *being made a curse for us* (Gal. iii. 13). Cf. also Col. ii. 12—14.

The body of sin is our sinful body, not as a body, but as sinful.

Serve sin ; this idea of servitude is worked out from *v*. 16 to the end of the chapter.

7. *He who is dead is justified* (*i.e.* acquitted) *from sin*. A dead man does no wrong: the proof of death is the proof of innocence, simultaneous with death. So

x

St. Peter : *He that hath suffered* (ὁ παθών, a Greek euphemism for *he that is dead*) *in the flesh has ceased from sins.* See 1 Pet. iv. 1—3. So St. Chrysostom : " If you are dead in baptism, remain dead : for no dead man can sin any more." Cf. 1 John iii. 9 ; v. 18. But there remains with us, until the hour of our natural decease, an unhappy power of reversing our baptism, dying to justice, and reverting to a new life of sin.

8. *If we be dead* (or rather, *if we died*, ἀπεθάνομεν) *with Christ* in baptism, *we believe that we shall also live together with Christ*, *i.e.* we trust that we do live and shall go on living the supernatural life of grace, as explained *v.* 5, till it be turned into the life of glory,—*sanctification and the end life everlasting*, *v.* 22.

9. *Shall no more have*, κυριεύει, *has no more dominion over him*, is certainly the right reading.

10. This verse should stand as in the first Rheims edition : *For that he died, to sin he died once : but that he liveth, he liveth unto God.* Thus and not otherwise the apodosis of the first sentence in the verse answers the apodosis of the second : any other collocation of the words spoils the antithesis. Anyhow the difficulty remains, how Christ can be said to have *died to sin.* The answer is that He died to a world in which sin and death were dominant ; a world in which many of the penal consequences of sin and death to humanity fell likewise upon Him (cf. viii. 3, *in the likeness of sinful flesh*, with note) ; a world in which the sins of men were laid upon Him to expiate, so that He was said to be *made sin* (2 Cor. v. 21, and note).

Once, i.e. once for all, Heb. ix. 27, 28 ; x. 10, 12, 14. *Liveth unto God, in the glory of the Father, v.* 4.

11. *Alive unto God*, that is, in the grace of God, dealing with Him as a child with its father.

In Christ Jesus, in your union with Christ, for which see on *v.* 3.

12. *Let not sin reign, i.e.* concupiscence, the effect of sin (above on *v.* 1). A king reigns by the consent of his people. Concupiscence may attempt to tyrannize, but reign it cannot without the man's consent.

In your mortal body, because being *mortal*, the body is obnoxious to concupiscence, from which Adam's body, while it was deathless, was free.

13. *Neither yield ye your members as instruments* (or *arms*, *arma*, ὅπλα) *of iniquity to sin* (*concupiscence*). The *members* are the limbs and all the body, as subject to the control of the will. Take the example of anger. If, when anger arises in your heart, you break out into angry words, use your feet to pursue your enemy and your hand to strike him, you make your tongue, feet, and hands, *instruments of iniquity*, or tools of wickedness to abet anger : you have *armed* anger against yourself. If you had kept your hands and your tongue quiet, if you had simply done nothing to gratify your anger, anger would never have reigned in you. There are some celebrated words of St. Augustine on this subject (Serm. 128, n. 12) : "God has given thee power by His Spirit to withhold thy members. Passion rises, withhold thou thy members : what shall the passion do that has arisen ? Do thou withhold thy members : yield not thy members as instruments of iniquity unto sin : arm not thine adversary against thyself. Withhold thy feet, that they go not to places unlawful : withhold thy hands from all crime : withhold thine eyes from evil gazing : withhold thine ears from willingly listening to lustful speech : withhold thy whole body, flank, front, and rear : what shall passion do ? It knows how to rise, it knows not how to conquer ; and by constantly rising to no purpose it will learn even not to rise."

Your members as instruments of justice. It is a bad defence, that never assumes the offensive : we must do supernatural good works, or we shall not long hold out against sin.

14. *You are not under the law, but under grace.* " We are not under the law, which commands what is good but gives it not, but we are under grace, which, making us love what the law commands, can command us as free men " (St. Augustine).

Practically the text means, you have not only the ten commandments, but also the seven sacraments.

15. This verse stands to *v.* 14 precisely as *v.* 1 stands to v. 20. Twice in this short compass the Apostle guards his praises of grace from being taken as an encouragement to sin and neglect of good works, showing himself as far from Antinomianism as St. James.

16. This supposes the truth: *No man can serve two masters* (Matt. vi. 24).

17, 18. These two verses should be taken together, with only a comma between them. Verse 18 should run, *and being made free from sin, you were made servants of justice.* So it is in the Rheims Testament of 1583. There is a double error in the modern Rheims version: first, the conjunction *then*, representing an inferior reading οὖν for δέ, *autem* (Vulg.), *but*, for which the English idiom here requires *and:* second, a quite unauthorised substitution of the first person for the second, *we have been made*, for *you have been made*, against all other texts that ever were. The error arose from a mistaken desire to make a separate sentence of *v.* 18. This second error does not exist in the text which I have printed, which reads *you are become.*

Thanks be to God that you were the servants of sin, but, &c., is a Greek idiom, strange to an English ear. A Greek would say: 'It is intolerable, if other kings my ancestors are entombed in peace, but I shall be cast out from sepulture, an unclean thing' (cf. Is. xiv.

18, 19) : where what is really complained of stands in the second clause. Cf. vii. 25 (with note); viii. 10. The clauses are severally introduced by μὲν, *indeed*, and δὲ, *but:* for which English idiom prefers, *whereas . . . yet.* It may be noticed that St. Paul writes simply ἦτε, and not as classical Greek would have had it, ἦτε μὲν. On the other hand he gives the δὲ twice over, ὑπηκούσατε δὲ, *but you come to obey*, and ἐλευθερωθέντες δὲ, *but being set free.* It may be Englished : *Thank be to God that, whereas you were servants of sin, yet now you have come to obey*, &c.

That form of doctrine. So 2 Tim. i. 13 : *Hold the form of sound words, which thou hast heard of me in faith:* texts which, with many others, go to show how far the Apostle was from being averse to symbols, creeds, definitions, and fixed formularies of faith.

Into which you have been delivered, more clearly, *according to which you have been taught*, παρεδόθητε. The more usual construction of this verb is seen in 1 Cor. xi. 23 : *that which also I delivered unto you*, ὅπερ καὶ παρέδωκα ὑμῖν.

19. *I speak a human thing, i.e.* I give you a recommendation suited to human infirmity, *because of the infirmity of your flesh:* for *the flesh is weak* (Matt. xxvi. 41), —the nature of man makes its weakness felt for all that it is supported by grace. The recommendation is that they should do at least as much for justice sake, now that they are Christians, as they have done before for the gratification of sinful appetite. Human weakness apart, they might have been called on to do much more.

Unto iniquity, unto sanctification, means to the increase of those habits. The phrase, *justice unto sanctification*, argues that to be justified is to be sanctified, against the theory of imputed justice. See on iv. 5, seq.

20. *Free from justice.* "You were not subject to it, but altogether estranged from it : for you did not divide

the measure of your service, giving part to justice and part to sin, but you gave yourselves wholly to sin. So also now that you have transferred yourselves to justice, give yourselves over wholly to virtue, doing no evil at all, that you may at least render equal measure" (St. Chrysostom). Such is the theory, but in practice good and evil are strangely interchanged, the just falling into some sins (1 John i. 8), and the unjust doing some good actions. Still the broad difference remains between the just and the unjust, between those who are in the state of grace and those who are in mortal sin, the most unseen and withal the deepest of all differences among mankind.

21. *What fruit had you then in those things of which you are now ashamed?* This is St. Chrysostom's punctuation, adopted by the Latins generally, and is likely enough. But moderns incline to Theodoret's: *What fruit had you then? That whereof you are now ashamed;* which the Greek will equally bear.

The end of them is death, or according to Theodoret, *the end of that* (fruit) *is death,* the death of the soul, *the second death* (Apoc. xxi. 8), as Adam incurred the death of the body also by eating the forbidden fruit. *End* here is τέλος, *finis consummans,* crowning result and consummation; not πέρας, *finis finiens,* limit.

23. *The wages of sin is death,* another way of saying, *the end of them is death* (v. 21).

The death of the body, to one who dies in sin, is the beginning of his everlasting punishment, as to the just it is the vestibule of his everlasting reward. To the one it comes as a punishment, to the other as a release.

Wages, ὀψώνια, *stipendia,* the money given to a soldier for his daily keep (1 Cor. ix. 7), earned by his works, and due to him in justice: so men earn eternal damnation.

The grace, τὸ χάρισμα, *the gratuitous gift of God,* is *life everlasting,* because, as St. Augustine says, "it is rendered to those merits which grace has bestowed on man."

———

Chapter VII.

1. Know you not, brethren, (for I speak to them that know the law,) how the law hath dominion over a man as long as it liveth. 2. For the woman that hath a husband, while her husband liveth, is bound to the law: but if her husband be dead, she is loosed from the law of her husband. 3. Wherefore, whilst her husband liveth, she shall be called an adulteress if she be with another man: but if her husband be dead, she is free from the law of her husband; so that she is not an adulteress if she be with another man. 4. Therefore, my brethren, you also are become dead to the law by the body of Christ: that you may belong to another, who is risen again from the dead, that we may bring forth fruit to God. 5. For when we were in the flesh, the passions of sins, which were by the law, did work in our members to bring forth fruit unto death. 6. But now we are loosed from the law of death, wherein we were detained, so that we should serve in newness of spirit, and not in the oldness of the letter. 7. What shall we say then? Is the law sin? God forbid. But I did not know sin but by the law: for I had not known concupiscence, if the law had not said: Thou shalt not covet. 8. But sin, taking occasion by the commandment, wrought in me all manner of concupiscence. For without the law sin was dead. 9. And I lived some time without the law; but when the commandment came, sin revived. 10. And I died: and the commandment that was ordained to life, the same was found to be unto death to me. 11. For sin, taking occasion by the commandment, seduced me, and by it killed me. 12. Wherefore the law indeed is holy, and the commandment holy, and just, and good. 13. Was that then which is good made death to me? God forbid. But sin, that it may appear sin, by that which is good wrought death in me; that sin by the commandment might become sinful above measure. 14. For we know that the law is spiritual, but I am carnal, sold under sin. 15. For that which I work I understand not: for I do not that good which I will, but the evil which I hate, that I do. 16. If then I do that which I will not, I consent to the law, that it is good. 17. Now then it is no more I that do it, but

sin that dwelleth in me. **18.** For I know that there dwelleth not in me, that is to say, in my flesh, that which is good: for to will good is present with me; but to accomplish that which is good I find not. **19.** For the good which I will I do not: but the evil which I will not, that I do. **20.** Now if I do that which I will not, it is no more I that do it, but sin that dwelleth in me. **21.** I find then a law, that, when I have a mind to do good, evil is present with me: **22.** For I am delighted with the law of God according to the inward man: **23.** But I see another law in my members fighting against the law of my mind, and captivating me in the law of sin that is in my members. **24.** Unhappy man that I am: who shall deliver me from the body of this death? **25.** The grace of God by Jesus Christ our Lord. Therefore I myself with the mind serve the law of God: but with the flesh the law of sin.

1. *I speak to them that know;* γινώσκουσιν λαλῶ means *you to whom I speak know.*

As long as it liveth, rather, *as long as he liveth.* So the original Rheims edition of 1583. It was a saying of the Rabbis: "Man when he is dead, rests from the law." The Greek and Latin not expressing the pronoun, Origen and others understand *it lives:* but is it more obvious to speak of the life of a law or of the life of a man?

2. *Whilst her husband liveth, is bound to the law.* Say, *is bound to her living husband by the law.* The Greek is τῷ ζῶντι ἀνδρὶ, *to her living husband.* Tertullian reads the same, *viventi viro.* The Greek νόμῳ may be either *legi* (Vulg.), *to the law*, or *lege, by the law :* but the restoration of the previous dative, *to her living husband*, which all the Greek authorities require, requires also that we make of νόμῳ an instrumental dative, *by the law*, answering to the Latin ablative, *lege.*

The law here is not precisely the law of Moses, which allowed divorce (Deut. xxiv. 1, seq.; Levit. xxii. 12; Ruth i. 12), but the still older law of the Old Testament, given to Adam (Gen. ii. 24), and promulgated anew by our Lord (Matt. v. 31, 32; xix. 4, seq.), and after Him by St. Paul (1 Cor. vii. 10, 11).

She is released, κατήργηται, literally, *undone, made of no effect :* word recurs iii. 3 ; 2 Cor. iii. 11, 13, &c., and below, *v.* 6.

The law of her husband, i.e. respecting her husband. So Levit. xiv. 2, *the law of the leper.*

3. *Of her husband* in this verse is an unnecessary repetition, crept in from the previous verse, not in the Greek Fathers and MSS.

4. *Dead to the law by the body of Christ, i.e.* by your incorporation with the body of Christ, 1 Cor. xii. 13, 27, where see notes : also Eph. i. 22, 23 ; v. 29, 30.

For the strict application of the comparison we should have, *the law is dead to you :* but inasmuch as whichever of the two parties in a marriage dies, the deceased is dead to the survivor, and the survivor to the deceased, St. Paul makes his point by saying, *You are dead to the law,* and therefore free from the law : for *he that is dead is justified,* or set free from obligation (vi. 7) : *for the law* of marriage, or of any other relation, *hath dominion over a man* only *as long as he liveth* (*v.* 1). This abrupt and off-handed application of a comparison is quite in the Apostle's manner, not sufficiently recognised by too formal and over-nice commentators.

Bring forth fruit to God. Bearing fruit presupposes life ; and *fruit to God,* or *fruit unto sanctification* (vi. 22), presupposes a divine life, breathed into us by the Holy Ghost.

5. *When we were in the flesh. To be in the flesh* sometimes means to be in this mortal life, 2 Cor. x. 3 ; Gal. ii. 20 ; Phil. i. 22, 24 ; and Heb. v. 7, speaks of our Lord *in the days of his flesh.* That cannot be the meaning here. Another meaning is evident below, viii. 8 ; *They who are in the flesh cannot please God,* on which see notes. And that is the meaning in this place, namely, ' in our unregenerate state.'

The passions of sins, i.e. leading to sins, *which were by the law*, *i.e.* were aggravated by occasion of the law (below *vv.* 7, 8), *did work.* But ἐνηργεῖτο may be passive and be rendered, *were wrought out.* See on 2 Cor. i. 6; iv. 12.

Fruit in death, once more fruit corresponding to the life which it presupposes; for death, *the second death*, is the fruit of a sinful life. See on vi. 21.

6. *The law of death*, so called, if the reading be sound, as occasioning sin and eternal death. But all the best Greek MSS. read (Origen refers to the other reading, τοῦ θανάτου, and sets it aside): *But now when we died* (ἀποθανόντες, when we died with Christ in baptism, vi. 3, 4; Col. iii. 3), *we were loosed from the law, wherein we were detained.*

So that we should serve, still serve, not be our own masters.

In newness of the spirit, Eph. iv. 23, 24.

Not in oldness of the letter,—for *the letter killeth* (2 Cor. iii. 6, and notes). *The letter* is the letter of the Old Law, barely as a law, apart from grace to keep it.

In the passage that follows, *v.* 7 to end of chapter, St. Paul is not describing his own experience as he was a Christian and a minister of Christ; nor is he necessarily writing an account of his state before his conversion, after the manner of the *Confessions* of St. Augustine. All that we can say is that he is describing the state of a Jew, who has only the law to help him, and is not helped in his struggles against sin by the grace of Christ. We must observe that this was not the essential condition of all Jews before the coming of our Lord: for the grace of Christ was bestowed by anticipation even under the Old Testament, though not so abundantly as in the New. However, both in the Old and in the New Testament, many have thrust aside from them the grace of Christ. So this is not a mere ideal and abstract view of life, but a sketch of human life as it is often actually lived.

By *the law* St. Paul understands immediately the moral portion of the Mosaic law, that is, the Ten Commandments, one of which he quotes (*v.* 7). The passage however has its application also to the natural law (ii. 15), though less perfectly, as that law is less distinctly known by the light of nature than the ten commandments were by divine revelation. The Apostle's words find also an unhappy fulfilment in modern times, wherever moral obligations are accurately known, but the ordinary channels of grace, the sacraments, are neglected, abused, or denied. Those reformers might have found their condemnation here in St. Paul, who pulled down the Altar and banished the Blessed Sacrament, and then wrote up at the back of their Table the Ten Commandments.

7. *I did not know sin, i.e.* the sinful tendency of concupiscence (see note on vi. 1), *but by the law :—for by the law is the knowledge of sin* (iii. 20). Apart from some recognised external code, the sinfulness of indulged concupiscence is very imperfectly appreciated.

Thou shalt not covet, Exod. xx. 17; Deut. v. 21.

8. *But* (original) *sin taking occasion by the commandment,* just quoted, *wrought in me all* (*i.e.* extreme, cf. *all joy,* James i. 2) *concupiscence.*

Without the law sin was dead, i.e. did not come before the mind with such distinctness as to make the temptation formidable. A set prohibition both defines the obligation and provokes us to spurn it. As Ovid says (*Amor.* iii. 4) :

> Nitimur in vetitum semper cupimusque negata.
> Forbid a thing, we strive for it : deny it, we desire.

9. *And* (*now,* δὲ, *autem*) *I lived some time without the law,* in the early years of boyhood, when the law was not urgent upon me.

The commandment came, with the years of maturity and discretion.

Sin revived. Original sin in its effects of evil con-cupiscence *sprang up into life in its turn*, ἀνέζη.

10. *I died*, the spiritual death of actual mortal sin. See St. Augustine's *Confessions*, l. ii. c. 2. Cf. also note on Gal. ii. 19. Notice the antithesis in these three verses : *Sin dead, I lived : sin revived, I died*.

The commandment that was ordained to life, Levit. xviii. 5 ; Ezech. xx. 11 ; Matt. xix. 17.

11. *Sin seduced me, i.e.* concupiscence *deceived me*, ἐξηπάτησέν με, as Mother Eve said : *The serpent deceived me*, ἠπάτησέν με (Gen. iii. 13, a passage alluded to by St. Paul in two other places, 2 Cor. xi. 3 ; 1 Tim. ii. 14).

12. *The commandment* (quoted in *v.* 7) *is holy and just and good*, Psalm xviii. 9—13.

13. *Wrought*, in the Greek a participle, κατεργαζομένη. And this has suggested to commentators a way of making the sentence clearer thus : *But sin* (has been made death unto me), *that it may appear sin, working death in me by that which is good*.

Sin, that it may appear sin, i.e. concupiscence that it may realise its sinful tendency.

That sin might become sinful beyond measure, i.e. that concupiscence might work itself out to the last excesses of actual sin.

14. *For we know*, οἴδαμεν, or possibly οἶδα μέν, *I know indeed*.

The law is spiritual, inasmuch as perfect fulfilment of it is a work of grace.

I am carnal, away from grace, swayed by fleshly or sensual appetite. It must be borne steadily in mind that St. Paul in all this passage is not speaking as Paul the Apostle, but in the assumed character of the unregenerate Jew. St. Augustine and a large school of followers, who will have it that St. Paul here speaks in his own person, have involved themselves in difficulty and the passage in obscurity.

Sold under sin, as we say of a slave, that he was
'knocked down' to the master who purchased him. The
phrase is found, 3 Kings xxi. 20, 25; 1 Macc. i. 15, 16.
Sin here again is concupiscence.

15. *I understand not;* οὐ γινώσκω, for which the Vulgate
has, *non intelligo. Nihil moror, I don't approve of*, would
have been better. A good example of the phrase is
Thucydides, i. 86, which opens: τοὺς μὲν λόγους τοὺς πολλοὺς
τῶν Ἀθηναίων οὐ γιγνώσκω, 'I reckon nothing of the long
speeches of the Athenians.'

I will, I hate, means what my mind and conscience
wills and hates. But my conduct unfortunately goes
the other way. The words *good* and *evil* are absent in
the Greek.

16. *I consent to the law*, that is, my mind and conscience bears out the law. But my will falls in with my
concupiscence for all that.

It is no more I that do it, i.e. my better self protests,
even while permitting itself to be overcome. See the
celebrated picture of the charioteer with his two horses
(reason with the appetites) in Plato, *Phædrus*, 254.

Sin, i.e. concupiscence, *that dwelleth in me.* A man
might say: 'It is not I that drove over the child, but
my horse that ran away with me.' It would be a
question for a jury in such a case, whether the man
had mismanaged the horse, whether he could not have
restrained it at the beginning, also whether he had any
business to be driving out with an animal that he knew
he could not manage. So of concupiscence. It is
increased by mismanagement of oneself: it may be
checked by prayer. Still the principle holds, that God
will never be angry with any man for what was absolutely beyond his power to hinder.

18. *My flesh* here is my sensitive appetite. *That
which is good*, is that which befits man in that which
formally distinguishes him as man, namely, his reason.

Good then here is rational good. Now the sensitive appetite, the seat of the passions,—as such, and apart from any formation that reason, or grace, may give to it,—takes no cognisance of rational good, any more than a swine or an ape does.

The best Greek MSS. have a characteristic idiom : *To will is present to me, but to do that which is good, not,—* sentence ending with *οὔ*, which may throw light on the reading of 1 Cor. xv. 51.

To will is here the mere velleity of the will that fain would stand out against concupiscence, but weakly yields.

To accomplish, say, simply *to do,* as the same word, κατεργάζεσθαι, is properly enough translated in *vv.* 17, 20. *To accomplish* (*perficere,* Vulg.) lends itself rather to the Augustinian interpretation (above, *v.* 14). But *Græcum attende codicem,* as St. Augustine himself says (quoted on *v.* 15).

19, 20. See on *vv.* 15, 17.

21. *I find then a law.* A *law* would be νόμον τινὰ, which perhaps would better suit the explanation to be given, but the Greek is τὸν νόμον, *the law.* The expression usually in St. Paul means the Mosaic law. So all the Fathers understand it here; but hardly any two Fathers explain the text alike. The text in fact has no explanation on that understanding. The mass of modern authority, Catholic and non-Catholic, understands *the law* to mean no more than *the established tendency,* the same which in *vv.* 23, 25, is called *another law in my members,* and *the law of sin.* Thus explained, this much-vexed verse is clear enough.

22. *The inward man* is *the mind* (*vv.* 23, 25), reason and conscience. It is not the same as *the spirit,* which means the soul as the theatre of the operations of grace (Gal. v. 16—25). The man who is here the speaker is man away from grace : therefore the mention of the

inward man in 2 Cor. iv. 16, where St. Paul is really speaking of himself, is not quite a parallel instance.

23. The *other law in my members, the law of sin that is in my members*, is the animal tendency of concupiscence.

Fighting, ἀντιστρατευόμενον, *carrying on a warfare in opposition.* A warfare is not a perpetual fight, but a perpetual menace, with fighting sometimes.

The law of my mind is the law of God, revealed through Moses, borne out by my mind (*v.* 22). To a Gentile, it is simply the law of nature, or the unrevealed law of God, attested by human conscience (ii. 15).

Captivating me, αἰχμαλωτίζοντα, *taking me prisoner,* so that I am *sold under sin* (*v.* 14), as prisoners taken in war of old were sold into slavery. *Captivating* bears another meaning in modern English.

24. *The body of this death* is *the body of sin,* vi. 6, where see notes.

25. *The grace of God,* ἡ χάρις τοῦ θεοῦ. The Vatican MS. has χάρις τῷ θεῷ, *thanks be to God.* The Sinaitic and Alexandrine, εὐχαριστῶ τῷ θεῷ, *I thank God,* which is the received Greek text. It means: *Thanks be to God,* (we have deliverance) *through Jesus Christ our Lord.*

I myself, αὐτὸς ἐγώ, *I by myself,* away from the grace of Christ, *while with the mind,* τῷ μὲν νοΐ, *I serve the law of God, yet with the flesh,* τῇ δὲ σαρκί, *I serve the law of sin.* On this use of μέν and δέ, where the assertion falls principally on the second (the δέ) clause, see note on vi. 17.

Here ends the speech of the unregenerate Jew.

Chapter VIII.

1. There is, therefore, now no condemnation to them who are in Christ Jesus, who walk not according to the flesh. 2. For the law of the Spirit of life, in Christ Jesus, hath delivered me from the law of sin and of death. 3. For what the law could not do, in that it was weak through the flesh, God, sending his own Son in the likeness of sinful flesh, even of sin, condemned sin in the flesh; 4. That the justification of the law might be fulfilled in us, who walk not according to the flesh, but according to the spirit. 5. For they who are according to the flesh relish the things that are of the flesh; but they who are according to the spirit mind the things which are of the spirit. 6. For the wisdom of the flesh is death; but the wisdom of the spirit is life and peace. 7. Because the wisdom of the flesh is an enemy to God; for it is not subject to the law of God, neither can it be. 8. And they who are in the flesh cannot please God. 9. But you are not in the flesh, but in the spirit, if so be that the Spirit of God dwell in you. Now if any man have not the Spirit of Christ, he is none of his. 10. And if Christ be in you, the body indeed is dead because of sin; but the spirit liveth because of justification. 11. And if the Spirit of him who raised up Jesus from the dead dwell in you, he that raised up Jesus Christ from the dead shall quicken also your mortal bodies, because of his Spirit dwelling in you. 12. Therefore, brethren, we are debtors, not to the flesh, to live according to the flesh. 13. For if you live according to the flesh, you shall die: but if by the spirit you mortify the deeds of the flesh, you shall live. 14. For whosoever are led by the Spirit of God, they are the sons of God. 15. For you have not received the spirit of bondage again in fear; but you have received the spirit of adoption of sons, whereby we cry: Abba, (Father.) 16. For the Spirit himself giveth testimony to our spirit, that we are the sons of God. 17. And if sons, heirs also: heirs indeed of God, and joint-heirs with Christ: yet so if we suffer with him, that we may be also glorified with him. 18. For I reckon, that the sufferings of this present time are not worthy to be compared with the glory to come, that shall be revealed in us. 19. For the expectation of the creature waiteth for the revelation of the sons of God. 20. For the creature was made subject to vanity, not willingly, but by reason of him that made it subject in hope; 21. Because the creature also itself shall be delivered from the servitude of corruption, into the liberty of the glory of the children of God. 22. For we know that every creature groaneth, and is in

labour even till now. **23.** And not only it, but ourselves also, who have the firstfruits of the Spirit, even we ourselves groan within ourselves, waiting for the adoption of the sons of God, the redemption of our body. **24.** For we are saved by hope: but hope that is seen, is not hope: for what a man seeth, why doth he hope for? **25.** But if we hope for that which we see not, we wait for it with patience. **26.** Likewise the Spirit also helpeth our infirmity: for we know not what we should pray for as we ought; but the Spirit himself asketh for us with unspeakable groanings. **27.** And he that searcheth the hearts knoweth what the Spirit desireth, because he asketh for the saints according to God. **28.** And we know that to them that love God all things work together unto good, to such as according to purpose are called to be saints. **29.** For whom he foreknew, he also predestinated to be made conformable to the image of his Son, that he might be the firstborn amongst many brethren. **30.** And whom he predestinated, them he also called; and whom he called, them he also justified; and whom he justified, them he also glorified. **31.** What shall we then say to these things? If God be for us, who is against us? **32.** He that spared not even his own Son, but delivered him up for us all, how hath he not also, with him, given us all things? **33.** Who shall lay any thing to the charge of the elect of God? God who justifieth. **34.** Who is he that shall condemn? Christ Jesus who died, yea, who rose also again, who is at the right hand of God, who also maketh intercession for us. **35.** Who then shall separate us from the love of Christ? shall tribulation or distress, or famine, or nakedness, or danger, or persecution, or the sword? **36.** (As it is written: For thy sake we are put to death all the day long; we are accounted as sheep for the slaughter.) **37.** But in all these things we overcome, because of him that hath loved us. **38.** For I am sure that neither death, nor life, nor angels, nor principalities, nor powers, nor things present, nor things to come, nor might, **39.** Nor height, nor depth, nor any other creature, shall be able to separate us from the love of God, which is in Christ Jesus our Lord.

1. *There is now therefore no condemnation*, κατάκριμα, see note on this word, v. 16. The *general condemnation* of the race by reason of Adam's sin, is done away with in the case of *them that are in Christ Jesus*, namely, the baptized (vi. 3, with note). Rightly then is this text quoted by the Council of Trent (sess. 5, cap. 5) in support of the theological axiom, *In renatis nihil odit*

Y

Deus, "in the regenerate there is nothing that God hates."

Who walk not according to the flesh, has been put in from *v.* 4, as MSS. show.

2. As *the law of sin and of death* is original sin and death, so *the law of the Spirit of life* is the Holy Spirit, the Lord and Giver of life, guiding the conduct of the regenerate, in whom He dwells.

The phrase, *in* (through) *Christ Jesus,* is to be taken with the verb, *hath delivered.*

3. *For what the law could not do,* i.e. *in respect of what,* &c., τὸ ἀδύνατον being the nominative or accusative absolute.

It was weak through the flesh. "The law enjoined and fulfilled not, because the flesh, where grace was not, resisted most invincibly" (St. Augustine),—understand, in cases of protracted and severe temptation.

In the likeness of sinful flesh, in this that He was exposed to suffering and death, from which the flesh, or body, of man would have been protected but for original sin. Cf. Eph. ii. 7.

Even of sin. These words are not to be joined with *in the likeness,* nor with *hath condemned,* but with *sending.* The English is faulty in the translation, and the Latin in the punctuation. Translate, *et de peccato,* καὶ περὶ ἁμαρτίας, *and for sin,* just as we have, *Christ died for our sins,* περὶ ἁμαρτιῶν (1 Pet. iii. 18); and *shed for many,* περὶ πολλῶν (Matt. xxvi. 28). Christ then was sent *in the likeness of sinful flesh and for sin.*

Condemned and cast out *sin* by suffering *in the flesh.* We are not to join together *sin in the flesh.*

4. *The justification* (δικαίωμα, say, *righteous observance*) *of the law.* Cf. ii. 26, *the ordinances* (δικαιώματα) *of the law.*

5. *The things that are of the flesh* (Gal. v. 17—21), which are not according to the law.

6. *The wisdom* (or *mind, bent and purpose,* φρόνημα) *of*

the flesh; and similarly, *the mind, bent and purpose of the spirit, the flesh* here being man left to his animal and worldly desires, and *the spirit* man under the guidance of grace.

7. *The wisdom* (bent and purpose) *of the flesh is an enemy to God.* The Latin translator has confounded ἔχθρα, *enmity,* the reading of all the Greek MSS. and Fathers, with the adjective ἐχθρά, *inimica, hostile. The bent and purpose of the flesh is enmity with God.*

Not subject, neither can it be. " What means *cannot be?* Not that man cannot be, not that the soul cannot be, not that the flesh itself, as it is the creature of God, cannot be: but *the wisdom of the flesh* cannot be, vice cannot be, not nature. As if you were to say: ' Lameness is not subject to right walking, neither can it be.' The foot can, but lameness can not. Take away lameness, and you will see right walking: but so long as lameness is, it cannot be right. So, so long as the wisdom of the flesh is, it cannot be subject: let the wisdom of the flesh be no more, and man can be subject " (St. Augustine).

To which we may add that, even in the best Christians, there ever remains *the law of the members fighting against the law of the mind,* though it does not *take them prisoners* (vii. 23). Cf. on Gal. v. 16.

8. *They who are in the flesh cannot please God,* cf. vii. 5, and note. *In the flesh,* that is, in the state described, vii. 8—25, in the corruption of the first Adam, in sin, original and actual; out of the state of grace, and *without Christ* (Eph. ii. 12), and yet within reach of all mere natural gifts, secular education, arts, sciences and literature, laws and politics, commercial prosperity, military glory; yes, and of the mere natural virtues also, legal justice, truthfulness, philanthropy and courage. St. Paul does not say: ' They who are in the flesh can do no natural good : ' but, *They cannot please God,* in such

sort as to surmount sin, and obtain that vision of God for eternity which is promised to the clean of heart (Matt. v. 8).

9. *In the spirit*, in the grace of God, and corresponding with God's graces, the diametric opposite of being *in the flesh*.

If so be that, εἴπερ, *si tamen* (Vulg.), rather, *siquidem*, *if, as I must suppose*. The Spirit of God had been given to them in baptism, and the Apostle says he must suppose they have not already lost the gift by relapsing into their pagan vices.

He is none of his, is too strong a translation of οὗτος οὐκ ἔστιν αὐτοῦ, *hic non est ejus:* it should be simply, *he is not his*, or better still, *he is not of him*. The Christian who has driven the Holy Ghost from his soul by mortal sin, short of loss of faith and actual apostasy (Heb. vi. 4—6; x. 25, 26), is still a sheep of Christ, albeit a lost sheep (*my sheep that was lost*, Luke xv. 6); he is still a member of the Church,—the Church has condemned John Wycliffe, who taught the contrary; and being a member of the Church, he is still so far forth a *member of Christ* (1 Cor. vi. 15; xii. 27; Eph. v. 30), although a dead member, who if he repent not shall finally be *cast forth and wither, and they shall cast him into the fire* (John xv. 6). Remaining still a member, but dead, he is truly said to be *not of Christ*, because *the life of Jesus* (2 Cor. iv. 10, 11), which is the supernatural life, does not flow forth from the Sacred Heart unto him; and also because he is no imitator of Jesus, but rather of the devil, as our Lord told the Jews: *You are of your father the devil, and the desires of your father you will do* (John viii. 44).

The Spirit of God (the Father, 1 Cor. i. 3) is also *the Spirit of Christ*, first, because Christ as Man *sends* Him (John xv. 26), *i.e.* by His merits obtains that He shall be sent (John xiv. 16, 26); secondly, because as Christ is God, and is the Second Person of the Blessed Trinity, the Holy Ghost proceeds from the Father and from Him.

10. *If Christ be in you.* Cf. Col. i. 26, 27, *the mystery, which is Christ in you:* Gal. iv. 19, *until Christ be formed in you.* Christ is where the Spirit of Christ is, by that mystical union spoken of on Rom. vi. 3.

The body indeed . . . but, μὲν . . . δὲ. The English idiom is, *Though the body, . . . yet.* See on vi. 17; vii. 25.

The body was mortal ere ever original sin was, but by a special providence it would have been kept from dying. Now it is called *dead,* since *because of sin* it is not only mortal, but also certain to die.

The spirit (the soul supernaturalised, as in *v.* 6) *liveth* (certainly the reading is, *is life, i.e.* the formal cause of supernatural life).

11. *Spirit* in this verse means the Holy Ghost, The interchange of these two meanings of the word, seen in *vv.* 9, 10, is the reason why the Collects in which the word occurs are sometimes terminated *in unitate ejusdem Spiritus Sancti,* and sometimes the *ejusdem* is omitted. Cf. *v.* 13, *by the Spirit,* or *by the spirit.*

Because of his Spirit, διὰ τὸ πνεῦμα. Authorities are divided between this reading, and διὰ τοῦ πνεύματος, *by agency of his Spirit.*

This verse is an undoubted reference to the resurrection of the body. Cf. vi. 5, 8.

13. *Mortify,* θανατοῦτε, *do to death.* "This doing to death of the deeds of the flesh has to be carried out with patience, not suddenly, but gradually. First they must be abated, in beginners: then, as men begin to advance more ardently and to be filled more abundantly with the Spirit, the deeds of the flesh will begin not only to abate, but to fade away: when men reach the perfect state, so that neither in deed nor in word nor in thought

any indications of sin arise in them, then they are to
be reckoned altogether to have mortified and done to
death the deeds of the flesh " (Origen).

15. *You have not received the spirit of bondage again in
fear*, means, *The Spirit that you have received* (the Holy
Ghost in baptism) *is not a spirit of bondage back unto fear*
(πάλιν εἰς φόβον). In classical Greek the participle ὅν
would be expressed before δουλείας; ' you have not
received a spirit, being one of fear:' just as a Greek
would say, ' I tell you things being true,' for, ' What
I tell you is true.' The same idiom is noticed on
Gal. iv. 8. So 2 Tim. i. 7, *God hath not given us the
spirit of fear*, means, *The spirit that God hath given us,
is not one of fear*. The fear spoken of is that slavish fear
of God, which persists in seeing in him only the
Chastiser.

The spirit of adoption, whereby we cry Abba, Father. See
Gal. iv. 6, with note.

16. *Giveth testimony to our spirit*, better, *giveth testimony
along with our spirit* (συμμαρτυρεῖ).

The assurance founded on this testimony is not
faith, because the testimony itself is not a revelation.
It is no more than a *testimony along with our spirit*, the
voice of the Holy Ghost and of our own soul under
grace, the two speaking in unison. Now, conceivably,
our soul might take both parts, and speak for the Holy
Ghost as well as for itself. In that case the testimony
could not be depended on.

The testimony of which St. Paul speaks, when it
becomes sensible, that is, when it takes the form of
inward joy and comfort, is called by ascetic writers
' consolation.' The description of it in the Rules for
the Discernment of Spirits in the Spiritual Exercises of
St. Ignatius, helps very much to the understanding
of this verse. There are good men, high in God's
grace, without consolation. All good men have to go

without consolation at times.   There is also a false
consolation, which may delude a sinner, who is not
sincere with God, but never permanently delude a man
of good will.

The Council of Trent teaches: " As no person ought
to doubt of the mercy of God, of the merit of Christ, of
the virtue and strength of the sacraments, so any one
when he looks at himself, at his own weakness and
insufficiency, may entertain both fear and dread of his
own grace; since no one, with a certainty of faith,
beneath which nothing false can be concealed, can know
that he has received the grace of God " (sess. 6, cap. 9).

Still, short of the certainty of faith, as Suarez
teaches, " we can attain to such a degree of certainty
as, according to the ordinary course of things, morally
speaking, should exclude all alarm."   And he adds:
" I deem it in the highest degree probable, that it is
possible for a good man to reach a state of virtue, in
which he may be no less assured of the remission of
the sins he may actually have committed than he is
of the remission of his original sin " (Suarez, *De gratia,*
l. 9, c. 11, n. 10).

Such is the practical sufficiency of *the testimony the
Spirit giveth that we are the sons of God.*

17. *Heirs of God,* the subjective genitive, as we might
say, *God's heirs;* and also the objective genitive, as it
were, *heirs to God:* for God Himself is our inheritance,
since *we shall see him as he is* (1 John iii. 2: cf. 1 Cor. xiii.
12).   This inheritance we enter upon on condition of
our union with Christ, first in suffering, every man his
own trial in this life, then in glory, every man his own
crown (1 Cor. xv. 41, 42; Luke xxiv. 26).

18. *I reckon,* λογίζομαι.   St. Paul had some acquaintance with both sides of the reckoning,—of *sufferings,*
2 Cor. xi. 23—27,—and even of *the glory to come* he had
had some foretaste (2 Cor. xii. 2, 3).

Not worthy to be compared with, οὐκ ἄξια πρὸς, literally, *standing not in the balance against.* The adjective ἄξιος is from ἄγω in the sense of *I weigh.* Of sufferings in this comparison our Elizabethan writers would have said that they "kick the beam."

√ *Revealed in us,* because glory is but the revealing and uncovering (ἀποκαλυφθῆναι) of the sanctifying grace that is in us already. Hence sanctifying grace is itself called *glory,* iii. 23.

20. *The creature,* ἡ κτίσις. It is a great question what is meant by this word in this and the next two verses. Many will have it to mean the whole of the irrational creation, all beings below angels and men. Hence they draw a picture of the renovation of the material world, of the vegetable world, and the lower animals, a renovation that is to have place when there shall be *a new heaven and a new earth* (Apoc. xxi. 1). No man can take upon himself to say that such renovation will not take place: at the same time to assert it on the strength of these three verses, is to build upon an interpretation that is far from certain, perhaps even less probable.

Probably, by *creature* we should understand simply *mankind.* The word κτίσις sometimes means *creation, i.e.* the *creative act,* as in 2 Pet. iii. 4. Sometimes it is the *creature* as distinguished from the Creator, as above, i. 25. In Col. i. 15, 16, it means *men and angels.* In 2 Pet. ii. 13, we find the expression, *human creature, i.e.* mankind. Finally in Col. i. 23; and Mark xvi. 15, the word *creature* by itself means mankind only, since men only are the recipients of the gospel: *the gospel which you have heard, which is preached among all creatures,* ἐν πάσῃ τῇ κτίσει, *under heaven: preach the gospel to every creature* (πάσῃ τῇ κτίσει).

Expectation, ἀποκαραδοκία, literally, *waiting with neck outstretched.*

The revelation of the sons of God in the resurrection. On the word *revelation*, cf. note on *v.* 18. Our Lord was shown for what He really was on the day of His resurrection (Acts xiii. 33); and so, when their day comes, shall be shown *they that are of Christ* (1 Cor. xv. 23).

Mankind at large expect this *revelation, the redemption of our body* (*v.* 23), not definitely and expressly, but vaguely and confusedly, in that mankind are always looking for a better day to dawn for the race,—are ever catching at the words of prophets who promise them, *the morning cometh* (Isaias xxi. 12). This *expectation*, which had grown particularly intense just at the time that the gospel was first preached, was a great pre-disposing cause of the spread of the gospel. It is one of the bulwarks of Christianity to this hour, and ever will be. It has likewise nourished innumerable delusions, such as the Milennium, Humanitarianism, Socialism; to say nothing of the hopes built on Education, Reform, Civilisation, Progress, Evolution.

To vanity, to an aimless existence, to living for other ends than that for which man was created. This *vanity* is the whole theme of the book of Ecclesiastes. It took its commencement from the sin of Adam; and as that sin was not done by the actual will and consent of Adam's posterity, therefore mankind are said to be *subject to vanity, not willingly, but by reason of him who made it* (*the creature*, mankind) *subject, i.e.* by reason of Adam and his first disobedience. This understanding of τὸν ὑποτάξαντα, *him who made it subject*, to be Adam, has the authority of St. John Chrysostom.

In hope. No stop should follow these words. They belong to the next verse, *in hope that*, &c., and should be preceded by a comma.

21. *Because*, Vulgate *quia*, and the Sinaitic manuscript has διότι. But the better authenticated reading is ὅτι: so we have ἐπ' ἐλπίδι ὅτι, *in hope that*. The same

sense however may be obtained from the Vulgate, *in hope, because*.

The servitude of corruption, the bondage and misery of sin, original and actual, described vii. 8—25. Not that all mankind who now are shall be delivered from this bondage in the day of the resurrection: the wicked, who have thrown in their lot with the rebel angels, shall share their doom (Matt. xxv. 41 ; 2 Pet. ii. 4 ; Jude 6): but the mankind who shall then *possess the land* (Matt. v. 4), the race of men who shall inherit the *new earth* (2 Pet. iii. 13), they shall be delivered. The reprobate are the refuse and offscourings of humanity, and are left out of count accordingly. In the chapter on the resurrection (1 Cor. xv.), they are not so much as alluded to (at least according to what seems to be the true reading of *ib.* 51).

The liberty of the glory of the children of God is in its fulness in heaven, and of this the Apostle speaks. It may be observed however that this verse was in large measure fulfilled by the preaching of the gospel, and the deliverance of mankind from the darkness of heathenism and the bondage of Judaism to the liberty and light of Christianity (Gal. iv. 31 ; v. 1).

22. *Every creature groaneth and is in labour.* It needs no commentator to point out how true these words are of *every creature*, πάση κτίσις, in the sense of *all mankind*, from the first dawn of history *till now*.

23. It might have been thought that this heart-ache of humanity,—this ἀποκαραδοκία, or eager looking out for absent good (*v.* 19); this groaning and travailing (*v.* 22), —would have been cured by conversion to Christianity. The Apostle shows that the Gospel is not a cure, only a mitigation, and an earnest of perfect cure to come. Even to the Christian this life remains a period of groaning and waiting, but waiting for a definite and assured good,

Firstfruits of the Spirit (Eph. i. 13, 14; 2 Cor. i. 22).
As the payment of firstfruits signified that the whole
field belonged to God, and was a pledge that the entire
crop should be used according to His good pleasure
(Deut. xxvi.), so is the Holy Ghost given to us in this
life as an earnest of the perfect possession of God in
heaven.

24. *We are saved by hope, i.e.* our salvation is in hope,
not yet consummated,—*spe, non re,* as St. Augustine often
says.

What a man seeth, why doth he hope for? is hardly
English. Render: *What doth a man hope for, that he
seeth?* A better reading however is the reading of the
Vatican manuscript: ὃ γὰρ βλέπει, τίς ἐλπίζει; *who hopeth
for what he seeth?*

26. *As we ought,* as the context shows, refers not to
the manner but to the matter of our prayer. Only in
general do we know what is good for us: in particular
we are often mistaken in our petitions, as was St. Paul
himself on a notable occasion, 2 Cor. xii. 8, 9.

The Spirit himself (i.e. of Himself, preventing us with
His gratuitous grace) *asketh for us with unspeakable groanings.* "What is *asketh for us* but *maketh us ask?* To ask
with groanings is a sure sign of need, but it is impious
to suppose the Holy Spirit to be in need of anything.
But the word *asketh* means that He makes us ask, and
breathes upon us the impulse of asking and groaning,
according to the text (Matt. x. 20): *It is not you that
speak, but the Spirit of your Father that speaketh in you*"
(St. Augustine).

Unspeakable (or *unuttered*) *groanings.* A parent, himself
an uneducated man, brings his boy to school, and says
to the schoolmaster: 'I want you to make this boy a
scholar: prepare him for the University.' Thus the
end is laid down in general: but of the particular
course of studies to be pursued, the parent knows

nothing: all these details he leaves to the schoolmaster. Such details are by him *unuttered*, and even *unutterable* and *unspeakable*, because of his ignorance. So, moved strongly by the Holy Ghost, we desire and groan for salvation : but the detail of means that will lead to our individual salvation is, on many points, beyond our knowledge. Our *groanings* then, in respect of these particular means, are *unuttered* and *unspeakable*, because of our ignorance of detail.

27. *He that searcheth hearts* (God,—Psalm vii. 10; Apoc. ii. 23), *knoweth what the Spirit desireth, i.e.* understands the full meaning of the petitions which the Holy Ghost prompts us to make, though we understand our own requests only in the vague, or even positively misunderstand them. One may think of a loyal-hearted man, who hates Catholics, praying that he may find the true way to salvation, or of a child praying to be a priest.

He asketh for the saints, i.e. moves the saints to ask for themselves. *Saints* here (as in 1 Cor. i. 2, &c.) means all true followers of Christ.

According to God, things which lie within God's purpose to grant us in order to our salvation. Such things the Holy Spirit moves us to pray for ; and such prayers are always heard (Matt. vii. 7, 8 ; John xiv. 13, 14 ; 1 John v. 14, 15). When we pray for those things, we pray *as we ought* (*v.* 26). See St. Thomas, 2a 2æ, q. 83, art. 15, ad 2 (*Aquinas Ethicus*, vol. ii. p. 128).

28. *To them that love God.* St. Paul does not say, 'to them that believe in God,' or 'to them that are once justified.'

All things work together unto good. The Vatican and Alexandrine manuscripts alone read : *God worketh all things together unto good.* St. Paul is thinking especially of sufferings and persecutions, as appear from *vv.* 17, 18, 35—37.

The latter part of this verse should be read simply, *to such as according to purpose are called*, τοῖς κατὰ πρόθεσιν κλητοῖς οὖσιν, which is the reading of all the Greek MSS. St. Augustine and other Latin Fathers also omit *sanctis* (*saints*). *Called* in the New Testament means *those who have been called and have come* (Matt. xx. 16; xxii. 14; above, i. 6, 7). So Clement of Alexandria: "Whereas all men have been called (κεκλημένοι), such as have been willing to hear are termed *called* (κλητοί)" (*Strom* i. 18).

According to purpose. The human purpose of those called, say the Greek Fathers, for which use of the word there is authority in 2 Tim. iii. 10; Acts xi. 23; xxvii. 13. The divine purpose, or predestination, of God calling, say the Latin Fathers, according to ix. 11; Eph. i. 11; iii. 11; 2 Tim. i. 9. The latter opinion is more probable from the citations.

Predestination is either to grace in this life, or to glory in the next. That predestination to grace is antecedent to any foreseen merits, is a dogma of the Catholic faith, clearly taught in this Epistle, iv. 1—6; ix. 11, 12. Whether predestination to glory is also antecedent to any foreseen merits, or is consequent upon such merits, theologians dispute, and interpret St. Paul variously.

After his manner (see note on *v.* 21), St. Paul speaks as though all whom he was addressing were predestined to glory. Yet elsewhere he sufficiently indicates the danger of Christians falling away, 1 Cor. ix. 24—x. 12; Phil. ii. 12. In practice, the way to go to heaven is to live as if you were going there,—to *run* (1 Cor. ix. 26) as if you meant to win; to *fight* (*ib.*) as if you had no idea of being beaten (cf. *Imitation of Christ*, i. 25, 2). And similarly of the other place.

29, 30. *Foreknew*, προέγνω; more probably, *foreapproved*, for which sense of γιγνώσκω see on 1 Cor. viii. 3; Gal. iv. 9; Rom. vii. 15. Cf. Nahum i. 11, *the Lord is good, and knoweth them that hope in him.*

These two verses are difficult in construction, as
well as in doctrine. First as to the construction. The
first thing to notice is the thrice-repeated pronoun in
v. 30, τούτους, τούτους, τούτους, *hos, hos, illos.* But before
καὶ προώρισεν (*et praedestinavit*) there is no pronoun. This
should make us hesitate to supply the pronoun, and to
translate the καὶ (*et*) by *also* instead of by *and.* Then
again it is well known that the Greek δέ, and sometimes
the Latin *autem,* is used to take up the thread of a
sentence, like the English, *well then, I say.* For this use
of δέ see 2 Cor. v. 6, 8; x. 1, 2. We may then remove
the comma after προέγνω (*praescivit*), and construe thus:
*Whom he foreapproved and predestinated to be made conformable
to the image of his Son, that he might be the firstborn amongst
many brethren——whom I say he predestinated, them he also
called.* And this construction seems the more probable.
It makes *praescivit et praedestinavit* to express one idea,
the second verb bearing out the sense of the first. Only
the idea gains force and emphasis by the doubling of
the verb.

For doctrine it may be sufficient to explain the
literal meaning of the verses, and leave further discussion of predestination to theologians.

He called refers to an effectual call to the faith. See
note on *v.* 28 and on 1 Cor. i. 2. Comparing this with
Acts xiii. 48: *And they believed, as many as were appointed
unto life everlasting,* we have the interpretation: *Whom
he predestined to life everlasting, them he called* effectually
to the faith: *them he also justified* in baptism.

Conformable to the image of his Son. The Son of
God *took the form of a servant* (Phil. ii. 7), that, as the
Church prays in the Christmas Mass, *in ejus inveniamur
forma,* " we may be found in His form," which is
the form of God (Phil. ii. 6: cf. John i. 12, 14). We
shall bear the form of God, as perfectly as human
creatures are capable of bearing it, in the day of the

resurrection, when our whole humanity shall be conformed to the type of Christ risen: see 1 Cor. xv.
45—49; Phil. iii. 21. This supposes a previous conformity of our mortal life with His mortal life of
obedience and humiliation (Phil. ii. 5—8).

He predestinated, he called, he justified, he glorified, are
all in Greek the aorist tense, what is called the gnomic
aorist, which makes an assertion irrespective of time,
and is just as well rendered by the English present, *he
predestinates, he calls, he justifies, he glorifies.*

31. *What then shall we say?* seems to have been a
favourite connecting link in St. Paul's discourses. Every
speaker feels the need of such links. It occurs, vi. 1;
vii. 7; viii. 31; ix. 14, 30.

God for us, who against us? *Us* and *we* from this to the
end of the chapter mean *the elect of God* (*v.* 33). See
final note on *v.* 28.

32. *Spared not even his own Son,* some reminiscence of
Gen. xxii. 16: *Thou hast not spared thine only-begotten son
for my sake.*

Hath he not given, donavit, is a mistake for *donabit,* the
old Latin reading; χαρίσεται, the future, being the only
Greek reading; *will he not give?*

33. *Who shall accuse? God that justifieth.* This English
seems to imply that God will be the accuser, which is
very far from the meaning. The Greek and the Latin
mean: *God is he that justifieth.* That is to say: 'When
God pronounces and renders the elect just, innocent
and clear of sin, who shall venture to accuse them?'

St. Augustine reads with an interrogation: *God that
justifieth?* (shall He be the accuser?). But God is
never the accuser: He is the Judge.

34. *Christ Jesus that died.* Again the meaning is:
Christ Jesus is he that died, &c. This sentence also
St. Augustine reads interrogatively.

Christ—maketh intercession for us. An interesting text

in view of the development of the devotion known as
the Apostleship of Prayer.   Cf. Heb. vii. 25.   Without
prejudice to His Divinity, for of the Divinity the text is
not spoken ; and without prejudice to the glory of His
Humanity, enthroned, as the Fathers say, on the very
throne of the Godhead, Jesus Christ still *maketh intercession for us,*—as our *Advocate* (1 John ii. 1) and *High Priest*
(Heb. viii. 1), " by presenting to the sight of His Father
the Humanity, which He has assumed for us, and the
mysteries enacted in that Humanity," as St. Thomas
says, notably His Crucifixion, of which He still bears
the print of the wounds (John xx. 20, 25, 27).

35. The connecting particle *then* should be away,
according to the best authorities.   The three inter-
rogatories are more impressive for the asyndeton : *Who
shall accuse ?   Who shall condemn ?   Who shall separate ?*

The love of Christ (cf. v. 5, *the charity of God)* is not
exclusively either our love of Christ, or Christ's love of
us : it is the love of friendship, which is mutual and
includes both.

36. Psalm xliii. 22.

37. *We overcome,* ὑπερνικῶμεν, *we are victorious " with
advantages."*

*Because of him that hath loved us, and hath washed
us from our sins in His blood* (Apoc. i. 5).   *Because of*
(*propter,* διὰ τὸν ἀγαπήσαντα) means *thanks to the help of.*
But the three best Greek MSS. read διὰ τοῦ ἀγαπήσαντος
(*per*), *by the doing of,* which says the same thing more
directly.

38. *I am sure* even with the certainty of faith, as it
is question of the salvation of the predestinate and elect,
of whom our Lord says : *No man shall pluck them out of
my hand* (John x. 28).

Neither death nor life, neither the brief agony of
martyrdom, nor the longer agony of a confessor of the
faith.

Nor angels nor principalities, no evil angels, whether of lower or higher degree.

Nor powers, probably an interpolation.

Things present, painful or delightful.

Things to come, promises or threats.

Nor might, read οὔτε δυνάμεις, *nor powers:* understand the powers of this world.

Nor height nor depth, &c.   We cannot particularise any further.   St. Paul's inspired eloquence outruns our comments.

———

CHAPTER IX.

1. I speak the truth in Christ, I lie not, my conscience bearing me witness in the Holy Ghost, **2.** That I have great sadness, and continual sorrow in my heart. **3.** For I wished myself to be an anathema from Christ, for my brethren, who are my kinsmen according to the flesh : **4.** Who are Israelites ; to whom belongeth the adoption of children, and the glory, and the covenant, and the giving of the law, and the service of God, and the promises ; **5.** Whose are the fathers, and of whom is Christ according to the flesh, who is over all things, God blessed for ever.   Amen. **6.** Not as though the word of God hath failed.   For all are not Israelites that are of Israel : **7.** Neither are all they who are the seed of Abraham children : but, In Isaac shall thy seed be called ; **8.** That is to say, not they who are the children of the flesh are the children of God : but they that are the children of the promise are counted for the seed. **9.** For this is the word of the promise ; According to this time will I come ; and Sara shall have a son. **10.** And not only she ; but when Rebecca also had conceived at once, by Isaac our father. **11.** For when the children were not yet born, nor had done any good or evil (that the purpose of God according to election might stand), **12.** Not of works, but of him that called, it was said to her : **13.** The elder shall serve the younger ; as it is written : Jacob I have loved, but Esau I have hated. **14.** What shall we say then ?   Is there injustice with God ?   God forbid. **15.** For he saith to Moses : I will have mercy on whom I have mercy ; and I will show mercy to whom I will show mercy. **16.** So then it is not of him that willeth, nor of him that runneth, but of God that showeth mercy. **17.** For the Scripture saith to Pharao : To this

z

purpose have I raised thee up, that I may show my power in thee, and that my name may be declared throughout all the earth. **18.** Therefore he hath mercy on whom he will, and whom he will he hardeneth. **19.** Thou wilt say therefore to me: Why doth he then find fault? For who resisteth his will? **20.** O man, who art thou that repliest against God? Shall the thing formed say to him that formed it: Why hast thou made me thus? **21.** Or hath not the potter power over the clay, of the same lump to make one vessel unto honour, and another unto dishonour? **22.** And if God, willing to show his wrath, and to make his power known, endured with much patience vessels of wrath, fitted to destruction, **23** That he might show the riches of his glory upon the vessels of mercy, which he hath prepared unto glory, **24.** Even us, whom also he hath called, not of the Jews only, but also of the gentiles; **25.** As he saith in Osee: I will call them my people, that were not my people; and her beloved, that was not beloved; and her that had not obtained mercy, one that hath obtained mercy. **26.** And it shall be, in the place where it was said to them: You are not my people; there they shall be called the children of the living God. **27.** And Isaias crieth out concerning Israel: If the number of the children of Israel be as the sand of the sea, a remnant shall be saved. **28.** For he shall finish his word, and cut it short in justice; because a short word shall the Lord make upon the earth. **29.** And as Isaias foretold: Unless the Lord of sabaoth had left us a seed, we had been made as Sodom, and we had been like unto Gomorrha. **30.** What then shall we say? That the gentiles, who sought not after justice, have attained to justice, even the justice that is of faith: **31.** But Israel, in pursuing the law of justice, is not come to the law of justice. **32.** Why so? Because they sought it not of faith, but as it were of works: for they stumbled at the stumbling-stone; **33.** As it is written: Behold I lay in Sion a stumbling-stone and a rock of scandal: and whosoever believeth in him shall not be confounded.

With this chapter commences the second part of the Epistle. A new thought has seized upon the Apostle's mind. He has just been describing the happy assurance of the elect. By contrast there occurs to him how that his own kith and kin, the Jewish people, have become reprobate. Thirty years have elapsed since the death and resurrection of Christ; and already the prophecy of Daniel is manifestly realised in the

Jews: *The people that shall deny him shall not be his* (Dan.
ix. 26). Hence the outburst of anguish with which this
chapter opens.

1. *Witness in the Holy Ghost*, who is *the Spirit of truth*
(John xiv. 17).

3. *I wished myself to be an anathema from Christ.* On
the word *anathema* see on 1 Cor. xvi. 22. *I wished* does
not represent faithfully the Greek ἐβουλόμην, which is
equivalent to ἐβουλόμην ἄν, the conditional tense of an
unfulfilled condition, and means *I could wish* (were I
called upon to do so). The meaning then is: ' I could
wish, were it necessary, to be accursed myself and cast
off from Christ, so that my brethren, the Jews, could be
brought to join Him.' Instead of Paul being elect
(viii. 38, 39), and the Jewish people reprobate, let Paul,
if need be, become reprobate so that they be elect.

As to the morality of this wish, we may observe:
first, that it is wrong to wish, even with a will of
inefficacious desire, for anything that is in itself sinful.
But St. Paul here does not wish for anything sinful.
He could wish, he says, not to sin, but to bear that
separation from Christ which is the result and punishment of sin, even as Christ Himself, remaining all-holy
and all-pure, for us was *made sin* and *made a curse* (2 Cor.
v. 21 ; Gal. iii. 13, where see notes).

Secondly. There are events, not in themselves
sinful, yet which we cannot bring about except by
sinful means. To desire such events with an efficacious
desire would be a sin, because it would imply a com-
placency also in the employment of those sinful means.
But to desire such an event with an inefficacious desire,
while abhorring the means, is not of itself a sin—though
it may be for us not a safe thing to do, as it may tempt
us to approval of these wicked means. Such an event
would be the death of a persecutor of the Church.
And such an event is the separation from Christ, which

St. Paul here desires with a conditional and inefficacious desire,—certainly without any thought of ever using the only means to such a separation, which is grievous sin.

Nor, thirdly, can it be contended that St. Paul here sins against charity to himself, whom he was bound to love more than his neighbours and brethren the Jews (St. Thomas, 2a 2æ, q. 26, art. 4 ; *Aquinas Ethicus*, i. 366). For a man is bound to love God even more than himself (*ib*. art. 3 ; i. 365). And here, out of the exceeding great love he bore to Christ his Lord and God (*v.* 5), seeing that the salvation of many souls is more glorious to God our Saviour than the salvation of one, St. Paul was willing, if need be, to forego his own salvation to bring in to Christ the multitude of his brethren. Cf. the prayer of Moses, Exod. xxxii. 31, 32. Rightly therefore does St. Chrysostom extol this as the highest mark of St. Paul's great love for Christ. Thus he paraphrases it : " I would consent to be separated, not from the love of Christ [viii. 35],—impossible, for he was doing this for His love—but from His enjoyment and glory, that my Lord might be no more blasphemed."

4. *The adoption.* Not that spiritual adoption spoken of, viii. 15, but what we may call a political adoption, by which the people of Israel were God's *peculiar possession above all people* (Exod. xix. 5 ; Deut. xiv. 2). Cf. Osee xi. 1 : *Because Israel was a child and I loved him, and I called my son out of Egypt.* This political adoption of the *Israel according to the flesh* (1 Cor. x. 18) was a *figure* (1 Cor. x. 11) of the spiritual adoption of *the Israel of God* (Gal. vi. 16).

The glory, the Shechinah, or brightness, the visible mark of God's presence in *the tabernacle of the testimony* (Exod. xl. 32—36), and afterwards in the Holy of Holies (3 Kings viii. 6—12). Cf. Ezechiel x. It was lost at the destruction of the first temple by Nabuchodonsor, and seems never to have appeared again. Psalm lxxxiv. 10, is a prayer for its return.

The testament; a better supported reading is *the testaments,* i.e. *the tables of the testament* (Heb. ix. 4), which were in the ark of the covenant, *i.e. the two tables of stone* (3 Kings viii. 9), given to Moses, containing the ten commandments (Exod. xxxiv. 28). These were the "moral precepts" of the Mosaic Law.

The giving of the law, rather in one word, *the legisla-tion,* νομοθεσία, refers to the "judicial precepts" of the Mosaic Law, regulating social usage and civil procedure.

The service, λατρεία, as we say, *Divine Service,* the "ceremonial precepts" of the Mosaic Law.

The promises, Deut. xxviii. 1—14; xxx.; xxxiii.: but especially the promise of the Messias, Deut. xviii. 15; Acts iii. 22—26.

5. *The fathers,* the patriarchs, Abraham, Isaac, Jacob (Acts vii. 32).

Christ, . . . *who is over all things, God blessed for ever.* ὁ χριστός, ὁ ὢν ἐπὶ πάντων Θεὸς εὐλογητὸς εἰς τοὺς αἰῶνας. As the passage stands, it is an express testimony to the Divinity of Christ, to which St. Paul bears other witness, Phil. ii. 6; Col. i. 16, 17; Tit. ii. 13. And so it is understood by some forty Fathers of the first six centuries, quoted by Cardinal Franzelin in his dis-cussion of this text (*De Verbo Incarnato,* pp. 71—82). Attempt is made to thwart this evidence by putting a full stop either at *flesh* or at *things,* and so making what follows a pious ejaculation to the glory of God. Against which notable device we may quote the well-known story of the nuns who ended at *dicitur* the rubric, *Hic non dicitur Gloria Patri.* The doxology, or giving of glory to God, comes well at the end of an Epistle (xvi. 27; 2 Tim. iv. 18). Above, i. 25, it is put in as a sort of reparation, both for what has been

mentioned and for the odious subject presently to be
introduced. In 1 Tim. i. 17, it is St. Paul's thanksgiving for his own conversion, of which he has been
just speaking. And in all these cases it comes in
without ambiguity. Here, if the received interpretation
of the Fathers is right, the dignity of the Israelites, *of
whom is Christ according to the flesh*, is vastly heightened
by the clear statement of the Divinity of Christ, and an
Amen of praise to Christ as God. But if this is not the
sense of the author, there is, first, a most unfortunate
ambiguity, to which St. Paul, jealous alike as Jew and
as Christian of the honour due to *the only God*, cannot
have been blind. Secondly, the doxology is out of
place, and not to be looked for from a man who has
just said : *I have great sorrow and continual sadness in my
heart (v.* 2). Thirdly, this would be an exception to the
legal rule, that a document is to be read in its obvious
and natural sense, and in the sense given to it by
tradition, unless cogent reason be shown for setting
aside that obvious sense and that traditional interpretation. But here no reason is forthcoming, except the
reluctance of a certain school to admit the Divinity of
Christ, or any other Divinity but what they themselves
constitute.

6. *Not as though the word of God hath failed.* This
was the objection of the Jews against Christianity, that
if Christianity was true, God was false, in that His
promises to the Jewish people had failed, and a world
of Gentiles and sinners had stolen into the place of
favour reserved for Israel. The answer is that *all are
not Israelites* (or as the best Greek MSS. read, *all are not
Israel*), *who are of Israel.* It is the distinction which we
saw before between *Israel according to the flesh* (1 Cor.
x. 18) and *the Israel of God* (Gal. vi. 16). See on Gal.
iii. 7, 9, 26, 29; iv. 23, 28. The promises were made,
absolutely, to the latter, not to the former.

The first four words of this sentence in Greek, οὐχ οἶον δὲ ὅτι, are not easy to translate. The best explanation is that οὐχ οἶον is a later Greek idiom, equal to οὐχ οἶον ἂν ῥαδίως γένοιτο, "not a thing that easily would happen." Translate according: *It is not a thing to be thought of, that,* &c.

7. *In Isaac shall thy seed be called*, Gen. xxi. 12.

8. *Children of the flesh, children of the promise.* Ismael, born in the ordinary course of nature, is the type of the former. Isaac, born of a *body now dead* and of a *dead womb* (iv. 19, see notes), is the type of the latter. See also on Gal. iv. 23—29.

9. *According to this time, i.e.* about this time next year. Gen. xviii. 10—14, which see.

10. This verse should be read as follows: *And not only she* [had two sons, one of whom was preferred to the other], *but Rebecca also, having conceived of one husband, who was Isaac our father.* The Rheims version in the first edition of 1582 has: *And not only she* [had two sons, &c., as above], *but Rebecca also conceiving of one copulation, of Isaac our father.* This renders the Vulgate correctly. But it is certain that the Vulgate reading, *ex uno concubitu habens, Isaac patris nostri,* is an error, for which we should substitute the reading of the older Latin versions, *ex uno concubitum habens Isaac patre nostro,* which answers to the unvaried Greek reading, ἐξ ἑνὸς κοιτὴν ἔχουσα Ἰσαὰκ τοῦ πατρὸς ἡμῶν, the English of which is given above.

11, 12. There should be either no parenthesis, or the words, *that the purpose of God according to election might stand, not of works, but of him that calleth,* should be all put in parenthesis together, for they are to be taken together.

The elder (Esau) *shall serve the younger* (Jacob). Gen. xxv. 23.

13. The whole passage, Malachy i. 2—4, should be read. Briefly it comes to this, that God has been

willing to restore the descendants of Jacob, the Jews, after their captivity, while the land of Edom and its people, the sons of Esau (Gen. xxv. 30), is never to recover its prosperity.

As regards, *I have loved, I have hated*, according to a well-known Hebrew idiom, it means no more than : ' I have preferred one to the other.' So we read that Jacob *loved Rachael more than Lia*, and immediately, that *God seeing that Lia was hated* (Gen. xxix. 30, 31). Again our Lord's words : *He that hateth not his father cannot be my disciple* (Luke xviii. 26) appear in St. Matthew (Matt. x. 37), *He that loveth his father more than me is not worthy of me*. Thus *Isaac blessed Jacob and Esau* (Heb. xi. 20), but Jacob more (Gen. xxvii. 38—40). Of course *to hate* means *to hate*, in Hebrew as in any other language, and the Jews were good haters. This use of *to hate* for *to love less* is when the word is used relatively, not abso-lutely. So an Englishman says he loves riding, and hates walking, which means he will never walk when he can well ride : yet he will often walk when he might sit still.

Nothing is said here (nor indeed in Heb. xii. 16, 17) of Jacob being predestinate and elect, nor of Esau being reprobate and doomed to damnation; but only of their temporal fortunes, as types of the spiritual differences that were to obtain among the Jews, all brothers, come of one stock, yet some believing in the Christ and being saved, others rejecting their Saviour and being lost.

14. *Is there injustice with God ?* in calling one effectually to the faith, and leaving another in Judaism [or paganism, or heresy], apart from any antecedent merits in either party. Cf. iv. 4, 5, with notes, as to the gratuitousness of this call.

15. Exod. xxxiii. 19. As in many verses of the Old Testament, the second part is merely the first in other

words. Literally the Greek runs: *I will have mercy on whomsoever I have mercy; and will have pity on whomsoever I have pity.*

16. *So then it is not of him that willeth, nor of him that runneth,* that he is converted to Christianity, *but of God that showeth mercy.* Once more we have the statement, that no acts of will or of outward work can merit for any man the grace of his first justification by faith and baptism. This verse therefore is not at all parallel to, nor yet in contradiction with, 1 Cor. ix. 24: *So run that you may obtain:* for that is an exhortation to Christians to correspond with the graces given, and by good works, done in grace and by grace, to merit heaven.

17. Exod. ix. 16, which see. *I have raised thee,* ἐξήγειρά σε, *excitavi te,* Vulg. (better, *suscitavi te*), means, *I have raised thee to the throne.* So the word is used in Zach. xi. 16: *I will raise up a shepherd in the land,* ἐξεγείρω ποιμένα, a high priest or king. And 1 Kings ii. 35: *And I will raise me up a faithful priest.*

Those who choose to understand *excitavi te,* "I have excited thee to sin," create difficulties for themselves.

Just as God, foreseeing that the Jews in their wickedness would crucify His Divine Son, ordained that crucifixion to man's salvation; so having set Pharao on the throne, and foreseeing that he would not obey the Divine command to let the people of Israel go, God determined to use his obstinacy as an occasion for displaying His own power, and making the exodus of the people of Israel memorable to all posterity.

18. *He hath mercy on whom he will,* a repetition of *v.* 15.

Whom he will he hardeneth. This is implied in *v.* 15. The term *hardeneth* is taken from Exodus; and it is worth while seeing how it is used there. We read nine times of the Lord hardening Pharao's heart (Exod. iv. 21; vii. 3; ix. 12; x. 1, 20, 27; xiv. 4, 8, 17): seven times of Pharao's heart being hardened (vii. 13, 22;

viii. 19, 32 ; ix. 7, 35 ; xiii. 15) : once of Pharao's hardening his own heart (viii. 15). These are all so many
versions of the same fact. Pharao's heart was hardened :
he was obstinate in disobeying God : his obstinacy was
of his own choosing, yet in some sense God rendered
him obstinate, and that in two ways. First, foreseeing
that, for all the strong persuasions employed to move
his heart (as detailed, Exod. v.—xi.), Pharao would not
be mollified, God would not use stronger means from
the first to obtain his consent to let the people go, that
consent which He finally wrung from him by slaying
the firstborn (Exod. xii. 29—32). Secondly, seeing that
Pharao chose to be obdurate, God took occasion of that
obduracy for an extraordinary display of His power, a
display to be remembered by the Hebrew people with
awe and gratitude down to the latest times (Exod.
xv. 1—21 ; Psalm civ. 26—38, &c.).

So in regard of the obdurate Jews, who were
unmoved by the preaching of Christ and His Apostles.
God hardened them in this sense, that, foreseeing how
all the outward persuasions, and all the inward knock-
ings of His Holy Spirit at their hearts, which He
intended to employ, with a real desire for their conversion, would prove inefficacious, He was content with
these persuasions and solicitations, and would not press
them further, as He might. Where it is to be observed
that God communicates Himself to a man little by little,
as He finds him faithful ; and withdraws little by little
from the man who is unfaithful. The first step may be
to listen patiently to a preacher, who is God's messenger,
but without being convinced. The second step may be
to attend to some slight questionings of conscience, and
pray about them. The third may be to ask further
information of the Church, and so on. If a man will
not take the first step, God may refuse him the grace
which would have carried him to the second. A chain

of successive infidelities may provoke God finally to withhold that abundant flow of grace, without which it is not indeed impossible for the man to be converted, but God foresees that actually the conversion will never take place. This then is God's *hardening* of the sinner, in the Pauline sense of *hardening*: it is the holding back of any special abundance of grace, with the foreknowledge that, unless specially abundant, the grace given will not be efficacious. And such *hardening* the sinner draws upon himself by rejecting time after time God's earlier advances.

These remarks apply to conversions to the Catholic faith in modern times: also to the converting and reclaiming of bad Catholics from a state of sin to the state of grace.

The *hardening* of Henry VIII. is an historical instance.

19. The difficulty is formed upon the previous verse, which shows both submissive and refractory men coming under the will and disposal of God: hence it is asked, how God can find fault with any man, since His will rules all. A general reply, based upon the *power* of God, is given in *vv.* 20, 21. A more particular reply, based upon the *patience*, or rather *longsuffering* of God, appears in *v.* 22. The entire answer, abrupt and obscure to a degree, shows the need not of inspired Scripture alone, but of commentators and theologians to explain it, and of an infallible Church to check those commentators.

20. *O man, nay rather who art thou?* is the Greek. The Vulgate omits *nay rather*.

21. We may gain some preliminary glimpse of St. Paul's mind by reading these parallel passages: Isaias xxix. 16; xlv. 9, 10; Jerem. xviii. 1—10; Wisd. xv. 7; Ecclus. xxxiii. 11—15; 2 Tim. ii. 20.

To argue original sin from the clay being a "con-

demned lump" (*massa damnata*), is to bring in an idea
which is not in this verse, nor in any of the parallel
passages.

The answer is a general one; that just as the clay
is unable to understand why the potter makes some of
it into vessels for baser uses, and other some into
vessels for honourable use; so man is equally unable
to comprehend why God converts some sinners from
their evil ways, justifies, sanctifies, and glorifies them,
while others He leaves in their wickedness, and afterwards punishes them for the same. The potter is
master of his clay; and God is master of His creature
man, and knows what He does with him. Beyond
this general answer St. Paul does not travel in this
verse.

22. *What if?* some read, as though the Vulgate
were *Quid si?* But the Vulgate is *Quod si*, the Greek
εἰ δέ, *but if*. The original Rheims version is *And if*.
The sentence is elliptical: *But if God hath endured*, &c.,
[what will thou say to that?]. We have in this verse
the particular answer to *v.* 19, but in the form of a
suggestion, not of a direct statement.

The principal word in the reply is μακροθυμία, which
is ill translated *patience;* it should be *longsuffering.* The
word, with its derivatives, occurs twenty-five times in
the New Testament, generally denoting a virtue that
man has to practise, but five times it denotes an
attribute of God, always the same attribute of *longsuffering*, whereby God bears with the sins of men.
This noun determines the sense of the verb ἤνεγκεν,
to be rightly rendered by the Vulgate *sustinuit*, our
endured.

In contrast with this principal term, *longsuffering*,
we have the terms, *wrath, power, destruction.* They are
contrasted, but subordinate. It is the longsuffering of
God that is asserted in the verse, not His wrath, nor

His power, not the destruction which He deals to sinners.

The participle, *willing*, does not show cause why God *endured*. It would be absurd to say that, because God was *willing to show his wrath*, therefore He *endured with much patience*. If that were the construction, we could only say that a negative must have dropped out, and that we should read οὐ θελων, *not willing*. But that is not to be thought of. As it is, we can only translate the participle, *though willing*.

The sentence then is: *But if God (though willing to show his wrath and to make his power known*, in His own good time) *endured with much longsuffering vessels of wrath, fitted for destruction*, &c. (*v.* 23)—[what will the objector say to that?]

St. Paul's answer, wrapped up in a sentence certainly *hard to be understood* (2 Pet. iii. 16), is simply this, that *the longsuffering of our Lord* is *salvation* (2 Pet. iii. 15) to such as are willing to avail themselves of it and be converted,—at the same time that it is damnation aggravated to those who hold out and harden themselves in sin, as explained under the type of Pharao (*v.* 18).

23. This verse assigns the cause and reason why God *endured ;* it was, *that he might show the riches of his glory upon the vessels of mercy*. Where observe that these *vessels of mercy*,—in particular such Jews as in process of time were converted—were at one time *vessels of anger* like the rest, and but for the *endurance* spoken of in *v.* 22, in which all these *vessels of anger* alike participated, their end would have been swift destruction. The same *longsuffering*, which mollified some, hardened others. As St. Augustine puts it : the same heat, which melts wax, hardens mud. *The Lord dealeth patiently,* μακροθυμεῖ, says St. Peter, *for your sake, not willing that any should perish, but that all should return to penance* (2 Pet. iii. 9).

There are also Our Lord's own words, giving this same reason for longsuffering, *lest perhaps gathering up the cockle, you root up the wheat also together with it* (Matt. xiii. 29). Thus God meets out His endurance alike to *vessels of wrath* and to *vessels of mercy*. To adopt another Pauline phrase, He endures all that anyhow He may save some (1 Cor. ix. 22, as read in the notes ; also below, xi. 14). Those who are not saved are hardened. Consequently upon their perversity, God withdraws His special aids ; and under that withdrawal their hearts grow harder and harder still. But that hardness of heart all has its origin in their own perverse will, resisting God's antecedent will to save, although not His consequent will to punish ; and for that voluntary perversity and resistance God justly *finds fault* (*v.* 19) with them and punishes them.

24. *Not only of the Jews, but also of the Gentiles.* So above, ii. 10, 11, *the Jew first, also the Greek, for there is no respect of persons with God.*

Read the whole passage, ii. 4—11, which is the best elucidation, being St. Paul's own, of these difficult verses, 18—24.

25. The citation is from Osee i. 23, 24, also cited by St. Peter (1 Pet. ii. 10).

And her that had not obtained mercy, &c. All the Greek MSS. and Fathers omit this clause, which has arisen simply from a double translation of one Hebrew word, which means both *beloved* and *having obtained mercy*.

Osee speaks immediately of the conversion of the people of Israel, who had become a separate kingdom from Juda. But as Israel was now a stranger to Juda, the conversion of Israel included the conversion of strangers, that is, of Gentiles.

26. From Osee i. 10.

27. This verse is from Isaias x. 22. Read the whole passage, Is. x. 20—23. A remnant of the Jews should escape the devastations of the Assyrians under

Sennacherib; and that remnant was a type of the small portion that should follow the Christ and be saved.

28. *For he shall finish his word, and cut it short in justice: because a short word shall the Lord make upon the earth.* Such is St. Paul's reading of Isaias x. 22, 23, where we now read from the Hebrew text translated by St. Jerome: *The consumption abridged shall overflow with justice: for the Lord God of hosts shall make a consumption, and an abridgment in the midst of all the land.* How recognise the text in these two different dresses?

The first thing is to secure better English versions, for the above are neither elegant nor intelligible. The quotation as it stands in St. Paul may be rendered thus: *For he shall accomplish (συντελῶν) the thing that he has spoken, and bring it to a speedy conclusion (συντέμνων,* with these two participles understand *ἔσται) in justice: because a work speedily concluded shall the Lord do upon the earth.* For *work* we have λόγον, *verbum, word,* which in Hebrew constantly stands for a *work,* considered as matter of promise or discussion. The latter part of the verse is in sense a mere repetition of the former, and is not found in the three best Greek MSS., the Vatican, the Sinaitic, and the Alexandrine.

The passage in Isaias in the Hebrew is obscure. The following version from the Hebrew is probably more accurate than St. Jerome's Latin, and certainly more intelligible than the Douay English: *Destruction is decreed, bringing justice: for destruction and a firm decree the Lord of hosts carrieth out in the midst of all the land.*

But—guided as we cannot doubt by the Spirit of God, the Inspirer of the Scriptures—St. Paul does not quote from the Hebrew, but, as the Apostles often did, from the Septuagint Greek version; and this he quotes exactly, with the mere verbal substitution of *upon the earth* for *in the whole world.*

As explained, this verse (Is. x. 23) does no more than emphasise the previous verse (22). It says nothing about the saved of Juda being few, which is the point that St. Paul is arguing. Hence some would translate συντέμνων *cutting down* [the people of Juda] *to a small number ;* and λόγον συντετμημένον, *a deed of cutting down :* certainly more to the point, if the translation may be admitted.

29. From Isaias i. 9. The text confirms the doctrine of the *remnant* (*v.* 27). If any one will argue that, because comparatively few Jews escaped the sword of the Assyrian in Isaias' time, and comparatively few Jews were converted to Christ in St. Paul's time, which is the meaning of these verses, therefore comparatively few men, or comparatively few Christians, are saved, he will need to enter into a long and arduous elucidation of the theory of Scripture types to make good either inference.

30. *The gentiles, who followed not after justice,* as abundantly shown (i. 18—32).

The justice of faith and baptism (iii. 28 ; vi. 4).

31. This text should be read, with the three best Greek MSS.: *But Israel, by following after the law, is not come to the law of justice.*

The law is the Mosaic law.

The law of justice is that observation of the law which carries with it supernatural justice, or sanctity, which can only be by faith in Christ,—under the Old Law, still to come ; in the New Law come already.

32. *Of works,* mere natural works, done without faith and grace (iv. 4—6).

They stumbled at the stumbling-stone,—Christ crucified, unto the Jews a stumbling-block (1 Cor. i. 23). Cf. Luke ii. 34.

33. The quotation is a blending of two texts, Isaias viii. 14, and xxviii. 16, the latter according to the

Septuagint, where the Hebrew has the meaningless, *He that believeth, let him not hasten.*
See the quotation also in St. Peter (1 Pet. ii. 6—8).

———

Chapter X.

1. Brethren, the will of my heart, indeed, and my prayer to God, is for them unto salvation. 2. For I bear them witness, that they have a zeal of God, but not according to knowledge. 3. For they not knowing the justice of God, and seeking to establish their own, have not submitted themselves to the justice of God. 4. For the end of the law is Christ, unto justice to every one that believeth. 5. For Moses wrote, The justice which is of the law, the man that shall do it shall live by it. 6. But the justice which is of faith speaketh thus : Say not in thy heart : Who shall ascend into heaven ? that is, to bring Christ down ; 7. Or who shall descend into the deep ? that is, to bring up Christ again from the dead. 8. But what saith the Scripture ? The word is near thee, even in thy mouth, and in thy heart : this is the word of faith which we preach ; 9. That if thou confess with thy mouth the Lord Jesus, and believe in thy heart that God hath raised him up from the dead, thou shalt be saved. 10. For with the heart we believe unto justice ; but with the mouth confession is made unto salvation. 11. For the Scripture saith : Whosoever believeth in him shall not be confounded. 12. For there is no distinction of Jew and Greek ; for the same is Lord over all, rich to all that call upon him. 13. For whosoever shall call upon the name of the Lord shall be saved. 14. How then shall they call on him in whom they have not believed ? or how shall they believe him of whom they have not heard ? and how shall they hear without a preacher ? 15. And how shall they preach unless they be sent ? as it is written : How beautiful are the feet of them that preach the gospel of peace, of them that bring glad tidings of good things ! 16. But all do not obey the gospel. For Isaias saith : Lord, who hath believed our report ? 17. Faith then cometh by hearing, and hearing by the word of Christ. 18. But I say : Have they not heard ? Yes verily, their sound went over all the earth, and their words unto the ends of the whole world. 19. But I say : Hath not Israel known ? First Moses saith : I will provoke you to jealousy by that which is not a nation ; by a foolish nation I will anger you. 20. But Isaias is

AA

bold, and saith: I was found by them that did not seek me: I appeared openly to them that asked not after me. **21.** But to Israel he saith: All the day long have I spread forth my hands to a people that believeth not, and contradicteth me.

1. *The will of my heart*, εὐδοκία, which St. Chrysostom says means *strong desire*: so the corresponding verb is used, 2 Cor. v. 8; 1 Thess. ii. 8. It means in fact the *set of my heart (beneplacitum cordis)*.

2. *A zeal of God*, better, *zeal for God*. St. Paul (Acts xxii. 3) describes himself as *zealous for God* (so the Greek text) before his conversion. Of *zeal not according to knowledge*, young Saul was a conspicuous example.

3. *The justice of God*, the state of being just before God, which in the present order can only be by the grace of Christ.

To establish their own justice, by the natural performance of works of the law.

Have not submitted themselves to the justice of God,—even the justice that is of faith (ix. 30). They have not received the faith, and have been content with certain works of their own, as many men are now.

4. *The end* (τέλος) *of the law is Christ*. The law was given to the Jews on purpose to excite their faith in the coming Christ by its mysteries, which were types of the Christian mysteries, and by its precepts to lead them to the school of Christ (Gal. iii. 24, with note). When the end is achieved, the means are superfluous. The Mosaic institutions therefore are superfluous, now that Christ and His redemption is come.

5. *The man that shall do it shall live by it* (Deut. xxx. 12), quoted and explained, Gal. iii. 12, with note.

There was promised to the observers of the law, first, a life of temporal blessings (Deut. xxviii. 2—13; xxx. 9, 10): secondly, life everlasting (Matt. xix. 17; Luke x. 25—28), but that only on condition of their imitating their father Abraham's faith in the Christ to come (Rom. iv. 11), and sharing in the anticipated grace of Christ, without which indeed they were incapable of keeping the moral law in grievous temptation (vii. 22—25). But the Jews thought to live by mere doing of the law, of their own sheer will and natural strength. That attempt the Apostle deprecates.

6—8. To understand how Deut. xxx. 12—14 is here quoted, we must know what is meant by the " accommodated sense" of Scripture. Just as we often quote Horace or Shakespeare to illustrate some event or peculiarity of modern life, which never entered into the mind of either of those poets, so we may quote Scripture merely by way of illustration, not as exposing the sense of Scripture, whether literal, mystical, or moral. Thus the words of Caiphas: *And the Romans will come and take away our place and nation* (John xi. 48), have been put in the mouth of an Anglican clergyman. *The Romans* does not mean *the Roman Catholics* except in a decidedly "accommodated sense." Other instances of St. Paul's use of the accommodated sense of Scripture occur below, *v.* 18; xv. 21; 2 Cor. viii. 15, where see notes.

In this passage (Deut. xxx. 12—14) Moses is not speaking of the Incarnation (*v.* 6), nor of the Resurrection of Christ (*v.* 7), nor of *the word of faith* (*v.* 8), to all of which St. Paul accommodates his words, but simply of the observance of the law which he has just promulgated.

In verse 8 all good MSS. read: ἀλλὰ τί λέγει; *sed quid dicit? but what saith it?* The unexpressed nominative to *saith* is not *Scripture*, but from *v.* 6, *the justice which is of faith.*

9. *Confess the Lord Jesus*, literally, *that Jesus is Lord.* The word *Lord*, as applied to the Messias, stands for *Adonai*, which in Hebrew is a substitute for Jehovah. This implies then a confession of the Divinity of Christ.

St. Paul here by no means limits the creed necessary

for salvation to the two articles of the Divinity and Resurrection of Christ, but he proposes them to the Jews as Test Articles, which carry with them the rest, *e.g.* the doctrine of original sin, laid down in ch. v. See what he says to the Galatians (Gal. i. 6—12; iii. 1, 2), who yet seem never to have wavered about the Divinity or the Resurrection of their Saviour.

To confess with the mouth that Jesus is Lord, probably refers to the confession of faith required before baptism, *e.g.* Acts viii. 37 (in the Vulgate).

10. *Justice, i.e.* justification, is inchoate *salvation*. The text merely means that faith must be ever in our heart, and at times on our lips.

11. For the quotation see on ix. 33. It is immaterial whether we read, as here, πᾶς ὁ πιστεύων, *every one that believeth*, or as the best authorities read on ix. 33, ὁ πιστεύων, *he that believeth*. The proposition is universal in any case. As noticed above, we have the authority of St. Paul for preferring the Septuagint reading of these words of Isaias to the received Hebrew text; and St. Paul was an inspired commentator.

12. iii. 29, 30. The word *Lord* here points to the Word Incarnate (Acts x. 36; Phil. ii. 11).

13. Joel ii. 32, where there is also mention of *the residue whom the Lord shall call*: cf. *the remnant* (above, ix. 27). The text was quoted by St. Peter in his Pentecostal address (Acts ii. 21).

14. *How shall they believe him of whom they have not heard?* scarcely makes sense. I may well believe the statement of a man I never heard of. The original Rheims edition reads: *How shall they believe him whom they have not heard?* which is an accurate translation of the Vulgate: *Quomodo credent ei, quem non audierunt?* and that is quite a possible, indeed the more obvious rendering of the Greek, πῶς δὲ πιστεύσωσιν οὗ οὐκ ἤκουσαν; But from the context it is not a question of believing Christ,

or of hearing Christ, but of hearing of Him and believing in Him. We must therefore fall back upon a construction, common in Homer, by which ἀκούειν with the genitive means *to hear of or about* a person. Thus we have the translation required: *How shall they believe in him of whom they have not heard?*

15. *How shall they preach unless they be sent?* To preach, in Greek κηρύττειν, means *to act as herald*. Now a herald is essentially a person sent by authority, to make a proclamation dictated to him by authority. When St. Paul says twice over, *I am appointed a preacher and an apostle*, κήρυξ καὶ ἀπόστολος, he says, literally, *I am appointed a herald and one sent*. We read of false prophets, God saying, *I did not send prophets, yet they ran: I have not spoken to them, yet they prophesied* (Jerem. xxiii. 21).

St. Paul's quotation is from Isaias lii. 7. It is spoken literally of the messengers who announce the fall of the Babylonian monarchy and the return of the Jews from captivity.

16. *Lord, who hath believed our report* (Isaias liii. 1), literally, *our hearing, i.e.* what they hear from us, our preaching.

17. *Faith cometh by hearing, i.e.* by preaching, *and hearing* (preaching) *by the word, i.e.* by the mandate *of Christ*. For this sense of ῥῆμα, *word*, cf. Luke v. 5.

18. The quotation is from Psalm xviii. 5, taken here in an "accommodated sense," since the Psalmist is speaking, not of the spread of the gospel, but of the glory of God declared by the heavens. See above on *v.* 6.

St. Paul means to say that already, twenty years after our Lord's Ascension, the gospel was widely spread in the Roman Empire, and therefore could not be unpublished in the hearing of the Jews. Cf. Acts i. 8.

19. Deut. xxxii. 21. As an idol is *that which was no god* (Deut. l.c.), so the Gentiles, who worshipped idols,

are *that which is not a nation*, and for the same reason also they are called *a foolish nation*. God says that by the temporal blessings that He would bestow upon the Gentiles, He would *provoke* the Jews *to jealousy;* and this jealousy was renewed by the spiritual blessings conferred upon the Gentiles, when the Messias came.

20. *Isaias is bold*, or *outspoken* (Is. lxv. 1). In this verse, the people spoken of are the Gentiles.

21. Isaias lxv. 2. In this verse the people spoken of are the Jews.

CHAPTER XI.

1. I say then: Hath God cast away his people? God forbid. For I also am an Israelite of the seed of Abraham, of the tribe of Benjamin. 2. God hath not cast away his people which he fore-knew. Know you not what the Scripture saith of Elias; how he calleth on God against Israel? 3. Lord, they have slain thy prophets, and have dug down thy altars; and I am left alone, and they seek my life. 4. But what saith the divine answer to him? I have reserved to myself seven thousand men, who have not bowed their knees to Baal. 5. Even so, then, at this present time also there is a remnant saved according to the election of grace. 6. And if by grace, is it not now by works; otherwise grace is no more grace. 7. What then? that which Israel sought he hath not obtained; but the election hath obtained it, and the rest have been blinded 8. (As it is written: God hath given them the spirit of insensibility, eyes that they should not see, and ears that they should not hear) until this present day. 9. And David saith: Let their table be made a snare, and a trap, and a stumbling-block, and a recompense to them: 10. Let their eyes be darkened, that they may not see, and bow down their back always. 11. I say then: Have they so stumbled that they should fall? God forbid. But by their offence salvation is come to the gentiles, that they may be emulous of them. 12. Now if the offence of them be the riches of the world, and the diminishing of them the riches of the gentiles, how much more the fulness of them? 13. For I say to you gentiles: As long indeed as I am the apostle of the gentiles, I will honour my ministry, 14. If by any means I may provoke to emulation those who are my flesh, and may save some of them. 15. For if the loss of them be the reconciliation of the world, what

shall the receiving of them be, but life from the dead ? **16.** For if
the firstfruit be holy, so is the lump also; and if the root be holy,
so are the branches. **17.** And if some of the branches be broken,
and thou being a wild olive-tree, art ingrafted in them, and art
made partaker of the root and of the fatness of the olive-tree ;
18. Boast not against the branches : but if thou boast, thou bearest
not the root, but the root thee. **19.** Thou wilt say then : The
branches were broken off, that I might be grafted in. **20.** Well :
because of unbelief they were broken off ; but thou standest by
faith : be not high-minded, but fear. **21.** For if God hath not
spared the natural branches, fear lest he also spare not thee.
22. See, therefore, the goodness and the severity of God : toward
them indeed that are fallen, the severity ; but toward thee the
goodness of God, if thou continue in goodness ; otherwise thou
also shalt be cut off. **23.** And they also, if they abide not still in
unbelief, shall be ingrafted : for God is able to ingraft them again.
24. For if thou wert cut out of the wild olive-tree, which is natural
to thee, and contrary to nature wert ingrafted into the good olive-
tree ; how much more shall they that are the natural branches be
grafted into their own olive-tree ? **25.** For I would not have you
ignorant, brethren, of this mystery, (lest you should be wise in your
own conceits,) that blindness in part has happened in Israel, until
the fulness of the gentiles should come in. **26.** And so all Israel
should be saved ; as it is written : There shall come out of Sion
he that shall deliver, and shall turn away impiety from Jacob :
27. And this is to them my covenant, when I shall take away their
sins. **28.** According to the gospel, indeed, they are enemies for
your sake ; but according to election, they are most dear for the
sake of the fathers. **29.** For the gifts and the calling of God are
without repentance. **30.** For as you also in times past did not
believe God, but now have obtained mercy through their unbelief ;
31. So these also now have not believed, for your mercy that
they also may obtain mercy. **32.** For God hath concluded all in
unbelief, that he may have mercy on all. **33.** O the depth of the
riches of the wisdom, and of the knowledge of God ! how incomprehensible are his judgments, and how unsearchable his ways !
34. For who hath known the mind of the Lord ? or who hath been
his counsellor ? **35.** Or who hath first given to him, and recompense shall be made him ? **36.** For of him, and by him, and in
him are all things : to him be glory for ever. Amen.

1. *Hath God cast away his people ?* In Psalm xciii. 14,
we read : *The Lord will not cast away his people.*

2. *Which he foreknew*, προέγνω. See note on viii. 29. It means here, 'which he formerly recognised as his own.' The clause is not to be taken as restrictive, 'that portion of his people, which he predestined:' for the consolation which St. Paul seeks and finds, is not in the certainty of predestination, which is obvious, but in this, that the Jewish people as a whole is not to be finally cast off by God.

Against Israel, the kingdom of Israel, then ruled by Achab.

3. 3 Kings xix. 10, 14.

4. 3 Kings xix. 18, except that there we read: *I will leave me seven thousand men.* Baal is feminine in the Greek, τῇ βαάλ, which is supposed to be because the Hellenist Jews objected to pronounce the idol's name, and called him ἡ αἰσχύνη (*the shame*).

5. *A remnant* (ix. 27) of the Jews *saved* by conversion to Christianity, *according to the election of grace*, *i.e.* according to a gratuitous election,—gratuitous, because the grace of first conversion can never be merited.

6. This verse is explained by the Council of Trent (sess. 6, cap. 8): "Nothing of those things which precede justification, neither faith nor works, can merit the grace itself of justification." Cf. iv. 5, 6. The text does not refer to the works of those who are already justified and in the state of grace.

The Vatican MS. and some others add here: *But if of works, it is no longer grace : otherwise the work is no longer a work.*

7. *The election*, the elect remnant (*v.* 5). *Blinded*, or *hardened*, ἐπωρώθησαν.

8. *God hath given them the spirit of insensibility*, from Isaias xxix. 10, where we read : *For the Lord hath mingled for you the spirit of a deep sleep.* In what sense God can be said to do this, we have seen in the texts on the harden-

ing of Pharao (ix. 18, seq.). The rest of the quotation is from Deut. xxix. 3, where we read: *And the Lord hath not given you a heart to understand, and eyes to see, and ears that may hear, unto this present day.*

9, 10. Psalm lxviii. 23, 24.

11. *Have they* (the Jews) *so stumbled that they should fall?* "like Lucifer, never to rise again."

By their offence salvation is come to the Gentiles: not that, if the Jews had been converted, the Gentiles would never have been called to the faith (Mark xvi. 15; Acts x.); but that the Gentiles have come in first, before the Jews, and have become the ruling element of Christ's kingdom on earth instead of the Jews. Cf. Acts xiii. 46; xviii. 6; xix. 9; xxviii. 28. Rome, once Babylon (1 Pet. v. 13), is now Jerusalem.

That they may be emulous of them is a mistranslation of εἰς τὸ παραζηλῶσαι αὐτούς, which means, *to provoke them* (the Jews) *to emulation,* as the verb is rightly translated below, *v.* 14. The reference is to Deut. xxxii. 21, quoted on x. 19, which see.

12. *Diminution,* ἥττημα (classical ἥττα), properly, *defeat.* But a defeat involves a diminution in numbers: therefore the rendering *diminution* may stand, especially as there seems to be some antithesis to the succeeding *fulness* (πλήρωμα, *full complement, full muster*). For another instance of the word see on 1 Cor. vi. 7.

13. *As long as I am the apostle of the gentiles, I will honour my ministry.* Rather; *Inasmuch as I am the apostle of the gentiles, I do honour my ministry.* The present, δοξάζω, *honorifico, I do honour,* is the reading of St. Augustine, of the Greek Fathers, and of nearly all the Greek MSS. The reading *honorificabo, I will honour,* has led the Vulgate to translate ἐφ' ὅσον by *quamdiu, as long as* (as in Matt. ix. 15). But there is nothing else in the context to determine the meaning to duration. It is better to assign to the phrase its general sense

(Matt. xxv. 40, 45, where again the Vulgate gives *quamdiu* for *in quantum*).

I honour my ministry,—as we say, "I do honour to my ministry:" I perform it in a creditable way.

St. Paul relates how our Lord sent him to the Gentiles rather than to the Jews, Acts xxii. 17—21.

14. The verse means, in continuation with the preceding: 'I make the most of my ministry among the Gentiles, on the chance of provoking to emulation, and so to Christianity, the Jews, who are my kith and kin.'

May save some of them: for the time was not yet come (and still it is not come), for *all Israel* to *be saved* (*v.* 26).

15. *The loss of them the reconciliation of the world.* The Gentiles have gained spiritually what the Jews have lost, pardon and reconciliation with God (*vv.* 11, 12).

The receiving of them, πρόσληψις, as we talk of " receiving one into the Church."

Life from the dead. The phrase is used in quite a general sense, as we speak of "light out of darkness." It means simply a grand and unlooked for restoration. High authorities see in it a reference to the general resurrection, which is shortly to follow the conversion of the Jews: but that interpretation appears strained.

16. The *firstfruit* and the *root* are the patriarchs, Abraham, Isaac, and Jacob. The *lump* and the *branches* are their descendants, the Jewish people. From the sanctity of their forefathers the Jews received a certain aptness for holiness, and as we may say, dedication, though not the actual endowment of sanctifying grace. In the same way it is said: *The unbelieving husband is sanctified by the believing wife;* and, *your children are holy* (1 Cor. vii. 14): where see note. The metaphor of *firstfruit* and *lump* is taken from Numbers xv. 21: *You shall give firstfruits of your dough to the Lord.* When an

Israelite kneaded dough for his bread, he first set aside
a small portion of it, which he made into a cake, and
either burnt it as an offering to Heaven, or gave it to
the priest.   This was to sanctify all the rest of the
lump, which was taken for domestic use.

17. There is an horticultural difficulty here, in the
fact that the fruit tree is grafted upon the wild tree,
not the wild tree upon the fruit tree.   St. Augustine
supposes this fact to have been borne in mind by
St. Paul as part of his metaphor, and to be referred
to in *v.* 24: *thou, contrary to nature, wert ingrafted in the good
olive-tree.*   But two Roman writers, Columella, *De re
rustica,* v. 9, and Palladius, *De insitione,* xiv. 53, refer to
a practice of grafting the wild olive upon the cultivated
variety in order to render the latter fertile, when it was
old or sterile.   Whether the process would lead to any
good, is another matter: but it would be enough for
St. Paul's metaphor, if he had seen such an operation
performed.   It might even help the metaphor, to consider the outworn stock of Judaism rejuvenescent by
the ingrafting of Gentile converts.

Ingrafted in them, not in the *branches* that are *broken,*
but among the other *natural branches* (*v.* 21).

Cf. Eph. ii. 11--22, also addressed to the Gentile
converts, to humble them for what they were, and to
move them to gratitude for what they have been made
by the *word of the Lord* that has *gone out from Jerusalem*
(Isaias ii. 3), for *salvation is of the Jews* (John iv. 22).

18. *Thou bearest not the root, but the root thee, i.e.* thou
art as little necessary to the Church, which is the true
family of Abraham and *the Israel of God* (Gal. vi. 16),
as those Jews were, who for their obstinate unbelief
have been cut off from the family of Abraham, the
father of the faithful (Gal. iii. 6—9).   No individual
is necessary to the Church, or to any Religious Order
in the Church.   The promises of Christ are absolute

to the Church, not to the individual. The salvation of the individual is conditioned on his holding on to the Church in faith and charity.

19. *That I might be grafted in*, as a better substitute.

20. *Well*, καλῶς, slightly ironical. St. Paul declines to discuss whether the substitution be a gain or not.

Because of unbelief, τῇ ἀπιστίᾳ, say, *by unbelief*, answering to τῇ πίστει, *by faith*.

21. *Lest perchance he also spare not thee.* The Greek of the best MSS. is more direct : οὐδὲ σοῦ φείσεται, *neither will he spare thee*, corresponding with the *severity*, or *abruptness*, ἀποτομία, of the next verse (22), *thou also shalt be cut off*.

23. This passage, *vv.* 23—31, is the chief Scripture witness of that obscure, because yet unfulfilled prophecy, of the final conversion of the Jewish race before the end of the world. The event is taken to be connected with the reappearance of Elias : *Elias indeed shall come and restore all things* (Matt. xvii. 10, 11 ; Apoc. xi. 3—8).

24. *Contrary to nature, contra naturam* (Vulg.). But the Greek, παρὰ φύσιν, is better rendered, *præter naturam*, *beside the* (ordinary) *course of nature*, which is diverted into another course by grafting.

The natural branches come by nature of the stock of the patriarchs. Belief in the Old Testament and the expectation of the Messiah are elements in a Jew, which render his conversion to Christianity always more *natural* than that of a pagan. By more *natural* we mean, more easily to be expected from his antecedents. Unfortunately, the obstinacy of the Jewish character prevails the other way (cf. John ix. 39).

25. *I would not have you ignorant, brethren :* St. Paul's favourite phrase for giving a confidence or calling attention (above, i. 13 ; 1 Cor. x. 1 ; xii. 1 ; 1 Thess. iv. 12).

Wise in your own conceits, from Prov. iii. 7 : *Be not wise in thy own conceit.* The warning however is not against self-opiniatedness, for there is no question of opinions, but against self-conceit and despising others, notably the unbelieving Jews. *Be not self-conceited*, would be a more apposite rendering here, and possible in the Book of Proverbs also. The Greek in both cases is ἐν ἑαυτῷ, or παρ' ἑαυτῷ, φρόνιμος.

This mystery, this divine secret which I am about to tell you. Cf. 1 Cor. xv. 51.

Until the fulness (πλήρωμα, as in *v.* 12, *the full muster*) *of the gentiles should come in* (εἰσέλθῃ, shall have come in).

26. *And so all Israel should be saved.* There is no doubt that St. Paul wrote, καὶ οὕτως πᾶς Ἰσραὴλ σωθήσεται, *And so all Israel shall be saved :* which is the only Greek reading, and the reading of all the versions but the Latin. It is the statement of the same fact, but more direct and clear.

The quotation should be read, according to the Vatican, Sinaitic and Alexandrine manuscripts : *There shall come out of Sion the deliverer* (ὁ ῥυόμενος) *: he shall turn away impieties from Jacob.* The quotation is from Isaias lix. 20, according to the Septuagint, where we now read *for Sion's sake* instead of *out of Sion*, which alters not the sense.

27. *And this is to them my covenant* (from Isaias lix. 21) : *when I shall take away their sins* (from Isaias xxvii. 9, where we read in the Septuagint : *And this is his—* Jacob's—*blessing, when I shall take away his sin*).

In these verses, 25—27, we have three unfulfilled prophecies, two of them of the highest interest :—

(*a*) That before the end of the world, all nations of the Gentiles shall be converted to Christianity, that is to say, such a large portion of every nation, that it will be morally true to say that the nation has been converted.

" *The fulness of the gentiles,*" says St. Thomas, " is not some individuals from the Gentiles, as converts were

being made then, but it stands for the whole or the
greater part of all nations."

(*b*) That before the end of the world, the Jews, as
a people, shall become Christian. This does not mean
that each and every Jew will be converted, any more
than it is meant that there will be no outstanding
pagans among the Gentiles.

(*c*) That the general conversion of the Gentiles will
happen before the general conversion of the Jews. The
Jews will be the last to be converted ; and the conversion of the rest of the world will *provoke them to emulation*
(παραζηλώσει, above, 11, 14, and x. 19).

These prophecies should be pondered by all who
feel tempted to announce the immediate advent of the
Day of Judgment. See however note on xiii. 11.

28. *According to the gospel*, now preached to them in
vain, *they* (the Jews) *are enemies*, hated of God, *for your
sake, i.e.* to the benefit of you Gentiles, as explained on
v. 11 : *but according to election*, by which of old they
became God's chosen people, Deut. iv. 7, 8, &c., *they
are most dear* (ἀγαπητοί, *well-beloved*) *for the sake of the fathers*,
Abraham, Isaac, and Jacob.

29. *For the gifts and calling of God are without repentance.*
The best parallel to this remarkable verse is perhaps
John vi. 59 : *He that eateth this bread shall live for ever.*
It means that God holds fast to His favourites : that
He does not easily abandon for ever any nation or
individual on whom He has bestowed special graces.

The text forms a plausible argument for the salvation
of the majority of Catholics who go to the sacraments,
for the recovery to Christendom of a city like Constantinople, and to Catholicism of a nation like England.
There are apparent exceptions to the rule ; and we
have to speak with modesty of any particular case, and
to think with most modesty and holy fear (above, *v.* 20 ;
1 Cor. ix. 26, 27 ; x. 12) of our own case.

There is a certain distinction which may be made in the schools, but is not really applicable to the text ; namely, that the *gifts of God are without repentance*, not absolutely, but conditionally on our fidelity. This distinction is not applicable, because the Apostle must be speaking absolutely ; otherwise his words would not cover the case for which they are alleged, God's final mercy to the Jews, a nation that have been and are most unfaithful and most perfidious.

30. *Have obtained mercy through their unbelief.* As above, *v.* 28, *enemies* (hated of God) *for your sake : vv.* 11, 12, *their offence the riches of the world :* see notes.

31. *Your mercy* means 'the mercy of God extended to you, Gentiles, in converting you to the faith.' So in Deut. xi. 25 : *your dread and fear upon all the land, i.e.* the dread and fear of you. It is a common use of the Greek possessive pronoun, *e.g. Odyssey,* xi. 202, σὸς πόθος, *regret for you.*

For your mercy, may be either joined with *have not believed,* and explained as above, *v.* 30, or with what follows, thus : *that they also may obtain mercy by the mercy extended to you.*

32. *God hath concluded all in unbelief.* Cf. Gal. iii. 22 : *The scripture hath concluded all under sin :* see notes there.

The Greek is συνέκλεισεν εἰς ἀπείθειαν, *has shut them up unto unbelief.* Some understand this in the same sense as that in which it is said of God, *he hardeneth* (ix. 18, with notes). But the passage from Galatians determines us in favour of the interpretation of the Greek Fathers, who take this *concluding,* or *shutting up,* for a logical process. 'God has brought all men to be found guilty of unbelief : He has convicted them and shown them up for unbelievers, formerly the Gentiles, and now the Jews.' Cf. iii. 23.

Omnia, all things, of the Vulgate is a less supported

reading than τοὺς πάντας, *all men.* But in the passage from Galatians we read τὰ πάντα, *all things.*

That he might have mercy on all, converting the Gentiles in apostolic times the sooner for the rejection of the gospel by the Jews; and the Jews at the end of the world the more effectually by the example of the Gentiles (*v.* 11, with notes).

33. All the Greek MSS. and Fathers read: *O depth of riches and of wisdom and of knowledge of God.* Thus riches, wisdom, and knowledge are three coordinate attributes.

O depth of riches! St. Paul often speaks of the *riches* of God and of Christ : *the riches of his goodness and patience and longsuffering* (ii. 4) : *the riches of his glory on the vessels of mercy* (ix. 23) : *the abundant riches of his grace* (Eph. i. 7, 8 : ii. 7) : *the riches of his glory* (Eph. i. 18 ; iii. 16) : *the unsearchable riches of Christ* (Eph. iii. 8). These quotations, taken along with what has gone before, leave no doubt that here we should understand the *riches of God's mercy.*

O depth of wisdom! Wisdom here is a sort of Divine prudence in the adaptation of means to ends, the end being man's salvation to be worked out consistently with God's glory.

O depth of knowledge! Knowledge lights up the region within which wisdom works: it covers the facts and conditions under which the end has to be wrought out.

How incomprehensible (ἀνεξερεύνητα, *unsearchable*) *are his judgments!* particularly of *mercy* (*v.* 32),—*a deep abyss* (Psalm xxxvii. 7).

How unsearchable (ἀνεξιχνίαστοι, *untraceable*) *his ways! All the ways of the Lord are mercy and truth* (Psalm xxiv. 10). Cf. Isaias lv. 6—9.

34. *Who hath known the mind of the Lord,*—and hath fathomed His *knowledge?* It is a quotation from Isaias

xl. 13, according to the Septuagint, where we read : *Who hath forwarded the spirit of the Lord ?*
. *Or who hath been his counsellor* (Isaias xl. 14),—and hath seconded His *wisdom !*

35. *Or who hath first given to him,*—and hath increased His *riches ?* The quotation is from Job xli. 2 : *Who hath given me before that I should repay him ?*

Nor is this inconsistent with the Catholic doctrine of merit, laid down by the Council of Trent (sess. 6, cap. 16), and by St. Paul himself (2 Tim. iv. 8). So St. Augustine (Serm. 158): "God has been made our debtor, not by receiving anything from us, but by promising what it pleased Him to promise. It is one thing to say to a man: ' You are in my debt, because I have given you something:' and another thing to say: ' You are in my debt, because you have promised.' When you say: ' You are in my debt, because I have given you:' a benefit has proceeded from you, but a benefit in the shape of a loan, not of a present. But when you say: ' You are in my debt, because you have promised me:' you have given nothing; and yet you exact; for the goodness of him who has promised will give, lest his word of honour turn to evil-mindedness: for he who breaks his word is evil. But do we say to God : 'Give back to me, because I have given to Thee?' What have we given to God, when all that we are, and all the good that we have, we have from Him ? We have given Him nothing. We cannot in any such terms exact anything of God as our debtor, especially since the Apostle says to us: *Who hath first given to him, and recompense shall be made him ?* In this way then we can exact something of our Lord by saying : ' Render what Thou hast promised, because we have done what Thou hast commanded ; and that is Thy doing, because Thou hast helped us in the labour.' "

36. *Of him, and by him, and in him* (say, *unto him,*

BB

εἰς αὐτὸν : the Vulgate *in ipso* represents a period of Latin when *in* with the ablative was often put for *in* with the accusative, as above, vi. 3 ; and Phil. ii. 11), *are all things*.

Of him, as Creator—efficient cause.

By him, as Preserver—sustaining cause.

Unto him, as Last End—final cause.

Again :

Of him, of His Power, which is appropriate to the Father.

By him, by His Wisdom, which is appropriate to the Son.

Unto him, unto His Goodness, which is appropriate to the Holy Ghost.

To him be glory for ever, Amen. This doxology terminates the dogmatic portion of the Epistle. The remainder is moral exhortation and personal commendations. At the end of every Homily of St. John Chrysostom on Holy Scripture, after the exposition of the text, there is an ἠθικόν, or *Moral Instruction*. Such an ἠθικόν are these chapters xii.—xv.

One word ere we quit this part of the subject. St. Paul certainly saw further into the mysteries of predestination and election than any of his readers or commentators. What he saw prompted this outburst of amazement and gratitude, *vv.* 33—36. The more we penetrate the real mind of St. Paul, the more we shall be struck with awe and gratitude for the unfathomable depths of God's mercy.

CHAPTER XII.

1. I beseech you, therefore, brethren, by the mercy of God, that you present your bodies a living sacrifice, holy, pleasing to God, your reasonable service. **2.** And be not conformed to this world; but be reformed in the newness of your mind, that you may prove what is the good, and the acceptable, and the perfect will of God. **3.** For I say, through the grace that is given me, to all that are among you, not to be more wise than it behoveth to be wise; but to be wise unto sobriety, and according as God hath divided to every one the measure of faith. **4.** For as in one body we have many members, but all the members have not the same office: **5.** So we, being many, are one body in Christ, and each one members one of another. **6.** And having gifts different, according to the grace that is given us, whether prophecy, according to the proportion of faith; **7.** Or ministry, in ministering; or he that teacheth, in teaching; **8.** He that exhorteth, in exhorting; he that giveth, with simplicity; he that ruleth, with solicitude; he that showeth mercy, with cheerfulness. **9.** Love without dissimulation; hating that which is evil, adhering to that which is good; **10.** Loving one another with brotherly love; in honour preventing one another: **11.** In solicitude not slothful; in spirit fervent; serving the Lord; **12.** Rejoicing in hope; patient in tribulation; instant in prayer; **13.** Communicating to the necessities of the saints; pursuing hospitality. **14.** Bless them that persecute you: bless, and curse not. **15.** Rejoice with them that rejoice; weep with them that weep: **16.** Being of one mind one to another; not high-minded, but condescending to the humble. Be not wise in your own conceits: **17.** Render to no man evil for evil: provide things good not only in the sight of God, but also in the sight of all men. **18.** If it be possible, as much as is in you, have peace with all men. **19.** Revenge not yourselves, my dearly beloved, but give place to wrath; for it is written: Revenge is mine, I will repay, saith the Lord. **20.** But if thy enemy be hungry, give him to eat; if he thirst, give him drink: for doing this, thou shalt heap coals of fire on his head. **21.** Be not overcome by evil, but overcome evil by good.

1. *I beseech*, παρακαλῶ, *I exhort. By the mercy* (διὰ τῶν οἰκτιρμῶν, *by the mercies*) *of God*, extended to you in your conversion, enlarged upon in the previous chapter.

Your bodies a living sacrifice, by the subjection of bodily desires to the law of God, vi. 12.

The word *sacrifice* connotes the death of the victim ; and still the victim is to be *living*. It is the *death* and the *life* described, vi. 4—11.

Your reasonable service, *rationabile obsequium*, λογικὴν λατρείαν. This is not a caution against injuring one's health by excessive asceticism. The only other place in the New Testament where the adjective occurs is 1 Pet. ii. 2, λογικὸν γάλα, *rational milk*, which is the spiritual milk of God's word, as distinguished from material milk. In Plato's *Republic*, book vi. (ad fin.) there is a contrast between νοητὸς τόπος and αἰσθητός, "the region of intellect and the region of sense." St. Peter's and St. Paul's λογικός is Plato's νοητός. We had better translate, *spiritual service*, as distinguished from the *sensible service*, by which victims were slaughtered in the Jewish ritual : not in that concept of the word *spiritual* (πνευματικός) in which it stands opposed to *carnal* (σαρκικός, or ψυχικός, *e.g.* 1 Cor. ii. 14, 15, where see notes). Eusebius (*Demonstratio Evangelii*, i. 6 and i. 10) speaks of the Holy Eucharist as ἄναιμος καὶ λογικὴ θυσία, "a bloodless and spiritual sacrifice," in distinction from the Jewish sacrifices. This throws light on the phrase, *oblationem rationabilem*, in the Canon of the Mass.

By a common Greek construction, the words λογικὴν λατρείαν are in the accusative in apposition, not with σώματα, but with the whole phrase preceding. In plain English : *Present your bodies a living sacrifice*, &c., *which presentation is your spiritual worship*.

The Vulgate *obsequium* does not well render λατρείαν (above, ix. 4; Heb. ix. 1, 6). It should be *cultum* (worship); and the whole phrase *spiritualem cultum vestrum* (your spiritual worship).

2. *Be not conformed to this world.* He will appreciate

this injunction, who knows what shape *this world* bore in Rome in the days of the early Cæsars.

Conformed, reformed. This play upon words is not in the original, συσχηματίζεσθε, μεταμορφοῦσθε. *Fall not in with the fashion of this world, but be transformed by the renovation of your mind*, would be a literal translation. For *newness*, or rather, *renovation*, see Col. iii. 9, 10. It is a process that has to be kept up continually, so long as the baptized man lives, environed with concupiscence, which *is not subject to the law of God, neither can it be* (viii. 7, with note).

The good and the acceptable and the perfect will of God. So the Vulgate. But the Greek admits of a more likely rendering, τὸ θέλημα τοῦ θεοῦ, τὸ ἀγαθόν καὶ εὐάρεστον καὶ τέλειον, *the will of God, in respect of what is good and well-pleasing and perfect. Good* is good : *well-pleasing* is better : *perfect* is best. We have here some inkling of a difference between commandments and counsels. Thus marriage is *good*, but virginity is *well-pleasing* (1 Cor. vii. 27, 28) : martyrdom is *perfect* (John xv. 13). Ordinarily, the *good* alone is obligatory : not the *well-pleasing*, not the *perfect*, except in certain cases, when it is thrust upon us by special circumstances as an alternative to sin, as martyrdom may be, or virginity either, *e.g.* in case of lunacy of one married party ; or poverty, in the case of the greater part of mankind (Luke vi. 20, 21). In practice, what is recommendable for the individual, is not what is absolutely *well-pleasing* or *perfect*, but what is relatively so for him, the better or best course with his character and under his circumstances.

3. *By the grace that is given me, i.e.* by the authority of my apostolate (i. 5 ; xv. 15, 16).

Not to be more wise than it behoveth to be wise, but to be wise unto sobriety. There is a play upon words in the Greek, quite unrepresented in the Latin and English :
μὴ ὑπερφρονεῖν παρ' ὃ δεῖ φρονεῖν, ἀλλὰ φρονεῖν εἰς τὸ

σωφρονεῖν, *not to be high-minded beside what we should be minded, but to be minded unto sober-mindedness.*

The measure of faith, not here the theological virtue of faith, but the gratuitous miraculous gifts that then often went with baptism (1 Cor. xiv. with notes). This is apparent from *vv.* 6, 7.

4—8. This idea of what we may call the ' differentia-tion' of the members of the body of the Church, is worked out at greater length in 1 Cor. xii. 5—30, which see. See too 1 Pet. iv. 8—11, which is almost a transcript of this passage.

The Vulgate is right in beginning a new sentence here. But the sentence is elliptical, the finite verbs being left out, which have to be supplied somehow in this sort: *But having different gifts according to the grace that is given us, either prophecy*, (let us prophecy) *according to the proportion of faith, or ministry*, (let us serve) *in ministering: or he that teacheth*, (let him abound) *in doctrine; he that exhorteth*, (let him be assiduous) *in exhor-tation; he that giveth*, (let him give) *with simplicity; he that ruleth*, (let him rule) *with carefulness; he that showeth mercy*, (let him show mercy) *with cheerfulness.*

The rule of faith, ἀναλογίαν πίστεως, *rationem fidei*, means just the same thing as the *measure of faith*, μέτρον πίστεως, *mensuram fidei, v.* 3, as there explained. *Rule of faith* is a bad translation both of the Latin and of the Greek; and is misleading, as introducing a modern term of theology, which signifies quite a different thing from what is here meant by St. Paul. He means, not the standard of things to be believed, but the proportion in which the miraculous gift of prophecy is held by its possessor. Say *proportion of faith.*

7. *Ministry.* From the context, and from 1 Cor. xii. 5, 10, 28 (where see notes), we must not explain this of the sacred orders of diaconate or priesthood, which are ordinary and permanent gifts in the Church, but of

those extraordinary and transient graces of *healings*, *helps, interpretations of speeches*, of which there is question in the passage cited.

He that teacheth (1 Cor. xiv. 26).

8. *He that exhorteth* (*ib.*) Not in the way of ordinary *teaching*, or ordinary *exhortation*, such as we may hear in Christian pulpits now, but of special, miraculous eloquence. At the same time the Apostle's words serve to guide the preacher, catechist, or religious writer of our time, who commonly has no miraculous powers.

Or may we not say that still, unless the Spirit of the Lord seize upon the preacher and change him into another man (1 Kings x. 6), his preaching is all lifeless and fruitless? Are there not times, when he looks on his own production with wonder, like the grafted tree in Virgil? (*Georgics*, ii. 82)—

Miraturque novas frondes et non sua poma.

Whoever has had experience of preaching, can witness to this.

He that giveth his goods to the poor under divine inspiration (1 Cor. xiii. 3; Acts iv. 34—37).

In simplicity. See on 2 Cor. viii. 2; ix. 11.

He that ruleth, seems to refer to that obscure gift called *governments* (1 Cor. xii. 28), a miraculous gift.

9. *Love without dissimulation* is the same as *charity unfeigned* (2 Cor. vi. 6: cf. 1 John iii. 18). After referring to the miraculous gifts, common at that time, he insists on charity, as the *more excellent way* (1 Cor. xii. 31, with note).

Hating that which is evil, cleaving to that which is good. The one is the only way of doing the other, provided always that our hatred be of things, not of persons. " For example," says Origen, " if one proposes to guard purity, he cannot guard it safely, unless he conceives a certain hatred and execration of impurity : for difficult

and very difficult is that continence, in which the thing
abstained from is desired, and the yearning of the heart
is bridled solely by the fear of future judgment."

10. *Preventing one another*, getting the start of one
another, being the first to show civility and respect.

11. *In solicitude* for one another's good, not for one's
own skin or for one's own pocket.

Serving the Lord Jesus Christ (Eph. vi. 5—7; Matt.
xxv. 45). There is an inferior reading, *serving the time*
(τῷ καιρῷ for τῷ κυρίῳ), which reads like the emendation
of some cynic, with the mind of an historian rather
than of a moralist.

12. *Rejoicing* in the eternal happiness that is *in hope*
(*in spe*): *patient in* the temporal *tribulation*, that is in fact
(*in re*); and meanwhile *instant in prayer* to pass through
the one to the other.

13. *Communicating to the necessities of the saints*, imparting
aid to saints (fellow-Christians, Acts ix. 32; Eph. i. 1)
in want. Or it may be taken, *sharing in the necessities of
the saints*, considering their need your need.

Pursuing hospitality, which means going after guests,
—as it were chasing them and bringing them in: not
simply enduring their presence when inevitable.

15. "None is so stony-hearted as not to weep for a
person in distress: but it requires a very generous soul,
when your neighbour prospers, not only not to envy
him, but even to rejoice with him: therefore he puts
this recommendation first, *Rejoice with them that rejoice*"
(St. Chrysostom).

16. *Being of one mind one towards another*. Better, from
the Greek, τὸ αὐτὸ εἰς ἀλλήλους φρονοῦντες, *being of the same ·
mind towards one another* as each is towards himself.
Nothing could be more Pauline than St. Chrysostom's
explanation: "Be affected towards your neighbour as
towards yourself. If you take yourself for a great
personage, take him for a great personage also. If you

look down on him as mean and inconsiderable, take
the same view of yourself, and eliminate all inequality."

But condescending to the humble ; τοῖς ταπεινοῖς συνεπα-
γόμενοι, *being carried along with the humble.* The verb
recurs Gal. ii. 13 ; 2 Pet. iii. 17.

*Be not wise in your own conceits. Hast thou seen a man
wise in his own conceit ? there shall be more hope of a fool than
of him* (Prov. xxvi. 12). And again (xvii. 12) : *It is better
to meet a bear robbed of her whelps than a fool trusting in his
own folly.* Here is a rendering of some Greek verses,
that Socrates loved to quote :

Best man by far the genius is, who sees all by himself :
Again a worthy man you find, who takes another's word.
But whosoe neither sees himself, nor heeds the word he hears,
Go write him down a worthless wight : there's no doing aught
with such.

17. *To no man rendering evil for evil* (Matt. vi. 43—47).
To the Greek mind revenge was as much a man's part
as gratitude.

Providing good things, i.e. taking forethought to give
edification, *in the sight of all men* (Matt. v. 16). This is
the best reading : the rest of the clause has been put
in from 2 Cor. viii. 21.

19. *Give place unto wrath, i.e.* to Divine wrath : leave
it to God to be angry. The quotation is from Deut.
xxxii. 35.

20. Prov. xxv. 21. *Doing this, thou shalt heap coals of
fire upon his head,* merely means that you will bring your
enemy to reason more effectually by kindness than by
heaping coals of fire upon his head.

Chapter XIII.

1. Let every soul be subject to the higher powers: for there is no power but from God; and those that are, are ordained of God. **2.** Therefore he that resisteth the power, resisteth the ordinance of God; and they that resist purchase to themselves damnation. **3.** For rulers are not a terror to the good work, but to the evil. Wilt thou then not be afraid of the power? Do that which is good, and thou shalt have praise from the same: **4.** For he is the minister of God to thee for good. But if thou do that which is evil, fear; for he beareth not the sword in vain: for he is the minister of God, an avenger to execute wrath upon him that doeth evil. **5.** Wherefore be subject of necessity, not only for wrath, but also for conscience sake. **6.** For therefore also you pay tribute: for they are the ministers of God, serving unto this purpose. **7.** Render therefore to all their dues: tribute to whom tribute is due; custom to whom custom; fear to whom fear; honour to whom honour. **8.** Owe no man any thing, but that you love one another: for he that loveth his neighbour hath fulfilled the law. **9.** For, Thou shalt not commit adultery; Thou shalt not kill; Thou shalt not steal; Thou shalt not bear false witness; Thou shalt not covet: and if there be any other commandment, it is comprised in this word, Thou shalt love thy neighbour as thyself. **10.** The love of the neighbour worketh no evil. Love, therefore, is the fulfilling of the law. **11.** And that knowing the time, that it is now the hour for us to rise from sleep; for now our salvation is nearer than when we believed. **12.** The night is passed, and the day is at hand: let us, therefore, cast off the works of darkness, and put on the armour of light. **13.** Let us walk honestly as in the day: not in rioting and drunkenness, not in chambering and impurities, not in contention and envy: **14.** But put ye on the Lord Jesus Christ, and make not provision for the flesh in its concupiscences.

For the philosophy of the first six verses, see *Ethics and Natural Law* in the Stonyhurst Series of Manuals of Catholic Philosophy, pp. 317, 318. St. Paul may have been afraid lest neophytes should abuse his doctrine of Christian liberty (1 Cor. vii. 23; Gal. iv. 31), especially since, as St. Jerome tells us, the opinions of Judas of Galilee (Acts v. 37) were still current among the Jews,

that none but God should be called Lord, and that tithe
to the Temple released from the obligation of tribute to
Cæsar (Matt. xxii. 17—21).

1. *Let every soul be subject to the higher powers.* " Every
soul, be he apostle, evangelist, prophet, or any one
else," says St. Chrysostom. *Be subject,* ὑποτασσέσθω (the
middle voice), 'range himself under,' 'bow down to'"
(said of our Lord at Nazareth, Luke ii. 51).

To the higher powers, that is, to the State; understand,
in civil matters and things that come within the purview
of the State's authority. Cf. Acts v. 28, 29.

There is no power but from God: for God is the supreme
guardian of law and order; and provides for man
through man that the law and order necessary for civil
society, and therefore necessary for human kind, be
maintained. The mediate Providence—the middle-
man, so to speak—in this work of conservation is the
civil ruler.

Those that are: the Anglican version is a household
word: *the powers that be.* But the word *powers* is not
repeated in the best MSS.

Lest any one should confine his veneration to power,
or authority, in the abstract, while disobeying actual
existing authority, on the ground of its incompetence,
or wickedness, St. Paul is careful to add that the
existing authorities, *the powers that be,* are to be obeyed
as part of God's ordinance,—so far as they are in
possession, and so far as their command is within the
competence of their office.

2. *He that resisteth,* ὁ ἀντιτασσόμενος, *he that rangeth
himself against,* in contrast with ὁ ὑποτασσόμενος, *he that
rangeth himself under.* The play upon the word is kept
up in *ordinance,* διαταγῇ, say *arrangement.*

They that resist purchase to themselves damnation, ἑαυτοῖς
κρίμα, *judgment to themselves.* " The same phrase is used
as in 1 Cor. xi. 29 of the unworthy communicant, as

though it were the like sin to rend our Lord's mystical
Body by civil discord as to profane His natural Body
by sacrilege " (*Ethics and Natural Law*, p. 318).

3. Cf. 1 Pet. ii. 13, 14.

4. *He beareth not the sword in vain*, the instrument and
emblem of capital punishment, the right to inflict
which is called 'the right of the sword,' and is the
distinctive feature of sovereignty.

5. *Be subject of necessity.* Read, *There is need to be
subject*, ἀνάγκη ὑποτάσσεσθαι, the undisputed Greek
reading.

Not only for wrath, his anger, who *beareth the sword*.

6. *Therefore also*, (i.e. *for conscience sake* also) *you pay
tribute*, when the tax-gatherer finds you out and calls
for it. We must not use force against a public official,
nor fraud against any man.

They (the officers of the revenue) *are the ministers of
God*, λειτουργοί; this word, whence our *liturgy*, is used
here in no religious sense, but as we have it in Phil.
ii. 25, λειτουργὸν τῆς χρείας μου, *a minister to my want.* See
note on 2 Cor. ix. 12.

Serving, προσκαρτεροῦντες, *waiting assiduously upon*, so
xii. 12; Acts vi. 4; Mark iii. 9.

7. *Tribute*, a poll-tax or land-tax.

Custom, tolls, custom-duties.

8. *Owe no man anything but to love one another.* It
means: 'Have no debts but the debt of love.' That
debt can never be paid off, but however much has been
paid, more remains due. Cf. 1 Pet. iv. 8. The reason
is given by St. Thomas: "First, because we owe our
neighbour love for the sake of God, whom we can never
sufficiently recompense (1 John iv. 21): secondly,
because the motive of love always remains, being
likeness in nature and grace (Ecclus. xiii. 19): thirdly,
because charity does not diminish but increases by
loving (Phil. i. 9)."

He that loveth his neighbour hath fulfilled the law. If a
man loves himself rationally and spiritually, he will not
fail in taking due care of himself. If he loves his
neighbour as himself, he will not fail in due care of
his neighbour. But no one loves his neighbour rationally
and spiritually, who does not love God supremely, the
supreme rational and spiritual good of man. The two
precepts of charity are inseparable. Cf. Gal. v. 14;
Matt. xxii. 35—40; 1 John iv. 20, 21.

9. The key to St. Augustine's saying: *Ama, et fac
quod vis :* "Love, and do as you like."

10. The Greek is: *Love worketh no evil to our neighbour.
Charity is kind* (1 Cor. xiii. 4).

Love is the fulfilling of the law,— 1 Tim. i. 5; 1 Cor.
xiii. 1—3; xvi. 14.

11. Punctuate: *And that, knowing the season, that it is
now the hour,* &c.

And that. Cf. note on vi. 6, *And that, knowing.* Also
1 Cor. vi. 6, 8; Heb. xi. 12 (καὶ ταῦτα).

The season, or as we should say now, *the situation.*

Now our salvation (our final deliverance in soul and
body) *is nearer than when we believed* (ἐπιστεύσαμεν, the
inceptive aorist, like ἐβασίλευσεν, *reigned,* i.e. *came to the
throne,* 3 Kings xi. 43; xiv. 20, 31, &c.: here it means,
than when we first came to the faith). Our final deliverance
in soul is when we die and are admitted into heaven:
in body, at the day of the resurrection. Both events
are nearer now than on the day when we were baptized:
the former much nearer, relatively to the time yet to be
run; the latter perhaps not much nearer. Of St. Paul's
ignorance of the time of the Second Coming (he knew
no more of that than we do, Mark xiii. 32), of his hopes
and conjectures thereupon, see notes on 1 Cor. xv. 50,
seq.; vii. 29—31; 2 Cor. v. 1—4. He must have
reflected at times that the conversions which he
announced to take place before that last consummation

of all things (xi. 25, 26), must needs take years, perhaps centuries, to effect. The Apostles were inspired to utter their anticipations on this head, while warning their hearers that they were not certainties and definitions :—so 2 Pet. iii. Our Lord would have us live in constant looking for the day of judgment (Matt. xxiv. 36—47). As for St. Paul's prophecy just referred to (see note on xi. 27), which seems to give the present world a long lease to run, it is, like other prophecies, not without its obscurities. Origen writes : " God only knows, and His only-begotten Son, and any friends that may be privy to His secrets, what is *all Israel* that is to be *saved*, and what is *the fulness of the gentiles* that is *to come in*."

12. *The night is past,* προέκοψεν, say, the *night is far advanced.* Some of the old Latin versions read *processit*, a correct rendering of the Greek, as above. *Processit* has got altered into *præcessit*, an error. If a train had passed you all but the guard's carriage, you might say, *processit, it is well on its way :* not *præcessit, it is past.* St. Paul's idea is of rising just before daybreak.

The day is *the day of the Lord* (2 Thess. ii. 2), *the brightness of his coming* (ἐπιφανείας, *appearance, ib.* 8), the Sun of Justice appearing in judgment. Hence all the time before the judgment day is comparatively *night.* Now however that our Lord has come for the first time as Saviour, we may say that the night is *well on* (προέκοψεν), that its darkest hours are past, and that the *day* of full *salvation is at hand.*

In John ix. 4, the metaphor is inverted. The working time of this life is the *day ;* and *the night cometh,* when we die and do no more work of merit or demerit.

The works of darkness. Cf. Eph. v. 11, 12 : *For the things that are done by them in secret* (*the unfruitful works of darkness*), *it is a shame even to speak of. Works of darkness* are then in the first place works of indecency and

shame, referred to in *v.* 13. Secondly, they are works
of ignorance, often culpable ignorance, of God, and the
blindness of the sensual man to the things of the Spirit
(1 Cor. ii. 14). Thirdly, they are eminently unchristian
works, works that our Lord came into this world to
scatter and expel (John i. 9—13; iii. 19; Luke i. 79;
xi. 33—36). One of the early names of baptism is
illumination : cf. Eph. v. 14, probably a quotation from
an early Christian hymn.

Put on the armour of light, Eph. vi. 13—17. A man
puts on his clothes,—or his armour, if he is a soldier
in the field—at rising. It is called the *armour of light,*
because it suits the coming light, and prepares one to
go abroad without shame. A man would not walk in
the light of day in a night-dress.

13. *Let us walk honestly,* εὐσχημόνως, *decently,* no reference to commercial dealings. Such too is the meaning
of the Latin *honeste :* cf. 1 Cor. vii. 35 ; xii. 24.

*Not in rioting and drunkenness, not in chambering and
impurities,* the text that converted St. Augustine, as he
relates in his *Confessions,* l. viii. c. 12.

Rioting, the κῶμος, the last stage of a Greek drinking-
bout, when they went out singing in the streets : cf.
Gal. v. 21.

14. *Put ye on the Lord Jesus Christ,* like baptized
persons, Gal. iii. 27 : cf. also Gal. ii. 20, and above,
vi. 4—12, with notes.

In its concupiscences : εἰς ἐπιθυμίας, *unto lusts.*

CHAPTER XIV.

1. Now him that is weak in the faith take unto you, not in disputes about thoughts. 2. For one believeth that he may eat all things: but he that is weak, let him eat herbs. 3. Let not him that eateth despise him that eateth not; and he that eateth not, let him not judge him that eateth: for God hath taken him to him. 4. Who art thou that judgest another man's servant? to his own master he standeth or falleth; and he shall stand: for God is able to make him stand. 5. For one judgeth between day and day; and another judgeth every day. Let every man abound in his own sense. 6. He that regardeth the day, regardeth it unto the Lord; and he that eateth, eateth to the Lord, for he giveth thanks to God: and he that eateth not, to the Lord he eateth not, and giveth thanks to God. 7. For none of us liveth to himself, and no man dieth to himself. 8. For whether we live, we live to the Lord; or whether we die, we die to the Lord: therefore, whether we live, or whether we die, we are the Lord's. 9. For to this end Christ died, and rose again, that he might be Lord both of the dead and of the living. 10. But why dost thou judge thy brother? or why dost thou despise thy brother? for we shall all stand before the judgment-seat of Christ. 11. For it is written: As I live, saith the Lord, every knee shall bow to me, and every tongue shall confess to God. 12. So, then, every one of us shall render account for himself to God. 13. Let us not, therefore, judge one another any more: but judge this rather, that you put not a stumbling-block or a scandal in your brother's way. 14. I know, and am confident in the Lord Jesus, that nothing is unclean of itself; but to him that esteemeth any thing to be unclean, to him it is unclean. 15. But if, because of thy meat, thy brother be grieved, thou walkest not now according to charity. Destroy not him with thy meat for whom Christ died. 16. Let not, then, our good be evil spoken of. 17. For the kingdom of God is not meat and drink; but justice, and peace, and joy in the Holy Ghost. 18. For he that in this serveth Christ pleaseth God, and is approved of men. 19. Therefore, let us follow after the things that are of peace, and keep the things that are of edification one toward another. 20. Destroy not the work of God for meat. All things, indeed, are clean; but it is evil for that man who eateth with giving offence. 21. It is good not to eat flesh, and not to drink wine, nor any thing whereby thy brother is offended, or scandalized, or made weak. 22. Hast thou faith? have it to thyself before God. Happy is he

that condemneth not himself in that which he alloweth. **23.** But
he that discerneth, if he eat is condemned, because not of faith :
for all that is not of faith is sin.

1. *Him that is weak in faith*, *i.e.* him that has a *weak
conscience* (1 Cor. viii., with notes), him that is scrupulous
in his food. It was among those of the Roman Christians
who had been converted from Judaism that these
scruples prevailed : due partly to the Levitical traditions in which they had been brought up of clean and
unclean meats, partly to the commandment of the early
Church to *abstain from things sacrificed to idols, and from
blood, and from things strangled* (Acts xv. 29). These good
people seem to have concluded that the one sure way
of observing these various injunctions was by abstain-
ing from meat altogether, for their own practice :
but they made no attempt to impose it upon the
remaining portion of the Christian flock, the converts
from heathendom. Hence St. Paul addresses them
himself, and bids others treat them, tenderly and
gently. He spares them all that invective which he
pours out upon the intolerant Judaizers (2 Cor. xi.
13—15; Gal. iii. 1—3 ; v. 1—12). This use of *faith* for
conscience appears again in *vv.* 22, 23.

Take unto you this good, scrupulous man as a friend,
for so *God hath taken him to him* (*v.* 3 : cf. xv. 7, *receive one
another*, where the verb is the same, προσλαμβάνεσθε).

Not in disputes about thoughts, μὴ εἰς διακρίσεις διαλογισμῶν,
non in disceptationibus cogitationum (Vulg.), the usual late
Latin use of *in* for the ablative for *in* with the accusative, of which above, xi. 36; xiii. 14, &c. Translate
the Greek, *not unto* (rash) *judgments of thoughts*, *i.e.* of
beliefs about what is right and wrong. The preposition
διὰ, used here twice in composition, may well bear its
classical signification of reciprocity. The meaning then
is : 'Not proceeding to mutual rash judgments of one
another's ideas as to things right and wrong to eat.'

cc

2. *Let him eat herbs*, a decidedly bad rendering, which obscures the sense. Read, *he that is weak eateth herbs*, and avoids all meat, as explained above. All the Greek MSS. of value read ἐσθίει; Tertullian, *vescitur;* St. Jerome, *manducat* (eateth).

4. *Who art thou* (ix. 20) *that judgest another man's servant?* ἀλλότριον οἰκέτην, *another's domestic.* The word *man's* in our version is awkward, as there is question of a domestic of God.

To his own lord he standeth, or falleth, i.e. by the judgment of his own master he is acquitted or condemned.

And he shall stand : this scrupulous Christian shall be acquitted : *for God is able to make him stand*, giving him such grace as shall secure his fidelity and acquittal.

5. *Judgeth between day and day, i.e.* keeps one day as holier than another, as we keep the 25th of December for a holier day than the 23rd.

Another judgeth every day, keeps every day as equally holy and proper for prayer.

But this sense is clearer from the Greek, κρίνει ἡμέραν παρ' ἡμέραν, *judgeth day in preference to day.* For this sense of παρά see i. 25 ; Luke xiii. 2 ; Heb. i. 9.

It would appear that these Jewish converts observed certain Jewish holidays, sabbaths and new moons, which their brethren from the Gentiles neglected. Cf. Gal. iv. 10: *You observe days and months and times and years.* St. Paul is not angry with the Romans as with the Galatians, because they did not put justification in the observance of the Jewish festivals, but rather clung to them as old customs, which they themselves were loth to forego, though they would not impose them on others.

Let every man abound in his own sense. This text lends no countenance to the Protestant error of private judgment, which St. Paul abhorred (Gal. i. 6—9). The translator doubtless has the Vulgate, *unusquisque in suo sensu abundet*, to support him : but the meaning of this not very intelligible phrase must be drawn from the Greek, ἕκαστος ἐν τῷ ἰδίῳ νοΐ πληροφορείσθω, *let every man be sure in his own conscience: i.e.* before you do a thing, ascertain and make up your mind that it is a right thing for you to do: do not act, thinking all the while that possibly you are committing a sin. The verb πληροφορεῖσθαι is used in this sense in iv. 21, where our versions have, *plenissime sciens, most fully knowing;* and the substantive πληροφορία, Col. ii. 2; 1 Thess. i. 5; Heb. vi. 11; x. 22.

For the consonance of this precept with the doctrine of Probabilism, see *Ethics and Natural Law*, pp. 152—159. What is called the direct and speculative uncertainty is undergirt by a reflex and practical certainty.

6. *He that regardeth the day*, or *has a devotion to* (φρονῶν, cf. viii. 5) *the day*, as a holiday.

He that eateth flesh meat (*v.* 2).

He giveth thanks, as St. Paul did (Acts xxvii. 35). Read 1 Tim. iv. 3—5.

7. *Liveth to himself*, to *please himself* (xv. 1).

Dieth to himself, quits this world as it were on an errand of his own, or merely because he is tired and wants to go.

8. In this verse *the Lord* is Christ Jesus, to whom we are dedicate in baptism (vi. 3), and who has *bought* us *with a great price*, so that we are *not our own* (1 Cor. vi. 19, 20).

9. *Died and rose again*, ἀπέθανε καὶ ἔζησε (inceptive, cf. ἐπιστεύσαμεν, xiii. 11), *died and came to life*, is probably the right reading. For the sentiment, 2 Cor. v. 15. The dominion that belonged to our Saviour as *the only-begotten of the Father*, made flesh (John i. 14), He did not fully enter upon till He could claim it by right also of redemption (Matt. xxviii. 18; Luke xxiv. 26, 46, 47; John xiii. 31, 32; xvii. 1—5; Phil. ii. 6—11).

Lord of the dead, as He proves Himself by judging

men after their death (Acts x. 42). For Luke xx. 38, see the previous verse, 27, and Acts xxiii. 8.

10. *But thou (weak in faith, i.e.* scrupulous in conscience, *v.* 1), *why judgest thou thy brother,* for eating meat (*v.* 2)? *Or thou (the stronger,* xv. 1), *why dost thou despise thy brethren,* for his scruples which confine him to *herbs?*

We shall all stand before the judgment-seat of Christ. So 2 Cor. v. 10: cf. 1 Cor. iv. 5. But here the better MSS. have, *before the judgment-seat of God.* And so the following quotation rather suggests, the words being in the mouth of God as God.

11. Isaias xlv. 23, 24. *Confess to God, i.e.* acknowledge Him. The reading we find in Isaias, both in the Hebrew and the Greek, is: *Every tongue shall swear.* But *swearing by the Lord of hosts* (Is. xix. 18) is taken as the equivalent of confessing Him as God.

13. *Judge this rather that you put not.* There is a play on the word κρίνειν (to judge) used twice. The second time it means to *determine : determine this rather, not to put.* Cf. Tit. iii. 12: *There I have determined* (κέκρικα) *to winter.*

A stumbling - block, offendiculum, πρόσκομμα, is any obstacle in the way, great or small, that one may stumble over. *A scandal,* σκάνδαλον, is properly the wood of a trap, that falls down and catches the animal inside. You trip up over a *stumbling-block,* but are caught by a *scandal.*

14. *Nothing is unclean of itself.* The distinction of clean and unclean animals (Leviticus xi.) was a mere legal observance, abolished by the coming of Christ (Matt. xv. 11 ; Acts x. 13—15 ; xv. 28, 29). Even meat that had been portion of a sacrifice to false gods was not of itself a sinful food (1 Cor. viii. 4—7 ; x. 19, 25—27).

But to him that esteemeth anything to be unclean, it is unclean. This is the principle laid down by St. Thomas, that "an erroneous conscience is binding" (1a 2æ, q. 19, art. 5 ; *Aquinas Ethicus,* i. pp. 67—70). See too *v.* 23.

Similarly, but more severely, St. Paul writes to
Titus : *All things are clean to the clean : but to them that are
defiled and to unbelievers nothing is clean : but both their mind
and their conscience are defiled* ('Tit. i. 15).

15. It is a rule of moral theology, that we are bound
in charity to avoid grieving our neighbour without proportionate cause.

Destroy not him with thy meat for whom Christ died.
This is explained by 1 Cor. viii. 9—13 ; x. 27, 28.

16. *Let not then our good*—our Christian liberty to use
all meats—*be evil spoken of* (cf. 1 Cor. x. 30) by fellow-
Christians, whom we shock by parading this our liberty
in defiance of their prejudices. This admonition has
or had in modern times some application in the matter
of Sunday observance.

17. *The kingdom of God,* the reign of Christ in our
souls, *is not meat and drink.* So 1 Cor. viii. 8.

Peace is the fruit of *justice ;* and *joy* as it were the
efflorescence of *peace.*

19. The best MSS. read: *Therefore we follow after*
(διώκομεν) *the things that are of peace, and the things that are
of edification one towards another,*—omitting *keep.*

20. *Destroy not* (μὴ κατάλυε, go not undoing) *the work of
God,* the Redeemer, in the soul of thy fellow-Christian.
Above, *vv.* 14, 15.

21. *Is offended* (stumbles) *or scandalized* (see note on
v. 13) *or made weak, i.e.* unsettled in his conscience, by
coming to imitate your use of meat or wine, all the time
thinking it sinful.

Not to drink wine. How this gave scandal, we do
not exactly know. The Nazarites did not drink wine
(Num. vi. 3; Luke i. 15); nor the Rechabites (Jer.
xxxv); nor the priests actually ministering in the
temple (Lev. x. 9). St. Augustine explains: " The
heathen used to pour libations to their idols from
the firstfruits of their wine, and offered sundry sacrifices

438 ROMANS xiv. 22, 23.

at the wine-presses themselves." Hence some Christians
may have thought the whole vintage defiled.

22. *Hast thou faith ? i.e.* a strong and clear conscience,
free from scruples (*vv.* 1, 23).

Have it to thyself before God : let it guide your own
private practice.

*Blessed is he that condemneth not himself in that which he
alloweth.* Better as the version of 1582 had it: *Blessed
is he that judgeth not himself in that which he approveth :*
which means : ' Blessed is he whose conscience
questions not the rectitude of the course which he
adopts.'

23. *He that discerneth*, say, *he that doubteth*, ὁ διακρινόμενος, which verb is translated *to stagger*, iv. 20; Matt.
xxi. 21 ; Mark xi. 23: *to doubt*, Acts x. 20: *to waver*,
James i. 6. The Vulgate, *qui discernit*, takes διακρινόμενος
for διακρίνων. He that doubts whether his food be
lawful, sins if he eats it, because his action is not borne
out by his conscience.

All that is not of faith is sin, *i.e.* every action that has
not the approval of *a well made up conscience* (such is the
meaning of *faith* here, cf. *vv.* 1, 2—*believeth*, 22) is a sin.
So St. Thomas explains the text (1a 2æ, q. 19, art. 5,
ad 4). It certainly does not mean that all the works of
infidels are sins.

1. Now, we that are stronger ought to bear the infirmities of the weak, and not to please ourselves. 2. Let every one of you please his neighbour for his good unto edification. 3. For Christ did not please himself; but, as it is written: The reproaches of them that reproached thee fell upon me. 4. For what things soever were written were written for our instruction; that through patience and the comfort of the Scriptures we might have hope 5. Now the God of patience and of comfort grant you to be of one mind one toward another, according to Jesus Christ; 6. That with one mind and with one mouth you may glorify God, and the Father of our Lord Jesus Christ. 7. Wherefore receive one another, as Christ also hath received you, to the honour of God. 8. For I say that Christ Jesus was minister of the circumcision for the truth of God, to confirm the promises made to the fathers: 9. But that the gentiles are to glorify God for his mercy, as it is written: Therefore will I confess to thee, O Lord, among the gentiles, and will sing to thy name. 10. And again he saith: Rejoice, ye gentiles, with his people. 11. And again: Praise the Lord, all ye gentiles; and magnify him, all ye people. 12. And again Isaias saith: There shall be a root of Jesse; and he that shall rise up to rule the gentiles, in him the gentiles shall hope. 13. Now the God of hope fill you with all joy and peace in believing that you may abound in hope, and in the power of the Holy Ghost 14. And I myself also, my brethren, am assured of you, that you also are full of love, replenished with all knowledge, so that you are able to admonish one another. 15. But I have written to you, brethren, more boldly in some sort, as putting you in mind, because of the grace which is given me from God, 16. That I should be the minister of Christ Jesus among the gentiles, sanctifying the gospel of God, that the oblation of the gentiles may be made acceptable, and sanctified in the Holy Ghost. 17. I have, therefore, glory in Christ Jesus toward God. 18. For I dare not speak of any of those things which Christ worketh not by me, for the obedience of the gentiles, by words and by deeds, 19. By the virtue of signs and wonders, in the power of the Holy Ghost; so that from Jerusalem, round about as far as to Illyricum, I have fully preached the gospel of Christ. 20. And I have so preached this gospel, not where Christ was named, lest I should build upon another man's foundation: but as it is written: 21. They to whom he was not spoken of shall see; and they that have not heard shall understand. 22. For

which cause also I was hindered very much from coming to you, and have been kept away till now. 23. But now, having no more place in these countries, and having a great desire these many years past to come to you; 24. When I shall begin to take my journey into Spain, I hope that, as I pass, I shall see you, and be brought on my way thither by you, if first, in part, I shall have enjoyed you. 25. But now I shall go to Jerusalem, to minister to the saints. 26. For it hath pleased them of Macedonia and Achaia to make some contribution for the poor saints who are in Jerusalem. 27. For it hath pleased them ; and they are their debtors. For if the gentiles have been made partakers of their spiritual things, they ought also in carnal things to minister to them. 28. When, therefore, I shall have accomplished this, and consigned to them this fruit, I will come by you into Spain. 29. And I know that when I come to you I shall come in the abundance of the blessing of the gospel of Christ. 30. I beseech you, therefore, brethren, through our Lord Jesus Christ, and by the charity of the Holy Ghost, that you assist me by your prayers for me to God, 31. That I may be delivered from the unbelievers that are in Judæa, and that the oblation of my service may be acceptable in Jerusalem to the saints; 32. That I may come to you with joy, by the will of God, and may be refreshed with you. 33. Now the God of peace be with you all. Amen.

1. *Not to please ourselves*, not to use our strength selfishly.

2. *Please his neighbour unto good, to edification.* Not that unprincipled complaisance of which St. Paul says elsewhere : *If I yet pleased men, I should not be the servant of Christ* (Gal. i. 10).

3. " What means, *Christ did not please himself?* It was open to Christ not to bear reproaches, and not to suffer what He did suffer, had He chosen to regard His own feelings : but them He would not regard. He regarded our interest and neglected His own " (St. Chrysostom). Especially He would take no advantage of His divine power to screen Himself, but *the reproaches*, &c. (Psalm lxviii. 10).

4. *What things soever were written* (or προεγράφη, *were written beforehand, i.e.* in the Old Testament) *were written*

for our instruction. Read 1 Cor. x. 11: cf. 2 Tim. iii. 16, 17.

5. *To be of one mind one towards another:* τὸ αὐτὸ φρονεῖν ἐν ἀλλήλοις, *to be of the same mind one with another.* The phrase is not the same, nor the meaning either, as in xii. 16, where see note. The unanimity is to be in religious matters, as the next verse shows; and in civil matters to the extent of avoiding quarrels.

6. *God and the Father of our Lord Jesus Christ,* τὸν θεὸν καὶ πατέρα: say, *the God and Father of our Lord.* See 2 Cor. i. 3; xi. 31, where the phrase recurs. Cf. John xx. 17: *my Father and your Father, my God and your God.*

7. *Receive one another,* προσλαμβάνεσθε, note on xiv. 1.

8. *Minister of the circumcision,* that is, of the circumcised. So Gal. ii. 7—9; Phil. iii. 3; and above, iv. 12, Abraham is *father of the circumcision.* While He was on earth, our Lord confined His ministrations to the Jews (Matt. xv. 24; x. 5, 6). He looked forward to being glorified among the Gentiles only after His death (John xii. 20—25). Our Lord preached to the Jews *for* (ὑπέρ, on behalf of) *the truth of God,* that is, God's truthfulness, in fulfilment of God's promises: or, as St. Paul has it, *to confirm the promises made unto the fathers, i.e.* to the Jewish patriarchs. To them and to their descendants in the flesh the promises were made primarily, though by no means exclusively (iv. 11, 12, 16, 17; Gal. iii. 7—9), nor altogether absolutely (xi. 7—11, 29).

9. *But that the gentiles are to glorify God for his mercy.* This version is faithful neither to the Latin nor to the Greek. Much better the original Rheims: *But the gentiles to honour God for his mercy.* We must look back at the construction of the previous verse. *To confirm,* &c., is εἰς τὸ βεβαιῶσαι, the aorist infinitive. This verse 9 opens with another aorist infinitive, δοξάσαι, joined to βεβαιῶσαι by the particle δέ, and like it depending on

εἰς. In other words, the infinitive δοξάσαι (*to glorify*), equally with the infinitive βεβαιῶσαι (*to confirm*), expresses a purpose. We may translate : *Christ was minister of the circumcision on behalf of the truthfulness of God*, for a twofold purpose, first, *to confirm the promises made unto the fathers ;* secondly, *to the end that the Gentiles should glorify God for his mercy*, in admitting them by faith and baptism to become children of Abraham (iv. 12, 16, 17; vi. 3, 4; Gal. iii. 26—29), and so to share in the promises (xi. 17).

The connection of these verses 8 and 9 with verse 7 is this. The converts to the faith from heathendom despised the converts from Judaism for their scrupulosity about meat and drink and holidays. St. Paul bids them receive their brethren of Jewish stock as friends, and not to scorn them. To this effect he humbles the pride of the converts from heathendom, by reminding them that Christ preached only to the Jews, in fulfilment of the promises of God to the children of Abraham, and with the intention that the Gentiles should afterwards be admitted by a gracious act of mercy through faith and baptism into the line of Abraham's posterity, and so inherit the promises. Cf. Eph. ii. 11—13.

In the Vulgate, *honorare* cannot like δοξάσαι be the infinitive of purpose, but must depend upon *dico* (*I say that the gentiles glorify*), which is in several ways less likely.

The quotation is from 2 Kings xxii. 50; Psalm xvii. 50. In these words David celebrates his conquest of heathen nations. But David was a recognised type of Christ, and in their typical sense St. Paul understands them of Christ.

10. Deut. xxxii. 43, according to the Septuagint.

11. Psalm cxvi. 1.

12. Isaias xi. 10, according to the Septuagint. From the Hebrew, through the Latin, the Douay version reads : *In that day the root of Jesse, who standeth for an*

ensign of peoples, him the gentiles shall beseech. An *ensign of peoples* means a standard round which they rally, and therefore an authority which they obey. And *beseech* gives the idea of supplication, which involves *hope.*

13. *Peace in believing* supposes rest on a firm foundation of faith. There is no rest in an earthquake, no peace in doubt.

The hortatory part of the Epistle, which began at xii. 1, is here concluded. The rest is epilogue, consisting of (*a*) personal confidences, like those addressed to the Corinthians, but less intimate (xv. 14—33): (*b*) salutations to friends (xvi.).

14. *Full of love,* ἀγαθωσύνης, *goodness, kindness.*

15. *More boldly in some sort,* a good rendering. The words are to be taken together. The *boldness* probably consists in such sayings as: *All have sinned, and do need the glory of God* (iii. 24); and still more perhaps in the extolling of the Jewish stock (iii. 2; xi. 1; xv. 8, &c.) to the Romans, most of whom had been Gentiles.

Putting you in mind, rather than telling you what you did not know. Thus for example the account of original sin (v. 12—19) is rather allusive than expository.

It is an evil practice putting full stops at the end of every verse, particularly in a continuous writer like St. Paul. This verse should end with a comma.

16. *The minister* (λειτουργόν) *of Christ Jesus among the gentiles* (i. 5, 13, 14; xi. 13; Gal. ii. 7—9).

Sanctifying the gospel of God, sanctificans evangelium Dei, is an unfortunate rendering, particularly as the word *sanctified* occurs in the same verse, representing another word in the original and another idea. Nor can any man tell what *sanctifying the gospel of God* can mean. The Greek is ἱερουργοῦντα τὸ εὐαγγέλιον τοῦ θεοῦ, *making a sacrificial work of* (preaching) *the gospel of God.* So in the Fourth Book of Maccabees (vii. 8), they who die for the law are said to be ἱερουργοῦντας τὸν νόμον ἰδίῳ

αἵματι, 'making of the law a sacrifice in their own
blood.' Preaching to the heathen is a sacrificial work,
inasmuch as it prepares the victim, who is to be incorporated with Christ, the Great Victim, to die with
Him in baptism (vi. 4, 5), *a sacrifice, holy, pleasing unto
God* (Rom. xii. 1). This sacrifice may be and should
be continually renewed, as St. Paul says : *I die daily*
(1 Cor. xv. 31). The idea of the *living sacrifice*, the
continual death of the faithful in union with the death
of Christ, is a grand and fertile ascetic idea. The first
step to this sacrifice is the preaching and hearing of
the word of God ; and that step also, that sacrificial
work, has to be continually repeated. So much for the
sacrificial character of preaching, here insisted on.

The oblation of the gentiles is the offering of the
world, converted and *sanctified* (ἡγιασμένη), in Christ
to God.

18. *I dare not speak of any of those things which Christ
worketh not by me*, is a modest and somewhat involved
way of saying, ' I dare speak only of such things as
Christ worketh by me.'

19. *Illyricum*, the north and east shore of the
Adriatic. We have no other mention of St. Paul
preaching there.

Fully preached, for which some editions have *replenished*, not very intelligible English. The verb
πεπληρωκέναι appears in the same sense, Col. i. 25;
Luke vii. 1 ; Acts xii. 25.

20. *I have so preached :* οὕτως δὲ φιλοτιμοῦμαι εὐαγγελί-
ζεσθαι, *I so make a point of preaching*, or *I so make it a
principle to preach*. This principle of *not building upon
another man's foundation*, he refers to, 1 Cor. iii. 10 ; 2 Cor.
x: 15, 16. It did not prevent his preaching as he passed
by, in a church which another apostle had founded,
but only his settling there, and making that church a
centre of his missionary work, as he made Ephesus and

Corinth, and proposed to make Spain (*v.* 24, where see note).

21. The Septuagint reading of Isaias lii. 15. Another instance of the "accommodated sense," for which see note on x. 6.

22. *For which cause, i.e.* because I continually had new churches to found, *I was hindered very much* (τὰ πολλὰ, *those many times, i.e.* very often : there is another reading, πολλάκις, *often*).

And have been kept away until now, repeated from i. 13, not in the Greek.

23. *No more place in these countries, i.e.* in Corinth, where he wrote from (xvi. 1), and the parts about. The Corinthian church was now well founded. It is interesting to note that the Apostle saw no footing to gain in Athens.

24. *My journey into Spain,* which never came off, for sufficient reasons (Acts xxi.—xxviii.).

As I pass, I shall see you. He did not intend to stay in Rome. The Roman Church had been founded by another,—as Catholic tradition says, by St. Peter. See *v.* 20 and note. St. Paul did see Rome, and did stay there, but as a prisoner (Acts xxviii. 15—31).

25, 26. For these transactions see 1 Cor. xvi. 1—4 ; 2 Cor. viii. ix.; Acts xx. 3—16; xxi. 1—17.

27. *They are their debtors,* &c. 1 Cor. ix. 11.

28. *Consigned to them this fruit :* σφραγισάμενος αὐτοῖς τὸν καρπὸν τοῦτον, *set my seal* (2 Cor. i. 22) *for them upon this fruit.* When the fruit was gathered in, it was customary to set a seal upon the store, that it might not be pilfered by the slaves. So the sealing up was the last process of gathering in. St. Paul seems to mean : 'When I shall have fully assured to them (*the saints in Jerusalem*) the fruit of this contribution.'

31. He feared *the unbelievers in Judæa,* with what cause appears by Acts xxi. 28; and was not sure that

his *service* would be *acceptable* even to those he came
to relieve, *to the saints in Jerusalem,—all zealots for the law*
(Acts xxi. 20). The latter fear proved groundless (Acts
xxi. 17).

CHAPTER XVI.

1. And I commend to you Phœbe, our sister, who is in the
ministry of the church that is in Cenchrea ; **2.** That you receive
her in the Lord, as becometh saints, and that you assist her in
whatsoever business she shall have need of you : for she also hath
assisted many, and myself also. **3.** Salute Prisca and Aquila, my
helpers in Christ Jesus, **4.** (Who have for my life exposed their
own necks : to whom not I only give thanks, but also all the
churches of the gentiles,) **5.** And the church which is in their
house. Salute Epenetus, my beloved, who is the firstfruit of Asia
in Christ. **6.** Salute Mary, who hath laboured much among you.
7. Salute Andronicus and Junias, my kinsmen and fellow-captives,
who are renowned among the apostles, who also were in Christ
before me. **8.** Salute Ampliatus, most beloved to me in the Lord.
9. Salute Urbanus, our helper in Christ Jesus, and Stachys, my
beloved. **10.** Salute Apelles, approved in Christ. **11.** Salute them
that are of Aristobulus's household. Salute Herodion, my kinsman.
Salute them that are of Narcissus's household, who are in the
Lord. **12.** Salute Tryphena and Tryphosa, who labour in the
Lord. Salute Persis, the dearly beloved, who hath much laboured
in the Lord. **13.** Salute Rufus, chosen in the Lord, and his mother
and mine. **14.** Salute Asyncritus, Phlegon, Hermas, Patrobas,
Hermes, and the brethren who are with them. **15.** Salute Philo-
logus, and Julia, Nereus, and his sister, and Olympias, and all the
saints who are with them. **16.** Salute one another with a holy
kiss. All the churches of Christ salute you. **17.** Now I beseech
you, brethren, to mark them who cause dissensions and offences
contrary to the doctrine which you have learned ; and avoid them.
18. For they that are such serve not Christ our Lord, but their own
belly ; and by pleasing speeches and good words seduce the hearts
of the innocent. **19.** For your obedience is published in every
place. I rejoice, therefore, in you : but I would have you to be
wise in good, and simple in evil. **20.** And may the God of peace
crush Satan speedily under your feet. The grace of our Lord Jesus
Christ be with you. **21.** Timothy, my fellow-labourer, saluteth

you, and Lucius, and Jason, and Sosipater, my kinsmen. **22.** I,
Tertius, who wrote this letter, salute you in the Lord. **23.** Caius,
my host, and the whole church, saluteth you. Erastus, the
treasurer of the city, saluteth you, and Quartus, a brother. **24.** The
grace of our Lord Jesus Christ be with you all. Amen. **25.** Now
to him that is able to establish you according to my gospel and
the preaching of Jesus Christ, (according to the revelation of
the mystery kept secret from eternity, **26.** Which now is made
manifest by the Scriptures of the prophets, according to the commandment of the eternal God, for the obedience of faith known
among all nations;) **27.** To God the only wise, through Jesus
Christ, to whom be honour and glory for ever and ever. Amen.

1. *Phœbe our sister,* fellow-Christian. Tradition names
her as the bearer of this letter from Corinth to
Rome.

Who is in the ministry; οὖσαν καὶ διάκονον, *who is
deaconess.* The deaconesses discharged in the early
church those works of charity to the sick and poor,
which are now the occupation of the active orders of
nuns.

Cenchrea—properly Cenchreæ—is the east po   of
Corinth.

3. Aquila and Prisca his wife, whom St. Luke calls
Priscilla, harboured St. Paul when he first came to
Corinth. They followed him to Ephesus, where they
were the means of the conversion of Apollo. By this
time they must have been back in Rome, from whence
they originally came (Acts xviii. 2, 3, 18, 19, 26; 1 Cor.
xvi. 19; 2 Tim. iv. 19).

5. *The church which is in their house,* the congregation
who meet there to celebrate the divine mysteries. Such
domestic churches, or congregations, in early Christian
Rome were called 'titles,' from the name that they
bore, either of the master of the house, or of the locality,
or of some martyr buried hard by.

The firstfruit of Asia in Christ, the first Christian
convert in the Roman Province of Asia, which was the

south-western portion of Asia Minor. This is the meaning of *Asia* always in the New Testament.

6. *Mary*, quite an unknown person.

7. *My fellow-prisoners.* We do not know on what occasion. Paul was *in prisons often* (2 Cor. xi. 23). He was not in prison at this time.

Of note among the apostles. Apostle with the article prefixed, as here, means an Apostle in the strict sense of the word. Andronicus and Junias (or Junia, a woman, according to some) were held in esteem by the Apostles.

Who also (Andronicus and Junias) *were in Christ before me*, converted before St. Paul was.

9. *Stachys*, said to have been made by St. Andrew first Bishop of Byzantium (Constantinople).

11. *Aristobulus's household, Narcissus's household.* There was an Aristobulus, a nephew of Herod the Great, brought up at Rome, a friend of the Emperor Claudius. He is likely enough to have adopted a not uncommon practice of making the Emperor his heir. Narcissus, a prominent figure in the pages of Tacitus, was a potent freedman of Claudius. He was put to death by Nero, and his property went to the Emperor. St. Paul, writing afterwards a prisoner from Rome, has this salutation: *All the saints salute you, especially they that are of Cæsar's household* (Phil. iv. 22). Merged in *Cæsar's household*, we may recognise *Aristobulus's household* and *Narcissus's household*. It is likely that Aristobulus and Narcissus were both already dead, but their slaves and freedmen, now gathered in the Palace, bore their former masters' names.

12. *Tryphena and Tryphosa.* The Roman Martyrologium joins them with St. Thecla.

13. *Rufus* is pretty plainly the son of Simon of Cyrene, *the father of Alexander and Rufus* (Mark xv. 21).

St. Mark wrote at Rome for the Romans, and mentions Alexander and Rufus as names familiar to the Christian community there.

His mother and mine, an expression of gratitude and respect. St. Paul may have known her at Jerusalem, when he was being *brought up at the feet of Gamaliel* (Acts xxii. 3).

16. 1 Cor. xvi. 20; 2 Cor. xiii. 12; 1 Thess. v. 26; 1 Pet. v. 14.

All the churches of Christ, all the various congregations in Greece and Macedonia.

17. *Offences*, σκάνδαλα, *scandals*, see on xiv. 13.

Contrary to the doctrines you have learnt. Cf. Gal. i. 6—9. St. Paul was not 'comprehensive.' This is probably the one allusion to the Judaizers, who gave so much trouble at Corinth, and who might possibly trouble the Church at Rome.

18. *Serve their own belly*, preach novelties and flatteries in expectation of a dinner,—of the same Judaizers: so Phil. iii. 18, 19; 2 Cor. xi. 13; Tit. i. 10—16.

19. *Your obedience* (*obedience of faith, v.* 26) is *published in every place;* εἰς πάντας ἀφίκετο, *has reached all*. So above: *Your faith is spoken of in the whole world* (i. 8). These are testimonies to the flourishing estate of Christianity in the primitive Roman church. St. Paul wishes it to appear that what he does mention of evil is meant by way of precaution, not of correction. There is a tone of deference and respect in everything that he addresses to Rome.

Wise in good; in bono, εἰς τὸ ἀγαθόν, *unto good* (cf. note on *in ipso*, xi. 36).

Simple in evil, εἰς τὸ κακόν, *unto evil*: as it were not understanding it, and therefore not taking it up. Cf. 1 Cor. xiv. 20.

20. *The God of peace crush* (the best MSS. have συντρίψει, *will crush*) *Satan* (the adversary, Apoc. xii. 9)

DD

450 ROMANS xvi. 21—25.

under your feet (Gen. iii. 15) *speedily.* A glorious prophecy of the Church of Rome!

21. *Jason* of Thessalonica, Acts xvii. 5—9. *Sosipater,* or Sopater, of Beroea, Acts xx. 4.

22. *I, Tertius, who wrote* (*have written* from dictation) *this epistle.* See on 1 Cor. xvi. 21 ; Gal. vi. 11.

23. *Caius my host,* a wealthy and hospitable Corinthian, one of the few whom St. Paul baptized with his own hand (1 Cor. i. 14). He seems to be the Caius to whom the third Epistle of St. John is addressed (3 John i. 5).

And the whole church. Manuscripts and sense alike bear out the reading—*and of the whole church.* Caius is called *the host of the whole church* from his readiness in entertaining strangers.

Erastus, the treasurer of the city, possibly father or uncle of the Erastus mentioned in Acts xix. 22; 2 Tim. iv. 20.

Quartus, a brother, possibly slave of Caius or Erastus (1 Cor. i. 26).

24. This verse is omitted in the three best MSS. It is repeated from *v.* 20.

The next three verses, 25—27, have been questioned. But they are in the best MSS., the Vatican, the Sinaitic, and the Alexandrine, in the latter twice over, here and at the end of ch. xiv.

25. *The mystery which was kept secret from eternity,* namely, *that the gentiles should be fellow-heirs,* &c.: see Eph. iii. 4—6. The revelation of this mystery astonished St. Peter, *and the apostles and brethren:* see Acts x. xi.

Read *vv.* 25, 26 together . . . *mystery, kept secret,* σεσιγημένον, *from eternity, but now made manifest* (another participle, φανερωθέντος), *and* (τε) *by prophetic writings, according to the precept of the eternal God, for the obedience of faith, made known* (γνωρισθέντος, a third participle) *to all the nations.*

The parenthesis begins at *according to the revelation,* and ends at *nations.* The key to the understanding of it is to observe well the three participles above marked. The Vulgate, which resolves the second participle into a relative clause, and joins together *patefactum est per scripturas prophetarum (made manifest by the scriptures of the prophets),* is obscure and misses the construction.

The *mystery* then in question, and the theme of this Epistle, is the call of the gentiles by faith to share in the spiritual promises made to Abraham. This mystery is *known by prophetic writings;* or, as St. Paul elsewhere puts it, *witnessed by the law and the prophets.* The witness of the prophets is abundantly alleged in this Epistle (ix. 25, 26; x. 13, 15, 18, 20; xv. 9—12): cf. also Acts xiii. 47; xv. 16, 17, &c.

27. *To God the only wise . . . to whom.* This relative *to whom* mars the construction of the sentence, and in point of syntax should either be omitted (with some MSS.), or (with others) altered to *to him.* But the best MSS. have it, and we must regard it as an irregularity due to the author.

The only wise. There should be a comma here. The words, *through Jesus Christ,* go with what follows. The *wisdom* of God is aptly glorified in reference to a *mystery* (*v.* 25: cf. xi. 33—36).

We may be allowed to terminate our labours on St. Paul with a doxology, supplied partly hence and partly from 1 Tim. vi. 15, 16:

To God the only wise, blessed and only mighty, the king of kings and lord of lords, who only hath immortality and inhabiteth light inaccessible, whom no man hath seen nor can see, to him through Jesus Christ be honour and glory and empire everlasting for ever and ever, Amen.

INDEX TO NOTES.

CATALOGUE

OF THE QUARTERLY SERIES,

AND OTHER BOOKS

WRITTEN OR EDITED BY

FATHERS OF THE SOCIETY OF JESUS.

London: BURNS AND OATES, LIMITED.

English Manuals of Catholic Theology.

OUTLINES OF
DOGMATIC THEOLOGY.

BY

SYLVESTER JOSEPH HUNTER, S.J.

Three Volumes. Price 6s. 6d. each.

TREATISES.

LONDON : LONGMANS, GREEN, AND CO.

IN this work an attempt is made to offer to the English reader an outline of the dogmatic theology of the Catholic Church as one connected whole. The language is rich in works of controversy, some of which deal with the Rule of Faith, while others defend particular doctrines, such as Purgatory and the worship of Saints, from the attacks that are made upon them by popular writers ; these works are very valuable, and are useful in showing the worthlessness of the ordinary objections made to the Catholic faith, which most commonly rest upon misrepresentation : but works written to suit particular phases of controversy are necessarily confined to the points which happen to engage attention at the moment, and they fail to exhibit the science of theology as a whole, and to show its essential unity. Courses of theology for the use of students exist in abundance, varying in fulness and excellence, but they are written in Latin, so that they are of less use to a wide circle of readers who would wish to know something on the subject ; they are little known beyond the ranks of the clergy. So far as is known, there is no modern work in the English language comparable to those which France owes to Gousset and Germany to Scheeben, who endeavour to deal with the matter in the vernacular, in such a manner as to satisfy the curiosity of all intelligent readers. An attempt is now made to supply this defect.

The work is divided into three volumes, containing twenty-three Treatises, the distribution of which is appended. The treatment may strike the professed theologian as meagre, but it was necessary to compress the vast material, to reduce it to a reasonable compass. No attempt has been made to enforce the rigid exclusion of all matter that is not strictly dogmatic, but portions of history and the like have been admitted as often as they seemed suitable to illustrate the subject. Other Treatises might have been added, as on Hope, on Charity, on Sin, and the like : but it is believed that what are here given hang together sufficiently well, and that these Outlines will admit of being filled up by the readers who go on to study more elaborate Treatises.

Opinions of the Press.

" It is the desire of the Church that all who have the opportunity should study her theology. She by no means desires to confine this useful and interesting pursuit of truth to those whose official duty it is, or will be, to teach the truths of faith. Father Hunter, in publishing his present work, has endeavoured to place in the hands of all a suitable means of carrying into effect this wish of the Catholic Church. . . . The style is for the most part sufficiently attractive for subjects of the nature discussed in the volume. The arguments are nearly always cogent. Hence its utility, especially in countries where Protestantism is the principal error to be avoided, cannot be doubted."—*Irish Ecclesiastical Record*, March, 1895.

" The style of Father Hunter is remarkably clear ; his diction has a legal accuracy, and is entirely free from any technicalities of foreign turns. This instances a distinct development of the English language as now handled by Catholic writers, who make it rich in Catholic phraseology without detracting from its purity. And, apart from the phraseology, this work enriches the literature itself with a new addition of what has been so long denied to it, the classic statement of truths, which it is the one thing necessary to know and to embody in thought and life."—*American Ecclesiastical Review*, April, 1895.

" Altogether an admirable and very useful work, filling a place not previously supplied."—*The Weekly Register*, February 9, 1895.

" The contents of this volume deserve high praise. The style is clear and fresh and forcible, and well adapted to the subject-matter. Altogether there are few works of the kind which more accurately fulfil their aim, or which will prove more interesting to the student. The layman will find many a useful lesson here which may avail him in any department of life. Some of the explanations are really profound, and touch upon current difficulties."—*The Catholic Times*, March 22, 1895.

" Father Hunter is supplying what many are likely to consider just the book we want. This is the first of three volumes, covering the whole ground of Dogmatic Theology. . . . It is a repertory of happy illustration and popular exposition for the preacher, and the theological student will find it a valuable help to master the contents of the regular text-book. We are looking forward with pleasure to the publication of the other two volumes."—*The Glasgow Observer*, March 15, 1895.

" In undertaking to give us a text-book of dogmatic theology in English, Father Sylvester Hunter has broken new ground. . . . Of his fitness for the task there can be no question. In addition to the scientific accuracy which in these matters is almost an inseparable accident of the publications of the illustrious Order to which he belongs, the author comes before us with the weightiest of personal qualifications for a task by no means easy ; the training of a lawyer, and a long and distinguished career as a writer on some of the most difficult points of legal practice, followed by a no less earnest devotion to the higher studies of theology in the schools of St. Beuno's. . . . It is in the chapters dealing with modern objections to Revelation, and the miraculous preparation for the advent of

Christ, that the value of Father Hunter's work becomes immediately apparent. . . . It will prove a welcome boon to our hard-working clergy and the growing band of educated laymen who are spreading in so many places where our priests can find no entry, the saving faith of Christ."—*The Tablet*, June 8, 1895.

"The second volume of Father Hunter's *Outlines of Dogmatic Theology* has just reached us, and we hasten to lay before our readers some of the impressions which a necessarily hasty perusal of a lengthy closely-reasoned book of nearly six hundred pages has made upon us. To our thinking the learned author has succeeded admirably in his praiseworthy purpose of putting before the English-speaking public, Catholic and otherwise, the outlines, at least, of those scientific treatises of dogmatic theology whose more detailed and fuller study is the proper duty of the ecclesiastical student. . . . Many interesting pieces of information about the tenets of the numerous non-Catholic sects around us are to be found up and down this volume; information which we ought to have at hand, but which it is difficult to procure. . . . The student will find it a very valuable companion to the lengthier works in common use in our seminaries; even the ordinary reader, anxious to gain a fuller knowledge of 'the faith once delivered to the saints,' will be charmed by the easy style and logical sequence of the treatises and chapters, which open out a vista of those magnificent truths which have for eighteen centuries employed the prayerful studies of generations of learned men, and which will be for all eternity a wonder ever new when faith has given place to vision. . . . The book is a learned, valuable, and frankly honest introduction to the noblest and most necessary of sciences."—*The Tablet*, August 31, 1895.

"Father Hunter's work is of distinct advantage, and should be widely read. His exposition is all that could be desired—lucid and cogent. Keeping close to the principles of St. Thomas Aquinas, the Rev. author does not refuse to glance at modern errors, which gives his book a decided value. The opening treatise of the volume before us [vol. ii.]—that on "The One God"—introduces such difficult matters as the *scientia-media*, free-will, the problem of evil, and is, therefore, one of a character to test the powers of a writer. Father Hunter's account of them leave nothing to be desired. We wish the work a wide circulation, alike among Catholics and non-Catholics.' —*Freeman's Journal*, August 16, 1895.

"To Catholic laymen who have sufficient appreciation of their faith to desire a detailed and systematic acquaintance with Catholic doctrine, we recommend the *Outlines of Dogmatic Theology*. But it is not to laymen only that the *Outlines* will be useful. They might be of much assistance to students in our theological seminaries. In some of our seminaries there is, in addition to the ordinary course, what is known as the "short course" of Theology. The "short course" is intended for students who are a little older or a little less bright than the average, and the lectures in this course are delivered in English. To the students that follow the short course the *Outlines* ought to be particularly acceptable, and indeed we think that for them it might very well serve as a text-book."—*Dublin Review*, October, 1895.

Some Opinions of the Press.

"The 'Stonyhurst Series' is not a mere translation of old scholastic treatises on Philosophy. Each volume differs so much in treatment of its matter from what a mediævalist philosopher would have penned, that at first sight these English Catholic Manuals would seem to have set up systems of their own. But the discrepancy is only apparent, not real. In its philosophical system, the series is scholastic to the core. But it has taken up scholastic principles to apply them to the problems raised by modern writers."
—*Bombay Advertiser*.

"These Manuals are worthy of the widest circulation. They will clear away many popular delusions, much confusion of thought and language. They will help to strengthen many minds to strive fearlessly and perseveringly in the search of truth."—*Bombay Catholic Examiner*.

LOGIC.

"We must congratulate the editor of the series of Catholic Manuals of Philosophy on affording such a valuable contribution to English Catholic literature. The easy style throughout, the clearness of exposition, and the well-chosen examples, make the book at once attractive to the general reader, and of inestimable use to the special student. But the highest excellence of the work, and the one which characterises the series conceived and edited by the author, is sympathy with the intellectual atmosphere in which we live, with its difficulties, with its strength, and with its weakness."—*The Tablet*.

"An excellent text-book of Aristotelian logic, interesting, vivid, sometimes almost racy in its illustrations, while from first to last it never, so far as we have noticed, diverges from Aristotelian orthodoxy."—*Guardian*.

"Though Father Clarke mainly concerns himself with Formal Logic, he occasionally, for the sake of edification, makes excursions into wider fields. Adopting the standpoint of 'moderate realism,' he directs his chief attack against the limitation of the Principle of Contradiction, the nominalist statement of the Principle of Identity, and the theory of conception set forth by Mill. The arguments usually employed in these time-honoured controversies are marshalled with much vigour. . . . The uncontroversial portions of the book are extremely clear, and the descriptions of the various forms of syllogism as little dry as their subject-matter permits."—*Saturday Review*.

FIRST PRINCIPLES OF KNOWLEDGE.

"It is a hopeful sign of the times that a Catholic professor should freely enter the lists of debate in opposition to acknowledged masters of recent philosophy. The Jesuit Father is no respecter of persons."—*Journal of Education*.

"In the two volumes named below (*First Principles of Knowledge* and *Logic*), we have set forth in clear and vigorous English the doctrine of knowledge and the principles of reasoning taught by the learned and subtle Aquinas in the thirteenth century, but adapted to the needs of students and controversialists of the nineteenth century by teachers who, like St. Thomas himself, are able to discuss doubts without doubting, to hold converse with sceptics of every school, and still to hold to the faith. . . . To those who would like to know exactly the form that philosophy takes when she enters the service of 'The Church' the volumes may be commended."—*Inquirer*, Sept. 21, 1889.

MORAL PHILOSOPHY.

"The style of the book is bright and easy, and the English (as we need not say) extremely good. . . . The manual will be welcome on all sides as a sound, original, and fairly complete English treatise on the groundwork of morality."—*Dublin Review*.

"The style is popular and easily intelligible; the principles are fully illustrated by concrete examples."—*Church Quarterly*.

"As regards the style of the book, it is, as a rule, clear, terse, and simple; and there are many passages marked alike by sound sense and by elevation of tone."—*Journal of Education*.

"Father Rickaby, with his Aristotelian and scholastic training, is always definite and clear, distrustful of sentiment, with an answer ready for every assailant."—*Mind*, No. 54.

"It is one of a series of 'Manuals of Catholic Philosophy' in course of issue, and embodies the substance of lectures delivered by the author during eight successive years to the students of the Jesuit Society at Stonyhurst. The book is marked with several of the merits usually found in the educational writings of the Jesuits: orderly method, lucid arrangement, clear, definite, and incisive wording, competent familiarity with the literature of the subject, both ancient and modern."—*Church Times*, May 3, 1889.

NATURAL THEOLOGY.

"This volume considerably increases the debt which English-speaking Catholics owe to the Jesuit Fathers who have brought out the 'Stonyhurst Series' of philosophical manuals. It is really a treatise *de Deo* dealing with the proofs of the existence of God, the Divine attributes, and the relation of God to the world—in plain intelligible English, and adapted to the difficulties raised in our own country at the present day. The author is evidently well acquainted with Mill, Spencer, Huxley, and other contemporary writers; they are quoted freely and clearly answered."—*Dublin Review*, October, 1891.

"Father Boedder's *Natural Theology* will be read with eagerness. The proofs of the existence of a Personal God are given with a completeness and clearness I have never before seen."—*Bombay Advertiser*.

PSYCHOLOGY.

"We regard Father Maher's book on Psychology as one of the most important contributions to philosophical literature published in this country for a long time. . . . What renders his work especially valuable is the breadth of his modern reading, and the skill with which he presses things new, no less than old, into the service of his argument. His dialectical skill is as remarkable as his wealth of learning, and not less notable is his spirit of fairness. . . . Whether the reader agrees or disagrees with the author's views, it is impossible to deny the ability, fulness, and cogency of the argument."— *St. James's Gazette*, July 8, 1892.

"Father Maher's joining of old with new in his *Psychology* is very skilful; and sometimes the highly systematized character of the scholastic doctrine gives him a certain advantage in the face of modern psychological classifications with their more tentative character. . . . The historical and controversial parts all through the volume are in general very carefully and well managed."—*Mind*.

"This work cannot be too highly recommended."—*The Tablet*, November 1, 1890.

GENERAL METAPHYSICS.

"*Metaphysics* is not a popular study, but Father Rickaby has done his best to popularize it. He expounds the idea of Being with its nature, existence, and attributes, and other notions less general, as substance, causality, space, and time. He ought to succeed in dissipating the common prejudice that metaphysics is mere cobweb spinning."—*Bombay Advertiser*.

"It will be seen, then, that we deny the merit of profundity to Father Rickaby's work; it will, however, do more good than harm; it is full of a learning rare and curious in England, and is tempered by an English common sense and a real acquaintance with English thought."—*Athenæum*, April 18, 1891.

POLITICAL ECONOMY.

"A concise but extraordinarily comprehensive text-book, with plenty of human interest, attractive—if now and then rather slight —illustrations from real life—and last, but not least, a clear, and on the whole a correct, exposition of the elements of economic science." —*Speaker*.

"We incline to consider Mr. Devas' Manual one of the most valuable contributions made for a long time to the study of economics. It is closely reasoned, for Mr. Devas possesses strongly the sense of the syllogism. . . . In the greater part of what he advances in his book we entirely follow him. It is constructed upon the right lines. It is especially valuable for the high ethical tone which pervades it from first to last."—*St. James's Gazette*, March 11, 1892.

*

QUARTERLY SERIES.

85. **The Life of the Venerable Joseph Benedict Cottolengo**, Founder of the Little House of Providence in Turin. Compiled from the Italian Life of Don P. Gastaldi, by a Priest of the Society of Jesus. 4s. 6d.

86. **The Lights in Prayer** of the Ven. Louis de la Puente, the Ven. Claude de la Colombière, and the Rev. Father Paul Segneri. 5s.

87. **Two Ancient Treatises on Purgatory.** A Remembrance for the Living to Pray for the Dead, by Father James Mumford, S.J. And Purgatory Surveyed, by Father Richard Thimelby, S.J. With Introduction and an Appendix on the Heroic Act, by Father John Morris, S.J. 5s.

88. **Life of St. Francis Borgia.** By A. M. Clarke, author of the *Life of St. Francis di Geronimo*. The first Life of the Saint written in English. 6s. 6d.

89. **The Life of Blessed Antony Baldinucci.** By Father Francis Goldie, S.J. 6s.

90. **Distinguished Irishmen of the Sixteenth Century.** By the Rev. Edmund Hogan, S.J. 6s.

91. **Journals kept during Times of Retreat** by Father John Morris, S.J. Selected and Edited by Father J. H. Pollen, S.J. Second Edition. 6s.

92. **The Life of the Reverend Mother Mary of St. Euphrasia Pelletier,** First Superior General of the Congregation of Our Lady of Charity of the Good Shepherd of Angers. By A. M. Clarke. With Preface by His Eminence Cardinal Vaughan, Archbishop of Westminster. With Portrait. 6s.

93. **Jesus.** His Life in the very words of the Four Gospels. A Diatessaron. By Henry Beauclerk, S.J. 5s.

94. **First Communion.** By a Religious of St. Mary's Convent, York. Edited by Father Thurston, S.J. With many Illustrations. Cheap Edition, 3s. 6d. Gift Book Edition, 7s. 6d., with new Illustrations.

95. **Life and Letters of Father John Morris, S.J.** 1826—1893. By Father John H. Pollen, S.J. 6s.

96. **The Story of Mary Aikenhead,** Foundress of the Irish Sisters of Charity. By Maria Nethercott. 3s.

97. **Life of the Blessed Master John of Avila.** Secular Priest, called the Apostle of Andalusia. By Father Longaro Degli Oddi, of the Society of Jesus. Edited by J. G. MacLeod, S.J. Translated from the Italian. 4s.

WORKS ON THE LIFE OF OUR LORD.

BY THE REV. H. J. COLERIDGE, S.J.

Published in the Quarterly Series.

---

31. **The Training of the Apostles.** Part I. 6s. 6d.

37. **The Training of the Apostles.** Part II. 6s. 6d.

45. **The Training of the Apostles.** Part III. 6s. 6d.

51. **The Training of the Apostles.** Part IV. 6s. 6d.

57. **The Preaching of the Cross.** Part I. 6s. 6d.

63. **The Preaching of the Cross.** Part II. 6s.

64. **The Preaching of the Cross.** Part III. 6s.

HOLY WEEK.

68. **Passiontide.** Part I. 6s. 6d.

72. **Passiontide.** Part II. 6s. 6d.

76. **Passiontide.** Part III. 6s. 6d.

78. **The Passage of our Lord to the Father.**
7s. 6d. Conclusion of *The Life of our Life.*

———

38. **The Return of the King.** Discourses on the
Latter Days. By the Rev. H. J. Coleridge, S.J. Second
Edition. 7s. 6d.

44. **The Baptism of the King.** Considerations on
the Sacred Passion. By the Rev. H. J. Coleridge, S.J. 7s.6d.

55. **The Mother of the King.** Mary during the
Life of our Lord. By the Rev. H. J. Coleridge, S.J. 7s. 6d.

60. **The Mother of the Church.** Mary during the
first Apostolic Age. By the Rev. H. J. Coleridge, S.J. 6s.

The Prisoners of the King. Thoughts on the
Catholic Doctrine of Purgatory. By the Rev. H. J.
Coleridge, S.J. New Edition. 4s.

The Seven Words of Mary. By the Rev. H. J.
Coleridge, S.J. 2s.

WORKS BY THE REV. JOHN MORRIS, S.J.

The Life and Martyrdom of St. Thomas Becket. Second and Enlarged Edition. In one vol. large post 8vo, 12s. 6d. Or in two volumes, 13s.

Catholic England in Modern Times. Royal 8vo, cloth, 1s. 6d. net.

Two Missionaries under Elizabeth. A Confessor and an Apostate. Demy 8vo, cloth. 14s.

The Catholics of York under Elizabeth. Demy 8vo, cloth. 14s.

The Life of Father John Gerard, S.J. Third Edition, re-written and enlarged, 14s.

The Letter-Books of Sir Amias Poulet, Keeper of Mary Queen of Scots. 3s. 6d.

The Venerable Sir Adrian Fortescue, Knight of the Bath, Knight of St. John, Martyr. With Portrait and Autograph. 1s. 6d.

Canterbury: Our old Metropolis. 9d.

The Tombs of the Archbishops in Canterbury Cathedral. 1s. 6d.

Canterbury. A Guide for Catholics. With Plans. 1d.

The Heroic Act of Charity in behalf of the Souls in Purgatory. 1d.

Daily Duties : An Instruction for Novices. 6d. net, by post 7d.

Meditation : An Instruction for Novices. 6d. net, by post 7d.

Vocation : or Preparation for the Vows, with a further Instruction on Mental Prayer. 6d. net, by post 7d. The Three Instructions together, in cloth, post free, 2s. net.

EDITED BY THE REV. JOHN MORRIS, S.J.

Manual of Prayers for Youth. A new Edition. Imperial 32mo. 264 pp. cloth. 1s. net, post free.

The Devotions of the Lady Lucy Herbert of Powis, formerly Prioress of the Augustinian Nuns at Bruges. 3s. 6d.

LONDON : BURNS AND OATES, LIMITED.

Fasti Apostolici. An Annual Record, from our Lord's Ascension to SS. Peter and Paul's Martyrdom. With copious Notes and Appendix. Second Edition. Small 4to, 184 pp. Cloth, 3s. 6d.

Britain's Early Faith. With copious Notes and Appendix. Seventeen chapters, 244 pp. Cloth, 3s.

Afternoons with the Saints. Tenth Edition. 394 pp. Cloth, 3s. 6d. French Edition. Wrapper, 2s.

Evenings with the Saints. Cloth, 3s. 6d.

Bracton : A Tale of 1812. Second Edition. Cloth, 2s.

In the Snow. Ninth Edition. Cloth, 2s.

The Catholic Crusoe. Ninth Edition. With Twelve Illustrations. Cloth, 3s. 6d.

Some Verses of Various Dates. Cloth, 6d. ; wrapper, 4d.

Luther. In Four parts. 172 pp. Cloth, 1s. ; wrapper, 6d.

Is Ritualism Honest ? Three Lectures. Third Edition. Including **Begging the Question.** 6d.

Via Crucis: translated from the original of St. Leonard of Port Maurice. Stanzas of the *Stabat*, chiefly by Aubrey de Vere. Seventh Thousand. 3d. and 2d.

The Old Religion of Taunton. 2d.

What is the Bible ? Is yours the right book ? 1d.

Confession to a Priest. 1d.

Five Minutes' Sermons for the Sundays throughout the Year.

PART THE FIRST. From Trinity Sunday to the Twelfth Sunday after Pentecost. 6d.

PART THE SECOND. From the Thirteenth to the Twenty-fourth Sunday after Pentecost. 6d.

HISTORICAL PAPERS.

17. England's Title: Our Lady's Dowry: Its
History and Meaning. By the Rev. T. E. Bridgett,
C.SS.R. 1d.

18. Dr. Littledale's Theory of the Disappearance
of the Papacy. By the Rev. Sydney F. Smith, S.J. 2d.

19. Dean Farrar on the Observance of Good
Friday. By the Rev. Herbert Thurston, S.J. 1d.

20. Savonarola and the Reformation. By the Very
Rev. J. Procter, O.P. 3d.

21. Robert Grosseteste, Bishop of Lincoln. By
Mgr. W. Croke Robinson. 2d.

The above numbers in four volumes, bound in cloth, 1s. each.

22. The English Coronation Oath. By the Rev.
T. E. Bridgett, C.SS.R. 2d.

23. Blessed Thomas Percy, Earl of Northumber-
land. By the Rev. G. E. Phillips. 3d.

24. The Landing of St. Augustine. By the Rev.
Sydney F. Smith, S.J. 1d.

25. The Hungarian Confession. By the Rev.
Sydney F. Smith, S.J. 1d.

BY THE REV. R. F. CLARKE, S.J.

Theosophy. Its Teaching, Marvels, and True
Character. Wrapper, 6d.

Spiritualism. Its Character and Results. Wrapper, 2d.

The Existence of God: A Dialogue. New Edition.
Wrapper, 6d.

A Pilgrimage to the Holy Coat of Treves. With
an Account of its History and Authenticity. With
Twelve beautiful Illustrations. Crown 8vo, cloth, 4s.

The Pope and the Bible. Wrapper, 6d.

The Adorable Heart of Jesus. By Father Joseph
de Galliffet, S.J. With Preface and Introduction by the
Rev. R. F. Clarke, S.J. Third Edition. Fcap. 8vo. 3s.